D0209243

The Wedding Game

Also by Jane Feather in Large Print:

Kissed by Shadows
To Kiss a Spy
The Accidental Bride
Virtue

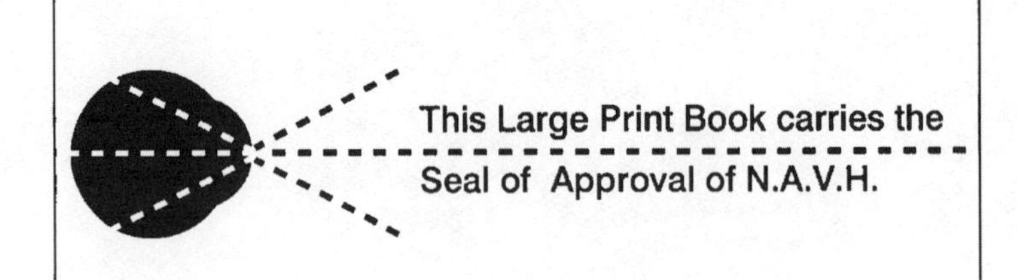

The Wedding Game

Jane Feather

Published in 2004 by arrangement with Bantam Books,
an imprint of the Bantam Dell Publishing Group,
a division of Random House, Inc.

Wheeler Large Print Hardcover.

The text of this Large Print edition is unabridged.
Other aspects of the book may vary from the original edition.

Set in 16 pt. Plantin by Al Chase.

Printed in the United States on permanent paper.

Library of Congress Cataloging-in-Publication Data

Feather, Jane.
The wedding game / Jane Feather.
p. cm.
ISBN 1-58724-725-9 (lg. print : hc : alk. paper)
1. Matrimonial advertisements — Fiction. 2. Poor — Services for — Fiction. 3. Marriage brokerage — Fiction. 4. London (England) — Fiction. 5. Physicians — Fiction. 6. Sisters — Fiction. 7. Large type books. I. Title.
PS3556.E22W43 2004
813′.54—dc22 2004049215

The Wedding Game

As the Founder/CEO of NAVH, the only national health agency solely devoted to those who, although not totally blind, have an eye disease which could lead to serious visual impairment, I am pleased to recognize Thorndike Press* as one of the leading publishers in the large print field.

Founded in 1954 in San Francisco to prepare large print textbooks for partially seeing children, NAVH became the pioneer and standard setting agency in the preparation of large type.

Today, those publishers who meet our standards carry the prestigious "Seal of Approval" indicating high quality large print. We are delighted that Thorndike Press is one of the publishers whose titles meet these standards. We are also pleased to recognize the significant contribution Thorndike Press is making in this important and growing field.

Lorraine H. Marchi, L.H.D.
Founder/CEO
NAVH

* Thorndike Press encompasses the following imprints: Thorndike, Wheeler, Walker and Large Print Press.

Chapter 1

The gentleman standing at the top of the steps of the National Gallery closely scrutinized the assumed art lovers ascending towards the great doors of the art museum at his back. He held a prominently displayed copy of the broadsheet *The Mayfair Lady*. He was looking for someone flourishing a similar article.

A cloud of pigeons rose in a flurry from Trafalgar Square as a figure hastened across the square, scattering corn to the birds as she came. She crossed the street directly below the museum and paused at the bottom step, crushing the paper bag that had held the corn in her hand as she gazed upwards. She held a rolled-up newspaper in her free hand. The man made a tentative movement with his own broadsheet and the figure tossed the scrunched bag into a litter bin and hurried up the steps towards him.

That the figure was small and female was about all the gentleman could discern. She was swathed in a loose alpaca dust coat of the kind that ladies wore when motoring, and wore a broad-brimmed felt hat, her face obscured by an opaque chiffon veil.

"Bonjour, m'sieur," she greeted him. "I think we are to meet, *n'est-ce pas?*" She waved her copy of *The Mayfair Lady.* "You are Dr. Douglas Farrell, is it not so?"

"The very same, madam," he said with a small bow. "And you are . . . ?"

"I am ze Mayfair Lady, of course," she responded, her veil fluttering with each breath.

With the phoniest French accent he'd ever heard, Dr. Farrell reflected with some amusement. He decided not to call her on it just yet. "The Mayfair Lady in person?" he questioned curiously.

"The representative of ze publication, m'sieur," she responded with a note of reproof.

"Ah." He nodded. "And the Go-Between?"

"One and the same, sir," the lady said with a decisive nod. "And as I understand it, sir, it is ze Go-Between that can be of service to you." *This damnable French accent always made her want to laugh,* reflected the Honorable Chastity Duncan. Whether she or one of her sisters was using it, they all agreed they sounded like French maids in a Feydeau farce. But it was a very useful device for disguising voices.

"I had expected to meet in an office," the

doctor said, glancing around at their rather public surroundings. A chill December wind was blowing across the square, ruffling the pigeons' feathers.

"Our office premises are not open to ze public, m'sieur," she said simply. "I suggest we go inside, zere are many places in ze museum where we can talk." She moved towards the doors and her companion hastened to open them for her. The folds of her alpaca dust coat brushed against him as she billowed past into the cavernous atrium of the museum.

"Let us go to the Rubens room, m'sieur," she suggested, gesturing towards the stairs with her newspaper. "Zere is a circular seat where we may talk without drawing attention." She moved authoritatively ahead of him towards the staircase to the central hall. Dr. Farrell followed obediently, both intrigued and amused by this performance.

At a landing halfway up the stairs she turned aside, hurrying through a succession of rooms hung with massive Renaissance canvases of atrocious martyrdoms, pietàs, and crucifixions. She cast not so much as a sideways glance at these cultural icons, stopping only when they emerged into a circular chamber, graced with a circular sofa in its center.

The room was hung most notably with two of Rubens's canvases of the Judgment of

Paris. With quiet amusement, the Duncan sisters had chosen this location for meetings with prospective Go-Between clients. The three buxom, naked renditions of Venus, Juno, and Minerva had somehow struck them as rather appropriate to the business at hand.

" 'Ere it is quiet and we may be private," she declared, settling herself on the sofa, gathering her skirts close to her to give him room to sit beside her.

Douglas glanced around with interest. It wasn't so much private, he reflected. There were other people in the chamber moving from painting to painting, conversing in undertones, but the circular sofa, although publicly situated, somehow provided an oasis where two people could sit close together and talk without drawing attention to themselves. He sat down beside her, aware of her perfume, a light flowery fragrance that seemed to waft from beneath the veil.

Chastity turned her veiled head towards him. She had the advantage on Dr. Douglas Farrell in that she had seen him once before, when he had visited Mrs. Beedle's corner shop to buy a copy of *The Mayfair Lady* and Chastity had watched the transaction unobserved. He was as she remembered him, a very big man, certainly not easily forgotten. Both tall and broad, with the muscular heft of a sporting man. A boxer or a wrestler, she thought. The prominent bump on a once-broken nose seemed to support the guess. His features were strong and uneven, his mouth wide, his jaw of the lantern variety. His eyes were the color of charcoal beneath thick black eyebrows that met over the bridge of his nose. His hair was as black, rather curly, but cut short and businesslike. Everything about him indicated someone who cared little for the nuances of appearances. He wore an unexceptional greatcoat, buttoned to the neck, with muffler and gloves, and he held a plain trilby hat on his lap.

She became suddenly aware of the length of the silence that had accompanied her assessment of her companion and said quickly, "Now, 'ow exactly can ze Go-Between 'elp you, m'sieur?"

He cast another slightly baffled glance around the gallery. "So, this is the office of *The Mayfair Lady*?"

She detected the faint Scottish lilt to his voice that she had noticed when she'd first observed him at Mrs. Beedle's. "*Non,* but we do not see clients in our office," she informed him firmly. Chastity kept to herself the reflection that their office was either the tearoom at Fortnum and Mason or the upstairs parlor of her father's house, which had been the Duncan sisters' mother's sanctum. Neither space was conducive to official client interviews.

"Why is that?" he inquired.

"It is necessary for ze Mayfair Lady to be anonymous," she stated. "Could we proceed with business, m'sieur?"

"Yes, of course. But I confess, madam Mayfair Lady, that I am curious. Why is this anonymity necessary?"

Chastity sighed. " 'Ave you read ze publication, m'sieur?"

"Yes, of course. I would not have known to seek the services of the Go-Between otherwise."

"You can read advertisements without reading the articles," she pointed out, forgetting her accent for a second.

"I have read the articles."

She gave a very Gallic shrug. "Zen surely you must see that the opinions expressed are controversial. Ze editors prefer to remain anonymous."

"I see." He thought he did. "Of course, creating a sense of mystery must add to the publication's appeal."

"That is true," she conceded.

He nodded. "As I recall, there was a libel case several months ago. *The Mayfair Lady* was sued for libel by . . ." He frowned, then his brow cleared. "By the earl of Barclay, I believe."

"A suit that was dismissed," Chastity stated.

"Yes." He nodded. "So I remember. I also remember that the publication was represented by an anonymous person in the witness box. Is that not so?"

"It is so."

"Intriguing," he said. "I'm sure you saw the volume of your sales increase considerably after that."

"Maybe so," she said vaguely. "But it is not for zat reason that we choose to conceal our identities. Now, to business, m'sieur."

Douglas, fascinated and curious though he remained, accepted that for the present, question time was over. "As I explained in my letter, I am in need of a wife."

She took the letter in question from her handbag. "That is all you say, 'owever. We would need to know more details of your situation and the kind of wife you are looking for before we can know whether we can 'elp you in your search."

"Yes, of course," he agreed. "As it happens, there are only two essential qualities I require in a wife." He drew off his gloves as he spoke, thrusting them into his pockets. "I am hoping in your registry you will have someone who would serve my purpose. Apart from the two essential issues, I am not unduly particular." His voice was very cool and matter-of-fact as he laid out the situation for her, tapping off the points with a finger on his palm as he made them.

"As I mentioned in my letter, I am a member of the medical profession. I have recently arrived in London from Edinburgh, where I received my medical degree and where I practiced for some years. I am in the process of opening a surgery on Harley Street, one that I trust will generate considerable income once I have become well enough known in London society."

Chastity made no response, merely clasped her gloved hands in her lap and regarded him through her veil. She was beginning to get a bad feeling about this interview, and her intuition rarely failed her.

The doctor unwrapped his muffler. He seemed to find it too warm in the round chamber despite the inadequate heating. Chastity, who was still chilled by her walk in the cold December wind, envied him. She reflected that perhaps such a large man generated extra body heat.

"Anyway," he continued, "I must find myself a wife who is first and foremost rich."

And at that point Chastity realized that her intuition had indeed been absolutely correct. But again she made no response, merely stiffened slightly.

"As you will appreciate," he continued in the same detached tone, "it's an expensive business setting up such a practice. Harley Street rents are very high, and wealthy patients expect to be treated in surroundings that reassure them they are receiving the best of care from a practitioner who treats only people who expect and can afford the best."

Chastity thought she could detect just a hint of sarcasm in his voice. She said distantly, "In my experience doctors who practice on Harley Street generally do very well for themselves. Well enough to support a wife, I would assume."

He shrugged. "Yes, once they're established, they do. But I am not as yet established and I intend to become so. To do that, I need some help. You understand me?"

"I am not generally considered obtuse," she said.

If her frigid tone disconcerted the doctor, he gave no sign of it. He continued as calmly as before. "I need a wife who can bring to the marriage a certain financial stability in addition to having the social graces and connections that would enable her to advance my practice. A lady, in short, who would be able to persuade the . . ." He paused as if looking for the right word. His lip had curled slightly. "The ladies with megrims, with the imaginary ailments that arise from having nothing to think about, nothing sensible to do with their lives, and the gentlemen with gout and the other ailments that arise from a lazy and overindulged existence. I need a wife to fish for those patients for me and to instill them with utter confidence in her husband's medical skill."

"In short, m'sieur, what you require is not

so much a wife as a banker and a procuress," Chastity stated. She wondered for a minute if she had been a little too offensive in expressing her outrage, but she need not have feared.

"Precisely," he agreed equably. "You understand the situation exactly. I prefer to call a spade a spade." He peered at her. "Is it possible to see your face, madam?"

"*Absolument pas,* m'sieur. Absolutely not."

He shrugged. "As you wish, of course. But apart from the fact that I prefer to do business with someone whose identity is known to me, this mystery seems a trifle unnecessary. Could you at least drop the fake accent?"

Chastity bit her lip behind her veil. She hadn't expected him to believe in it for a minute, but she also knew that it successfully disguised her voice, and when the time came for her to meet him face-to-face, as it would if they took him as a client, he must not link the lady from the National Gallery with the Honorable Chastity Duncan.

She chose to ignore the question and asked coldly, "Is ze Go-Between to assume, then, that you 'ave no interest in a marriage where affection or respect is of any importance? It is only money and social status zat matter to you?"

This time he couldn't fail to hear the asperity in her tone. He slapped his gloves into the palm of one hand. “They are my priorities,” he said. “Is it any business of the Go-Between to question those priorities? You are an agency that provides a service.”

Chastity could feel her cheeks grow hot beneath her veil. “In order to serve you, m’sieur, we must ask the questions we consider necessary.”

He frowned, then shrugged again as if in acceptance. “I would prefer to say that my choice of a wife is a simple matter of practicality.” He regarded her now with a measure of frustration. What had seemed simple enough to him was becoming difficult for some reason, and made all the more so when he had no visual clues to work with.

Chastity watched him through her veil. She could see him quite clearly and could read his mind with some accuracy. Her instinct was to refuse the man as a client without further ado. Her finer feelings, of which she had more than her fair share, were revolted by the idea of simply finding some blatantly mercenary individual a rich wife. But she couldn’t make such a decision without consultation with her sisters and she knew that they would scoff at such fine principles. They ran a business and could not afford to turn away a paying client, however much they despised him. Chastity knew she had to listen to Prudence’s coolly pragmatic voice rather than her own immediate emotional response.

And she could hear too how Constance, whatever she might think of the good doctor, would say that a paying client was a paying client. And there were women desperate enough for a husband who would probably find such a proposal convenient. Constance would say that such women needed to be educated to a degree of self-reliance, but until they were, one had to deal with them on their own terms.

And both Prudence and Constance would be right. *The Mayfair Lady* and the Go-Between ensured the independence of the Duncan sisters, and kept their father in relative comfort. While Prudence and Constance now had husbands well able to take care of them financially, neither woman was prepared to give up that independence.

At the thought of her father, Chastity gave an involuntary sigh. One that her companion heard, even as he saw the slight puff of her veil.

"Is something the matter?"

"No," she said. "Our business for today is concluded, I believe, m'sieur. I will go back to my office and consult with my si— my colleagues. You will 'ear from us by letter within ze week." She stood up, holding out her gloved hand.

He took it. "How will I meet suitable prospects?"

"You will be told," she said. "Always assuming that we can find a woman as willing as you to settle for a convenient marriage devoid of respect and affection. Good afternoon, Dr. Farrell." She left him in the embrasure before he had time to recover his wits.

He took a step after her, anger replacing incredulity at her tart tone as much as her words, but she was hurrying through the busy gallery and he couldn't see himself arresting her to demand an apology in such a public place. But he would have one nevertheless. Of all the stiff-necked, self-righteous statements. How could she possibly know the realities of his work?

Of course, a little voice reminded him, he hadn't told her of those realities, of the other side of his work, but that was not something he chose to broadcast to all and sundry. And besides, it was not relevant to the service the Go-Between was offering.

For all the progressive views put forward in *The Mayfair Lady*, it was clear that its writers and editors were people — women, he assumed — of means as well as education. They would know nothing of the dismal streets of Earl's Court, the tumbledown row houses where rats ran freely and the stench from the outhouses poisoned the air. They would know nothing of the realities of the tuberculosis and dysentery that lurked in every dark corner, of the desperate mothers trying to scrape together a penny for milk for their rickety children, of the men out of work, many of them drinking away whatever coins they could get, in the noisome public houses that littered every street corner. Oh, no, it was one thing to pontificate about women's suffrage and equal rights under the law, quite another to pit such grandiose views against the grim realities of the underclasses.

Douglas Farrell strode from the gallery, still seething. Growing up fatherless in a household that comprised his mother and six older sisters, a household of chattering, squabbling, yet smothering women, he was inclined to sympathize with fellow Scot John Knox and his complaint about the monstrous regimen of women. True, Knox was referring to the queens who three hundred years ago had ruled England and Scotland, but Douglas, as he had threaded his way through the maze of womanhood that had dominated his youth, took a certain savage satisfaction in applying the comment to his own situation. An abundance of love could be as much of a disadvantage as too little, he had decided some years ago, and had managed to reach the age of thirty-five without succumbing to the trap of matrimony.

It had been a narrow escape with Marianne, the voice of honesty reminded him, but the little murmur was ruthlessly suppressed. The past was the past, and now he was ready to sacrifice the peace of bachelordom to the interests of his passionate commitment to the poor of London's underworld, and whose business was that but his own?

He could see no reason why the wealth of some privileged aristocratic woman shouldn't go towards improving the lot of the suffering men, women, and children whose existence he was certain she would barely acknowledge. And he could see no reason why he shouldn't put his considerable medical skills to work to the same philanthropic end, exploiting the hypochondriacs who could well afford to pay for his services. So, by what right did that undersized veiled creature with that ridiculous fake accent prate to him about love and respect in a marriage? She advertised a service and it was none of her business why her clients chose to avail themselves of it. He'd been cured of love matches, and if he'd wanted one now he'd have gone and found one for himself.

Fuming, he stalked down the steps of the museum and marched off in the direction of St. James's Park, hoping that the cold air would cool his temper, as indeed it did. By the time he'd crossed the park and reached Buckingham Palace, his customary sense of humor had reasserted itself. He had learned from the age of five that when dealing with women a sense of humor was essential if a man was not to court insanity.

* * *

Chastity hurried across Trafalgar Square, this time ignoring the pigeons who rose up in a flapping, cooing flock from around her feet. She hailed a hackney at Charing Cross, gave the cabbie the address of 10 Manchester Square, and climbed in, wrinkling her nose at the smell of stale tobacco that clung to the squabs.

She had been looking forward to meeting Douglas Farrell. That day when he'd walked into the corner shop to buy a copy of *The Mayfair Lady*, she'd found something intriguing about a doctor who practiced in the wretched area around Earl's Court. And she'd been very intrigued by one who bought several pounds of sweets. Far more licorice and humbugs than any one person could consume, and Chastity knew her own capacity when it came to the consumption of sweets to be more than ordinary. She had wondered if he'd been buying them for the poor children who attended his surgery at St. Mary Abbot's. It was an idea that had sparked her own empathetic nature and had made her eager to meet the man. But he was very different in person from how she had imagined him.

She put back her veil with a little sigh of relief as the cool air laved her overheated complexion. Mrs. Beedle had seemed to like him, but of course it stood to reason that the keeper of a small corner shop wouldn't have intimate knowledge of her customers. Was he living in Kensington? It seemed likely if he patronized Mrs. Beedle's shop. It was respectable enough, but hardly a fashionable address for an up-and-coming Harley Street physician. Convenient enough, of course, for an Earl's Court surgery. And presumably cheap enough. And money, of course, was one of his problems.

Chastity told herself that the Go-Between was a matchmaking service and passing moral judgment on its clients was not part of that service. If you looked at it from one point of view, the doctor had merely been blunt and to the point in stating his objectives.

It was just a hard point of view for Chastity to take. Dr. Farrell was coldly calculating. He wanted a wife who was both rich and influential, a woman that he could use for his own purposes. It made her scalp crawl. She was aware of an overwhelming sense of disappointment.

The cab drew up outside the imposing facade of No. 10 and she stepped down to the curb before paying the driver. She then hurried up the steps to the front door, shivering in a gust of wind that swept across the square garden. Jenkins, the butler, opened the door for her before she reached the top step.

"I saw the cab draw up, Miss Chas," he

said by way of explanation. "There's a bitter wind this afternoon."

"It smells like snow," Chastity said, stepping into the hall that was warmed by a fat steam radiator. "Is my father in?"

"His lordship hasn't left the library, Miss Chas," Jenkins said. "He says he thinks he's getting a bit of a chill."

"Oh, dear." Chastity frowned as she took off her gloves and hat. "Should we call the doctor?"

"I asked, but he said no."

Chastity nodded. "I'll go and see him. Perhaps he'd like some tea with whisky."

"I took the whisky decanter in just after luncheon," Jenkins said.

Chastity frowned again. Lord Duncan had become increasingly depressed since the libel case that had exposed the perfidy of his erstwhile bosom friend, the earl of Barclay. The case had exposed both his friend's betrayal and his own blind stupidity in trusting him. It was the latter that troubled Lord Duncan the most, or so his three daughters believed. Through his own stupidity he had lost the family fortune, entrusting it to a man who could be trusted only to deceive and defraud. As a result, Lord Duncan's daughters had turned *The Mayfair Lady* and the Go-Between into paying propositions whose income for a while had kept their father in ignorance of the true state of the family finances. That fact too was eating away at Lord Duncan's pride. The fact that his daughters had kept the truth from him while making shift themselves to keep the household from bankruptcy was something with which he could not come to terms.

Chastity went towards the library and hesitated, her hand raised to knock. Since Prudence's marriage six weeks earlier, Chastity was the only daughter living at 10 Manchester Square and the burden of Lord Duncan's increasing depression lay heaviest upon her shoulders. It was not that her sisters wouldn't share the burden, but simple physical distance from the house separated them from the moment-by-moment recognition.

She tapped lightly and then went into the room. It was in the semidarkness of late afternoon, with only the glow from the fire providing any illumination. "Wouldn't you like the lamps lit, Father?" she asked, closing the door behind her.

"No, no, I'm fine as it is. We don't want to waste the gas," Lord Duncan declared heavily from the depths of his armchair beside the fire. "Time enough to light them when it's dark."

Chastity frowned. One way her father dealt with his new knowledge of the true state of the household's finances was to insist on small and pointless economies. "Jenkins said you're not feeling too well, Father. Should we call Dr. Hastings?"

"No, no. No need for the expense of a quack," his lordship declared. "It's just a chill." He reached for the whisky decanter and Chastity noticed that the level was down about two-thirds. She knew that Jenkins would have brought it in full. Her father didn't seem the worse for wear, but he had a very strong head. He probably wasn't drinking any more than usual, she reflected, it was just that he was drinking alone, whereas in the old days he would have been at his club with his cronies. She couldn't remember when he'd last gone to his club.

"Are you dining out tonight?" she asked, forcing a cheerful note into her voice.

"No" was the unadorned negative.

"Why don't you go to your club?"

"I'm not up to it, Chastity." He took a deep draught of his whisky.

"Well, why don't you change your mind and come with me to Prudence and Gideon's dinner party?" she coaxed.

"I declined the invitation, my dear. I'm not going to change my mind on a whim and upset your sister's table arrangements." He leaned forward and refilled his glass.

Chastity gave up. Her father could never be met head-on, one had to approach obliquely. She leaned over and kissed him. "Stay in the warm, then. I'll see what Mrs. Hudson has for your supper."

"Oh, just some bread and cheese will do."

Chastity sighed, reflecting that her father's economic martyrdom was actually harder to handle than his blithe spending of the past. "I'm going to Prue's early to dress for dinner there, so I'm going to get my things together now. I'll pop in and say good-bye before I leave."

"Very well, my dear."

Chastity left the library and encountered Jenkins lighting the gas lamps in the hall. Lord Duncan, even if he could have afforded the innovation, considered electric light an abomination of the modern world. "Could you light the ones in the library?" she asked. "Father says he doesn't need them, but he can't go on sitting in the dark, it's so depressing."

"If you ask me, Miss Chas, his lordship needs something to take him out of himself," Jenkins said.

"I know. My sisters and I are racking our brains trying to come up with something," she responded. "Maybe Christmas will cheer him up. He always likes the Boxing Day hunt."

"We'll hope so," Jenkins said, sounding somewhat doubtful. "I wanted to make sure about the timing for Christmas, Miss Chas. Mrs. Hudson and I will be going down to

Romsey Manor on the day before Christmas Eve."

"Yes, and the rest of us will come down late afternoon on Christmas Eve, after Lord Lucan and Hester Winthrop's wedding," Chastity said. "The reception is a luncheon affair, so we should be able to catch the four o'clock and be there in time for the caroling."

"Very nice it will be to have a grand family Christmas again," Jenkins said.

Chastity smiled a little wistfully. "Yes, we haven't really had a proper one since Mother died. But with Prue and Gideon and Sarah, and Mary Winston, and Constance and Max and the aunts, it's going to be wonderful."

"In the old tradition," Jenkins agreed. "I'll go and light the library lamps now. I've told Cobham you'll be needing him at six. He'll bring the carriage around. You'll be staying the night with Miss Prue . . . Lady Malvern, I should say," he added.

"Not to her face, she won't know you're talking to her," Chastity said with a chuckle. "But, yes, I'm staying the night, and Sir Gideon's driver will bring me back in the morning." She left him in the hall and went towards the kitchen regions to consult with the cook, Mrs. Hudson, on the subject of her father's dinner.

"Oh, don't you worry, Miss Chas," Mrs. Hudson said comfortably. "I've a fine brace of pheasant for his lordship, with applesauce, just as he likes it. And there's his favorite chestnut soup, and I've baked a cream custard. Tempt his appetite nicely, that will."

"I knew you'd have it organized," Chastity said. "It certainly smells delicious in here." She smiled, bade the cook a cheerful farewell, and hastened upstairs to get together her clothes for the evening.

It still felt strange and rather lonely sometimes being the only one left in the house. In the old days the sisters would dress together, moving around between bedrooms, sharing clothes, jewels and trinkets, curling irons, asking one another's opinions of particular items of dress. Both Constance and Prudence were very aware of Chastity's possible loneliness and went out of their way to ensure that she spent almost as much time with them now as she had when they were all together under the same roof. Very rarely did Chastity dress alone if she and one or both of her sisters were attending the same social event; she had a standing invitation to stay at both houses. Natural delicacy kept her from overusing the invitation. Much as she liked her brothers-in-law and knew that the liking was mutual, she didn't want to intrude on her sisters' marriages.

Now she frowned to herself as she examined the contents of her wardrobe, contemplating the upcoming discussion with her sisters about her encounter with Douglas Farrell. Part of her cherished the secret wish that they would be as repulsed by the doctor's mercenary attitude as she herself was and would agree to decline his request for the Go-Between's service. She might wish it, but she also knew it was a fond hope. They would not turn down a paying client. But where were they going to find a suitably wealthy, suitably compliant, suitably socially positioned candidate for the doctor?

She chose an emerald-green silk gown with a low-cut neck and a small train that fell in graceful folds at the back from the high waist set just beneath her bosom. It was one of Doucet's creations, bought for Chastity by Constance in Paris on her honeymoon. She draped the gown over the back of a chair and selected the accessories, packing them in a small valise with her nightdress, toothbrush, and hairbrush. When all was assembled she gathered the gown over her arm, picked up her valise, and hastened downstairs just as the clock struck six.

Jenkins took her burdens and carried them out to the waiting carriage while she went to say good night to her father. Lord Duncan seemed a little more genial now. The lights burned cheerfully and the fire blazed. His whisky decanter was recharged and the good smell of roasting pheasant drifted from the kitchen. "Give your sisters my love, my dear," he instructed. "Tell them to come and see me once in a while."

"Father, really," Chastity protested. "They were here only yesterday. You know they come almost every day."

"Yes, but not to see me so much as to get on with the business of putting out that disgraceful rag you're all so proud of," Lord Duncan declared. "What your mother can have been thinking of when she started that publication, I can't imagine."

"Women's suffrage, as you know very well," Chastity told him, refusing to be drawn into this conversation. "And we're simply carrying the banner for her."

Lord Duncan harrumphed and waved her away. "Off you go, you don't want to be late."

"I'll be back in the morning," she said, kissing the top of his head. "Enjoy your dinner. Mrs. Hudson's cooked all your favorites, so be sure to thank her."

Shaking her head, she left him to his whisky. Cobham was waiting beside the carriage when she ran lightly down the steps, drawing her coat closer about her against the cold. The electric streetlights were lit and bright white pools glittered on the cobbles. It was a much less friendly light than the golden glow of gas, Chastity reflected, as she greeted the coachman and climbed into the carriage.

"My sister tells me you're retiring in the new year, Cobham," she said, settling the lap rug over her knees.

"Aye, Miss Chas. 'Tis time enough to go out to pasture," he said, whistling up the horses. "It's a nice snug little cottage Miss Prue . . . Lady Malvern . . . offered me an' the wife. Pleased as Punch is the wife. Nice little vegetable garden there. Happy as clams we'll be, I reckon."

"I'm sure you will," Chastity agreed, and huddled closer under the lap rug until they drew up outside the Malvern residence on Pall Mall Place.

Chapter 2

"Hello, Aunt Chas."

"Hello, Sarah." Chastity greeted her sister's eleven-year-old stepdaughter with a kiss. "How's school?"

"Boring," the girl said with an exaggerated, world-weary sigh. "Utterly tedious."

Chastity laughed. "I don't believe you, Sarah."

Sarah laughed back. "Well, I suppose there are *some* things I like, but you have to say it's all boring or people think there's something the matter with you."

Chastity correctly assumed that the people in question were Sarah's fellow schoolgirls. "I can understand that," she said sympathetically. "But it must be hard to pretend you're not enjoying yourself when you are."

"Oh, I'm quite a good actress," Sarah said blithely. "Is that the gown you're going to wear this evening? Let me take your valise."

"Yes, it is, and thank you." Chastity relinquished her burdens to the eager child. “Is Prue upstairs?”

“Oh, yes, and Daddy’s still in his chambers. They had words at breakfast, so I think he’s going to come home at the very last possible minute,” the girl confided with total lack of concern over a not infrequent event in the Malvern household.

“What did they have words about?” Chastity followed Sarah across the narrow hallway to the stairs.

“Something to do with a case that Daddy’s taking and Prue thinks he shouldn’t. I didn’t understand all of it, something about a man refusing to support a child.” Sarah danced ahead of Chastity up the stairs.

Chastity nodded to herself. If Prudence disapproved of something, she could be counted upon to say so. And Gideon could be counted upon to tell her to mind her own business. They were a somewhat flammable pair.

“Shall I put your things in the guest room? Prue’s in her sitting room.” Sarah paused outside a closed door on the landing above.

“Yes, thank you, Sarah. I’ll just go and say hello to Prue.” She smiled and hastened down the corridor to a pair of double doors at the far end. The door opened at her light knock and Prudence greeted her with a hug.

“Oh, I’m so glad you’re here,” she said, drawing her sister into a pretty, square sitting room that adjoined the large marital bedroom. "I am quite out of sorts with Gideon."

"Yes, Sarah said something." Chastity unbuttoned her coat. Ever the peacemaker, she prepared to listen to her sister's side. "Something about a man refusing to support a child."

"Sometimes I think Sarah hears far more than she should," Prudence said with a rueful frown, adjusting her spectacles on the bridge of her nose. "I wonder if we speak too freely in front of her."

"She's far too bright to get the wrong end of the stick," Chastity reassured. "And she's not afraid to ask if something puzzles her."

Prudence smiled. "No, you're right as usual. Gideon's always been very open with her, it would be a bad thing to change that just because I appeared on the scene."

"Exactly," her sister agreed, draping her coat over the back of a tapestry-covered chair. "So, tell me what happened."

Prudence filled two glasses from a sherry decanter that stood on a console table between two long windows, their rich amber velvet curtains drawn to shut out the winter night. She brought the glasses over to the sofa. Chastity took one and sat down, crossing her ankles, regarding her sister expectantly. She was accustomed to the role of sympathetic listener with both her sisters.

Prudence took a sip of sherry and began.

"Gideon's going to defend a man who's refusing to support a child born out of wedlock to his former mistress. It means that Gideon's going to be attacking the woman . . . her morals, her motives. Greed, he says, is what motivated her. She deliberately got pregnant in order to tie the man to her and is now trying to ruin his marriage and his career."

Chastity grimaced. She could sympathize absolutely with her sister. Any other viewpoint would be completely antithetical to any of the Duncan women. "Does Gideon really believe that?"

"No, I'm sure he doesn't. He says he takes any case that interests and challenges him regardless of guilt or innocence." Prudence shook her head disgustedly. "He said if he only took cases that fitted my moral framework, we'd all be out on the streets."

Chastity couldn't help laughing. "I'm sorry," she said. "But you must admit he's probably right. If we vetted every case offered to him according to our views of right and wrong, he'd have no practice."

Prudence smiled reluctantly. "It's not that I'm not practical about such things myself, but this just caught me on the raw."

"Yes, I can see why it would." Chastity sipped her sherry. "Is Con coming early this evening?"

Prudence glanced up at the clock on the

mantel. “She should be here soon. She said by seven at the latest, so that we can have time to discuss business before the guests arrive.”

“I’ll go and dress for dinner before she gets here, then.” Chastity stood up. “Could I borrow your topaz shawl? It goes so well with the green dress.”

“Of course. And you’ll need the matching ribbon for your hair. I’ll look them out while I’m dressing. Do you want a bath? I’ll send Becky to help you.”

“No, I bathed this morning and I can manage to dress myself,” Chastity said. “Somehow I don’t think I could get used to a lady’s maid.”

“Oh, you’d be surprised how quickly one can,” Prudence said. “Just wait until you’re living in the lap of luxury.”

Chastity just shook her head with a smile and made her way to the guest room where Sarah had hung up her gown. A jug of hot water steamed on the washstand beside a pile of thick towels. She unpacked her valise, reflecting that both her sisters had adapted with remarkable ease to the luxuries of life supplied by wealthy husbands. She could hardly blame them after all the time they had spent on the verge of bankruptcy, gradually giving up all the little luxuries they had known when their mother was alive, before Lord Duncan lost his shirt to the earl of

Barclay. For herself, though, she thought she would find the attentions of a lady's maid too intrusive. She was perfectly capable of dressing herself, after all.

She returned to her sister's sitting room within twenty minutes, fastening the wrist buttons of the tight sleeves of her gown as she went. Prudence, dressed now in an evening gown of black and gray silk, her cinnamon-colored hair piled in a pompadour, emerged from the bedroom as Chastity closed the sitting room door behind her.

"I do love that dress," Prudence said admiringly. "That shade of green is just magnificent with your hair. Here, let me fasten the ribbon." Deftly, she threaded the topaz ribbon into Chastity's artfully arranged red curls and then draped the matching shawl over her shoulders. "There, you look lovely, as always." A slight frown crossed her light green eyes. "You look thinner, Chas."

"Yes, I thought this gown was a bit looser." Chastity smoothed the folds down over her frame with a pleased air. She was the shortest of the three sisters and more inclined to roundness than either the much taller Constance or the much more angular Prudence. "I'm probably not eating so much cake," she said, cheerfully dismissing the subject.

"Who did you invite for me this evening?" She stood on tiptoe to examine her completed coiffure in the overmantel mirror. She licked a finger and smoothed her arched eyebrows over her hazel eyes.

"Roddie Brigham. That's all right, isn't it?" Prudence asked a little anxiously.

"Yes, of course it is. He's easy to talk to and we always enjoy each other's company," Chastity responded.

"You don't sound overwhelmed with enthusiasm," her sister observed.

"I'm sorry." Chastity turned back from the mirror and smiled at her. "I like Roddie and I like not having to stand on ceremony with him." She regarded Prudence with a slightly quizzical air. "But even though he's asked me to marry him at least three times, I am not looking for a husband, Prue, so don't get your hopes up."

"In my experience, you don't have to look for one, they just turn up," Prudence replied.

"What just turn up?"

They both spun to the door at the new voice. Their eldest sister, Constance, came into the room, preceded by a waft of exotic fragrance.

"Husbands," Prudence said.

"Oh, yes." Constance nodded. "How true. They tend to appear where least expected." She kissed her sisters. "You haven't found one, have you, Chas?"

"Not since yesterday," her sister informed her with a laugh. "But, as I just said, I'm not looking. At least," she added, "not for myself."

"Ah, did we acquire a new client this afternoon?" Prudence asked, remembering that Chastity was keeping an appointment as the Go-Between.

Chastity's small nose wrinkled. "I'd much rather tell him to go and fish in some other pool," she said. "He's really obnoxious."

Constance poured sherry for them all. "But that's not really the point, Chas," she said slowly. "We don't have to like our clients."

"I know." Chastity took the offered glass and arranged herself on the sofa again.

"What was his name? Doctor something . . ." Prudence sat down on the opposite sofa.

"Farrell. Douglas Farrell." She sipped her sherry. "He wants a rich wife, first and foremost. An essential *quality,* if that's the word." She couldn't disguise her distaste.

"Well, at least he's honest," Constance pointed out.

"Oh, yes, he's that all right. Not only must this wife be rich, she must also be willing and socially positioned to entice rich patients for him."

"Where does he practice?"

"Harley Street. He's just beginning to build a practice, hence the need for a procuress."

Her sisters grimaced. "Must you put it like that, Chas?" asked Prudence.

"I did to him and he said it was exactly right. He liked to call a spade a spade."

"You really didn't like him," Constance stated.

"No, I did not." Chastity sighed. "He's so cold and calculating. And he was so scornful of the Harley Street patients that he wants to enroll, basically said they were hypochondriacal malingerers. I can't imagine what his bedside manner must be like."

Her sisters regarded her in silence for a minute. It was so unlike Chastity to take such a determined stance against someone. Of the three of them she was the most charitably inclined, the least willing to criticize.

"It's not like you to be so dead-set against someone, Chas," Constance said.

Chastity shrugged. "He put my back up, I suppose." For some reason that she did not understand, she had not confided to her sisters her first unwitting sight of Dr. Farrell at Mrs. Beedle's. And for the same inexplicable reason she couldn't bring herself to tell them how her dislike of the man was rooted in disappointment. It seemed so illogical to have formed expectations of someone based on a clandestine observation behind a shop curtain.

"But you didn't tell him we wouldn't take him on as a client?" Prudence sounded a little anxious. Chastity could sometimes forget the financial priorities of their business, although that usually meant she pressed her sisters to take on clients just because she felt sorry for them, regardless of their ability to pay for the Go-Between's services.

"I wouldn't tell him that without consulting you two," Chastity said. "But that's what I would like to do. I can't imagine condemning any woman to such a cold and sterile relationship."

"Not every woman would see it your way," Prudence reminded her. "Successful Harley Street physicians are highly desirable on the marriage mart."

"Maybe so, but is it right to take advantage of a woman so desperate for a husband that she would basically sell herself? Because that's what it comes down to."

"Now, why am I not surprised to find the cabal gathered?" Sir Gideon Malvern's melodic voice interrupted the tête-à-tête. He entered the sitting room still in his street clothes. "Good evening, Constance, Chastity." He bent to kiss Prudence, who hadn't moved from the sofa. "And how are you, madam wife? In a better frame of mind, I trust."

"You could ask yourself that question," Prudence returned with asperity.

"Oh, I have," he said cheerfully. "And the answer is definitely in the affirmative."

Prudence felt the wind had been taken from her sails. Her husband had a way of disarming her that never failed. "Hadn't you better dress?" she said, a smile flickering at the corners of her mouth. "Guests are expected at eight-fifteen."

He nodded and moved towards the bedroom, asking over his shoulder, "Is Max coming this evening, Constance?"

"He certainly expects to," she said. "Parliament is in recess."

"Oh, good. I want to discuss something with him."

"Your case?" Prudence inquired.

"No, Christmas, as it happens," he replied, pulling his tie loose. "I'll be in my dressing room if anyone wants me." He disappeared into the bedroom.

"A quarrel?" Constance inquired of her sister with a knowingly raised eyebrow.

"Just a case he's taking that I don't agree with." Prudence put her in the picture and was gratified to see that Constance was at least as outraged as she by the defense Gideon intended to mount.

"Well, there's not much that can be done about it now," Chastity said. "Maybe you can work on him behind the bed curtains."

"I doubt it, he's as stubborn as an ox." Prudence sounded resigned.

"Speaking of which," Chastity said. "Father."

Her sisters were all attention. "Is there something new?" Constance asked.

Chastity shook her head. "Not since you

saw him yesterday. But he's not improving. His frame of mind . . . he's so depressed, and he just sits in his chair making inroads into the whisky decanter, staring into space, blaming himself for everything."

"We need to take him out of himself," Prudence said.

"That's what Jenkins said."

"Easier said than done, though," Constance stated.

"I had an idea on the way over here." Chastity looked at her sisters in turn, her gaze a little hesitant, a tentative note in her voice. "I don't know what you'll think of it."

"Well, tell us, love." Constance leaned forward attentively.

"I was thinking that maybe a companion . . ." Chastity paused, unsure how to go on. What she was about to propose could upset her sisters, could seem like an act of disloyalty to their mother's memory. "A wife," she said, making up her mind. "I thought, since we find wives and husbands for people all over town, maybe we could find a wife for Father. It's been nearly four years since Mother died. I don't think she'd mind. In fact —"

"In fact, she would applaud the idea," Constance interrupted strongly. "It's a brilliant idea, Chas."

Prudence was still silent, and they both looked to her. After a minute, she said slowly, "A woman of independent means would be perfect."

"Or even better, a wife of more than independent means," Constance said.

"But that's just as bad as Douglas Farrell," Chastity protested. "It's so mercenary. I just thought he might enjoy a loving companion. She doesn't have to be rich."

"No. No, of course not," Prudence soothed. "But if perhaps she was, well, wouldn't that really gild the lily? Father wouldn't be thinking about money, and of course we wouldn't put someone in his way whom we didn't like. But . . ." She shrugged. "Money has its uses, Chas."

"As if I didn't know that," Chastity said. "So, you think I'm being too nice in my objections to Farrell's mercenary attitude?"

"Quite frankly, yes," Prudence said, glancing at Constance, who nodded her agreement.

Chastity frowned into her sherry glass, then she said, "Very well. I thought you'd say that anyway. But you didn't meet him, don't forget. He's a dour, calculating, mercenary Scotsman."

"But he's also a doctor," Prudence reminded her. "He must have an interest in helping people. That should appeal to you, Chas."

"It would if I thought it was true," her sister said. "But he reminded me of some

Victorian industrialist who couldn't care what tools he used to advance himself, or whom he trampled on to get his way. He seemed to think that so long as he was honest about his greed, there was nothing to object to."

"You got all that in just a brief meeting in the National Gallery?" Constance asked in astonishment.

Chastity flushed slightly. "It does seem a little extreme," she admitted.

"Maybe when you see him in an ordinary social situation you'll see him in a different light," Prudence suggested.

"Well, we can't issue any invitations until we have some prospective brides," Chastity pointed out. "Who do we know rich and desperate enough to enter into a mutually convenient business partnership under the guise of marriage?"

"At least we know they don't have to have beauty or brains," Prudence said.

"Or even character," Chastity said with a touch of acid. "We do know our client is not in the least fussy about such minor matters."

"You've made your point, Chas." Prudence rose to her feet. "We'd better go down to the drawing room, the first guests will arrive any minute." She stuck her head around the bedroom door and called, "Gideon, we're going down. Hurry up."

Her husband appeared immediately, fastening his cuff links. "Is Sarah going to be in the drawing room before dinner?"

"She's hoping so, but I said you'd have to decide." Gideon had been Sarah's only parent for close to seven years and Prudence was still learning the moves of the stepparent dance — when it was appropriate to disagree or to make her own suggestions, and when to keep her opinions to herself.

"Do you think she's old enough?" he asked, turning back to get his coat.

"I would say so."

"Then, by all means. I'll be down in a couple of minutes."

The three women went to the drawing room. Sarah was hovering in the hall as they came down the stairs. "Can I stay for a little, Prue?"

"Yes, until we go in to dinner," her stepmother said. "Your father said it would be all right." She examined the girl, who, in anticipation of this permission, had donned her best party dress. The ink on her fingers rather spoiled the effect, but Prudence didn't think it worth mentioning. She adjusted a hair clip to catch up a drifting lock of hair behind Sarah's right ear. "Perhaps you could pass around the canapés."

"Oh, yes, I could certainly do that," Sarah agreed. She noticed Constance for the first time. "Hello, Aunt Con, I didn't hear you arrive. I must have been getting dressed."

"Yes, I'm sure that must be it," Constance

agreed gravely. "Your ears are far too sharp to have missed my arrival otherwise."

Sarah regarded her doubtfully for a second, as if trying to decide whether she was being made fun of, but then decided that it didn't matter if she was. She liked her newly acquired aunts. They never talked down to her, never excluded her, and were all amazingly competent when it came to tricky areas of homework. And they were great favorites with her father.

They went into the drawing room and Prudence cast a swift eye over the arrangements. All seemed in place.

"Who are our fellow guests, Prue?" Constance asked. "Anyone we don't know?"

"Only the Contessa Della Luca and her daughter, Laura. Everyone else you know."

Chastity cocked her head. "They sound exotic, Prue."

"The contessa was a client of Gideon's."

"One you approved of," Chastity put in with a hint of mischief, her habitual equanimity restored.

"Yes, Chas," Prudence said with an answering laugh. "A simple matter of helping her reclaim an estate. She's English, was married to an Italian count, and was recently widowed, so she decided to come back to London with her daughter. I haven't met either of them, I only know what Gideon told me. He asked me to invite them . . . to introduce them socially. I don't think he's met the daughter. Gideon, have you met Laura Della Luca?" she asked as her husband entered the room.

"No, only her mother. She's a pleasant woman. I assume the daughter is the same." He went to pour himself a whisky. "Can I get you all another sherry?"

The doorbell chimed and they heard Max Ensor's voice greeting the butler with easy familiarity. Max came into the drawing room, accompanied by Sarah, who announced, "The Right Honorable Max Ensor, Minister of Transport and Member of Parliament for Southwold."

"Cheeky madam," Max said, lightly tapping her cheek. Sarah ducked and grinned. She liked this newly acquired uncle as much as she liked her aunts.

"May I get you a drink, Uncle Max?"

"Whisky, please, Sarah." He kissed his wife, then his sisters-in-law, and shook hands with his brother-in-law.

"Busy day?" Constance asked, smiling up at him as he perched on the arm of the sofa beside her.

"No, an indolent one," he said, twisting one of her russet side curls around his finger. "I played billiards all afternoon."

"And did you win?" Constance knew her husband was as competitive as she was.

"Need you ask?"

She laughed. "No, of course you did."

The butler announced the first dinner guests and the time for intimate family chat was over.

Chastity dutifully devoted her attention to Lord Roderick Brigham, who was to take her in to dinner. It was no particular hardship, since she'd known him for years and he had an easy, accomplished manner. They performed the obligatory steps in the social dance automatically and were exchanging pleasantries about family matters when the Contessa Della Luca and her daughter were announced.

"Do you know them?" asked Lord Brigham in an undertone.

"No," Chastity said. "Do you?"

"Only by repute. My mother met them at tea at Lady Wigan's the other day."

Chastity glanced up at him, hearing something left unsaid. Lord Brigham's mother was a somewhat fearsome lady but an excellent judge of character. "And?" she asked with the ease of established friendship.

He lowered his head so that his mouth was close to her ear. "My mother found the contessa charming, but the daughter . . ." He let the sentence trail off.

"You can't stop there," Chastity declared in an undertone, looking covertly at the new arrivals, who were being greeted by their host and hostess.

"A bore," he whispered. "A priggish bore, to be exact."

Chastity told herself it was uncharitable to be amused by gossip, but she couldn't help a stifled chuckle. She could hear the formidable Lady Brigham pronouncing the condemnation in her elegantly articulated tones, probably with her long nose lifted in disdain.

"We had better be introduced," she murmured, and moved away from him towards the knot of people gathered by the fireplace.

"Contessa, may I introduce my sister, the Honorable Chastity Duncan," Prudence said as her younger sister came up to them. "The Contessa Della Luca . . ." She waved an introductory hand between them.

Chastity shook the hand of a woman well into her middle years, coiffed in somewhat spectacular style with ostrich plumes swaying in her graying pompadour. Her gown was of blue and gold damask, bustled and tightly corseted, with leg-of-mutton sleeves. It was slightly old-fashioned but it suited the woman's rather stately figure. The diamonds at her throat and ears were magnificent.

"Welcome to London, Contessa," she said, smiling warmly.

"Why, thank you, Miss Duncan. Everyone has been so kind." Her voice had a slight hesitancy, the barest trace of an accent, not as if she was speaking a foreign language, Chastity thought, but more as if her English was overlaid by a language she was more accustomed to speaking.

"And this is Miss Della Luca," Prudence said. "Miss Della Luca, my sister Chastity."

Laura Della Luca looked down upon Chastity. She was very tall and thin, dressed in a high-collared, very decorous gown of dove gray that hung from her narrow shoulders as if from a clothes hanger. Her hair was severely parted in the center and drawn back over her ears in two neat, braided circles. Her gaze was supercilious. Her narrow mouth moved in the semblance of a smile. "Delighted," she said in a voice that quite failed to express delight. "I am so unaccustomed to being called *miss*," she said. "I am so much more comfortable with *signorina*."

"We must try to remember that," Prudence said with a smile that came nowhere near her eyes. "Foreign ways are so new to us."

Chastity caught Gideon's eye. He seemed to be well aware that this particular guest was sailing a little close to the sharp edge of his wife's tongue. Not that anyone but Prudence's immediate family would be aware of it. Signorina Della Luca would be entirely oblivious of the darts of mockery that would puncture with unerring accuracy any attempts at pretension.

"Yes, I find the English are so poorly traveled," the lady said. "Travel is so broadening for the mind."

"Indeed," Constance said with a smile very similar to her sister's. "How strange, then, that it should so often breed contempt for the natives of these backward lands."

Max and Gideon exchanged looks that mingled reluctant amusement with a degree of desperation. Once their wives were up and running in this fashion, very little could stop them.

Chastity, however, came to the rescue. "Oh, you must tell me all about Italy," she said. "My sisters and I spent some time in Florence with our mother, but it was a long time ago. Or it seems so," she added. "You know Florence intimately, I'm sure."

"Oh, *Firenze,* of course," said the lady with a trill. "We have a villa just outside. I sometimes think that the Uffizi is my second home."

"How fortunate for you," Chastity said. "We were only able to spend a month there ourselves."

"A month is long enough to get to know the gallery very well, Miss Duncan," said the contessa with a pleasant smile.

"With due study, of course," her daughter put in. "But I hardly think, Mama, that a tourist visit to *Firenze,* even for a month, can be any substitute for living there."

"Dinner is served, Lady Malvern." The sonorous tones of the butler brought a timely conclusion to the conversation and Gideon breathed again.

He offered his arm to the contessa. Max, at a nod from his sister-in-law, performed the same service for the signorina, and the party fell into couples, the procession moving in stately fashion across the hall and into the dining room.

Prudence had seated the contessa in the place of honor on Gideon's right. The signorina she had placed between a judge colleague of Gideon's, who sat on her own right, and Max. She was thus in close proximity to her guest. Fortunately, Chastity and Roddie Brigham sat opposite at the same end of the table, so there was some conversational relief. Constance, up at Gideon's end, would be unable to participate in any conversation at the far end of the table.

"Did Gideon do any of the cooking this evening, Prue?" Chastity asked her sister as she sat down.

"No, but he did choose the menu," Prudence responded. She turned to the signorina. "My husband, Miss Della Luca, is a considerable chef."

"Oh, really . . . how unusual." Laura looked askance. "You would never find an Italian man in the kitchen. Most unmasculine."

"Ah, yes," Prudence said. "But the Italian character is perhaps a little different from the English. Englishmen are perhaps less concerned about their masculinity. It is perhaps more innate, would you not say, gentlemen?" She smiled at the men on either side of her.

"I think it's probably more to do with the type of cuisine," Max suggested swiftly. "Pasta, as I understand it, is very time-consuming to create. Women, by the very nature of things, have more time at their disposal."

"Oh, that's a generalization, Max," Chastity put in, hoping to divert the conversation from the competitive advantages of Italy over England. "Not all women have nothing to do but lie around reading magazines and gossiping all day. Apart from anything else, they make up the majority of the domestic workforce."

"My point exactly." He was deliberately goading now. "Domesticity is a woman's natural inclination, and the preparation of food is but one example. Wouldn't you agree, Judge?"

"Just so, just so," the judge agreed, nodding vaguely as he dipped his spoon with rhythmic concentration. "Excellent soup, Lady Malvern. I congratulate your cook."

"Perhaps you can explain why so many of the best chefs are male," Chastity said, seeing Laura Della Luca open her mouth. "In France, in particular. Are you well acquainted with France, signorina?"

"Oh, *mais oui*. Paris is my second home."

"I thought that was the Uffizi," Prudence remarked into her plate, but too softly for the signorina to hear, since she was expatiating at great length on the glories of the Louvre, in which she seemed to take a personal pride.

It continued in this fashion throughout dinner. Laura Della Luca dominated the conversation, dragging it remorselessly back to her own opinions whenever someone managed to create a diversion. Even Chastity gave up.

It was with relief that Prudence caught Gideon's eye at the end of the meal and rose from the table. "Ladies, shall we withdraw?"

The gentlemen all rose to help the ladies to their feet and waited until the female half of the dinner party had left the dining room.

Prudence led the way back to the drawing room, where coffee was laid ready for them. "I understand, Contessa, that you have bought a house in Mayfair," she said, pouring coffee and handing the cup to the footman to deliver.

"Yes, in Park Lane," the contessa said. "A very gracious house."

"Not as large or commodious as our villa outside *Firenze*," put in her daughter.

"It is quite large enough for our purposes," her mother said, taking the coffee from the footman. "With a very pleasant garden."

"And, of course, you have Hyde Park opposite," Constance said. She glanced at Chastity, who seemed to be sunk in reverie. "We always used to enjoy riding there. Do you remember, when we were children, Chas?"

Chastity looked up from her contemplation of her coffee cup. "I beg your pardon . . ."

"Riding in Hyde Park," Constance said. "We used to enjoy it."

"Yes, oh, yes." Chastity seemed visibly to pull herself back into the room. "I still do, but we don't often get the chance. Our horses are in the country, and I don't really like the job horses the stables have for hire."

"Oh, I would never hire a riding horse," declared the signorina with a wave of her thin hand. "Their mouths are so hard."

"My stepdaughter rides there quite often," Prudence said, sweeping past the interruption.

"Only the best in horseflesh will do for me," the lady continued, ignoring her hostess. "I had the most beautiful filly at home, did I not, Mama?"

Her mother consented and the signorina continued to expatiate on the delights and concerns of owning an Arabian mare, while somehow managing to convey to her companions that of course no one else could possibly have experienced either the delight or the concern.

The woman was impossible, Prudence thought disgustedly. She wasn't worth the time or effort to snub.

Chastity asked suddenly, "Signorina Della Luca, do you intend to be presented at

Court? You will find it necessary if you intend to participate in the London Season."

"Oh, most certainly, I do," the lady declared. "Why else would we come to London? After Christmas, Mama will present me. She was herself presented to Queen Victoria, of course."

"Of course." Chastity's smile was a little vague and she seemed to return to her reverie. If Laura Della Luca was intending to participate fully in the Season in the new year, then she must be on the lookout for a husband. She was, by even the kindest assessment, approaching the shelf. How anxious was she to get herself to the altar? Chastity mused.

Chapter 3

"What a pill," Prudence declared when the door had closed on the last of their guests. "Not even you, Chas, could find any redeeming features in *Signorina Della Luca*." She imitated the woman's affected accents.

"Oh, I don't know," Chastity said. "There might be some external redeeming features if one looked for them."

Constance looked at her sharply. "You've been very absorbed all evening, Chas," she observed. "You hardly said anything after we left the dining room."

Chastity only smiled and helped herself to a chocolate from the silver bonbon dish on the low marquetry table in front of the sofa where she sat.

"Cognac, Constance?" Gideon asked, well aware of his sister-in-law's tastes.

"Thank you." She accepted a goblet.

"Liqueur, Prudence?"

"Grand Marnier, please."

"And the same for you, Chastity?"

"No, Benedictine, I think," Chastity responded. "It goes better with chocolate."

Gideon smiled. Chastity's sweet tooth was something of a family joke.

Prudence took the tiny glass filled with the sweetish orange liqueur and remarked, "Did you say earlier that you wanted to talk to Max about something, Gideon? Something about Christmas, wasn't it?"

"Ah-ha," Max said. "I get the impression we're being dismissed, Gideon."

" 'Tis ever thus," Gideon said with a mock sigh as he rose from a deep armchair beside the fire. "Thrown out of my own drawing room, cast into the cold."

"There's nothing cold about the library," Prudence pointed out, removing her glasses from her nose and holding them up to the light to see if she could detect a smudge. "Take the cognac decanter with you and go and smoke a cigar."

"As you command." Gideon, shaking his head, picked up the cut-glass decanter. "Come, Max, my fellow exile." The two men went out, leaving the laughing sisters in sole possession of the drawing room.

"Now," said Prudence, replacing her glasses and coming to sit beside Chastity. "What have you been concocting, Chas?"

Chastity took another chocolate and followed it with a tiny but delicious sip of Benedictine. "Those monks certainly knew what they were doing," she said, holding up her glass to the light.

"Come on, Chas." Constance leaned forward and moved the bonbon bowl out of her baby sister's reach.

"Oh, unfair," Chastity said, but she set down her liqueur glass.

"External redeeming features," Prudence reminded her.

"Yes, well, I had a thought . . . two, actually. I do seem to be having rather a number of them just recently." Chastity sounded a little smug. "Our friend Laura is indeed a pill, but it's possible that for some people the 'pillness' of her would be irrelevant, if other features could be seen as compensations."

"Yes . . . ?" Constance said with an interrogatively raised eyebrow.

"Do you think she's in the market for a husband?" Chastity asked. "It's the only reason why anyone would go through all the palaver and expense of presentation at Court and the Season. Particularly at her age."

Her sisters were nodding in unison. "How old do you think she is?" Prudence inquired with a frown. "Late twenties, early thirties?"

"Without being ungenerous," Constance said, clearly unconcerned about generosity, "I would say more likely early-to-mid thirties. Did you notice the lines at the corners of her mouth, and under her eyes?"

"They could just come from a disagreeable

nature," Chastity pointed out judiciously. "People who frown a lot and pull down their mouths often get premature lines, I've noticed."

"Let's assume that she *is* on the marriage mart and rather anxious. What are you suggesting, Chas?" Prudence came to the point.

"Well, I think she must have money. Her mother clearly does and she's an only child, at least as far as we know. Houses in Mayfair aren't cheap, and neither is bankrolling a Court presentation and a Season."

"Not to mention Arabian mares and villas in *Firenze*," Constance put in. "I think I know where this is going, Chas."

Chastity smiled and sat back against the sofa cushions. "An up-and-coming Society physician who has no particular interest in a congenial wife, merely a rich one . . ."

Her sisters sat in silence, examining the prospect from every angle. "But do you think our Laura would be interested in a man who is still only up-and-coming?" Prudence asked eventually.

"I should imagine she would welcome the opportunity to help and instruct him in the right way to go about arriving at the pinnacle of his ambition," Chastity said. "I can just see her presiding over dinner parties, lecturing all and sundry on the cultural marvels of foreign parts, boring her guests into total submission."

She leaned forward to retrieve the bonbon bowl with the tips of her fingers and took another chocolate before adding thoughtfully, "She has something of the bully in her, I think. I'm sure she would relish rounding up patients regardless of objections and delivering them with open wallets to his surgery. It could well be a perfect match." She popped the chocolate into her mouth and leaned back against the cushions again.

"Your Dr. Farrell is a bully?" Prudence asked, exchanging a quick, frowning glance with Constance.

Chastity shrugged. "I don't know, really, but his tone when he talked of his potential patients was so contemptuous . . ." She hesitated, then said, "Anyway, I think they might deserve each other. I certainly wouldn't feel we were condemning a defenseless woman to a marriage of convenience with an unfeeling man."

"All right," Constance agreed. "Let's put them together and see what happens. We can't *make* them decide to marry. If they don't suit, they'll decide that for themselves."

"Your next At Home, Con?" Prudence suggested.

"No, I think it should be mine," Chastity said quickly. "At Manchester Square, next Wednesday."

"Any particular reason?" Prudence asked.

"Well, I had two ideas, if you remember."

Chastity was smiling now, the frown that seemed to accompany any discussion about Dr. Douglas Farrell no longer in evidence. "What do you think of Father and the contessa?"

"I think I like it," Constance said. Then she frowned. "You do realize that would make Laura our stepsister. And we couldn't possibly condemn Father to having her under his roof."

"No," agreed Chastity. "But if we married her off beforehand, it wouldn't be that bad. We wouldn't have to spend time with her except for obligatory family occasions, and neither would Father."

"I should think that the prospect of her mother remarrying might encourage the daughter to get herself to the altar as soon as possible," Prudence remarked.

"Yes, precisely," Chastity said with some satisfaction. "One hand washing the other, really."

"So, you invite both women for next Wednesday and we twist Father's arm to be there, and we send Douglas Farrell the usual instructions," Constance said. "That means flowers for every woman, and a white one for Laura."

"It'll have to be carnations," Prudence said. "They're the only buttonhole flowers easily obtained at this time of year."

"Then that's settled." Chastity nodded. "A

good evening's work."

A slight alerting tap on the door brought the return of Max and Gideon. The two men had no difficulty reading the slightly self-conscious start given by all three sisters at the interruption. "Just what miserable souls' lives have you been rearranging now?" Max asked.

"You know perfectly well we only suggest helpful things," his wife said with dignity as she stood up. "We work only in the interests of good."

"Tell that to some of those pathetic people who've had their lives ruthlessly turned upside down without their even knowing it," said Gideon.

"Can you give me one example of a couple we've put together who are unhappy about it?" his wife demanded.

Gideon threw up his hands in defeat. "Since I don't know half of them, what can I say?"

"Leave us to do our business just as we leave you to do yours," Prudence said.

"You still express opinions," he commented mildly. "Is a husband to be accorded the same right?"

"If you're ready, Constance, I believe it's time we went home," Max said.

"And I think it's time I went to bed," Chastity said, jumping up from the sofa.

"Now look what you've done," Prudence accused her husband, but with a laugh in her voice. "Driven away our guests by being quarrelsome."

"Not a bit of it," he denied. "They were going anyway." He moved to the door. "Constance, Max, let me see you out."

"By the way, what were you discussing about Christmas?" Constance asked as they all walked into the hall.

"Now, that is truly none of your business," Max said.

"Surprises?" Chastity asked, her hazel eyes glowing. "I love surprises, particularly Christmas ones."

"Then I hope you won't be disappointed. Good night, Chastity." Max kissed her and bade farewell to his hosts. Constance hugged her sisters and the Ensors went out into the crisp night to their motor, waiting at the curb, engine running, the chauffeur huddled into a heavy driving cape.

Chastity yawned. "I'll bid you good night, Gideon."

"I'll come up with you and make sure you have everything you need," Prudence said, linking arms with her. "Will you be long, Gideon?"

"No, I'll just turn out the lights and lock the door," he said. "I sent the staff to bed an hour ago."

Prudence examined the arrangements in the guest room with a critical eye. "I think you have everything," she said, smoothing down the already smooth coverlet before going to the dresser. "There's milk and chocolate and the spirit stove here if you'd like hot chocolate." It was a reference to the sisters' nightly ritual in their father's house, when they would gather together over hot chocolate in their own private sitting room to talk over the events of the evening.

Chastity shook her head, smiling. "Not after chocolates and Benedictine," she said. "Everything is perfect, Prue, so go to bed and I'll see you in the morning."

Prudence nodded but hesitated, her hand on the doorknob. "This Douglas Farrell," she said, "you seem to have developed such an antipathy towards him. Do you think you'll be able to meet him face-to-face . . . do what we have to do for him as a client without betraying something?"

Chastity unthreaded the topaz ribbon from her hair before answering. Then she said, "I don't see why not. We'll only be meeting in social situations. He won't have any idea that we're the Go-Between. Even if he senses I dislike him, it's not going to matter. People dislike people all the time, but they're perfectly polite about it. Anyway, I'm sure I can hide it. There's no reason why I should ever be alone with him, and when we're in company I'll just keep the conversation on neutral subjects."

"I suppose so," her sister said, sounding

unconvinced. " 'Night, Chas." She went out, closing the door behind her.

Chastity surveyed the closed door for a minute. She understood her sister's puzzlement. She was as puzzled herself by this violent dislike of a man she'd only met once. Maybe, she thought, as she got to know him better she'd find something in him to ameliorate that dislike. First impressions couldn't always be relied upon. But she didn't seem to be able to convince herself, however hard she tried, as she brushed her thick, vivid red curls the requisite one hundred strokes and completed her nighttime ablutions, hanging the emerald-green gown in the armoire before slipping into her nightgown.

She climbed into bed and lay propped on the pillows, watching the firelight dance on the molded ceiling. For some reason she wasn't sleepy. She reached out and turned on the bedside light again. An easy matter since Gideon, like Max, embraced all modern conveniences of daily life with a vengeance, whether it be electric lights, motorcars, or telephones.

There was a small secretaire in the guest room, with pen, ink, and a writing tablet. Chastity got out of bed and went to sit at the desk. She began to compose the Go-Between's letter to Dr. Douglas Farrell. He was to present himself at 10 Manchester Square on Wednesday next at three o'clock, when the lady of the house, the Honorable Miss Chastity Duncan, would be holding her weekly At Home. He was to give the butler his card and explain that he needed to talk with Lord Buckingham, whom he had been told he could meet there that afternoon.

Chastity leaned back in the spindly chair, tapping her teeth with the top of her pen. There was, of course, no Lord Buckingham. The fictitious character was merely the excuse the Go-Between routinely used to bring prospective clients together.

She put pen to paper again, explaining that Miss Duncan herself would have no idea who Dr. Farrell was, but since she was acquainted with Lord Buckingham would welcome the doctor without question. *Intimately acquainted with Lord Buckingham,* Chastity reflected with a grin. Since he had sprung for the first time from her imagination.

A lady whom the doctor might find of interest in his search for a bride would be wearing a white carnation. If, after observation, he wished for an introduction, his hostess would furnish it, again without question.

Chastity set down her pen and read through the letter. It was one she had written many times before, so she could find no fault. She signed it *The Go-Between,* blotted the sheet, folded it, and slipped it into an envelope that she addressed to the doctor, care of Mrs. Beedle's corner shop, as Douglas Farrell's original letter had requested. Mrs. Beedle acted as a poste restante for more clients than *The Mayfair Lady* and the Go-Between, and Chastity had been puzzling for some time over why a London doctor should need a poste restante. Did he not have an address of his own? It was a question that came into the same category as what such a man with his social ambitions was doing frequenting such an unfashionable part of town.

She frowned, thinking about the surgery just off St. Mary Abbot's. Chastity had never set foot in that area of London, but she knew, or thought she did, that Earl's Court, the Warwick Road, and the Cromwell Road were not just unfashionable but downright slums, for the most part. He couldn't make much money practicing medicine there, which was presumably part of his problem. But just why would a man who was openly and unashamedly trawling for a rich wife and a wealthy practice waste any time at all on the poor and infirm of the London slums? Perhaps he had no choice, she decided. Perhaps he was such a bad doctor, only the poor who had no alternative would go to him. From what she'd seen of his general attitude, he'd have a hard time buttering up the wealthy socialites who required a mixture of obsequiousness and authority in their medical practitioners. He probably realized that, hence the need for the well-connected wife who could smooth out the rough edges, or, in the case of the Signorina Della Luca, ride right over them, herding prospective patients to his Harley Street practice like so many stunned cattle to the abattoir.

Chastity yawned, somewhat dismayed by her own malice. It was not at all like her. She set the letter on the secretaire, intending to give it to Prue's butler to post in the morning, then returned to bed, this time to sleep.

It was cold in the bare back room despite the miserable flicker of a coal fire in the grate. The woman on the straw-filled mattress writhed in silence, stoically enduring what she had endured six times before.

Douglas Farrell straightened from his examination and said softly, "Bring that candle closer, Ellie."

The girl, who looked to be no more than eight, hurriedly brought the stub of a candle over to the doctor. She held it high, as he instructed, but averted her eyes from her mother's agony.

"Did you boil the water?" Douglas asked, his tone still soft and gentle as he palpated the swollen abdomen.

"Charlie's doin' it," the child replied. "Ma's goin' t'be all right, i'n't she, Doctor?"

"Your mother knows what she's doing," he

replied. The woman jerked, and his hands moved swiftly now between the blood-streaked thighs. "Hold the candle steady, Ellie."

The woman cried out abruptly for the first time, her body convulsed, and a blood-soaked scrap appeared between the doctor's hands. He worked fast and deftly, clearing the infant's nasal passages. A thin cry emerged and the blue body took on a pinkish hue. "A boy, Mrs. Jones," he said, cutting the thick cord and tying it. He laid the child on his mother's breast. "Small but healthy enough."

The woman gazed in blank-eyed exhaustion at the infant, then with experienced fingers she attached his mouth to her nipple. " 'Tis to be 'oped I've some milk this time," she murmured.

Douglas turned to wash his hands in a basin of cold water, the hot would be for the mother and child. There wasn't enough fuel in this hovel to heat more than one bowl. "I'll get the midwife to you," he said.

"No, Doctor. Us can manage," the woman protested weakly. "Our Ellie there can 'elp clean up. No need to disturb the midwife."

Douglas offered no objection. He knew there was no money here for a midwife's services and the eldest daughter had enough experience by now. He bent over the woman, felt her brow, said softly to Ellie, "If there's fever, send for me at once. You understand?"

"Yes, Doctor." The child nodded vigorously.

He opened the girl's hand and laid a coin on her palm, closing her fingers tightly over it. "Get candles, a bucket of coal, and milk for your ma," he said. "Don't let your da see it."

She nodded solemnly, tucking her closed fist against her ragged skirt. He patted her shoulder and left the room, bending his head below the low lintel of the narrow door that separated the back room from the front. A room that was in no better case when it came to fire, light, and furniture than the other. Piles of rags scattered across the floor served as beds, a broken chair stood beside a fireplace, where a saucepan with a miserly quantity of water stood on a trivet over two or three coals, tended by a boy of around five, although judging by his stunted growth he could be several years older.

"Where's your da, Charlie?"

"Down the pub," the boy said, staring into the pan as if willing the water to boil.

"Run down and tell him you've a new baby brother," Douglas said, lifting the pan off the coals.

" 'E'll be drunk," the child said listlessly.

"Tell him to get back here. Tell him *I* said so." For the first time a sternness entered his voice. It was enough to bring the boy to his feet.

" 'E'll clip me one," he said.

"Not if you duck," Douglas said aridly. "You can move faster than he can when he's drunk. I've seen you."

A faint grin lit the grimy face. "Aye, that I can, Doctor," he said. He went to the door. "Is Ma all right?"

"She's fine, and the baby," Douglas returned. "I'm going to take the water to Ellie. Run and fetch your da." The boy scampered off, his bare feet slapping on the icy cobbles of the street.

Douglas took the water into the back room, gave the child some further instructions, and then left, ducking through the door into the street, fastening the buttons of his greatcoat as he went.

He stood for a minute, pulling on his gloves, turning up his collar, looking up and down the alleyway. He glanced towards the pub on the far corner, watching for Daniel Jones to emerge, red-eyed and bleary, into the gray day. He waited until the man limped out, Charlie dancing just a little ahead of him, and then Douglas went on his own way. Daniel wasn't a bad man when he was sober, and even when he was drunk had a tendency to maudlin sentimentality rather than violence. He'd be pleased enough at the advent of yet another mouth to feed, not feeling himself in general responsible for putting the bread in that mouth or any of the others he had sired.

Douglas stopped off at Mrs. Beedle's on his way to his surgery behind St. Mary Abbot's. She greeted him with her usual cheery warmth. "Bit parky, isn't it, Doctor? Been busy, have you?"

"Delivering a baby," he said. "Fine healthy boy."

"Oh, that's nice," she said. "Postman brought a couple of letters for you this morning." She reached up to the shelf behind the counter and handed him his post.

He took it with a murmur of thanks, bade her good afternoon, and went out into the street, examining the envelopes as he emerged from the warmth of the shop. One was from his mother. The handwriting of the other, on thick vellum, was also immediately recognizable. He had a response from the Go-Between.

He tucked them both into his coat pocket and walked briskly to his surgery. It was the lower rooms of a two-up, two-down row house just behind the church. As usual the front room was thronged with women and runny-nosed children. It was cold and gloomy, the fire in the grate burning low. He greeted them all by name as he threw more coal on the fire and lit the candles. Then he beckoned to a woman with a baby at her breast and a toddler clinging to her apron. "Come on in, Mrs. Good. How's Timmy today?"

"Oh, the rash is summat awful, Doctor," the woman said. She turned on the scratching child and clipped him over the ear. "Stop that, you 'ear." She sighed as the child rubbed his ear and whimpered. " 'E won't stop scratchin', Doctor. Not no 'ow."

Douglas sat down behind the scarred table that served as his desk. "Let's have a look, Timmy." He examined the oozing eczema sores on the child's arms and reached up to a shelf to take down a tub of ointment. "Put this on three times a day, Mrs. Good. It should clear up quickly, but bring him back in a week."

"Thank you, Doctor." The woman put the tub into the capacious pocket of her apron. Hesitantly she drew out a copper coin. "What do I owe you, Doctor?"

The coin, as Douglas could see, was a penny. It would buy a loaf of bread or a pint of milk. It would go nowhere towards the cost of the ointment. But these people had their pride; indeed, in general, it was all they had. He smiled. "Just a penny, Mrs. Good."

She laid it on the table with the firm nod of one discharging an obligation. "Well, I thank you, Doctor. Come along now, Timmy, and don't you be scratchin' again."

Douglas leaned back in his chair, running

his hands through his thick hair as the door closed behind his patients. He looked at the penny on the table, then scooped it into the palm of his hand and dropped it into a tin box. It made a hollow *clink* as it joined the very small group of its fellows at the bottom.

A baby wailed from beyond the surgery door and Douglas pushed back his chair to go and call in his next patient.

It was a long and as always frustrating evening. He couldn't help everyone; so many of his patients suffered from the intractable ailments of poverty, and while medicine could help, he couldn't lay hands on sufficient free medicine for everyone in need. He was bone-weary as he locked up and headed for home.

Home was a lodging house on the Cromwell Road. The usual smell of boiling cabbage and fish heads greeted him as he stepped into the dark, narrow hallway and closed the door.

His landlady popped her head out of the kitchen. " 'Evenin', Dr. F. You're late. I 'ope the fish is not dried up."

"So do I, Mrs. Harris, so do I," the doctor murmured, heading for the stairs. "I'll be down in a minute."

" 'Tis all laid out in the parlor for you," she said. "A nice piece of bream, it is."

"Or was," murmured the doctor, mounting the linoleum-covered stairs.

"Should I send our Colin to the Red Lion

to get a jug o' mild-and-bitter for you, Dr. F?" the landlady's voice drifted up the stairs after him.

Douglas contemplated dried-up bream and the inevitable mashed potatoes and soggy cabbage, accompanied only by water, and dug into his pocket. He returned downstairs and handed Mrs. Harris a threepenny piece. "A pint, if you please, Mrs. Harris."

"Right y'are, Dr. F." She ducked back into the kitchen and shouted for her son.

Douglas went upstairs to take off his outdoor clothes. The bathroom, usually occupied by the tenant from No. 2, was free for once. He washed his hands and face, combed his hair, and went down for his supper.

He chewed his way through the bream, which was as dried-up and flavorless as he'd feared, and opened the letter from his mother. Folded within the five pages was a bank draft for one hundred pounds. The attached note said, "I'm sure you must have some good cause that could benefit from this. Fergus says it's due you from the trust."

Douglas folded the draft and put it in his breast pocket. Fergus was the family banker and he was not in the habit of pressing hundred-pound drafts on his clients, even if the trust in question was a substantial one, which this one most certainly was not. It had been set up by Douglas's father for his son's education, and Douglas was well aware that very little now remained in it. There was very little loose change in the Farrell finances. His mother was well provided for. His sisters all had husbands who were comfortably situated, but they also all had children. Douglas was to have kept himself and a suitable Society wife in proper style by continuing his father's practice.

He drummed his fingers on the stained tablecloth, the memory of Marianne once again rising in his mind. By giving up the lucrative practice in favor of a slum clinic that absorbed all his personal finances, he had lost Marianne, the prospective suitable Society wife, and effectively reduced himself to penury, although he did his best to hide the latter fact from his overly solicitous mother. Not too successfully, it would seem, judging by the bank draft. It was typical that she had couched the gift in such terms that he couldn't possibly refuse it.

He turned to the letter itself. It was five pages covered with her tiny handwriting, full of news of his sisters and their various progeny, of the antics of their neighbors, of whom his mother in general did not approve, the whole interlarded with advice as to the well-being of her youngest born, who also happened to be her only son.

Douglas took a deep draught of his ale and laughed softly. What his mother would say if she could see him in this miserably dreary boardinghouse on the Cromwell Road, forking cold, overcooked fish into his mouth at the end of an unbelievably long day, he couldn't imagine. She would be sitting at this moment in the elegant Farrell mansion on Prince's Street in Edinburgh, probably preparing the menus for tomorrow, if she was not playing bridge with her friends or instructing one of her daughters on some aspect of child rearing or the domestic running of her household.

It wasn't that he didn't love his mother; he did. But Lady Farrell was a grande dame of the old sort, an overbearing Victorian of rigid principles. She had given her Society-physician husband seven children before his death at forty. The last child was the longed-for son. Widowed, she had been obliged to assume the mantle of both parents. A mantle she had taken to with both relish and competence. All her children were in awe of her. Only her son had managed to shake off the maternal shackles and pursue his own course. And he'd only managed to do that with a fair degree of deceit.

Douglas folded the letter and returned it to its envelope. It would require an answer very soon, and a careful one, since his mother must continue to be kept in the dark about the realities of his life and work. The truth would at the very least bring on an attack of angina. He had his own theories about his mother's heart condition, but whether or not he believed it simply to be a useful weapon in her arsenal of control, its effects were very real.

He shook his head reflectively. His mother had never understood why he'd abandoned his destiny, left the lucrative practice that had earned his father a knighthood and kept the Farrell family at the top of Edinburgh's social tree. She had done her best to cope with the breaking of his engagement to Marianne, but at the first mention of her son's going to London to develop a practice there, she'd taken to her bed for a week, enlisting the desperate pleas of her daughters to keep him at her side. He'd resisted with grim fortitude and, if his sisters were to be believed, a total lack of compassion. He knew the latter was not true, just as he knew they would never understand why he was doing what he was doing.

On which subject . . . He picked up the other envelope that sat beside his plate and slit it with his knife. He read the contents twice. It was a very straightforward, very practical letter. He tapped it thoughtfully into the palm of his hand. He didn't think it could have been penned by the veiled lady he had met in the National Gallery. Here there was no hint of condescension or moral superiority, just a simple list of instructions, as befitted a business arrangement. Personalities and personal opinions had no place in a business arrangement, and it was a relief to know that whoever *really* ran the Go-Between understood that. Their representatives could do with some training, he thought somewhat caustically. Perhaps he should drop a line to *The Mayfair Lady* and mention that he'd been dissatisfied with their emissary's less than professional manner. It certainly didn't look as though he'd ever meet one of the editors or managers in person.

He read the letter again. The Go-Between had a prospect in mind for him. A lady sporting a white carnation at an At Home at a prestigious address in Manchester Square. Businesslike but completely anonymous, as he'd been told it would be.

He glanced around the parlor, at the yellowing net curtains on the windows, the greasy antimacassars on the chairs, the stained tablecloth. The game had started. It was time to make a move. A man who frequented At Homes in Manchester Square held by the Honorable Miss Chastity Duncan could not continue to live at Mrs. Harris's boardinghouse on the Cromwell Road.

The bank draft crackled in his pocket as he pushed back his chair. It would certainly go to a good cause, one that even Lady Farrell might support.

Chapter 4

Chastity bent back her father's newspaper and kissed him on the cheek when she entered the breakfast room on Wednesday morning. "Good morning, Father."

"Good morning, my dear," he said, returning his newspaper fastidiously to its creases.

"I want to ask you a favor," she said, pouring coffee into her cup. "It's a very big favor, actually, so you'll have to think about it before you answer."

Lord Duncan regarded his youngest daughter uneasily. "Not sure what you mean."

"No, I haven't explained it yet," she said, giving him a quick smile as she reached for the toast rack. "Could you pass the marmalade?"

He pushed the silver pot across to her and looked down at his own plate of cooling eggs with obvious distaste.

"You can't waste those," Chastity said

gravely. "We can only afford a dozen eggs a week. There must be at least two there."

Her father shot her a sharp and startled look, then saw her teasing smile. "It's no laughing matter," he declared, picking up his fork again. But Chastity had seen just the glimmer of reluctant amusement in his eye and it gave her some encouragement. "If you and your sisters had kept me apprised of the situation in the first place, we wouldn't find ourselves in this absurd position now." It was a statement repeated so often, it had become something of a mantra.

"There's nothing absurd about it, Father," Chastity said, spreading butter lavishly on her toast. "We have plenty of money to live quite well, particularly now that Con and Prue are no longer a household expense." She gave a heavy sigh, shaking her head. "You can have no idea how expensive *they* were to keep."

"I do wish you wouldn't talk nonsense at the breakfast table," Lord Duncan said, burying his nose once more in the newspaper.

Chastity smiled to herself and ate her toast, waiting. She didn't have long to wait. Her father suddenly peered at her around the side of the paper. "Did you say something about a favor?"

"Yes," she said. "It's Wednesday." She took a second piece of toast.

He glanced at the front page of his newspaper as if to reassure himself of that fact. "It is. And what of it?"

"It's the day for my At Home," she explained. "Wednesdays have always been At Home days. It was Mother's day too."

He was looking puzzled. "I remember. Am I being obtuse?"

"No, not at all. It's just that I would like it if you would be there this afternoon. Con and Prue will come, of course."

He shook his head. "Not my kind of thing, Chastity. You know that."

"Yes, that's why I said it was a big favor," she said, refilling his coffee cup. "I need you to help me out with someone. A widow, from Italy. She doesn't know anyone in London, and she's . . . how shall I put it . . . she's more in your age group than ours. You would only need to stay for about ten minutes, just to drink a cup of tea with her."

"Tea!" her father expostulated. "You expect me to drink tea with some foreign woman on a perfectly good Wednesday afternoon?"

"For a start, she's not foreign," Chastity said. "She's as English as you or I, but she was married to an Italian. And if you don't want to drink tea, there's always whisky or sherry. And in the last place, what else were you intending to do on a perfectly good Wednesday afternoon?" Now there was a distinct challenge in the hazel eyes and in her lightly teasing tone.

"Making small talk with a roomful of insipid women is not my idea of a pleasant afternoon," her father said, vigorously turning the page of the newspaper and folding it back with a crackle.

Chastity propped her chin on her hand and regarded him steadily. After a minute he looked around the paper and said with resignation, "No more than ten minutes."

"Thank you, Father, you're a sweetheart," she said. "I promise it won't be that bad. Nothing can be too bad for only ten minutes. And she's a nice woman, but a little uncertain about London. If you would just put her at her ease . . ."

"Make sure Jenkins puts the whisky decanter out." Lord Duncan returned once more to the paper.

"Of course," Chastity said, rising from the table. "Have you finished? Shall I tell Madge to clear away?"

"Is that the name of the new parlor maid?" her father asked. "Thought she looked unfamiliar."

"She's one of Mrs. Hudson's nieces. A nice girl. She'll be coming down to Romsey with us at Christmas." Chastity went to the door.

"Oh, yes, Christmas. I suppose it'll be a small party?"

"Not particularly," Chastity said. "Just family at present. But we might pick up some strays between now and then."

"An expensive business, house parties at Christmas," her father said.

"I thought we'd pawn the Stubbs," Chastity responded, referring to the George Stubbs that hung over the wall safe in the library. She whisked herself from the room before her father could react to the joke.

Jenkins was crossing the hall from the front door with a handful of letters. "Has the postman been, Jenkins? Anything interesting?" she inquired.

Jenkins looked suitably shocked. "I wouldn't know, Miss Chas. I haven't looked at them."

Chastity took the letters from him. "You know perfectly well, Jenkins, that nothing of significance passes you by, just as you know there are no secrets from you in this house."

"I don't go about prying, Miss Chas," he protested.

"No, of course you don't," she said, giving him a kiss on the cheek that brought a dull flush in its wake. "I have to go to the florist's to buy some carnations this morning. We need to arrange them in the usual way before the At Home."

"Very well, Miss Chas. Another client for the Go-Between, I assume?"

"Yes, exactly. The gentleman, a Dr. Farrell, will ask for Lord Buckingham, as usual. The white carnation goes to a lady who likes to be called Signorina Della Luca."

"An Italian lady, I take it."

"No, not a bit of it," Chastity said, wrinkling her nose. "She just likes to affect Italian airs."

"I see," the butler said.

"Oh, and Lord Duncan has promised to put in an appearance, but he won't drink tea."

"I'll make sure the whisky decanter is on the sideboard, Miss Chas." Jenkins nodded and went on his way.

Chastity glanced through the letters as she went upstairs. Household bills mostly. Nothing of any great significance, and nothing to trouble her father with. She put them on the secretaire where Prue, the family mathematician, who still largely managed the household finances, would go through them when she came round later that afternoon. Then she went to fetch her coat and hat for her trip to the florist's.

She returned with her arms full of red and pink carnations, a single white bloom buried in the colorful depths, and ran into her sisters just alighting from a hackney at the bottom of the steps. "We thought we'd come for luncheon," Prudence said. "In case Father needed some more persuasion. Did you have any luck?"

"He agreed to show his face for ten minutes," Chastity said, unlocking the front door. "But very reluctantly, so if you could add your voices to the pot it might keep him up to the mark."

"Is he in the library?" Constance asked, taking off her hat.

"Unless by some miracle he's gone to his club," her youngest sister said. "Jenkins, is Lord Duncan in?"

The butler relieved her of her armful of flowers, saying, "He did go out for a stroll for half an hour, but he came back a few minutes ago. Good morning, Miss Con, Miss Prue. You'll be here for luncheon?"

"If it's not too much trouble for Mrs. Hudson," Constance said.

"No, it's always a pleasure to see you both. I'll put these in water for the time being." He carried the flowers towards the kitchen.

"Let's go and see Father." Constance was already halfway to the library door. Her sisters followed her.

Lord Duncan was standing at the window looking out at the wintry garden. He turned as his daughters came in. "Well, you're a sight for sore eyes, m'dears," he said with a clear attempt at joviality. "If you've come to bully me about the At Home this afternoon, there's no need. I told your sister I'd be there, and I will be."

"We don't only come to bully you, Father," Prudence said reproachfully. "We came to see how you are."

"Well enough," he said. "How's Gideon?"

"Busy defending a cad," Prudence told him with a chuckle.

"And Max is writing a White Paper on the need for more tar macadam on the main roads out of London so that motor vehicles can travel more easily," Constance said. "He wants to know if you'd like to drive down to Romsey with him on Christmas Eve. We're going to take the train."

"I'll think about it," Lord Duncan said. "Unreliable things, motorcars." Ever since his own disastrous attempt at owning one some months before, he'd developed a considerable aversion to motorized transport.

"Max's Darracq isn't unreliable."

"Neither is Gideon's Rover," Prudence chimed in. "But he'll have Sarah and Mary, as well as all our luggage and presents." She laughed. "Sarah's presents and belongings actually take up enough space for a railway carriage."

"Well, I'll think about it," Lord Duncan repeated. "Let's go in to luncheon."

The sisters managed to keep their father entertained throughout the meal. He spent so much of his time immured in the house that reminding him of the existence of the outside world had become one of their main endeavors. They all hoped that sooner rather than later these frequent reminders would act to bring him out into the world again.

At the end of luncheon, he rose from the

table with a benign smile and a rather rosy countenance. "I think I'll take a glass of port in the library," he said. "Leave you girls to your own chatter."

"Don't forget the At Home," Prudence reminded him. "Jenkins will come and tell you when the Contessa Della Luca arrives and you can make your appearance then."

"Oh, very well," he said, sounding resigned. "I trust the woman is capable of holding a sensible conversation."

"You'll find her very easy to talk to," Chastity assured him. "She's very cultivated."

Lord Duncan shook his head and went off to his port in the library.

"Are you changing, Chas?" Prudence asked, running an eye over her younger sister's simple navy-blue linen blouse and gray skirt.

"Yes, I suppose so," Chastity said. "Since you two have come dressed to the nines."

"I wouldn't say that," Constance said. "Elegant, yes. But dressed to the nines, no. That's so vulgar, Chas." She smoothed down the skirts of her blue-and-white-striped silk afternoon dress with a mock pained air.

Chastity laughed. "Well, you both look very elegant, then, so I had better go and do something about my own costume." She went upstairs, leaving them to arrange the carnations on the hall table. Jenkins would be responsible for giving every lady visitor a flower before he announced them, ensuring that the one white bloom went to the signorina.

In her own bedroom, Chastity opened the armoire and gazed at its contents. She caught herself wondering how Douglas Farrell was preparing himself for this afternoon. He had struck her as a man not overly interested in his appearance, and since it was to be assumed he had very little money, it was also to be assumed that his wardrobe would be rather limited. But he would surely have a best suit. He couldn't expect to charm a rich wife into his hand without the correct clothes and accessories. Unless he was intending to announce up front to a prospective bride that he was only after her money, he must be prepared to appear to be something that he was not.

Chastity took out a cream crepe de chine blouse with a shirred bodice and a high, close-fitting neck that encircled her throat in bands of lace. It was one of her favorites, as was the skirt of russet-colored poplin that she laid beside it on the bed. It was an outfit in which she always felt confident. A pair of black, buttoned boots and a wide black belt completed the effect. She put her hands at her waist and decided with some satisfaction that she was definitely slimmer than she had been a few weeks earlier.

She sat at the dresser to deal with her hair. Unlike her sisters, whose hair waved in a very convenient fashion, lending itself to many different styles, Chastity's was a mop of thick and unruly curls that were hard to tame. Where her sisters had hair that could be called auburn, shading from such attractively subtle colors as russet to cinnamon, Chastity's was unashamedly red. But at least it was definitely red, not orange, she told herself as she twisted it into a knot that she fastened on top of her head with long and firmly inserted pins. She combed out the side ringlets that clustered around her ears, and teased a few tendrils to wisp on her forehead.

She examined the whole with a critical eye and decided that it was as good as it was going to get.

"Chas, are you ready? It's nearly three." Prudence stuck her head around the door. "Oh, you're wearing that lovely blouse. It suits you so well. I love that collar."

"So do I," Chastity said, turning on the stool. "Could you fasten the buttons on my right wrist? They're so tiny, my fingers become all thumbs." She held out her right arm.

Prudence obliged, deftly inserting the minute pearl buttons into the silk loops. "I wonder if our Dr. Farrell will arrive early and eager," she commented. "Or saunter in nonchalantly at the very end of the afternoon."

"I don't know," Chastity said. "I hope he

doesn't come before his quarry. We'll have to talk to him ourselves if he does." She stood up, smoothing down her skirts. "Let's go down."

Prudence followed her downstairs, reflecting that she was looking forward to meeting this ogre who had caused such an extraordinary reaction in her placid, sweet-natured sister.

Douglas Farrell was in no hurry to present himself at the door of No. 10 Manchester Square. He sauntered twice around the square, observing the carriages pulling up outside the house, trying to guess which of the female visitors was the one earmarked for his consideration. They seemed to come in pairs and trios of all shapes, sizes, and ages, some with male escorts, some alone. The Wednesday At Home at No. 10 seemed to be a popular event. He wondered about the Honorable Miss Chastity Duncan. Some elderly spinster, probably. Rich enough, certainly, judging by the imposing double-fronted edifice of the house. But then, of course, she could be some poor relation acting as companion or carer to an elderly relative. Some charity case responsible for walking overfed pug dogs and listening to the valetudinarian complaints of her benefactor.

He'd met plenty of women in such situations in his father's practice in Edinburgh, and he supposed that once he had established himself on Harley Street he would meet the English variety. But it would be unusual for a woman in such a subordinate position, little more than an upper servant, really, to be hosting the At Home. Passing the cakes, yes, fetching and carrying, yes, but hostess, unlikely.

Well, he wasn't going to find out by circling the square, Douglas decided. He glanced at his fob watch. It was just after three-thirty. Time to go in and meet his fate.

He ascended the steps to the front door and banged the highly polished lion's head door knocker. The door opened while the clang was still resounding in the air. A stately, white-haired butler greeted him with a bow. "Good afternoon, sir."

Douglas handed him his visiting card. "Dr. Farrell," he said. "I need to talk with Lord Buckingham, who, I understand, is visiting Miss Duncan this afternoon."

"Ah, yes, of course, sir. His lordship has not arrived as yet, but if you'd care to come in, I'll inform Miss Duncan." Jenkins's scrutiny was sufficiently covert for Douglas to be unaware of it. The butler could find no fault with the visitor's appearance or demeanor. He was dressed in conventional black frock coat, gray waistcoat, black tie, striped trousers.

"May I take your hat, sir?" Jenkins held

out his hand for Douglas's bowler hat and silver-knobbed cane and placed them on the table with several others. The card, he held in his hand as he invited the visitor to follow him into the drawing room.

Douglas had missed the butler's scrutiny mainly because he was observing his surroundings. The faded elegance of old money, he decided. Aubusson rugs, a little threadbare but still charming, scattered casually over the parquet floor, a Sheraton table, and two Chippendale chairs. A collection of carnations in single-bud vases intrigued him, until he was shown into the drawing room and saw that every woman there had a flower pinned to her lapel.

Jenkins read from the card. "Dr. Douglas Farrell, Miss Duncan."

Chastity turned swiftly from the sideboard where she was pouring tea. Her first thought, quite unbidden, was that Douglas Farrell was a remarkably attractive man. How had she failed to notice that the first time? But she *had* noticed it the very first time she'd seen him at Mrs. Beedle's. It was the second time, when they'd actually met, that she had failed to register anything appealing about him.

She came forward, her hand outstretched, her expression composed, a slightly interrogative smile on her lips. "Dr. Farrell . . . I don't believe we've met."

Definitely not some elderly spinster. And defi-

nitely not some charity-case poor relation. He took her hand. "No. Forgive me for intruding."

Chastity looked down at her hand, registering with some surprise how completely it disappeared within the large palm enclosing it. It was a very firm, warm, and dry clasp and it seemed to last a fraction longer than necessary as he continued, "I was told I might meet Lord Buckingham here this afternoon. I need to speak with him and I keep missing him at my club." He smiled and at last released her hand.

Those charcoal eyes seemed to be dancing, Chastity thought, as if they were full of little sprites of humor. His wide mouth had parted in a crooked smile that absurdly produced a dimple in his chin. She realized she hadn't seen him smile before.

"Lord Buckingham usually comes to visit on Wednesdays," she said, trying to sound neutral. "But he's not here as yet. Let me give you some tea." She turned back to the sideboard.

"Dr. Farrell, I'm Miss Duncan's sister Constance Ensor . . . and this is my other sister, Lady Malvern."

Douglas turned his head to confront a tall, very elegant woman who, like the more angular lady at her side, bore a distinct family resemblance to Miss Duncan. Hair a slightly less vivid shade of red, eyes more green than

Miss Duncan's hazel. But definitely the same family.

He shook hands and explained his need to speak with Lord Buckingham, an explanation that they took with the same unquestioning ease as had their sister, who now reappeared at his side with a cup of tea.

"Sandwich, Dr. Farrell? Or would you prefer a tea cake?"

"Neither, thank you," he said. "I really am sorry to intrude."

"I am At Home this afternoon, Dr. Farrell," she said with a cool smile. "At home to any who care to visit. You are perhaps not from London."

"No, from Edinburgh," he responded.

"Ah." She nodded. "I'm sure they don't have the same social traditions up there."

For all the world as if he'd said he was from the islands of Samoa, Douglas thought with a prickle of annoyance. For some reason he could sense little shards of antagonism coming from the Honorable Miss Duncan, but for the life of him he couldn't understand why.

"The Contessa Della Luca, Miss Della Luca," announced Jenkins.

"Excuse me," Chastity said, and flitted from the doctor's side. "Contessa, signorina, how delightful you could come. Do have some tea and let me introduce you. Are you acquainted with Lady Bainbridge?" She drew the two women into a circle of ladies all balancing teacups on their laps. "My sisters, Constance and Prudence, you know, of course. And this is Lady Winthrop and her daughter, Hester. Hester is to be married in a couple of weeks."

A genteel chorus of greetings answered the introductions. Laura sat down beside Hester, fixed her rather protruding gaze on her, and said, "Where are you going on your honeymoon, Miss Winthrop? You should definitely go to Italy. No one's education is complete without a visit to *Firenze* and *Roma*."

"Isn't it a little cold at Christmas?" Hester ventured, somewhat intimidated by the authoritarian tone and the unmoving stare.

"No, no, not at all. *Firenze* is in the south," Laura declared with a wave of her mittened hand and a blithe disregard for the realities of geography.

"Naples or Sorrento are perhaps more southern," ventured Prudence with a gleam in her eye.

"Oh, there's nothing there to see," Laura said.

"Pompeii," murmured Chastity. "I was under the impression that Pompeii was definitely worth visiting."

"It would be even more so if they would allow women to see the erotic frescos," Constance said. "When we were there some years ago with our mother, we were not permitted to see them, while the men were welcomed with open arms and prurient winks."

"I hardly think such sights are suitable for a woman's eye," Laura announced, primly dabbing her lips with her handkerchief. "I would shudder to see them."

"I really think Michelangelo's *David* should be covered with a loincloth," Chastity suggested in a tone as sweet as chocolate as she handed the lady a teacup. "I had to avert my eyes." She turned to the doctor, who had approached the conversational circle, his eyes on the white carnation on Miss Della Luca's lapel. "What do you think, Dr. Farrell? Should women be permitted to view male anatomy as part of a work of art?"

He had the unmistakable sense that he was stepping into a trap. If he disagreed with the lady wearing the white carnation, then he could be ruining his chances with a prospective bride, but if he agreed with her, he would be exposing himself to the ridicule of this somewhat intimidating trio of sisters. He had not been fooled by Miss Duncan's sweet-voiced suggestion. It had been so heavily larded with irony, only the most obtuse ear could miss it.

He opted for diplomacy. "I think it's a matter of personal preference, Miss Duncan. I gather you know Italy well, Miss Della Luca?"

"It is my home, *Dottore*. The true home of

my heart." The lady launched into her favorite subject, and the sisters moved away with silent sighs of relief.

"That was accomplished simply enough," Constance murmured, picking up a plate of sandwiches. "Now all we want is Father."

Her wish was answered as it was spoken. Lord Duncan, dapper as always, his luxuriant white hair carefully brushed back from his broad forehead, entered the drawing room with a practiced smile. He greeted his daughter's guests with impeccable courtesy, kissing female hands and cheeks according to his degree of familiarity, clapping the men on the shoulder, exchanging a jovial remark. His daughters, watching, had difficulty reconciling this social ease with the recluse he had become.

"I suppose it's like riding a bicycle," Chastity whispered. "Once learned, never forgotten." She stepped forward. "Father, I'd like to introduce you to Contessa Della Luca."

"Delighted, my dear," he said, smiling, bowing to the lady. "New faces are always welcome, madam. I trust there are some compensations for London in dreary December."

"I find it quite delightful," the lady responded robustly. "I wonder, could you explain to me the history of that painting over the cabinet? I've been looking at it and wondering ever since I arrived. It is not a Fragonard, by any chance?"

Lord Duncan beamed. "Why, well spotted, madam. Indeed it is. But not his usual style. So few people recognize it. Come and take a closer look." He offered his arm. "I have another rather similar in the library. My late wife had a very good eye." He bore the contessa off on his arm.

"Do you have a practice in London, *Dottore?*" Laura asked, turning her full attention to the man sitting on a gilt chair at her side.

Chastity found herself concerned for the chair; it seemed too fragile to bear the size of its occupant. But she noticed how deft and delicate were his hand movements, how his fingers on the dainty teacup were long and elegant even though his hands were so big. He was a doctor, she reminded herself. He probably performed surgery in some cases, or he certainly would have done during his training. It wasn't surprising that his hands were so sure.

"In Harley Street, Miss Della Luca," he responded.

"Oh, and do you specialize, *Dottore?*" She leaned forward, clasping her mittened hands in her taffeta lap, her tongue rolling around the Italian pronunciation as lovingly as if it were sampling the finest beluga.

"I treat all complaints," he responded. "But

I specialize in diseases of the heart."

"Oh, how splendid," she cooed. "And how very important. You have a successful practice, of course."

"It's newly established," he demurred. Not for the first time his eyes were drawn to Miss Duncan, who was sitting in conversation with Lady Winthrop opposite, and he wondered why his attention kept wandering from the lady with the white carnation. He turned back to Miss Della Luca and gave her the warmly attentive, practiced smile that always reassured patients of his interest and sympathy. "I've only recently arrived in London from Edinburgh, where I had a flourishing practice. Of course, I hope to replicate that on Harley Street."

"I'm sure you will," Laura said. "Such a noble profession, the Hippocratic one. I salute you, *Dottore*." She patted his hand. "One could wish for nothing better than to help one's fellow man. So essential for those of us who have been blessed by fortune."

Douglas consented with a smile that was now a little forced. The sentiment was his own. So, why did he find the manner of its expression repellent? But then he reminded himself that that was not at issue. He knew better now than to expect in a wife a woman who combined wealth and social position with a true sympathetic understanding of his own calling. A rich woman who could at the very least voice the correct sentiments, even if it was only for effect, would suit his purposes very well. His smile became warmer.

The lady was not unattractive. One would not have to spend a great deal of time trying to converse with her. She would have all the right social connections. And he had a feeling she would be very persuasive when it came to advancing her husband's career and, not coincidentally, her own social position.

After half an hour, he rose to make his farewells. "I hope I may call upon you, Miss Della Luca."

"Oh, yes, indeed. Mama and I would be delighted. Twenty-six Park Lane. A delightful house. Not quite as commodious as our villa outside *Firenze,* but very pleasant . . . overlooking Hyde Park, you know." She let her hand lie limply in his. "But don't let us take you away from your patients, *Dottore*. They have much greater need of you than we do." A coy little laugh accompanied the instruction.

"I don't work all hours of the day," Douglas lied, raising the limp fingers to his lips.

The doctor had address, Chastity thought, watching this byplay with well-concealed scorn. It seemed he was willing to pursue the introduction, though, and the signorina didn't appear averse, quite the opposite. Her mother was still absent from the drawing room, presumably in the company of Lord Duncan, examining the more unusual works of art scattered around the house.

All in all, in terms of beginnings it could be counted a successful afternoon for the Go-Between.

"I must make my farewells, Miss Duncan."

She turned at the doctor's lilting voice. "Oh, but you haven't seen Lord Buckingham. I'm sure he'll come in the next half an hour."

"Unfortunately, I have patients to see," he said smoothly.

"Oh, what a pity. Should I tell him that you were here looking for him? Is there an address I can give him where he could find you later?" she asked, for some reason delighting in making mischief. How was he going to extricate himself from this one? The doctor believed there was a true Lord Buckingham who was well known to his hostess, who was now calling him on his manufactured excuse.

"No, don't trouble, please. I'll probably find him later at my club," he said.

"Is that White's?" she asked sweetly.

"No, Crocker's," he responded. "A gambling club, Miss Duncan. Lord Buckingham and I have a penchant for *vingt-et-un*."

Oh, nice. Chastity gave a mental bow in acknowledgment of the deft rejoinder. "Good afternoon, Dr. Farrell. I hope your practice prospers."

"Thank you." He bowed over her hand and left.

Outside on the pavement he looked up at the house. Signorina Della Luca — rich enough, eager enough, unless he was much mistaken. But he was under no obligation to pursue the Go-Between's introduction to the exclusion of all other prospects.

The Honorable Chastity Duncan? Rich enough, judging by her surroundings. Aristocratic enough, without a doubt. All the right social connections. And without doubt a much more interesting prospect than the one the Go-Between had presented. But he would have to get to the root of her strange but unmistakable antagonism. She'd met him for the first time that afternoon, so what had he done or said to put her back up?

Well, he'd always liked a challenge. With a little nod of his head, Douglas Farrell did a jaunty sword pass with his cane and strolled away towards Harley Street and the rooms he had just rented for his Society practice.

Chapter 5

"I rather liked your Dr. Farrell, Chas," remarked Constance when the last visitor had left and the clock had struck five, signaling the conventional end of visiting hours.

"He's not *mine,*" Chastity protested, gathering up plates from the sofa tables. "I'm hoping he's going to be Laura Della Luca's."

"He's attractive," Prudence said, handing a tower of teacups to the parlor maid. "Do you think he was a boxer at university? He has the physique for it."

"And the broken nose," Constance said. "There's certainly something very physical about him." She was watching Chastity as she said this and noticed just a hint of pink on her cheekbones. "Don't you think, Chas?"

Chastity shrugged. "He's just huge, that's all."

"Huge," exclaimed Prudence. "You make him sound like a fat grizzly bear, or a man mountain. He's just rather tall and very broad and muscular."

"Does it matter?" Chastity asked, shaking out sofa cushions with some vigor. "We've done our job. The question is, do we need to do more to promote the match, or can we leave them to it?"

"We can't leave them to it at this early stage," Prudence stated. "Anything — or anyone — could distract him. Constance had better have a dinner party."

"Unless Father could be persuaded to host one with the contessa as guest of honor?" Constance suggested. "Since that awful day in court, I haven't seen him as animated as he was this afternoon."

"Ten minutes certainly stretched close to an hour," Chastity agreed, relieved for some reason that the subject of Douglas Farrell had been dropped for the moment. "What puzzles me is how such a pleasant and civilized woman could have such a tiresome daughter."

"A lady of little brain and even less education," said Constance acidly. "Add to that an inflated sense of one's own worth and opinions, and you get tiresome."

"Where the contessa goes, so also goes the daughter, so we'd better get used to her if we're to stick to our plans," Prudence pointed out.

"However, the sooner we get the daughter off the mother's hands, the better. If Father has to spend too much time in Laura's company, he'll rapidly lose interest in her mother." Chastity shook her head. "Quite frankly, I don't know how I can endure the prospect of her as a stepsister, married or not. Do you think we've bitten off more than we can chew this time?"

"Oh, faint heart," chided Constance as she gathered up her handbag. "We have never yet been defeated. We'll find a way to curb the obnoxious signorina. It's three against one, after all."

Chastity still looked doubtful. "I know that, but this is the first time we've involved Father," she said. "These are not just random prospects we're putting together. We can't risk Father getting hurt."

"No, of course not," Prudence said, giving her a hug. "But this was your idea, love, remember? And it's a brilliant one. It'll all work out, don't worry."

Chastity was not totally reassured but she smiled anyway. "Yes, I'm sure you're right. I'll drop the idea of a dinner party into Father's ear, see if it finds fertile ground. Of course, he's bound to say we can't afford it," she added.

"And then he'll start fretting about the condition of his wine cellar and whether he has anything worth offering to guests," Prudence said with a knowing chuckle. "I don't think we can leave you to deal with this alone, Chas. We'll bring it up together. How about we come over for supper tomorrow evening? Are you free, Con?"

"Tomorrow, yes," her elder sister answered, drawing on her gloves. "But I have to go now. We're going to the theater this evening and meeting people for dinner first. Max gets all wrinkled up if we're late."

"Are you doing anything tonight, Chas?" Prudence asked, gathering up her own belongings.

"Roddie Brigham's put together a party for a concert at the Albert Hall. I believe it's that Italian virtuoso, Enrico Toselli," Chastity answered. "There's a supper party at Covent Garden afterwards."

"Sounds amusing," Prudence said.

"But you don't sound too enthusiastic, Chas," Constance observed.

Chastity shook her head. "Of course I am. I'm just feeling a little tired for some reason. Making small talk all afternoon will do it. I'll be right as rain once I've had a bath."

"Well, we'll leave you to it." Constance kissed her. "Supper here tomorrow evening, then?"

"Yes, that'll be lovely."

"On our way out, we'll tell Father we'll be here." Prudence went to the drawing room door. "Have a nice evening, Chas."

"You too." Chastity raised a hand in farewell as her sisters went out together. Alone, she wandered over to the French windows that opened onto the terrace at the rear of the house. It was full dark outside, the garden invisible. She opened the door and stepped out onto the terrace. A bitter wind sliced through her thin crepe de chine blouse and pressed the poplin skirt against her thighs. But she stayed where she was for a few minutes despite the discomfort. Something was the matter with her. It was as if she was sickening for something. She felt confused and restless and dissatisfied. Ordinarily the prospect of the evening ahead would have pleased her. She liked Roddie and she liked the members of the party he had put together. But at the moment the prospect seemed about as enticing as a bowl of vanilla pudding.

A particularly sharp gust of wind sent her back inside. She shut the doors and drew the curtains across. Madge, the parlor maid, had lit the gas lamps and was now building up the fire, and for a moment Chastity contemplated sending her excuses to Roddie and spending the evening alone, curled up with a book in front of the fire.

But that, she decided, was pathetic. If she was feeling depressed, the only thing to do was to shake herself out of the mood. It was strange, though. She had no reason to be depressed. But maybe she was still getting used to being without her sisters' constant company. That was an explanation she could understand. Feeling a little more positive, she poured herself a glass of sherry and took it upstairs to sip in a leisurely bath.

She lay back in the curling steam, her hair secured in a towel, and closed her eyes. She opened them again abruptly when her internal vision was entirely taken up with the image of Douglas Farrell. The mind was a very perverse thing, Chastity decided, and got out of the bath. She flung open the armoire and took out the most dramatic gown she possessed, a dark red silk creation with red velvet puff sleeves and a low, off-the-shoulder neckline that accentuated her well-rounded bosom. She twisted her hair ruthlessly into a braided chignon and fastened it on top of her head, inserting a silver and diamond ornament in the shape of a plume in the middle. Then she subjected the whole to a critical appraisal in front of the full-length mirror as she drew on long white gloves. She could find no fault.

The door knocker sounded as she left her bedroom. Roddie had said he would come for her just before seven. They would meet the rest of the party at a café for champagne and hors d'oeuvres before going to the concert. She had reached the head of the stairs, her evening cloak over her arm, when she heard the unmistakable Scottish lilt. Douglas Farrell was talking to Jenkins.

She half turned to return to her room and

then stopped, wondering what on earth she thought she was doing. She went downstairs. "Dr. Farrell, what a surprise," she said as she reached the bottom step, eyebrows lifted in faint interrogation.

"Dr. Farrell has mislaid his card case, Miss Chas," Jenkins explained. "He wondered if he had left it here this afternoon."

Douglas stepped adroitly around Jenkins and offered Chastity a winning smile. "Forgive me for intruding, Miss Duncan, I seem always to be doing it," he said. "You're on your way out, I see. Don't let me hold you up." He made no attempt to conceal his admiration. She was stunning. He had thought her attractive that afternoon, but the evening version was utterly breathtaking. A dramatic vision of perfectly matched shades of red.

Chastity couldn't fail to notice the admiration in his arrested charcoal gaze, or the change in his smile, from the practiced social version to one of genuine pleasure. A very female sense of satisfaction warmed her. However much she disliked the man, she was woman enough to enjoy having such an effect upon him. Her voice, however, was quite cool, neither welcoming nor unwelcoming. "I'm afraid I haven't seen a card case," she said. "Did anything turn up in the drawing room when Madge tidied up, Jenkins?"

"No, Miss Chas. Nothing was found."

"I'm so sorry, Dr. Farrell. Perhaps you left it somewhere else."

"I suppose I must have done," he said, just as there was another knock on the front door behind him.

Jenkins opened it. "Good evening, my lord." He stepped back to allow Viscount Brigham admittance.

"Good evening, Jenkins . . . Chas. Are you ready? My, don't you look stunning," Roddie said cheerily, revealing evening dress beneath an opera cloak. He looked a pleasant question at Douglas. "Brigham," he said, extending his hand.

"Douglas Farrell." Douglas shook the hand and explained his presence. "I mislaid something this afternoon and wondered if I'd left it here at Miss Duncan's At Home this afternoon. I just dropped by on the off chance."

"Oh, I see." Roddie nodded. "Easy enough to do, of course. I'm always losing things . . . half my possessions are scattered over town." He laughed his easy laugh. "Well, if you're ready, Chas, we should be going. The others are waiting for us at Blue Moon."

"I'm quite ready." She held out her hand to Douglas. "Good evening, Dr. Farrell. I hope you find your card case. Don't wait up for me, Jenkins. I have my key." She went out on the viscount's arm.

Douglas looked after her. A covered barouche waited at the curb, a pair of very fine chestnuts in the traces. He was a good judge of horseflesh and guessed that the pair had cost their owner several thousand guineas. Enough to equip a small hospital ward. He realized that Jenkins was waiting patiently beside the door, gazing into the middle distance, and hastily gathered himself together.

"What's Blue Moon?" he asked the butler.

"A café, sir. Rather select . . . situated in the Brompton Road. It is a favorite of the young people for early-evening gatherings," Jenkins informed him. "Viscount Brigham's party are going on to the Albert Hall afterwards, I believe."

"Ah." Douglas nodded. "Thank you." He left and walked briskly around the square. His visit to Manchester Square had been made on impulse, which in itself was unusual. He was not a man given to impulse. But he had had the thought that a surprise call on Miss Duncan might have interesting consequences. Maybe she would have agreed to an impromptu dinner invitation, or at least have invited him in for a drink.

He hailed a hackney. The cabbie leaned down from his box. "Where to, guv?"

To Douglas's astonishment, he heard himself say, "Albert Hall, please." He climbed in and sat in the dark as the cab clattered away. What the hell was he doing? While it was possible that there were spare tickets for the concert this evening and it was not beyond the realm of coincidence that he and Miss Duncan should find themselves at the same musical event, this spur-of-the-moment pursuit struck him as somewhat lunatic in its impulsiveness.

Roddie observed within the gloom of the barouche, "I didn't bring the motor because I thought it would be too cold for you tonight. There's a bitter wind."

"Yes," Chastity said rather vaguely, tucking her gloved hands beneath the lap rug.

"I hear this musician chappie is excellent," Roddie said.

"Yes," Chastity agreed. "I'm looking forward to hearing him."

"I'm looking forward to Guinness and oysters," Roddie said, rubbing his hands together. "Just the ticket on a night like this."

Chastity made no reply. He peered at her in the gloom. "You seem very thoughtful, Chas."

"Oh, do I?" She smiled at him. "It's probably the cold, it's numbing my brain."

"Oh, we'll soon take care of that." He slipped a hand beneath the lap rug and took one of hers. "You shall have onion soup, dear girl."

Chastity let her hand lie in his. Roddie had been pursuing a mild flirtation for so long, it was second nature to them both. He asked her to marry him on a fairly regular basis, but she was convinced he'd be shocked if she ever accepted him. He was as easy and comfortable to be around as wearing a pair of bedroom slippers. Not that she'd ever let him know that.

The only trouble was that tonight she seemed to want not bedroom slippers but a pair of impossibly high-heeled, very sexy buttoned boots.

Douglas left the Albert Hall ticket office in possession of a standing-room ticket. The prospect of standing didn't trouble him unduly, and it had the added bonus of only costing him a shilling. He was a music lover and particularly fond of the violin, so regardless of what lay behind this impulse, he was going to enjoy the evening.

He found a pub that offered steak-and-kidney pies and Guinness, and after he'd eaten he returned to the Albert Hall just before eight-thirty. He merged with the throng on the pavement, not too easy to do when one stood head and shoulders above the majority of one's fellow man, and glanced casually around. He saw Chastity's red dress immediately amid a lively, chattering group of elegantly dressed young people going into the Hall ahead of him, and followed at a distance to take up his humble standing position at the rear of the final tier of seats.

The orchestra struck up the opening

chords and he leaned back against the wall, arms folded, and settled into the music.

Chastity, in a prime seat, nibbled the sugared almonds supplied by her host. She was feeling much more relaxed, warmed by a bowl of rich onion soup and cheered by the bubbles of a vintage champagne. The music was sublime and she had completely recovered from her strange mood of earlier by the time the violinist drew his bow across his instrument in finale and the musical chords faded into the grand expanse of the Hall. The applause was, as always, conventionally discreet but nonetheless heartfelt. The musicians took their bows and left the stage.

"That was wonderful," Chastity said. "Thank you so much, Roddie."

"My pleasure, my pleasure," he said, beaming. "Not really my thing, though, this concert business. Prefer a good old singsong m'self, but a bit of culture never did any harm, did it?"

"Oh, Roddie, you're a lost cause," she said, laughing. "You're not nearly the Philistine you pretend to be." They slid out of the row, exchanging comments with the rest of the party. In the lobby, the women made their way to the cloakroom to refresh themselves and retrieve their cloaks. When they returned, Chastity gazed dumbstruck at the sight of Douglas Farrell chatting casually with Roddie and the men of his party.

"Wonderful musician, Toselli, don't you think, Miss Duncan?" Douglas commented as she came up. "A real privilege to have heard him."

"Yes," she said faintly. *Was he stalking her?* It was an absurd idea and she dismissed it on the instant. "What a coincidence," she said. "You being at the Albert Hall tonight. Perhaps you thought to find your missing card case here?"

His eyes sharpened. There was no mistaking the sardonic edge to her voice, or the challenge in the hazel eyes. Mind you, he could hardly blame her, there *was* something more than a little suspicious about his repeated appearances this evening. He didn't fully understand it himself. He managed a bland smile. "I hardly think so, Miss Duncan. And I hardly think it's that much of a coincidence. Toselli is only playing for this one night. What lover of his playing would miss the opportunity to hear him?"

"And you are a music lover, of course."

"A passionate one."

"Ah." She turned aside as if to dismiss him and said to one of her companions, a young lady sporting a diamond tiara, "Did you notice the gown Elizabeth Armitage was wearing, Elinor? Definitely Worth, don't you think?"

"Oh, definitely."

"Say, Farrell, why don't you join us? We're

just going on to the Piazza for supper. Plenty of room for another." Roddie issued the invitation with customary good nature, and Chastity ground her teeth. It was not an invitation for her to rescind. She kept her shoulder resolutely turned to Douglas and heard him accept the invitation.

"Why, that's very kind of you. I should be delighted."

"New to London, are you?" Roddie asked as they moved towards the open doors to the street. "Haven't seen you around."

Douglas lowered his head to be more on a level with his companion as he answered him. Chastity heard strands of their conversation as it drifted back. *Edinburgh . . . doctor . . . Harley Street . . .*

"He's a welcome addition to the scene," Polly confided in an undertone as they stepped into Roddie's barouche. "Oh, Roddie, there's no room for you in here," she cried as he attempted to follow them in. "Elinor is coming with us, aren't you, dear?"

"I suppose you want to gossip." Roddie stepped back with a resigned bow and handed the third lady into his carriage. "We'll follow in a hackney."

"So, tell us about this doctor, Chas. Where did you meet him?" Polly leaned forward across the narrow space that separated them as the carriage started forward.

"Oh, he came to the At Home this afternoon. He was looking for someone . . . I can't quite remember who," Chastity said vaguely. "I don't know anything about him, except that he's new to London and he's starting a medical practice."

"Oh, well, I shall definitely go to him," Elinor declared. "Large men seem to inspire such confidence." She dabbed at her cheeks with a *papier poudre*. "Anyone else need a touch-up?" She offered her companions the tiny book of paper impregnated with peach-colored face powder.

Chastity shook her head, though Polly availed herself of the offer. Chastity was still feeling somewhat stunned, as if she were caught up in a whirlwind. Was it more than coincidence that had brought Douglas Farrell to the Albert Hall that night, so soon after accosting her at home on an excuse that quite frankly had sounded trumped-up? Why wasn't he calling upon Laura Della Luca as he was supposed to be doing? Just what was going on? He certainly wasn't supposed to be forming part of *this* supper party. It was thoroughly disconcerting.

It was just as disconcerting to find herself sitting next to him at the round supper table in the noisy mirrored restaurant on Covent Garden's Piazza. One minute she had been about to sit between Roddie and Elinor's brother and the next she had Douglas Farrell adroitly displacing Roddie and sliding in on her left.

"This is a cheerful place," he said, shaking out his napkin.

"Yes, it specializes in serving the kind of food the costermongers in the market would eat," she said. "Good Cockney fare."

"Appropriate enough for my first opportunity to sample London's nightlife," he observed.

"You've been too busy starting up your practice to go out and about much, I daresay," she responded, accepting that the rules of etiquette now required her to engage her neighbor in small talk. "How does one go about doing that, exactly?"

She took a sip of water as her eyes roamed over the menu. She was actually interested in his response. As the Go-Between, she knew rather more of his plans than he would ever acknowledge, so it was at least amusing to see what web of fantasy he had spun for social use.

"I have some contacts from my father," he replied. "And, of course, some referrals from my previous patients in Edinburgh. It's a beginning. What are you going to eat? Do you recommend anything special?"

"The roast chicken is good," she said. She leaned forward around her other neighbor. "Excuse me, Peter. Roddie, was it the jugged hare that was so good last time we were here?"

A lively discussion ensued as to the relative merits of jugged hare or the *jarret de veau*. No one mentioned the merits of the roast chicken, Douglas noted. When Chastity sat back, he murmured, "Roast chicken seems somewhat pedestrian under the circumstances."

"That rather depends on your viewpoint. My brother-in-law, who is an excellent chef and an unashamed gourmand, always eats it here. He says it's the Platonic ideal of roast chicken — a perfect bird, perfectly cooked."

"Is that Lady Malvern's husband, or Mrs. Ensor's?"

"Prudence's husband. Sir Gideon Malvern." Chastity broke her roll and buttered a piece lavishly.

"Ah. The barrister."

"Yes," she agreed, then turned to the sommelier, who on Roddie's instructions was offering a choice of wine. "I'll have the red, please. I'm going to have the *jarret de veau*."

Douglas took a glass of the same. He was trying to remember where he'd heard the barrister's name before. Then it came to him. He snapped his fingers. "Wasn't Sir Gideon the barrister who defended *The Mayfair Lady*? Didn't he defend it in that libel suit?"

"Yes," Chastity agreed airily. "And a very fine job he did of it too."

Douglas ran the tip of his finger around the lip of his glass. "Forgive me, but wasn't your father involved in some way?" He gave her an apologetic smile. "I read about it in the papers."

"I'm amazed the story reached the Scottish newspapers," she said. "But, yes, my father was a witness for the broadsheet. It was one of the main reasons why Gideon took on the case . . . family, you understand." The lie was smooth as Jersey cream. It had been perfected in the weeks since the case had concluded, the story being that Gideon and Prudence had been secretly engaged at the time of the libel suit, and when Lord Duncan's possible involvement had come up, the prospective son-in-law had naturally enough stepped into the breach.

"Families have their uses," Douglas said with a somewhat ironic smile.

"Yes, they do. Did you just say that your father had medical connections in London?" The ironic smile puzzled her.

"Yes, he was a prominent physician in Edinburgh. I followed in his footsteps, although he died when I was very young. His partners in the practice took me under their wing." The smile didn't waver. "I've found that the name of Sir Malcolm Farrell can open quite a few doors for his son."

"You sound as if you disapprove."

He shrugged. "I believe a person should succeed on his own merits, so it rather goes against the grain to capitalize on my father's reputation. But needs must." He returned to his menu with an air that clearly indicated the subject was closed.

Now, just how did succeeding on one's own merits jibe with marrying for money, Chastity wondered. That was certainly ironic.

"What do you recommend to start . . . or should I ask, what would your brother-in-law recommend?" Douglas asked, breaking into her thoughts.

"Oxtail soup," she said promptly. She saw his look. "Oh, don't you like oxtail?"

Douglas's abused taste buds were reliving his landlady's braised oxtail that had appeared on the supper table a few nights back. It had been barely edible. "Not greatly," he said.

"Jellied eels?" she suggested. "They're a house speciality."

"Are you serious?" He turned to look at her and saw a dimple twitch at the corner of her mouth. "You're not," he said flatly.

"But they're very authentic," she protested. "Straight from Billingsgate. They're a Cockney delicacy, you must know that."

"I don't happen to be a Cockney," he said dryly, taking a sip of wine. "I think I'll stick to the kipper pâté. Kippers I understand."

"Don't they come from the Orkneys?"

"Among other places."

"It seems rather feeble to eat only what you're used to," she said. "I'd have thought you'd want to assimilate yourself to your new environment."

"Very well," he said, closing his menu. "Jellied eels it shall be, Miss Duncan, on condition that you eat them with me."

Hung by her own petard, Chastity acknowledged ruefully. But there was something in his tone that made it impossible for her to refuse the challenge. "A deal, Dr. Farrell."

"A deal." He offered his hand and she shook it, once again oddly fascinated by the way her own disappeared so completely within his.

"What are you two settling?" Roddie called from across the table.

"The issue of jellied eels," Douglas returned. "Miss Duncan has challenged me to sample a local delicacy. I've challenged her to sample it with me."

There was applause at this. The wine was circulating freely and in the noisy informality of the restaurant the usual strict rules of dining etiquette had gone by the board.

"Five guineas on Chastity," someone said. "She'll eat every last mouthful."

"Oh, I don't think so," someone else said, sizing up Dr. Farrell. "I think the good doctor here can see off a plate of jellied eels without even noticing. Six guineas on Farrell."

It went on, the bets mounting until the plates of jellied eels were served to the contestants. Chastity surveyed the pale shivering length on her plate and controlled a shudder. She glanced sideways at Douglas, who was regarding his own plate with all the resolve of Caesar about to cross the Rubicon. All eyes were on them, even those from other tables who had been drawn into the bidding. Waiters seemed to appear from nowhere, drawing closer to their table in their long white aprons, flipping dishcloths at tables that needed no cleaning, rearranging cruet sets and place settings.

"Oh, well," Chastity said, "they are a local delicacy for those whose budget doesn't run to *jarret de veau*. Who are we to despise what others enjoy?" She stuck her fork in the quivering fish.

Douglas, for a moment struck by the matter-of-fact comment that he would never have expected from such a creature of privilege as the Honorable Chastity Duncan, hesitated, then plunged in his own fork. They ate stolidly, stoically, fork after fork. Chastity concentrated on swallowing. She made no attempt to chew, merely gulped and forked, and gulped and forked. Every now and again she glanced sideways at her neighbor's plate. He seemed to be following exactly the same technique, but his mouth was bigger, so the contents of the plate diminished rather more rapidly than did hers. When he set down his fork in triumph, she still had at least three forkfuls to go.

Chastity did not look up. She cut, forked, swallowed. Cut, forked, closed her eyes, and swallowed, and with her eyes still tight shut, dealt with the last mouthful, then reached for her wineglass and drained it amid the laughing applause.

"A draw," Roddie, who'd been keeping the book, announced. "There were no bets on who would finish first."

"Considering how much smaller Chas is, she should have had a handicap," someone observed judiciously.

"Not established beforehand," Roddie said briskly. "I declare a draw."

"How are you feeling?" Douglas asked softly, seeing that Chastity's eyes were still closed.

"What do you prescribe for nausea, Doctor?" she murmured, reaching blindly for her refilled wineglass.

"Wine," he said cheerfully, following suit with his own. "In truth, they weren't that disgusting. It was the texture, not the taste."

"As my brother-in-law will tell you, the two are inseparable," Chastity returned with a mock groan. "Oh, pass me another roll, *please*."

Douglas reached for a roll in the basket in front of him, broke it, buttered a piece generously, and laid it on her plate. "That should take the taste away." He proceeded to butter the rest of the bread, his long fingers performing the task with the delicacy that had surprised her before.

Chastity blinked at the offering on her plate. She would have expected such an intimate gesture from a friend, Roddie, for instance, but Douglas Farrell was a stranger. But he was so matter-of-fact about it . . . obviously didn't think twice about it. Maybe as a doctor he was merely prescribing the correct medicine. With a mental shrug, she ate the bread.

He seemed to be sitting very close to her. She hadn't noticed his proximity before — the tables were all cramped and everyone sat cheek by jowl — but now, eating the bread newly delivered from those large hands, she became powerfully aware of his body. She remembered how Constance had commented on the man's sheer physical presence.

His forearm rested on the table and when he reached for his wineglass she noticed how the muscles of his upper arm pressed against the silky material of his coat. She glanced covertly at his profile. The long thin jaw gave his cheeks a hollowed-out, sculptured appearance, the whole dominated by the nose with its prominent bump on the bridge. Definitely a Roman nose, she thought. He had what she and her sisters had always referred to as a brainy brow, very broad, his hair springing back strongly from a pronounced widow's peak. There was, she thought, a certain ascetism to his uneven features that somehow didn't sit right with the force of his physical presence.

She dropped her eyes hastily when he turned suddenly towards her, a slightly quizzical look in his eye. The waiter's appearance to remove the empty plates was a welcome diversion. "Thank God for that," she murmured as the residue of eels was removed. She took another buttered bite of crusty roll and waited for the fishy taste and slimy feel on her tongue to go away, hoping all the while that he had not noticed her inspection.

"I'm in the mood for dancing," Elinor announced. "Who's for going on afterwards?"

"The Marrakech?" asked Roddie.

"Either there or Cleopatra's."

There was a lively discussion as to the differing merits of the two dance clubs as the main courses were served. Chastity took no part in the debate. She had no wish to go dancing tonight but if the whole group was in favor it was going to be difficult to extricate herself. Roddie, having invited her this evening, would feel obliged to take her home.

"Your brother-in-law was right about the chicken," Douglas commented, looking up from his platter of golden brown chicken and roast potatoes. "I don't think I've tasted anything as good as this since my childhood Christmases."

"Did you have chicken for Christmas? We always have goose," Chastity said. This was as safe and inane a topic of conversation as she could wish for.

"Chicken at Christmas, haggis at New Year," he said.

"Are you going home to Edinburgh this year?" she asked without much interest in the answer as she took a forkful of mashed potatoes.

He shook his head. "No, I'd have to go for at least two weeks to make the journey worthwhile and I have too much to do here."

"Oh. Work, you mean?"

"Work . . . and setting up house." He speared a baby turnip.

"Where are you living, Farrell?" Roddie asked, catching the end of this conversation.

"Wimpole Street," Douglas said. "Convenient for Harley Street."

"Oh, did you buy a house?" Elinor inquired. "Those Wimpole Street houses are magnificent."

"Actually, I've taken a lease on a flat for the time being," Douglas said. "It comes furnished and complete with a cook/housekeeper. Ideal for a working bachelor." He laughed lightly.

"Then setting up house can hardly be a major chore," Chastity observed somewhat tartly, leaning back for the waiter to refill her glass. "Not major enough to keep you away from your family at Christmastime, surely."

He looked at her and said with a hint of mockery at her sharp comment, "You don't let anything slip by, do you, Miss Duncan?"

Chastity had the grace to blush, even as Roddie said with a chuckle, "Oh, Chastity's quite benign when compared with her sisters. Can't make a careless remark around them without being called on it."

"We take after our mother," Chastity offered with an apologetic smile. "We were taught that accuracy is vital. One should only say exactly what one means."

"She sounds like a formidable woman," Douglas said.

"She was," Chastity agreed. "She died a few years ago."

"I'm sorry," he said, and his hand fleetingly brushed over hers where it rested on the table. There was so much natural empathy in the quiet, simple statement, in the light warmth of his fingers, that Chastity was oddly comforted. She began to wonder if her earlier negative assessment of Dr. Farrell's bedside manner had been rather harsh.

He was explaining his situation cheerfully now to the table at large. "I'm not entirely happy with my landlord's choice of furnishings. And I have some things of my own that require arranging. Books, for the most part. I am very particular about categorizing my library. It's likely to take me at least a week."

"That must be some library," said Elinor's brother with undisguised awe. "It takes me a year to read one book."

"That, Peter, my boy, is because you have the concentration of a gnat," Roddie said to general amusement. "Have we decided where we're going afterwards?"

"I get the impression you're not too keen on continuing the evening," Douglas said softly under cover of the renewed debate.

"Why? I haven't said anything," she responded with a frown.

"Exactly." He sat back as the table was cleared.

"Chas? What's it to be? Cleopatra's or the Marrakech?" Roddie asked.

"To tell you the truth, I'm rather tired," she said. "It's been a lovely evening, but would you mind terribly, Roddie, if I took a hackney home?"

"No, no, you can't do that," he protested. "I'll see you home. Of course I will."

"It's not necessary, Roddie."

"Indeed it is." And in Viscount Brigham's book it was. He had collected his guest from her house and he would return her from whence she came.

"If Miss Duncan is agreeable, I would be happy to see her home," Douglas said, twirling the stem of his wineglass between his fingers. "I'm not much of a one for dancing myself."

"What, no Gay Gordons, Dr. Farrell?" Elinor said. "No Eightsome Reels?"

He smiled. "Scottish reels, Lady Elinor, are in a rather different category. At those I excel. But I'm rather assuming they won't be on the dance program at the clubs tonight."

"True enough," Elinor conceded. "Do you wear a kilt when you dance reels, Douglas? I may call you Douglas?"

"I hope you will," he said. "And yes, I wear a kilt on the appropriate occasions."

Chastity reflected that Douglas Farrell was a master at putting paid to a conversation he didn't care for. He was never rude exactly, just very definite and to the point. He had turned back to her now and was saying pleasantly, "Would you give me the pleasure of seeing you home, Miss Duncan?"

And what could she say? Wimpole Street was but a half mile from Manchester Square. To refuse such a convenient escort would be bewilderingly discourteous to everyone but herself, and would require Roddie to miss his dancing. Chastity smiled and murmured her thanks.

Chapter 6

The party stood outside amid the swirling detritus of Covent Garden market. Roddie was efficiently summoning hackney cabs to take those would-be dancers who couldn't fit into his own carriage on to the Marrakech. He turned to Chastity and Douglas. "We're dividing the supper bill among us, Farrell. If you give me your card, I'll send you a note when I've worked out your share of the damage," he said easily.

"Dr. Farrell has mislaid his card case," Chastity said with a sweet smile, shooting him a rather pointed sidelong glance.

"Nevertheless, I do have a couple on me," Douglas said with a smile as smooth as her own. He reached into his pocket and took out a billfold from which he extracted a business card. "Both addresses are on there."

He handed the card to the viscount, who took it with a nod and offered his own in exchange. This led to a flurry of card exchanges between Douglas and the rest of the party.

"Are you sure you won't come and dance?" Roddie asked Chastity rather mournfully as this was going on. "I was looking forward to a quickstep with you."

"I'm sorry, Roddie, but I'm really tired," she said. "I've also got all those jellied eels swishing around inside me."

"What a revolting image," he said.

"It was a revolting experience," she returned with a laugh. "But other than that, it was a lovely evening. Thank you."

"Yes, and I thank you for including me," Douglas said, extending his hand. "A delightful introduction to London."

"Oh, my pleasure, dear fellow, my pleasure," Roddie declared, reaching up to clap the other man on the shoulder. "Tell me, if it's not an impertinence, did you get that nose in the ring?"

Douglas shook his head. "I could have quite easily since I was a heavyweight at school and went a good many rounds in my time, but it was actually on the rugby field."

"That is such a violent game," Polly said with a ladylike shudder.

"It has its moments," Douglas agreed, touching the bump on his nose reflectively.

"Oh, women don't understand the character-building value of sports," Elinor's brother said with a scornfully dismissive gesture. "If it's not a gentle pat-ball over a tennis net, they want nothing to do with it."

"That's not true," Chastity said. "Women play cricket and hockey, as well as tennis. They bicycle, they play golf and go mountain walking."

"But not what one might call contact sports," Douglas observed.

"If by that you mean we choose not to engage in physical wrestling with our opponents, then I suppose you have a point," Chastity responded. "But breaking limbs, not to mention heads and noses, strikes me as a thoroughly unintelligent way to win anything."

"A lost cause, I told you, Farrell," Elinor's brother said, shaking his head. Douglas merely smiled his agreement, deciding that the subject was best dropped. The Honorable Miss Duncan didn't pull any punches when it came to verbal sparring, whatever her opinion of physical sport.

The group piled into their various conveyances amid a chorus of good nights, leaving Douglas and Chastity still on the street.

Douglas looked around for a free hackney. "I think Brigham took them all," he commented.

"It's a busy time of night for hackneys," Chastity pointed out, turning up the collar of her evening cloak.

"There's one." Douglas put his fingers to

his lips and emitted a piercing whistle that would not have shamed a barrow boy. The hackney was going the wrong way but at the whistle the cabbie turned his horses.

"Oh, well done," Chastity approved. "That was some whistle. You must show me how you do it. If he'd got to the far corner we would have lost him. There's a whole crowd waiting over there."

Douglas opened the carriage door for her. "Allow me," he said, taking her lightly by the waist and lifting her into the interior before climbing in after her, slamming the door shut.

Chastity regarded him with a dangerous glint in her eye. "Clearly you belong to that group of men who believe that women find something charming about being made to feel like china dolls. I have to tell you, Dr. Farrell, that that is a thoroughly mistaken assumption. Women do not, in general, appreciate being scooped up willy-nilly by giants."

He looked surprised. "My sisters have never objected."

"Surely you can see the difference between family and complete strangers," Chastity demanded.

"Not complete strangers," he protested mildly. "We've eaten jellied eels together."

Chastity turned her head towards the window so that he wouldn't see the flickering smile she couldn't prevent.

After a minute he said in his usual tone, "When did Brigham settle that supper bill? I didn't see a piece of paper change hands."

"Roddie has an account there," she replied. "He has them all over town. He never carries money . . . he considers it vulgar. Probably because he has so much of it, he never has to give it a second thought."

"How fortunate," he said with an unmistakable touch of acid.

Chastity's eyes narrowed. She would not have this man criticizing her friends, however implicitly. She said with deliberate insult, "I'm sure, if you have difficulty paying your share, he would understand."

He sat up abruptly. "What are you implying?"

That if you're looking for a rich wife, one has to presume you need money to maintain your lifestyle.

"Nothing at all," she said. "What could I be implying?"

"I have no idea, that's why I'm asking." His voice was rather quiet and had a note that Chastity didn't like one bit. She was beginning to feel that she'd stepped into a rather hazardous quagmire.

"I wasn't implying anything," she said, aware of the inadequacy of the denial. She was going to have to watch her step around Douglas Farrell. She'd allowed her secretly formed adverse judgment of him to spill over, and that would never do. "I'm sorry if I offended you," she said. "I didn't mean to. I only thought that it must be an expensive business setting up a Harley Street practice."

Now, deny that, she thought. It was exactly what he'd said to the Go-Between.

"Certainly it is," he agreed readily. "But I don't believe, Miss Duncan, that I've ever given you any intimate information about the state of my finances."

"No," she said, lowering her eyes to her lap. *Not as far as you know, Dr. Farrell.* "I spoke out of turn," she said quickly. "But you annoyed me by criticizing my friends."

There was a short, loaded silence, then he said, "I apologize if I gave that impression." He leaned across the narrow space dividing them and laid a hand over hers. "Can we put this behind us, Chastity?"

She could feel the warmth and strength of his hand through her thin kid gloves. It was oddly unsettling but for some reason she made no attempt to withdraw her hand. She offered a tentative smile in answer to his question and he simply nodded, leaving his hand where it was as they sat in a silence that was both companionable and slightly confused until the carriage drew up outside the Duncan residence. Douglas jumped down and extended his hand to help Chastity alight. There was no overt familiarity this time, but his hand gripped hers firmly until she was on solid ground, when he released it almost reluctantly.

"Good night, Chastity." He gave her a half bow.

"Good night, Douglas. Thank you for bringing me home," she responded, and hastened up the steps to the front door.

Douglas waited until she had disappeared inside, then paid the hackney and sent him on his way. It was only a short walk to Wimpole Street and he could do with the air, cold though it was. He was puzzled and he needed to clear his head.

What had Chastity been getting at with that dig about his financial state? There had been something underlying her insult. He could accept that she'd been responding to a perceived criticism of her friends, but he still didn't understand why she'd said what she'd said. He'd certainly not given the impression of being short of money. At least he didn't think he had. There was nothing in his appearance, in his garments, in his manner, to indicate that he was not a gentleman of respectable means. In truth, he was, or would be if all his spare funds weren't swallowed in the great maw that was his slum practice.

Harley Street would redress the balance, once he could get it up and running. But to do that quickly and successfully he needed an injection of capital. He thought of Signorina Della Luca, conjured up the image of her narrow-faced countenance, only to have it superimposed by the Honorable Chastity Duncan's fuller features, glowing hazel eyes, and radiant complexion. She had a sweet smile too when she chose, but an adder's tongue when she chose. There was a puzzle there, a paradox of some kind, and he could not deny that he was drawn to her.

He didn't want to be drawn to her, or to any woman. As he knew from bitter experience, emotional ties merely led to painful complications. He simply needed a rich and suitably positioned wife who would be at least complaisant about his life's work. The Go-Between had offered such a prospect, it was up to him to follow through.

As if coming to some decision, he thrust his hands into his pockets and fingered the crisply engraved visiting cards he'd collected that evening. Contacts were as important as capital, and he'd made a few of those tonight.

Chastity spent a rather restless night. She was cross with herself for indulging her urge to sting the doctor a little, and she also felt miserably uncomfortable at having caused him pain just to satisfy what struck her now as a purely malicious self-indulgence. Avoiding pain to others came naturally to her and in general, despite the quickness of tongue shared by all the Duncan sisters, she went out of her way to avoid slights or unkind remarks. So, what had come over her last evening? She didn't like the man, but that was no real excuse, and he hadn't actually done anything during the evening to stimulate her dislike. Rather the opposite, if she was brutally honest.

She was awake at dawn when Madge crept in to rake out the ashes and rekindle the fire in the grate. "Oh, sorry, madam. Did I wake you?" The girl looked up from her knees in genuine distress when Chastity sat up in bed.

"No, I was awake." Chastity pushed aside the coverlet. "I'll light the fire, Madge, if you'd be a dear and fetch me some tea."

"*You* light the fire, madam?" Madge looked horrified.

"I'm quite good at it, actually," Chastity said with something approaching a grin. She knelt down in front of the grate. "Are you looking forward to Christmas, Madge?"

"Oh, yes, madam. Auntie — Mrs. Hudson, I mean — she told me all about the servants' dinner."

"We have a good time," Chastity agreed, poking the coals until a spark rose. And there would be a child this year, she thought. Sarah's presence would make the celebration even more special than usual.

Madge went off to fetch tea and Chastity remained on her knees in front of the fire, warming her hands as the fire crackled. The wind rattled the windowpanes and the flames spurted. There was something about winter that thrilled Chastity, gave her energy. Prudence and Constance both liked the summer, energized by the heat of a broiling day through which they always managed to remain cool and collected. Chastity wilted in the heat. She thought it was perhaps because her sisters were so much thinner and taller than she was. They were sunflowers. She was some other kind of flower, smaller and closer to the ground . . . a snowdrop that bloomed in the snow. But it was a fanciful metaphor and she gave it up with a little shrug of exasperation.

When she went downstairs later she was surprised to find the breakfast room empty. Her father's place had been cleared and the newspaper, read and refolded, placed at her own plate. Jenkins came in with a pot of coffee. "Good morning, Miss Chas."

"Good morning, Jenkins. Has my father breakfasted already?"

"He came down early and went out ten minutes ago. He said he had an errand to run."

"At this time of day?" she questioned, helping herself to toast. "How strange."

"Yes, I thought so too," the butler agreed. "Would you like a boiled egg, Miss Chas?"

Chastity thought about it, then shook her head. "No, just toast, thank you. I'll be going to Kensington to see your sister after breakfast, to pick up the post, and then I'll probably visit Prue, so I doubt I'll be back for luncheon, but Prue and Con are coming over for dinner this evening."

"Yes, so his lordship told me. I gather Mr. Ensor and Sir Gideon will not be joining us?"

"I doubt it. We want to ambush Father into giving a dinner party before Christmas."

"I see," Jenkins said. "Then I will check on the cellar. His lordship is bound to want to know what we have." He bowed and left her to her breakfast.

She finished quickly, skimming the newspaper as she ate, then hurried upstairs to fetch her coat and hat. She would collect the post for *The Mayfair Lady* and the Go-Between, but she also had another motive for visiting Mrs. Beedle this morning. It had occurred to her that the shopkeeper might have some more recent information on Douglas Farrell. Had he left the Kensington area and the insalubrious St. Mary Abbot's, now that he claimed to live on Wimpole Street and practice on Harley Street?

She was standing in the hall, checking the set of her hat in the mirror, when Lord Duncan came downstairs, impeccably clad in a gray tweed frock coat and matching trousers, and carrying a gray top hat. He also carried a large bouquet of chrysanthemums and autumn daisies and a parcel wrapped in brown paper tucked under one arm.

"Good morning," Chastity greeted him with a smile. "I didn't realize you'd come back. What lovely flowers, such wonderful autumn colors. Who are they for?"

Her father looked just the slightest bit self-conscious. "I promised the Contessa Della Luca that I would lend her that book of engravings that your mother bought when we were in Italy. Unfortunately, I couldn't lay hands on it yesterday afternoon, but I found it last night, so I thought I would call upon her this morning."

And the flowers? mused Chastity to herself. Her father looked like a man who was going courting, she thought. It would be a good idea to assess the situation for herself, see how he was received by the lady. "If you'd like some company, I'll come with you," she suggested casually. "I was going to pay a reciprocal call on Laura and her mother one morning soon. Today is as good as any other."

She couldn't tell whether her father really liked the idea or not, but he was too polite to refuse her company. "Well, that would be very pleasant," he said. "By all means, join me, my dear. But didn't you have other plans?" He glanced pointedly at her outdoor garments.

"None that were fixed in stone," she said

cheerfully. "Did you send for Cobham or will we take a hackney?"

"A hackney, I believe. We have to become accustomed to managing without our own transport now that Cobham is retiring," Lord Duncan said. "I understand Prudence has everything in hand."

"Yes," Chastity agreed. "Cobham mentioned to her that he was ready to leave London and retire to the country, so she found him a cottage on the estate."

"Your sister has her own household affairs to attend to now," Lord Duncan declared, gesturing that his daughter should precede him through the front door. "I must learn not to rely on her as much as I have been doing. Or you, Chastity, my dear. You'll be setting up house for yourself soon enough."

"I am not looking to do so, Father," she said. "It doesn't strike me as a matter of urgency."

"Well, maybe not, maybe not. But it's the way of things, my dear. I used to think I'd have all of you on my hands forever, and now look. Both your sisters married in less than a year." He shook his head, but he didn't sound displeased.

"Respectably too," Chastity said with a mischievous smile, linking her arm in his. "That's what *I* find surprising."

"It is rather surprising," Lord Duncan agreed, waving his cane at an approaching cab. "Considering that they are not in the least respectable themselves. Any more than you are. Although, to look at you, butter wouldn't melt, as they say. But then, your mother was the same." He opened the door for Chastity, offering his hand as she stepped in.

A perfectly ordinary, gentlemanly courtesy, Chastity reflected. Dr. Douglas Farrell could use the example.

They chatted idly as the hackney took them to Park Lane and drew up outside a substantial residence overlooking Hyde Park. The contessa was clearly a very wealthy woman, Chastity thought as she stepped onto the pavement, waiting while her father paid the cab. The contessa had said she had bought the house, not hired it. A mansion of this size and in this location would be worth a king's ransom. Now she was thinking like Douglas Farrell, she realized crossly. Assessing the woman's wealth with all the crudity of a fishwife.

However, the sensible little voice persisted, her father could do with a helping hand when it came to his bank balance, and the Signorina Della Luca would surely have sufficient inheritance to fulfill all the doctor's dreams.

A liveried footman opened the door to them. It was the most extraordinary livery, reminding Chastity of a costume at the opera, all gold braid complete with a cocked hat. The massive entrance hall was filled with Italian statuary and vast paintings in gilded frames. The ceiling moldings had been painted a Renaissance blue and etched in gold leaf. It was all quite dazzling, but what would be perfectly in keeping with a Florentine villa was startlingly out of place in a Georgian mansion on Park Lane.

Chastity glanced at her father and saw that he was looking utterly bemused. "I think our hackney was a magic carpet," she murmured in his ear as they followed the braided footman towards a set of double doors to the right of the hall. "We seem to be in Renaissance Italy."

Lord Duncan gave her a look that combined disapproval with amusement. The footman threw open the doors and announced with a thick Italian accent, "Lord Duncan . . . the Honorable Miss Chastity Duncan."

The contessa, with a warm smile of greeting, rose from a gold and white sofa with gilded scrolled arms. She was dressed in a silk saque gown of dark green with a pale yellow trim, her hair concealed beneath an elegant but old-fashioned turban. She came forward, hand extended. "My dear Lord Duncan, Miss Duncan, how good of you to call so soon."

Chastity's gaze was riveted to the couple

standing beside one of the tall windows looking out onto Park Lane. Laura Della Luca and Dr. Douglas Farrell. They had seemed to be in animated conversation, but now both turned towards the visitors.

"I'm tempted to say, 'We can't go on meeting this way,' Miss Duncan," Douglas remarked with a cool smile as he gave her his hand.

Last night they had been on a first-name basis, she remembered. Was he trying to erase the easy familiarity of the evening by returning to social formality? Perhaps he didn't want Laura to think that he'd been on such friendly terms with another woman. If so, that was quite promising and she would follow his lead. "We do seem to keep running into each other, Dr. Farrell," she agreed, shaking his hand quickly before turning to Laura. "How are you, Miss Della Luca?"

"Very well, thank you, Miss Duncan," Laura responded with the same formality. "It's so kind of you to call. I was just saying to the *dottore* that the door knocker hasn't been still this morning. That charming dinner party at Lady Malvern's the other evening has brought us many visitors."

"Yes, people have been very welcoming," the contessa said. "Oh, how delightful," she said as Lord Duncan, with a little bow, presented his flowers. "Laura, my dear, ring for Giuseppe to bring a vase and coffee. Do sit down, Lord Duncan, Miss Duncan."

"No coffee for me, dear lady," Lord Duncan said with a wave of his hand. "Never touch the stuff after breakfast." He sat down on the sofa beside his hostess and laid his parcel on the sofa table. "I found the book of engravings I was telling you about yesterday."

"Oh, how lovely," she exclaimed with clear, unfeigned pleasure as she unwrapped the book. "What will you have instead of coffee? Sherry, perhaps?"

Lord Duncan's preferred tipple was whisky but he consented to sherry. Laura pulled an ornately fringed bell rope by the fireplace. "Yes," she said, "apart from the *dottore*, we have received calls from Lady Bainbridge, Lady Armitage, and Lady Winthrop."

"Such charming people," her mother murmured absently as she turned the pages of engravings.

"You rang, signora." The braided liveried footman bowed in the doorway. Laura handed him the flowers and gave him instructions.

Douglas said quietly to Chastity, "No ill effects from the jellied eels, I trust."

She shook her head. "No, none. How about you?"

"Only bad dreams," he said with a chuckle.

"Oh, do you sleep badly, *Dottore?*" Laura rejoined them, her question sounding rather eager.

"Only when I eat jellied eels," he responded.

"Jellied eels?" She stared at him in blank incomprehension. "What are they?"

"A Cockney delicacy," Chastity told her. "And you'd be well advised to stay clear of them. They are quite revolting."

Lord Duncan looked up from his book. "What's this about jellied eels?"

"Dr. Farrell and I ate them in Covent Garden last night," Chastity explained.

"Good God, whatever for?"

"A very good question, sir," Douglas said. "Your daughter challenged me to eat them."

"Doesn't sound like Chastity's kind of thing at all," his lordship stated firmly. "You must be mistaken."

"No, sir, believe me, I am not."

"No, Father, he's not," Chastity said. "I did challenge him and he challenged me back, so we both ate them."

"What a very strange and indelicate thing to do," Laura said, looking down her long nose. "Jellied eels, how vulgar." She gave a fastidious little shudder.

"As in food pertaining to the common man," Chastity pointed out. "As I'm sure your Latin will tell you, Miss Della Luca. You must be very familiar with the ancient language of Rome after a lifetime spent in Italy."

Laura looked momentarily put out, almost

as if she had detected the snub, but the opportunity to pontificate was not to be missed. "But of course," she said with a decisive nod. "*Vulgar . . . vulgaris.* You must be familiar with the language of the ancients, *Dottore*. It is the language of medicine, is it not?"

"Some of the old textbooks, certainly," he agreed. "But I prefer to use modern texts."

"For modern ailments," said Chastity. "Do you think in our modern society we're developing new illnesses, Dr. Farrell?"

It was an interesting question and Douglas had opened his mouth to respond, when Laura cut off his opening words, stepping in front of Chastity so that she was excluded from the conversation. "I am a martyr to insomnia, *Dottore*. A martyr to it. Is there anything you would recommend? I have tried valerian and belladonna, to no avail. I hesitate to take laudanum, of course — the juice of the poppy, so addictive."

"I would normally recommend valerian," Douglas said, suppressing a sigh. In Edinburgh Society he had grown accustomed to being accosted for a medical consultation at social gatherings, and in general acceded with grace, while gently encouraging his questioner to visit his surgery. He assumed it would be the same in London and it was certainly one way to go about acquiring patients. It remained to be seen whether it was a way to go about acquiring a wife.

“Perhaps I should make an appointment to see you in your consulting room,” she said, feeding directly into his thoughts.

“I should, of course, be happy to do what I can for you,” he responded. “My consulting rooms are still not completely furnished, and the decor leaves something to be desired.” He gave a self-deprecating smile. “I have so little time to see to such details.”

“Oh, but *Dottore,* you must let me help you,” Laura said, one hand theatrically upon her heart. “I have, if I may say so with all due modesty, excellent taste in decoration and furnishings. It is an innate talent, I believe. Is it not so, Mama?” She turned to appeal to her mother.

The contessa looked up from her book. “Yes, my dear,” she said with a patient smile. “I leave all such details to you.”

Chastity cast an involuntary glance around the extraordinarily ornate drawing room and thought of the Renaissance hall beyond. Her eyes widened and then she met Douglas Farrell’s gaze and laughter welled unbidden and unwelcome to her lips. He was looking confounded, obviously trying to imagine the calm and comforting serenity of his consulting rooms given the Renaissance touch.

Chastity coughed, found her handkerchief in her handbag, and buried her face in its lavender-fragrant lace. Douglas leaned over and patted her back with some vigor.

"Choking on something?" he inquired solicitously.

"Only on absurdity," she murmured, stepping away from the vigorous hand on her back.

"Indeed, *Dottore,* I will come to visit your consulting rooms and we will discuss the decor," Laura stated with all the assertion of one who had made up her mind.

"No, please, you mustn't trouble —"

She swept his words aside. "No trouble, *Dottore*. No trouble at all. It will be my pleasure. A woman's pleasure . . . and a woman's touch." She nodded firmly. "You have far too much to do with the noble practice of medicine to concern yourself with things that are a woman's natural domain. I shall come around this afternoon."

Definitely a bully, Chastity thought. She glanced covertly at Douglas. He was looking mesmerized but then he said with a bow, "You are most kind, signorina."

"Oh, please, let us dispense with formality," she said with a coy trill of laughter. "Douglas, you must call me Laura."

He bowed again. "I should welcome your assistance, Laura."

Liar, thought Chastity. He was lying through his teeth. There was nothing he wanted less. But maybe he *had* seen the material advantages in pursuing Laura Della Luca. If she could ride roughshod over him, she could certainly round up patients for him.

"Chastity, my dear . . . ?"

She turned at Lord Duncan's voice. "Yes, Father?"

"I was suggesting to the contessa that perhaps she and her daughter would like to join us at Romsey Manor for Christmas. London will be deserted and very tedious. We're having a house party, I believe?"

"Yes," said Chastity after the barest instant of surprise. "Yes, indeed we are. What a splendid idea. I do hope you will accept, Contessa."

"Well, that's very kind of you, Miss Duncan." The lady showed well-bred hesitation. "We should be delighted to come if it wouldn't put out your numbers."

"Oh, no, not in the least," Chastity said with an airy wave of her hand. "The house has plenty of room. The more, the merrier."

Without giving herself time to think too much about it, she turned back to Douglas Farrell. "Dr. Farrell, you said you couldn't spare the time to go home to Edinburgh for the festivities; could we perhaps persuade you to join our little party for a few days? My father is right, London will be very dull."

A Christmas house party would be the ideal opportunity for wooing both potential wives and patients. Douglas said readily, "I should be delighted, Miss Duncan. How kind of you to invite me."

She smiled. "Perhaps we too should dispense with the formalities, Douglas, if we're to enjoy a family Christmas together."

He bowed his acknowledgment. "Thank you, Chastity. I am honored."

She thought he looked a little puzzled, a little speculative, and guessed he was wondering what had prompted the invitation. He was not to know that the Go-Between was at work. If Laura kept the good doctor busy, as she was intended to do, and as, it was clear, she had every intention of doing, then Lord Duncan could devote his attentions to the contessa without being put off by the daughter.

Chastity mentally rubbed her hands in satisfaction. The Go-Between's twofold task over Christmas would be to ensure that the doctor continued to see the advantages in a union with Laura Della Luca, while the sisters encouraged Lord Duncan's pursuit of the mother. A matter of two birds with one stone. And the three Duncan sisters were enough of a force to get them both.

Chapter 7

Douglas took his leave of the Della Lucas while the Duncans remained to discuss Christmas travel plans. Laura had insisted he give her the address of his consulting rooms and had promised him with a warm handclasp that she would call upon him that very afternoon with some of her ideas for the appropriate furnishings for a Harley Street practice.

He had no idea how he was going to steer clear of her more florid ideas. He found himself grinning as he thought of Chastity's reaction to the idea of giving ornate Florentine touches to what should be all leather, brass, thick carpets, reassuring shelves of medical texts, and inoffensive pictures on plain cream walls. Now, if Chastity would undertake the task . . .

He shook his head. It didn't seem like the kind of thing she would volunteer for. And on further reflection, he couldn't see the Honorable Miss Duncan volunteering to interfere in anyone's life. She seemed to be a very hands-off kind of woman, quite unlike the members of the female sex who had hitherto peopled his life. It was that, perhaps, that made her refreshing. That and a very sharp wit that had an almost masculine edge to it. Interesting contrast with her appearance, he caught himself thinking. She was a little person, softly rounded. He remembered being struck by the curve of her forearm in that wonderful red dress the previous evening . . . the curve of her forearm and the creamy swell of her breasts. Very feminine. He had enjoyed the minute when he had held her waist as he'd lifted her into the hackney, the feel of her warm flesh beneath the thin silk. No corset, he remembered. That was what had so surprised him. Her shape was most unfashionably her own. With all her own curves and natural indentations.

As a doctor he could only applaud the refusal of any woman to torture her body with whalebone and laces, but women in general were slow to follow medical advice. Vanity was a harsh taskmaster, as Marianne had taught him. His mouth took the rather bitter twist that thoughts of his ex-fiancée always produced, even after seven years. Marianne's vanity had been outraged at the prospect of being married to a charity physician. The twist to his mouth grew more pronounced as he remembered how she had recoiled physically from him when he'd confided his mission to found a practice in the Edinburgh slums. She'd reacted as if he'd brought typhoid fever and fleas into her mother's drawing room. Her withdrawal from the engagement had followed so swiftly and decisively, he'd had no choice but to accept that what he had thought was her genuine affection for him had been based entirely on his social eligibility as a husband. His bitterness and disappointment had been mitigated to some small extent by the knowledge that he'd discovered the truth in time.

He had no intention of coming anywhere close to that danger again. He needed a wife, a good, mutually convenient relationship with no emotional entanglements. He certainly found Chastity Duncan, who clearly scorned the rules of vanity, appealing, but there was something about her that set warning bells ringing. He had a feeling she was a little too complicated a character for the kind of wife he had in mind.

So, what about the Go-Between's suggestion? Signorina Della Luca. His professional eye had detected in her posture and movements the rigidity of a tightly corseted frame, although she seemed thin enough to do without such artificial reining in. But her rather prim and dowdy choice of dress didn't imply vanity, at least not of the physical variety. She was certainly opinionated and, like so many opinionated people, rather less than accurate in the facts and views she shouted from the rooftops. And she was undoubtedly a managing woman. But she was wealthy and those character flaws could be turned to advantage. He had the impression that once she took the bit between her teeth she would pursue any course with utter dedication, and helping her husband establish a successful Society medical practice would be a course that would lend itself to the bit.

Chastity Duncan, on the other hand, would be unlikely to take a bit of any description.

He turned onto Harley Street and walked towards the building that housed his new consulting rooms. It seemed he had made up his mind. The attraction he felt for the Honorable Miss Duncan notwithstanding, she would not make him the kind of wife he needed. Laura Della Luca . . . perhaps . . . and he didn't think the lady herself would be averse.

He inserted his key in the lock of the outside door, picked up from the table in the hallway the few pieces of post that had been delivered for him, and noticed that the other practitioners in the house all had significant piles of post. But give it time. He went up the carpeted stairs. A janitor kept them swept, the gilded banister highly polished. As he reached the first-floor landing, a door opened and a middle-aged woman with a pince-nez, her hair in a severe bun, emerged from the office behind.

"Good morning," she said. "It's Dr. Farrell, isn't it?"

"Yes," he agreed.

"I'm Dr. Talgarth's receptionist," she said, indicating the door behind her. "He was wondering if you'd stop in for a drink before you go home this evening . . . around five o'clock. He wanted to welcome you to the building."

"How very kind." Douglas smiled. "I should be delighted." He gave a slight nodding bow and continued up to the next floor. He would need a receptionist himself. Doughty Mrs. Broadbent had taken care of his Edinburgh practice as she'd taken care of his father's, but she could never be persuaded to abandon her legion of grandchildren to come to the city of sin. A true Calvinist was Mrs. Broadbent.

He opened the door onto the suite of rooms he had leased and looked around. They were sparsely furnished, the walls painted a dull green, the trim peeling in places. The windows needed washing, the carpet needed replacing. The furniture was scratched, the leather on the waiting room chairs cracked. He needed to throw everything out and start anew. An expensive proposition and beyond his present means, but he'd already arranged the bank loan that would get things started.

He walked through the waiting room and into the consulting room beyond. The practitioner who had had the suite before him had favored dark paneling and heavy mahogany furniture. It was enough to depress a patient who was fit as a flea, Douglas reflected, not to mention one who was riddled with gout or suffered intractable headaches. Light wood and paintwork and a warm thick-piled carpet were the answer. Then he thought of the blue and gilt and shuddered. Renaissance orgies were not the image he intended to present.

He looked at his watch. It was close to noon. He would have a surgery of desperate patients awaiting him at St. Mary Abbot's, he was ravenous, and Laura Della Luca was coming to rearrange his decor at four o'clock. He pushed his hands through his short curls in a familiar gesture of distraction and left Harley Street at close to a run.

Chastity and Lord Duncan left the contessa and her daughter shortly after the doctor.

"I can't possibly keep the book, Lord Duncan," the contessa protested as her visitor set the volume on the sofa table.

"Peruse it at your leisure, dear lady," he said, taking one of her plump hands with its heavily beringed fingers between both of his. "It gives me great pleasure that a book that delighted my late wife delights you."

The contessa's smile was both sympathetic and pleased. "Thank you, my dear Lord Duncan."

He patted the hand he held, then relinquished it to its owner and turned courteously to Laura. "Miss Della Luca, I look forward to furthering our acquaintance at Christmas."

"Yes, indeed, my lord," she said. "I shall be most interested to see how English festivities differ from the Italian."

Lord Duncan blinked. "Well, they're Catholic, aren't they? The Italians? Don't have any of that nonsense in a good English parish, Miss Della Luca."

"St. Jude's is high church, though, Father," Chastity interceded gently. "We do have incense and the Eucharist, Laura. I hope you won't find it too strange."

"I was thinking more of the secular celebrations," Laura said. "They are bound to be different."

"Oh, yes," Chastity said cheerfully. "We do have the Boar's Head procession on Christmas Day, although actually we eat goose. And we have the caroling and the Boxing Day hunt. I'm sure it will all be quite a revelation for you."

"And for Dr. Farrell," Laura said. "I doubt

the Scottish manner of celebrating Christmas is quite the same either."

"I'll look forward to Dr. Farrell explaining his country's customs," Chastity said sweetly. "Good morning, Contessa . . . Laura."

The operatic footman saw them out and when they reached the pavement Lord Duncan turned to look up at the house. "Peculiar woman, that," he observed somewhat obliquely.

Chastity made a stab. "Laura?"

"Yes, yes, of course. Not her mother . . . charming woman . . . quite charming."

"Yes," agreed Chastity. "I like her too."

"Not so sure about the daughter, though," Lord Duncan muttered, setting off up Park Lane towards Marble Arch. "Could be tiresome."

"I imagine she'll find a husband soon enough," Chastity said, half running to catch up with her father's suddenly energetic stride.

"Hmm," he commented. "Why'd you invite that Farrell fellow for Christmas?"

"As a possible husband for Laura," Chastity said coolly.

Lord Duncan stopped dead on the street. "Good God," he said. And then again, "Good God," before he started off again.

Chastity chuckled as she hurried to catch up. Her father knew nothing about the Go-Between. He knew only the secrets of *The Mayfair Lady.*

* * *

Douglas was back at Harley Street to welcome his interior decorator at four o'clock that afternoon. He was feeling rather worn and conscious that his Mayfair clothes of the morning could have acquired some stains during his time at St. Mary Abbot's. His patients were not always immaculately groomed. However, he straightened his collar, buttoned his coat, and installed himself behind his desk in the consulting room. When his visitor arrived, he opened the door to her and gestured with a wide-flung hand at the waiting room.

"So, Laura, tell me what I should do here."

"Oh, yes," she said, walking around, her handbag tucked tightly under her arm. "Oh, yes. I see exactly what should be done. We need pastels . . . chintz at the windows . . . nice, well-stuffed chintzy armchairs and comfortable sofas . . . we need flowers on the wall . . . flower paintings. So cheerful, so inviting." She turned to Douglas, her hands clasped fervently. "You must put yourself in my hands, *Dottore*. I know exactly how to make your patients feel welcome. I can see it all."

How to make his patients feel welcome. Now, that was definitely part of the program. Douglas looked around doubtfully, trying to envisage pastel colors. Anything would be better than the dull green . . . well, he amended, anything other than ornate gold. No reason why sober practical reassurance should be dark brown. Flowers *were* cheerful. Cushions *were* comfortable. He was a little unsure about the chintz, however. The country cottage atmosphere wasn't quite what he'd had in mind. He regarded his visitor thoughtfully.

"Maybe not pastel colors, exactly," he said. "I was thinking a plain cream."

She laughed. "You are not to give it a second thought, *Dottore* — oh, Douglas. In Italy we are always so formal in matters of address. I find these London ways so strange."

"Address me in whatever manner you wish," he told her.

"And you will leave this in my hands?" She was opening the door into the consulting room as she spoke.

Douglas gave a mental shrug. He didn't have the time to do it himself. What did he have to lose? "I would be most grateful," he said, suppressing a sudden flash of anxiety at an even more vivid memory of the Della Luca mansion on Park Lane. "I had in mind something very solidly comfortable, very much in keeping with London surroundings," he suggested.

She turned back to him, holding out her hands. "*Dottore,* you may have complete confidence. I will be so happy to do this for you.

I can never bear to be idle, you know, and this will be a project after my heart."

He took her hands. "Thank you," he said. And he was, he thought, truly grateful. It would be extremely unreasonable not to be. This was what he had asked the Go-Between to find for him. A woman who would participate actively in his Harley Street practice. Laura Della Luca seemed more than willing to take on that duty.

She let her hands lie in his until he took the initiative and gently but decisively released them. He escorted her through the encroaching dusk and hailed a hackney for her.

"I look forward to our association, Douglas," she said, pressing his fingers meaningfully when he gave her his hand to assist her into the hackney. And as he handed her in he was powerfully reminded of performing the same service for Chastity Duncan the previous evening. Or not quite the same service. He realized that he had not the slightest desire to lift Laura Della Luca into the cab. A thought to be quickly dismissed.

"I too," he said, and stepped back to the curb as the hackney moved away. Now to have a collegiate drink with his fellow tenant-practitioner. There were so many tedious social steps on the way to achieving his goal, but they couldn't be hurried. However impatient he grew with his present inability to deal adequately with the ever-lengthening lines of the sick and needy crowding the pavements of St. Mary Abbot's, he had to proceed with patience, ingratiate himself with the upper echelons of London's Society without giving away the slightest hint of his rising urgency.

"No, I'm serious, Con," Chastity insisted. "He really looked as if he'd walked off the stage set of *The Marriage of Figaro.* I expected him to break into an aria at any moment."

"And the house is truly a Renaissance palazzo?" Prudence inquired in laughing disbelief.

"Well, it's not from the outside. It's a large and perfectly respectable-looking piece of Park Lane, it's just inside. Almost as if they'd brought the contents of the Uffizi with them. I kept looking at the ceilings hoping they'd managed a corner of the Sistine Chapel." She shook her head. "Oh, dear, that's so unkind, and I truly don't mean to be. It was just so . . . so *unlikely.*"

"And they're coming for the *whole* of Christmas," Constance stated flatly. "We have to endure that dreadful Laura for an entire week."

"We'll have to endure her for longer than that if she becomes a stepsister," Prudence pointed out with customary bluntness.

"Yes, but we'll get her married off, and you

must admit the mother is a very nice woman," Chastity said a mite defensively. "I know we should have consulted you both before issuing invitations, but Father just sprang it on me out of the blue."

"Oh, but I think *that's* a very good sign," Prudence said. "And it *is* his house, after all. He's entitled to invite whom he pleases to it."

"Yes, I agree," Constance said. "And we can only be pleased that he's coming out of himself enough to issue invitations. Has he said anything yet about being able to afford to wine and dine all these people?"

"Not yet," Chastity said. "I think he's still a little starry-eyed and hasn't come down to earth."

"Well, if they're all coming for Christmas, there's no need to arrange a dinner party beforehand," Constance pointed out. "So, we don't have to ambush him about that this evening."

"I think that's him now." Chastity cocked her head towards the drawing room door. "He's talking to Jenkins."

Lord Duncan entered the room almost on the instant. "Well, well, my dears, this is quite like old times," he declared, rubbing his hands. He was looking rosy from his evening bath and several large glasses of whisky while dressing. "Do you have sherry?"

"Not yet," Constance said. "We were waiting for you."

"Let me do it." He went to the sideboard, where the decanters awaited. "So, is this some special occasion that brings us all together tonight?"

"No," Prudence said. "We just thought it might be pleasant to have a family evening."

He turned with two sherry glasses in his hands and regarded his three daughters with acute suspicion. They showed him smiles of pure innocence and good feeling. He handed the glasses to Prudence and Constance and turned back to the sideboard for Chastity's. He brought that over with his own and stood in front of the fireplace, every inch the paterfamilias in his black evening clothes, his gold fob watch gleaming on the round belly of a man who had never believed in stinting himself of the good things of life.

"What of your husbands?" he asked, taking a sip of whisky, his suspicion apparently unabated.

"Oh, they had other things to do . . . or at least Max did."

"Gideon is taking Sarah to a play," Prudence said. "*Twelfth Night*. She's studying it at school."

Lord Duncan frowned into his whisky. He could find nothing wrong with these explanations. "So, has Chastity told you about our Christmas houseguests?"

"Yes, it's a lovely idea," Constance said. "The contessa seems a very charming woman."

"A large party will be great fun for Sarah," Prudence said with enthusiasm. "And the aunts dote on her already, so she'll be spoiled rotten."

"Well, what kind of entertainments have you planned?" Lord Duncan asked.

"None so far," Chastity said, looking at her sisters. "Do we have to do special things?"

"I think the contessa will expect to be entertained," Lord Duncan said. "We should invite some of the neighbors, don't you think? For drinks if not for dinner."

"Boxing Day . . . in the evening, after the hunt?" suggested Constance.

"Dinner is served, my lord," Jenkins spoke from the doorway.

"Ah, good." Lord Duncan rubbed his hands. "Did you bring up the Chateau Talbot, Jenkins?"

"I did, my lord. Two bottles."

"Good, good." He sighed a little. "The last two bottles. Never see its like again. But then, I thought we'd have a treat tonight, my dears, since it doesn't happen very often these days that we all dine together as a family."

"Why won't we see its like again, Father?" Prudence asked as they crossed the hall into the dining room.

Lord Duncan gave another, heavier sigh. "Too rich for our budget, my dear. I paid an arm and a leg for it when I laid it down.

Goodness knows what it would cost now."

The sisters exchanged an exasperated glance as they sat down. "Father, there's no reason why you should deprive yourself of *everything*," Prudence said. "Certainly we have to be a little economical, but we'll be saving money on the horse and carriage when Cobham retires, and I've already found someone to rent the mews, which will bring in some extra income, more than enough to keep good wine in the house." Wisely, she made no mention of the increasing income from *The Mayfair Lady*. Her father did not care to be reminded of that source of revenue.

"Now, this is something else I wanted to talk to you girls about," Lord Duncan declared, picking up his soup spoon. "You and Constance have your own households to run now. There's no reason for you to be running this one as well."

"We've been doing it for so long, Father, I don't think we could stop," Constance said.

"Apart from anything else, we *like* doing it," Prudence added. "It's not as if it's much trouble."

"And we're actually rather good at it," Chastity said with a cajoling smile. "Mother taught us everything we know. And you know she would want us to continue in her footsteps, at least until . . . unless . . ." She stopped.

"Unless what?" her father asked, regarding her from beneath beetling white brows.

Chastity gave a tiny shrug. "You never know what might happen, do you?"

"Or who you might meet," said Constance.

There was an instant's silence while Lord Duncan absorbed the implications of this. A slight flush bloomed on his cheek then he shook his head vigorously. "Nonsense," he declared. "Arrant nonsense. I don't know what's come over you . . . all of you." He reached for his wineglass. "Now let's talk about Christmas, although how we're going to afford to entertain a large party, I really don't know. I was thinking I would tell the hunt that we can't have the meet at the Manor."

"We've always had the Boxing Day hunt meet at the Manor, Father," Constance protested. "We can't do away with tradition."

"The stirrup cup," Lord Duncan muttered. "That costs a pretty penny."

"Oh, Father, it doesn't," Chastity said, laughing. "Fifty little cups of shooting sherry, that's all."

"We'll manage the same way we've always done," Prudence said.

"Besides, not all the Christmas entertainments have to be lavish," Chastity pointed out. "We'll have one party for the neighbors, the hunt meet on Boxing Day, and the rest of the time we'll play Christmas games —

charades, for instance. How expensive can that be?"

"Three meals a day for . . . how many people is it?" Lord Duncan pointed out. "Breakfast, lunch, dinner, not to mention afternoon tea for . . ." He began to count in his head. "Twelve," he announced with a certain contrary triumph. "And the staff, of course. There's the staff dinner and ball, and their presents."

"Father, we've been doing Christmas traditionally every year since mother died, and in fact this year we have rather more money than in the past," Prudence said patiently. "Just don't fret about anything except the wine cellar. You and Jenkins can discuss what's laid down and ready to drink at the moment, and the account at Harpers is in credit now for anything else you need."

His lordship's response was a grunt that could have been acceptance, and an oblique change of subject. "You girls are going to the Lucan wedding first, then?"

"Yes, we'll take the train afterwards. Jenkins and Mrs. Hudson are going the day before," Chastity said.

"Then I think I'll go down with them. Make sure all the arrangements are satisfactory."

"That's a very good idea," Chastity said swiftly, happy to give her father the sense that he was not superfluous to requirements when it came to organizing the house party. "Which bedroom do you think the contessa should have?"

"Oh, the green room, definitely the green room," he said. "It's the most spacious of all the guest rooms and I particularly like the view over the park. I'm sure the contessa will appreciate it."

"Well, at least we sowed a little seed," Constance said after dinner, when their father had retired to the library with his port and the sisters had retired to their own parlor upstairs.

"Yes, and we let him know that we wouldn't have any objections to his remarrying," Chastity said from the depths of the sofa. "At least I think we did . . . I was trying to anyway."

"No, it was good," Prudence said. "But we don't want to rush anything. You know how stubborn he is."

"I just wish he wouldn't obsess about money, or the lack of it," Chastity said with a sigh.

"Poor soul. You have to put up with it all the time." Prudence gave her a sympathetic smile. "At least we go home at night."

"Oh, it's not that bad," Chastity said quickly.

Constance frowned at her, then changed the subject. "So, if the contessa has the green room, where does everyone else go? What about the good doctor, Chas? Any ideas?"

"Should we put him in an adjoining room with Laura?" Chastity asked. "Or would that be a little obvious?"

"I don't see why it should be," Prudence said. "Besides, I don't see the lady indulging in any bed-hopping, do you?"

They all laughed at an idea that seemed absurd. Laura Della Luca was far too prim and opinionated for any indiscreet forays at dead of night.

"But if they're next door to each other, they'll bump into each other all the time," Constance pointed out. "Going in and out, up and down the stairs, that kind of thing."

"Then, we'll give the doctor the Chinese room and his prospective bride the pink room next door," Chastity said, adding, "I expect she'd like the pink. It's not quite Italian but it's pretty-pretty, and the furniture in there is white and gold. She'll feel quite at home."

"Will they bring ladies' maids?" Constance asked, reaching behind her to the secretaire, where there was a notebook and pen. "We'd better start making notes."

"I would think they would bring their own personal servants," Chastity said. "Mrs. Hudson will know where to put them."

"What about the doctor?"

"I doubt he can run to a valet," Chastity

responded. “Unless he’s trying to make an impression, of course.”

“Men who live on Wimpole Street would tend to have valets,” Prudence mused.

“I know he has a cook/housekeeper,” Chastity said thoughtfully. “He said she came with the flat he’s leasing. But I’m not sure about a valet.”

“We’ll have to ask him,” Constance said. “Next time you see him.”

“Which will be when?” Chastity frowned. “I don’t have his address, so I don’t know how to contact him. We can’t write to him care of Mrs. Beedle, because that’s the address the Go-Between knows.”

“But he knows how to find you,” Constance reminded her, rising to her feet with a yawn. “And he’s bound to need to make contact before Christmas. To discuss travel arrangements and suchlike.”

“I could always ask Laura. She has the address of his office on Harley Street,” Chastity said. “I’ll write to him there. There’s no need for us to meet.”

“No, I suppose not,” Prudence said, regarding her younger sister with a slightly quizzical air. “If you don’t wish to, then of course there’s no need.”

“Exactly,” Chastity said.

Chapter 8

Chastity hurried along Kensington High Street in the teeth of an icy wind. Her coat was buttoned to the neck, the fur collar turned up around her ears. Her hat was pulled down low over her brow and a long, fringed scarf muffled her throat and streamed behind her. Her hands were encased in fur-lined leather gloves and her feet in high, buttoned boots. Even so, her breath steamed and the wind reddened her cheeks and the tip of her nose and made her teeth ache.

Mrs. Beedle's corner shop was a welcome haven and Chastity entered, setting the bell tinkling, almost slamming the door behind her in her anxiety to keep out the cold. She took a deep breath of the warm air that smelled of sweets and baking.

At the sound of the bell Mrs. Beedle emerged from behind the curtain that separated her kitchen from the shop. "Why, hello, Miss Chas." She beamed at her visitor. "Oh, my, don't you look cold. Come you in now and have a nice cup of hot cocoa. I've just made a Victoria sponge, straight out of the oven, it is." She lifted the hinged top of the shop counter.

"Yes, I can smell it," Chastity said, clapping her hands together in an effort to restore the circulation to her fingertips that despite the gloves were numb. "I can't think of anything nicer on such a day than cocoa and cake." She went behind the counter, dropping the top before following Mrs. Beedle through the curtain and into the kitchen.

"Oh, it's so lovely and warm in here," she said appreciatively.

"Sit you down by the range, m'dear." Her hostess was setting a pan of milk to heat on the stove. "There's a couple of letters for you on the shelf there."

"Thank you." Chastity took down the letters and then sat on a chair so close to the range, she was almost inside it. She glanced at the envelopes. They were all addressed to *The Mayfair Lady.* She thrust them unopened into her coat pocket before drawing off her gloves and unwinding her scarf. "That's better," she said. "It's the wind that's so fierce. It whistles around every street corner. Everyone looks blue with cold."

"Aye, there's not been too many customers today," the shopkeeper said, slicing a large piece of sponge cake oozing raspberry jam.

"When it's cold like this it keeps them at home. There you are now, Miss Chas. And the cocoa's coming up."

Chastity took the plate, smiling her thanks. Her hostess spooned cocoa powder into a mug and poured the steaming milk on top, stirring vigorously. This she placed on a low stool set beside her visitor's chair.

Chastity inhaled the rich chocolaty fragrance of the drink and broke off a small piece of cake with her fingers. "How have you been, Mrs. Beedle?"

"Oh, well enough, dear," the woman said comfortably. "Business has been busy with Christmas coming."

"I wonder if we'll have a white Christmas," Chastity said, happy to make idle conversation in this warm kitchen. The shop bell rang again and with a word of excuse Mrs. Beedle hurried through the curtain.

"Why, Doctor, haven't seen you in a while," she declared as she emerged into the shop. "Thought you'd up and left us."

"I moved away last week, Mrs. Beedle," Douglas Farrell explained. "Into central London."

Chastity sat very still, barely breathing, a piece of cake arrested in its journey to her mouth. *Of all the narrow escapes.* Five minutes either side and she would have run straight into him, and how in the world would she have explained her presence in unfashionable

Kensington, patronizing the shop that served as the poste restante for *The Mayfair Lady*? The man was no fool; it was at Chastity Duncan's At Home that he'd been introduced to a prospective bride. He would certainly have put two and two together.

"Central London, eh?" Mrs. Beedle was saying admiringly. "Now, that's a place I like to visit, particularly around Christmastime. I like to look at the shops all decorated with their window displays. So, what'll it be, Doctor?"

"Oh, the usual . . . licorice and humbugs, a pound each, if you please, Mrs. Beedle," Douglas said in his pleasant voice. "And I have a letter to leave for you to be collected."

"Oh, yes. Just drop it on the counter over there, Doctor." The sound of the shopkeeper shaking and weighing sweets reached Chastity, still sitting, almost paralyzed, behind the curtain.

She finally swallowed the piece of cake and licked the jam off her fingers, then sipped her cocoa, careful not to make the slightest scraping sound as she lifted the mug from the stool. Not that Douglas, as a mere customer, would have any interest in the sounds that came from the shopkeeper's private apartments, she reflected. It didn't make her less nervous, however.

She listened as the exchange was completed with a few cheerful pleasantries on both sides, and the chime of the doorbell signaled the customer's departure. Mrs. Beedle came back into the kitchen holding a letter. "Well, this is a strange thing, Miss Chas," she said. "Dr. Farrell there left a letter for *The Mayfair Lady*. Isn't that a coincidence . . . and you sitting right here in the flesh?"

"It is rather," Chastity agreed, taking the letter Mrs. Beedle held out to her. "But then, quite a lot of people write to the publication."

"I suppose that must be true," her hostess said, but she was shaking her head. "Doesn't seem quite like the doctor, though. What would he be doing writing to *The Mayfair Lady*?"

"I can't imagine," Chastity said cheerfully, thrusting the letter unopened to join the others in her pocket. She stood up, reaching for her gloves and scarf on the table. "I must run, Mrs. Beedle. Thank you so much for the cake and cocoa. I'm ready to face the outdoors again now."

"Right you are, Miss Chas. Give my regards to Miss Prue and Miss Con."

"I will. I probably won't see you before Christmas, so have a merry one, Mrs. Beedle, and a wonderful New Year."

"And to you too, m'dear." Mrs. Beedle followed her into the shop.

Chastity opened the door and peered cautiously out. Douglas was turning the far corner of the street. "Bye, Mrs. Beedle." She waved and stepped out onto the pavement. Douglas was headed in the opposite direction from her route home, and yet without giving the matter any serious thought she set off after him. She didn't want to meet him, but she *did* want to find out where he was going with his two pounds of sweets.

At the next corner, she saw him ahead of her, walking briskly towards the end of the street. She waited until he'd turned the far corner, then ran in the most unladylike fashion, anxious not to lose him at the next corner.

The streets were getting meaner, dirtier. There were few people about — it was too cold — and those who were standing around in aimless knots were uniformly poorly dressed, and the children who bobbed in and out of doorways were often barefoot. Chastity was so horrified, she could almost feel the freezing cobbles on her own feet. Still, she followed the doctor's unmistakable figure as he strode purposefully ahead, looking neither right nor left.

"Eh, lady, lady . . . penny, lady . . . go' a penny?" She had been so absorbed in wrestling with her horror at the frozen misery she saw around her that she became aware of the chanted question only belatedly. She turned round and found herself face-to-face with a group of ragged youths, grinning at her, hands stretched out towards her.

She felt in her pockets for her coin purse and shook a handful of pennies into her palm, aware of the deep-set eyes in thin faces fixed upon her, watching her every move. The group moved closer to her as the coins glinted, and there was a predatory look now in their collective gaze. Suddenly Chastity no longer felt safe. It had been a foolish impulse. Now it was too late to retrace her steps, even if she could find her way back to familiar ground through the twisting warren of streets. She was going to have to reveal herself to Douglas, and God only knew how he'd respond to being followed in this neck of the woods. She tossed the pennies to the street and spun on her heel, running after her quarry while the youths fell in a scrabbling, scrapping heap upon the coins.

Douglas turned into a narrow alley behind a church and stopped outside a door in the middle of the terrace of houses. He still wasn't aware of her behind him and instinctively Chastity slowed, catching her breath. He opened the door and disappeared within. An icy blast of wind roared down the narrow street, picking up refuse from the cobbles: manure-soiled straw, scraps of filthy paper, potato peelings, and other unidentifiable pieces of jetsam. Chastity shivered as the cold penetrated the thickness of her coat. She couldn't stand out here indefinitely. Squaring her shoulders she walked to the door and pushed it open. She stepped directly into a small, dreary front room that was filled with people — women and children, for the most part.

She gazed around her in confusion and dismay. She was overwhelmed by the misery all around her. It had a distinct smell that seemed to stifle the breath in her throat. The room was both cold and stuffy, and the coal fire gave off rank fumes that mingled with the burning oil in the lamps.

Douglas had his back to her and was bending over, talking to a woman seated on a rickety stool, a baby in her arms. He reached down and took the infant from her, cradling it against his shoulder with a completely natural ease. "Close the door," he said without turning, and Chastity realized that she was still standing in the open doorway, letting the frigid air into the house. She had no business here. She was about to step back into the street, closing the door behind her, when he glanced over his shoulder.

He stared at her in disbelief, his large hand still cupping the baby's head against his shoulder. "Chastity? What the *hell* —"

"I saw you back there and followed you," she said in a rush, interrupting him. "And then some youths started demanding money and I was suddenly scared. Silly of me, I know." She looked at him helplessly, knowing it was a pathetically inadequate explanation for what was clearly some monumental intrusion.

The baby wailed as if at a sudden pain and Douglas instantly turned his attention to the child, seeming to dismiss his unwelcome visitor. He touched the tiny ear and the child screamed. "All right," he said softly, rocking the infant as the mother looked up at him with a mixture of hope and helplessness in her tired eyes. "It looks like an ear infection; I think we can do something for him," he said, giving the woman a smile of reassurance. "Come into the office, Mrs. Croaker." Still carrying the crying baby he went through a door in the far wall, the woman on his heels.

Chastity remained standing by the outside door, wondering whether she should just slide away and pretend she'd never been there. But that didn't seem like an option somehow. She became aware of something tugging at her skirt and looked down into the hollow eyes of a whey-faced little girl of about four. Her nose was crusted and running. Chastity felt in her handbag for the packet of peppermints she always carried with her. She offered one to the girl, who regarded it for a moment with suspicion before grabbing it quickly and cramming it into her mouth as if afraid someone would take it from her.

The door to the inner room opened and Mrs. Croaker emerged, carrying her now quiet baby. Douglas appeared behind her. He beckoned Chastity, his expression rather dark. She was aware of dull eyes in thin grimy faces following her with little interest as she passed through them, following him into a smaller room, sparsely furnished with a table, two chairs, a shelf of books, and a screen in the corner.

"What the *hell* are you doing here?" Douglas demanded without preamble.

"I told you. I saw you and was trying to catch up with you," she said as if it was the most natural thing in the world. "I had a question I needed to ask you. Well, several actually."

His charcoal eyes were far from friendly as he said, "And just what could possibly have brought the Honorable Miss Duncan to this part of London?"

"I was visiting an old servant for tea," she lied glibly. "She lives on Kensington High Street, above a shop . . . a baker's shop. We — my sisters and I — take turns visiting her once a month. The poor old dear gets very lonely. I was just leaving when I saw you turn the corner of the street and I thought it would be a good opportunity to ask you my questions."

Douglas's gaze was incredulous. "You followed me for six relatively respectable streets into the depths of this neighborhood just to ask me a question?"

"Why is that strange?" Chastity asked with a touch of hauteur that she hoped would add verisimilitude to her tale. "If I see someone on the street that I want to talk to, what's strange about following them to attract their attention?"

Douglas shook his head impatiently. "Why didn't you just call out to me?" he asked. "When you first saw me."

Good question, Chastity thought, but she sensed that the truthful answer wouldn't serve her well at this point. Douglas did not look as if he'd have much sympathy for simple curiosity. "I did," she fibbed. "But you didn't hear me. And you were walking very fast. Before I realized it, I was lost and I had no choice but to keep following you. Where are we exactly?" she added.

His mouth tightened. He could see the revulsion in her hazel eyes, hear it in the question itself. He could almost hear Marianne asking the same question in the same tone. "Not your usual stomping ground, I'm afraid," he said with undisguised contempt.

Chastity flushed a little. "I wouldn't have thought it was yours," she said. "It's hardly Harley Street."

He gazed at her in silence for a minute and she began to feel like an insect under a microscope, then he agreed dryly, "No, it's not. But if you keep yourself to yourself, don't touch anything or anyone, and don't breathe too deeply, it's to be hoped you won't catch anything unsavory."

Her flush deepened. She had certainly intruded, but she didn't think she'd done anything to deserve this disdain. "I'll go and find a hackney," she said with as much dignity as she could muster.

"Don't be absurd," he snapped. "You don't really believe hackneys ply their trade in these streets."

Chastity took a deep breath and said with careful lack of expression, "If you would tell me exactly how to get out of this warren of streets to somewhere vaguely familiar, I'll leave you to your work. You have a lot of patients waiting."

He didn't answer immediately, but the angry frown creasing his forehead above the thick eyebrows deepened. The last thing he wanted was this Society lady poking her nose into his very private business. If she chose to blab about it, it would be all over town in no time. How many wealthy patients would be willing to patronize a physician who also had a surgery in the London slums? They'd run a mile. But the damage was already done and he couldn't in all conscience let her leave unescorted.

"I doubt you're capable of looking after yourself in that warren, as you put it," he said eventually. "And you'll certainly draw unwelcome attention to yourself. You may find these surroundings distasteful, but you need to wait until I'm ready to take you home. Take that chair over there." He gestured to a chair by the window.

She wanted to tell him that *distasteful* was not the word. She found the surroundings wretched, desperate; they filled her with horror and compassion, but in the face of his sardonic tone she was damned if she was going to tell him that. "I'll find a seat in the outer office," she stated, turning to go.

"I don't recommend that," Douglas said. "There are any number of infections hanging around in that room just waiting for a rarified flower such as yourself to host them."

"And *you* don't get them?" she inquired, the edge to her voice growing sharper. She couldn't understand his abrupt and hostile manner. He was entitled to some degree of annoyance, but this was too much, and she wasn't prepared to let him get away with it. "You don't consider you might pass them on to people you meet in your other life, Dr. Farrell?"

"You may rest assured, Miss Duncan, that I disinfect myself thoroughly," he said with that same flicker of contempt.

Chastity took herself out to the waiting room and found a spare seat. Children whined and sniffed; their blank-eyed mothers administered slaps and hugs indiscriminately. Everyone shivered. Chastity handed out the last of her peppermints and wished she had more. They were a small enough solace in the face of this collective misery but at least she felt as if she was contributing something. She huddled into her coat with her reflections as Douglas moved among his patients, talking softly to each one in the waiting room before taking them into his office.

This doctor was a very different man from the urbane physician of Wimpole and Harley Streets . . . and very different from the man who had a passion for music and who could be a charming and witty dinner companion, not to mention a liberty-taking carriage escort. He was a positive Jekyll and Hyde. But why was he working here? Were these the only patients who would come to him? Or was it simply that he didn't yet have a sufficiently established practice in the more salubrious office on Harley Street to give this one up? Could these people even pay him? Certainly not much.

Could it be choice? she thought suddenly, watching as he knelt on the dirty floor in front of an elderly woman whose badly swollen feet were wrapped in rags. He unwrapped the rags, holding her misshapen feet in the palms of his hands, tenderly palpating the ankles. It came to Chastity as a blinding revelation that he was treating these wretched folk with something akin to love. And they hung on his every word, their eyes following him as he moved among them. But how in the world did this scene jibe with a wealthy Harley Street practice?

And why had he been so contemptuous, so hostile towards her if he loved what he was doing? If he was proud of what he was doing? It was more as if he was embarrassed at being caught out at something that he was ashamed of.

For close to two hours, Chastity sat against the wall, trying to appear invisible. At least she'd solved the answer to the licorice and humbugs, she reflected, noticing that most patients as they left had some kind of medicine and the children without exception left his office with a handful of sweets. Finally he called in the last patient and she was the only person left in the waiting room. She got up from the rickety chair, feeling stiff and cold from sitting still so long, and went to the fireplace, stretching her hands to the meager glow.

She heard his office door open, heard him say, "Bring Maddie back in two days, Mrs. Garth. It's very important that I see her again. Don't forget." Chastity straightened and turned slowly to watch him show a thin woman and an even thinner child out the front door.

"Poor souls," she said rather helplessly.

"Yes, that's exactly what they are. Poor." He moved past her to the grate and bent to bank the fire, then rose and extinguished the lamps. "Did you find it an interesting afternoon? An enlightening one, perhaps?" That same adversarial note was in his voice. It was as if he was challenging her in some way.

"No, I found it depressing," she said. "I can understand why you would want to move to Harley Street."

"Can you?" he said with a short laugh. "Can you, indeed?" He opened the door for her and she stepped out into the icy street, wrapping the scarf around her throat while he closed the door.

"You're not locking it?"

"There's nothing to steal, and someone might need to come in from the cold," he said curtly. He looked down at her with that same frown creasing his brow. "Would it be too much to ask you to keep this little adventure of yours a secret?"

Chastity thought he sounded as if the request had been dragged from him by wild horses. She said rather coldly, "I'm not in the habit of gossiping. Besides, your business is no business of mine."

He looked unconvinced but then gave a short nod and said, "Let's hurry, I'm freezing to death."

He took her hand and pulled her along beside him as he strode rapidly away from the terrace and the church and along a series of miserable streets until they turned suddenly into the broad thoroughfare of Kensington High Street. "We'll take the omnibus from the corner," he said. "It goes directly to Oxford Street."

Chastity was about to say that in this cold she would prefer to take a hackney but bit her tongue. After what she'd seen this afternoon it wouldn't surprise her if the doctor didn't have the cab fare. *She* did, but remembering how he'd reacted when she'd hinted he might be a little short in the coin department, she wasn't prepared to risk a reprise by offering to pay for the ride herself.

Fortunately, the bus came quickly. It was fairly full but Douglas pushed her somewhat unceremoniously into the center, where there was a spare seat, or half a seat, the other half being occupied by a woman of very generous proportions who was also hung about with parcels and held a capacious handbag on her knee from which she had taken out her knitting. Chastity took the perch available and Douglas stood in the aisle, one hand on the seat back, the other holding the ceiling strap. He was so tall, it brushed his shoulder and he could reach it without so much as a stretch.

"So, what were these questions you wanted to ask me so urgently?" he inquired, handing the conductor sixpence for their fares as the omnibus lurched to a stop.

Chastity's large seat companion wanted to get off at the stop, giving Chastity time to consider her hastily manufactured excuse. It seemed rather feeble after the events of the afternoon. With mumbled apologies the woman banged her way past Chastity, parcels swinging precariously, knitting needles sticking out dangerously from the wide-open handbag. When she had finally staggered down the aisle trailing apologies, bruises, and scrapes in her wake, Chastity slipped over into the window seat, which was pleasantly warm from its previous occupant, and Douglas took the seat beside her.

"So?" he said.

It might be feeble but it was all she had. "I wasn't sure if we would meet again socially before Christmas and I didn't have your address," she said. "I wanted to know what arrangements you wanted to make about coming to Romsey."

"That was the question . . . the only question?" he asked incredulously. "You followed me into the darkest depths of Earl's Court to ask me something that trivial?"

"You might consider it trivial," Chastity snapped, well on the defensive now. "But as your hostess, I don't find it in the least so. Are you intending to arrive on Christmas Eve, or the day itself? How long do you intend to stay? Will you be bringing servants?

These are all vital matters."

He leaned his head back and laughed without the slightest hint of humor. "Vital matters. Dear God, I suppose for some people they are." He turned his head to look at her. "After what you saw this afternoon, how can you call — No, forgive me." He shook his head. "I know perfectly well I couldn't expect someone like you to understand."

Someone like you. Chastity was chilled by something quite other than the cold evening. *What kind of person did he think she was?* She'd been shocked, horrified, filled with pity for those people. And in different circumstances would have been overcome with admiration for Douglas Farrell. Except that his hostility rather blunted the edge of admiration, and besides, he must presumably be intending to leave that practice when he established himself instead among the rich socialites of the city, a wealthy wife upon his arm. But she couldn't say any of that, because she wasn't supposed to know about the wife part of his ambition, or about the contempt with which he viewed the rich socialites who would line his pockets. He had only revealed that to the representative of the Go-Between. And it was that same contempt he'd been directing at her all afternoon.

She said tartly, "Since you're abandoning those people in favor of a rather easier and more lucrative practice, I don't think you can throw stones, Dr. Farrell."

He said nothing. He had seen her distaste, the way she had shrunk from the unfortunates in his waiting room. He certainly wasn't going to waste his breath explaining himself to her.

Chastity said suddenly, "I'm getting off at the next stop. I'll take a hackney from there." She stood up, her face rather white under the flickering streetlights that illuminated the vehicle.

Douglas would have attempted to stop her, attempted an apology even, but he was rather alarmed by her pallor, which was particularly startling against the redness of her hair. She looked about to weep, he thought. "I'll take you —"

"No, you won't," she interrupted. "Thank you, but no. If you would let me pass, please?"

He stood up and she brushed past him, pushing her way towards the exit. He sat down again, tight-lipped. That had been nothing short of a debacle that threatened to throw all his plans into jeopardy. He had been furious at the position Chastity had put him in, the need to extract a promise from her as if St. Mary Abbot's was something of which he was ashamed. And he had hated her presence in his surgery, as much because he felt he was somehow exposing his patients' miseries to someone who couldn't empathize with them as by the threat she posed to his privacy and his plans.

But none of that was adequate excuse for having been so damnably and disastrously rude to her. In fact, he couldn't understand what had provoked him to such a foolish display of antagonism; he was usually expert at keeping his thoughts and feelings to himself. He knew that he couldn't realistically expect someone from Chastity's social circles and experience to feel anything but the revulsion she had made no attempt to disguise for the wretched inhabitants of the city slums, so it shouldn't have come as a surprise to him. He knew perfectly well that it wasn't realistic to expect any woman who would suit his marital purposes to sympathize with his mission. He had long ago accepted that a simple lack of objection from his spouse would serve his purpose perfectly well.

But now how was he to retrieve the situation? He could hardly spend Christmas as the guest of a woman he had so deeply offended, and if he was to court Laura Della Luca, he needed to have access to her. Christmas under the same roof was the perfect opportunity.

The omnibus lurched to a stop at Oxford Street and Douglas pushed his way to the exit. He stepped down onto the street, which despite the cold was thronged with Christmas shoppers, and strode off towards Wimpole Street debating his next move. He would have to try to make amends to Chastity without delay. Flowers first, a visit of apology afterwards . . . bearing, of course, the answers to her *vital* hostess questions, always assuming she was still interested in the answers.

Chastity arrived home still feeling emotionally winded. She hurried past Jenkins, who had the door open for her before she could get her key in the lock.

"Everything all right, Miss Chas?"

"Yes . . . yes, thank you, Jenkins. I'm just half-frozen," she called over her shoulder as she headed up the stairs to the welcome and familiar seclusion of her parlor. Here it was warm, the fire ablaze, the lamps lit. She unpeeled her outer garments and threw them over a chair by the door before dropping into a deep armchair by the fire. She propped her feet on the fender and closed her eyes for a minute.

Jenkins tapped on the door and came in with a tray of tea. "I thought you might like a cup of tea, Miss Chas, to keep out the cold." He looked at her with concern. "Are you quite well?"

"Oh, yes," she said. "Quite well, thank you. And tea would be lovely."

"There's some of Mrs. Hudson's gingersnaps too," he said, setting the tray on the small table beside her. "Now, is there anything else I can get you?"

She shook her head. "No, thank you. I'm just tired because of the cold, I think. It's exhausting trying to keep warm." She poured tea for herself. "Is Lord Duncan in?"

"He came back about ten minutes ago. He said he wouldn't be in for dinner tonight."

"Oh?" She sat up, her eyes widening. "Did he say where he was going?"

"Not in so many words," Jenkins said. "He asked that I have his evening dress pressed and that Cobham should be ready to take him out again at seven-thirty."

"His club?" Chastity speculated.

"I couldn't say, Miss Chas."

"But you don't think so," she observed shrewdly.

"His lordship seemed to be rather more concerned about the arrangements than for an ordinary visit to his club." Jenkins bowed himself out.

Chastity sipped her tea and thoughtfully broke a gingersnap between finger and thumb. Was he planning an evening with the contessa? That could be promising. She nibbled the biscuit between sips of tea and gradually began to feel a little less shocked by the afternoon's events. Of one thing she was certain, she wanted nothing more to do with either Dr. Jekyll or Mr. Hyde.

She remembered the letters in her coat pocket and set down her teacup before going over to retrieve them. Ordinarily, she and her sisters opened *The Mayfair Lady* post together and discussed their responses. Since the three of them were meeting tomorrow for coffee at Fortnum and Mason, where they conducted a fair number of their business meetings, she really should wait to open these until then. She tapped the one from Douglas Farrell against the palm of her hand. *What did he want of* The Mayfair Lady *now?*

It was irresistible. And he was very much her own special project, or at least, she amended, he had been. She set down the other letters and returned to her chair to open the missive, slitting the envelope with her thumbnail and drawing out the single sheet of writing paper. It had an address on Wimpole Street engraved at the head . . . rather different from his previous communication, which had used Mrs. Beedle's address.

To whom it may concern:

I have made contact with the lady you suggested I meet and have found her to be a potentially suitable connection. However, the contract states that you will offer me up to three prospects, so should you have other suitable possibilities on your books at this time, I would be happy to meet them. You may con-

tact me at the above address.

Yours very truly,
Douglas Farrell, MD.

Chastity read the note with increasing indignation. It was the arrogant tone of it that got to her. Laura Della Luca would do, but he'd like a few more choices up his sleeve. They were dealing with people here, she thought furiously, not loaves of bread — I like the whole-meal, but maybe I might like to sample the split-tin or the cottage-loaf before I make up my mind.

Well, if she had her way, the agency had fulfilled its contract to provide Dr. Farrell with the perfect candidate, and the Go-Between's obligation ended there. Except, of course, that he was quite right. They owed him two other introductions. She put the letter back in the envelope. They would discuss a response tomorrow.

Another discreet knock heralded the return of Jenkins. He was invisible behind the most enormous bouquet of hothouse roses that Chastity had ever seen.

"The florist's boy just delivered these for you, Miss Chas," he said from behind the floral wall.

"Ye gods!" she exclaimed jumping to her feet. "Who are they from?"

"The boy didn't say, but there's a note attached." Jenkins set the bouquet on the sideboard. "I'll fetch a vase . . . or perhaps two."

"Yes, bring that big crystal bowl and the Sevres vase, please," Chastity said, inhaling the fragrance that now filled the room. "They'll look beautiful in those. Oh, and some scissors. I should cut the stalks a little."

"Right away, Miss Chas." Jenkins, brushing stray leaves from his lapels, went off on his errand.

Chastity found the little card attached with silver ribbon to the stems. She recognized the handwriting immediately, which was hardly surprising since she'd been reading the same hand not two minutes earlier. She turned the card over.

My dear Chastity, can you ever forgive me for being such a bear? I behaved abominably this afternoon. I have no excuse and will not attempt to find one. Please accept my most profound apologies. Douglas.

Chastity read it again. It was graceful, elegant, and sounded utterly genuine. No fancy flourishes, no bombast. Did it come from Jekyll or Hyde? Either way, only the most ungenerous nature could refuse such an apology. And Chastity did not have an ungenerous nature.

And she was also very curious. How could such an urbane, charming, attractive man turn into a surly bear . . . good word that.

Not that he'd been in the least surly with his patients, she reminded herself, only with an unwelcome visitor. Admittedly, she'd ambushed him on his way to his very private business and she'd had the flimsiest of excuses for the ambush.

There *was* something inappropriate about wanting to talk about Christmas celebrations and servants to a man who had just spent two hours caring with the utmost compassion for the poorest of the poor. The most wretched inhabitants of this vast and uncaring city. If only she'd been able to think of a better excuse. But then, he'd been rude and abrupt before she'd even opened her mouth on the subject of Christmas. Was it simply because she'd intruded on a dark secret, or was there something else?

She wouldn't find out if she didn't accept his apology, let bygones be bygones, and renew the invitation for Christmas. And besides, she still had to play her role as Go-Between, she reflected. The prospective union of Laura Della Luca and Dr. Douglas Farrell was very much in all their interests. She could put aside her dislike sufficiently to play the courteous and helpful hostess for a few days.

Chapter 9

Lord Duncan was eating kidneys and bacon with a hearty appetite when Chastity went in to breakfast the next morning. She bent and kissed him. "Good morning, Father."

"Morning, my dear," he said, dabbing at his mouth with his napkin. "Excellent kidneys. I recommend them."

Chastity shook her head. "Not for me this early in the day." She gave him a quick, covert scrutiny. He was looking, she thought, remarkably smug, like a cat who's caught a larderful of mice. His cheeks were pink, his eyes very bright, his luxuriant white hair looking even more lush and well cared for than usual.

"Coffee?" She raised the pot in invitation and at his nod refilled his cup before sitting down. "So, did you go to the club for dinner last night?" she asked conversationally.

"No, no . . . Café Royal," he said. "Haven't been there in quite a while. Holds up nicely, I must say. Very pleasant dinner.

Nice bottle of Montrachet." He folded back his newspaper with a crackle.

"Pleasant company?" She kept her eyes on the toast she was buttering.

There was a pause, then the newspaper crackled again. "Yes, very pleasant," he said. "I dined with the contessa."

"She's a lovely woman," Chastity said warmly. "And very cultivated."

"Yes . . ." Another crackle from the newspaper. "Very good company . . . good conversation."

"I wonder if she plays bridge," Chastity mused. "At Christmas we thought we'd have a bridge tournament one evening."

"I'm sure she does," Lord Duncan said. He looked over his newspaper at his youngest daughter. "You're not thinking of playing in this tournament, are you?"

Chastity laughed. Bridge was not her forte. "I might be," she said.

"Good God. Well, I hope I don't draw you as a partner."

"Oh, that's unkind."

"Not a bit of it," he said. "Now, your sisters are a different matter. I can never decide which one of them is the better player."

"They get plenty of practice," Chastity pointed out. "Max and Gideon aren't exactly incompetent." She wondered whether Douglas Farrell was a bridge player. On reflection, she doubted it. He would be more inclined towards physical sport than idle evenings around a card table.

And on the subject of Douglas Farrell, she needed to consult her sisters.

Fortnum's tearoom was buzzing when Chastity passed through the swinging glass door at mid-morning. She saw her sisters at a table by a window overlooking Piccadilly and threaded her way through the tables towards them.

"Good morning," she greeted, unbuttoning her coat. "At least it's warm in here. Oh, yes, Gaston, you can take my coat, thank you." She smiled at the attentive maître d'hôtel as he helped her out of her coat. "I've been looking for a hat for David and Hester's wedding, but I couldn't find anything I liked."

"Great minds think alike," Prudence said. "We've been shopping for hats too."

"Successfully so," Constance said with a satisfied nod. "And what's more, we saw the most perfect hat to match your lavender shantung afternoon dress, so we bought it on approval."

"Yes, it'll be wonderful for the wedding," Prudence declared. "You were going to wear that dress, weren't you?"

"I will be now," Chastity said. Prudence's dress sense was always impeccable and her sisters trusted her sartorial judgment unreservedly. Chastity turned to examine the cake trolley that had appeared beside her. "A chocolate meringue, I think." She leaned back a little so that the waitress could put the plate in front of her and fill her coffee cup. "What's the hat like?"

"Pretty as a picture," Prudence said readily. "Turquoise felt with a wide brim, a tiny wisp of a veil, and a big lavender bow. I tell you, it could have been made expressly for that dress." She put a forkful of vanilla slice into her mouth.

"Well, that's one less thing to worry about," Chastity said, pouring cream into her coffee. "Did you know what Father was doing last night?"

Her sisters shook their heads. "Tell us," Constance demanded.

"He took the contessa out to dinner . . . to the Café Royal, no less." Chastity nodded significantly. "What do you think of that?"

"Promising," said Prudence.

"Very promising," said Constance.

"At breakfast he was so smug, you wouldn't believe," Chastity told them, forking into her meringue. "But there's something else, rather more urgent, that we have to discuss." She popped the airy forkful into her mouth and let it melt on her tongue in a chocolate and cream mélange while her sisters waited patiently.

Chastity swallowed, took another sip of coffee, then rested her elbows on the table and leaned forward, dropping her voice to a conspiratorial whisper. "I agreed not to tell anyone . . . of course, I don't count you two, but I expect Douglas would. Anyway, my promise is yours." She looked a question and received nods in return.

"Then let me tell you all about yesterday afternoon." The telling took close to an hour and another meringue, her sisters interjecting the occasional question, the occasional exclamation, but for the most part listening in silence.

"So," said Chastity at the end of the recital, "what do you think of all that?"

"I don't know," Prudence said. "What an extraordinary way to behave . . . to be so rude."

"Well, this is the card that came with the flowers." Chastity dug in her handbag for the card. "How could one resist an apology like that? It's as if the man has a double personality."

"A double life certainly," Constance said, reading the card and handing it to Prudence. "A practice in Harley Street and one in the slums." She shook her head. "And he's looking for a rich wife to help him with the rich practice. I hope he doesn't already have a poor wife to go with the poor practice."

Her sisters laughed, although the idea didn't strike any of them as completely ludicrous. Douglas Farrell was becoming a sufficiently mysterious character for one to believe almost anything of him.

"So, is he going to abandon the other practice as soon as he's properly set up on Harley Street?" Prudence asked.

"I assume so," Chastity said with a shrug. "That's got to be the point, surely. All he's ever said to the Go-Between is that he wants a rich wife whose money and position will go to establishing his practice. Oh, on which subject, he sent this letter to *The Mayfair Lady* as well." She handed over the letter from Dr. Farrell. "Nice tone, don't you think?" Her lip curled slightly.

"Arrogant certainly," Constance said. "But as we've so often noted, my dears, that's a very common trait among the male of our species. Some of them can be quite lovable despite."

"Somehow, I don't think *lovable* is a word one would ever be tempted to apply to Douglas Farrell," Chastity stated.

"But how did he end up at this St. Mary Abbot's in the first place?" Prudence asked, frowning as she took off her glasses and polished them on her napkin, an activity that often helped her to think. "He comes from a good family in Edinburgh — you said his father's connections have helped him in London, or will do as soon as he's ready to contact them. What took him to Earl's Court?"

Chastity shook her head. "I have no idea. Perhaps he had some kind of a row with his family and was disowned or something. It would explain why he's not going home for Christmas. He said it was because he was too busy setting up house but that sounded rather feeble to me since he's leasing a furnished flat. What's there to do?" She opened her palms in an expressive gesture.

Constance nodded. "So, perhaps he's penniless, with only his physician's shingle to his name, and he set up in the only place where he could do so really cheaply."

"Maybe," Chastity said, but she sounded a little doubtful. "I can't imagine he pays much rent on that miserable house. And I'm sure he doesn't have to tout for patients among those poor people living around there but . . ." She paused, sucking in her bottom lip.

"But what?" prompted Constance.

"I don't know. It was just a feeling I had." She stirred sugar into her coffee. "A feeling that he really *cared* for those patients. As if they mattered to him." She shook her head. "I don't know what to think, quite frankly."

"That kind of a practice can't bring in much money," Prudence pointed out, returning her glasses to her nose.

"No . . . so it would make sense to have a plan to move up in the world," Constance said. "He arrives broke, without friends, has to do something while he decides what he really wants to do, so sets up a surgery in the slums, and then goes about putting a grand scheme into practice."

"It makes some kind of sense, I suppose," Chastity said, still sounding doubtful. "He was certainly angry that I saw the place. I assumed he was embarrassed and obviously afraid that I'd let on and that would be the end of his grand scheme. Who's going to patronize a physician who's just had his hands on a patient from the slums?"

"Good question," Prudence said, finishing the last bite of her cake. "So, what do you want to do about him now, Chas?"

Chastity dabbed up a morsel of chocolate cream with her fingertip and licked it off thoughtfully before she said, "I'm intrigued. I want to know the answer."

"The answer to what?" Constance asked, watching her sister closely.

Chastity shrugged again. "To what kind of a man he *really* is. Is he just a socially ambitious gold digger, or is there something more to him? Watching him with those patients yesterday, it was . . . he was . . ." She shook her head. "I don't know how to describe it. It was beyond simple compassion, and then while he's doing that with one hand, with the other he's treating me with such incredible hostility. I want to know why."

She chased another morsel of chocolate cream with a fingertip, adding, "Besides, we did take him on as a client and we usually do what we can to foster the matches we make. Shouldn't we be trying to advance his courtship of Laura before we offer him any alternative prospects?"

"Particularly in the light of Father's definite interest in the contessa," Constance said. "We have to get the daughter out of the picture as soon as we can if we're going to promote *that* particular courtship."

"Not to mention protecting our own sanity from such a stepsister," Prudence said. "Chas can't possibly share a roof with her."

Chastity gave an exaggerated shudder. "Ghastly prospect. That was exactly why I invited Douglas for Christmas in the first place. But I'm sure he'll think the invitation is rescinded now."

"So, what does Chas do now?" Prudence asked, sipping her coffee.

"Wait for him to make the next move?" Constance suggested. "He's bound to follow up that apology with something."

"Unless he's waiting for me to acknowledge it," Chastity mused. "He might interpret a stony silence as a statement of rejection."

"You could always send a thank-you note for the flowers," Prudence said. "That would be appropriate."

Chastity nodded. "Yes, I think that's the answer. A cool but pleasant thank you should open the door again and give him the opportunity to follow up." She reached into her handbag and took out the other letters she had picked up from Mrs. Beedle's. "That takes care of the doctor for the time being, I believe, so let's look at our other post."

They parted company on the pavement outside Fortnum's, Chastity to go home and write her thank-you note to Douglas Farrell and get it in the post that afternoon, Prudence to the bank to deposit some payments made to *The Mayfair Lady*, and Constance to attend a meeting of the Women's Social and Political Union in Chelsea that she would then write up for the next edition of the broadsheet.

"Try the hat with the dress when you get home," Prudence instructed her sister. "It's on approval, so if it doesn't work we'll need to return it by tomorrow morning."

"It will work, I'm sure," Chastity said. "If you say it will." She swung the hatbox from its string then kissed her sisters and went off with a wave of farewell. She reached home to be told by Jenkins that Lord Duncan had gone to visit his wine merchants, Harpers of Gracechurch Street, and was not expected back for luncheon.

"It's good that he's getting out and about again," Chastity said.

"Yes, indeed it is, Miss Chas," Jenkins agreed. "His lordship's showing much more interest in things these days." He regarded Chastity with a question in his eye. "Quite suddenly, it seemed to me."

"Yes," Chastity agreed, then lowered her voice, saying with a mischievous smile, "Just between you, me, and the gatepost, Jenkins, I think there's a lady involved."

Jenkins made a visible effort to restrain an answering conspiratorial smile. He said with dignity, "Indeed, Miss Chas. Will you be taking luncheon?"

"Yes, please," Chastity said. "I'll be upstairs in the parlor. Some bread and cheese at my desk will be perfect since I have work to do." She hurried to the stairs, reflecting that if Jenkins realized that Lord Duncan's present female interest was different from his usual casual involvement with a lady of the town he might be less amused. The prospect of a new Lady Duncan with strange ways would not be relished by either Jenkins or Mrs. Hudson.

And where would it leave her? Chastity thought as she entered the parlor. It was a question she had been avoiding. But a stepmother taking over the household reins? She caught herself grimacing. Even if one liked the stepmother, it was still an awkward prospect. And if by some mischance they didn't get Laura married off beforehand, she'd have *her* under the same roof too. Not a prospect to be considered. She'd have to go and live with one or other of her sisters like some homeless poor relation.

Chastity realized she had been standing stock-still in the middle of the room for about five minutes contemplating the grimness of this picture. She shook her head vigorously as if she could dismiss the whole idea and went to the secretaire. The sooner she mended fences with Douglas Farrell, the better able she would be to throw him together with Laura on every possible occasion.

She had just taken up her pen when Jenkins tapped at the door. Presumably with her bread and cheese, she thought, turning in her chair as she called for him to come in. But Jenkins carried no luncheon tray; instead he had a silver salver on which reposed a visiting card.

"Dr. Farrell has left his card, Miss Chas. I didn't know whether you were at home for callers this morning." He presented the card.

"Did he leave straightaway?" She took the card, turning it around between finger and thumb.

"I suggested he wait in the drawing room while I ascertained whether you were at home or not," Jenkins informed her.

Chastity considered this, then said, "I believe I am, Jenkins. Will you tell Dr. Farrell that I'll be down in a few minutes?"

Jenkins bowed and retreated on his errand. Chastity played a tune on her lips with her fingertips. So, Douglas hadn't waited for a response to his initial overture. Her instinctive reaction was one of warm sympathy and understanding. He must be in agonies of remorse and embarrassment at his behavior and couldn't wait to put the whole wretched business behind him, and she certainly wouldn't prolong his misery another minute. But then her natural empathetic response faded a little as she reminded herself that this was the man with the dual personalities and a very clear strategy for gaining his goals. He wanted her on his side — no, *needed* her on his side. She was the person with the social introductions, the one who issued convenient Christmas invitations that would enable him to pursue one of those objectives.

Well, she had her own goals to pursue, one of which was to get this man married to Laura Della Luca with all due speed, so in this instance her goal meshed with his. It didn't really matter if his apology was genuine or not so long as it got them both where they wanted to go.

Chastity stood up and peered at her reflection in the mirror. Her hair was in an unruly mood this morning; the cold, dry air made it crackle and the curls tangled without any outside assistance. She tried to tame some of the wisping locks framing her face, pulling her fingers through them to untangle them, but they merely corkscrewed tighter. A veritable Medusa, she thought with a sigh.

She glanced down at her feet as if to remind herself of what she was wearing. It was one of her favorite suits, made of dark green wool with a matching braid trimming. It had a rather attractive pleated skirt with a long jacket, pleated at the back and flaring over her hips. She looked back in the mirror and made a minute adjustment to the high neck of the pale green silk blouse she wore beneath the jacket, then with a shrug both mental and actual decided it was a perfectly good outfit for receiving apologies and went to the door.

She walked quite slowly downstairs, trying to decide how she would greet her visitor. Cool and pleasant, she thought, opening the door to the drawing room.

Douglas was standing at the window looking out into the garden, his hands clasped at his back beneath his black frock coat. He turned at the sound of the door and a smile grew on his face as he saw her, his deep-set charcoal eyes warming in his lean face. He came towards her, his hands outstretched. "Chastity, it's so good of you to see me, I hardly dared hope you would."

This was the man she had discovered that first evening they'd spent together. There was not a hint here of the contemptuous arrogance of yesterday. How could he possibly be so different? But somehow under the genuine warmth of that smile all her resentment, her doubts faded into the mists. Her hands were lost in his firm all-encompassing clasp and she made no attempt to withdraw them. He raised both her hands to his lips and kissed them with a gesture that seemed so smooth and natural, Chastity didn't question it, even as she thought at the back of her mind that it was almost loverlike.

"Your flowers were beautiful," she said. "I was just this minute writing you a thank-you note actually."

He still held her hands, his fingers curling over hers with a warm strength that reminded her of the way he had held the old woman's feet in his surgery. He said quietly, "They can't begin to express my remorse."

Under the deep, penetrating gaze of his dark eyes, Chastity found herself curiously tongue-tied. She looked up into his face, searching his expression for some indication that he was not sincere, that he was only trying to correct a misstep, but she could read nothing there but this warmth, underlaid with an anxiety that surely could not be feigned.

"Can you forgive me?" he asked into the long-stretching silence.

She nodded, knowing that she had forgiven him the first moment she'd seen his face when she'd walked into the room, but she heard herself say, “I would like to understand, Douglas.”

“What would you like to understand?” He slowly, reluctantly, released his hold on her hands and she felt strangely bereft as the warmth of his skin left hers.

“You,” she said, rubbing her hands together as if they were cold. “I would like to understand you. Why are you working there . . . with those poor, poor people? I could understand if you were some kind of missionary, but you’re not. You have a practice on Harley Street.” She shook her head helplessly. “It doesn’t make any sense. But I know there must be a reason, and that’s why you were so horrid — angry and contemptuous — yesterday.”

Douglas steepled his hands, tapping them against his mouth as he looked at her. He’d trusted a woman once before to understand. At that time it hadn’t occurred to him in the youthful naiveté of his passionate commitment that anyone could fail to see matters as he did, could fail to feel the way he did . . . particularly a woman he believed loved him as he loved her. A woman he intended to spend his life with. That disillusion had been harsh enough to cure him of any desire to confide in anyone other than one or two of his peers and fellow medics, who, while they didn’t necessarily feel the same commitment, certainly didn’t regard it as some kind of lunatic infection. An oddity, perhaps, but not a failing.

"Have you got half an hour to spare?" he asked abruptly. It was probably foolish to confide in her but even if she reacted to his explanation in typical fashion, it wouldn't really matter. She knew enough now to make his life difficult if she chose, but he didn't believe she was the kind of person who would make that choice. And if she didn't sympathize with his mission, he would not be disappointed. This time he would be able to shrug it off. He wasn't in love with Chastity Duncan.

"Yes, I think so," she said readily. "Now?"

"Yes, now," he responded. "We'll go for a walk."

The suggestion surprised her. Why couldn't he simply answer her question here, in the quiet and the warmth of the drawing room? But then she had the sense that he was somehow and for some reason feeling confined, and once again she was conscious of his sheer physical size, the broadness and tallness, the muscularity of him. The room didn't seem big enough to hold him. And perhaps, she thought, it wasn't big enough to hold his secret, perhaps he needed open, neutral air for this confidence. "All right," she said. "I'll fetch my hat and coat."

His nod was brisk, his tone equally so as he said, "Don't be long."

As if he'd put apologies and remorseful anxiety behind him, he had reverted to his customary manner, relaxed and just a scrap too authoritarian for comfort. But then, Chastity reflected, that trait, like arrogance, was a very common one among professional men, as her sisters had noted. She could certainly handle it better than overt hostility.

"I'll be five minutes," she said, and left him. In her bedroom she retrieved the hat she had been wearing that morning. It was a fetching, dark green felt bonnet with a very long dyed green ostrich feather that curled onto her shoulder. Her hair, with its usual mind of its own, refused to stay completely beneath the hat and errant curls sprang in lively fashion over her forehead and framed her face.

She sat down before the dresser mirror and contemplated the small supply of cosmetics. Natural vanity insisted she look her best even for Douglas Farrell, in whom she had no interest other than as a client. Well, perhaps that wasn't entirely true, the ruthless voice of honesty corrected. She did have a personal interest now in finding out his story.

She picked up the little book of papers impregnated with face powder and leaned towards the mirror, looking for freckles. They didn't usually appear until the summer sun and she could find only a light sprinkling across the bridge of her nose. She dabbed at them with the papier rouge, thought about enlivening her mouth with lip rouge then dismissed the idea. It was so cold out her lips would dry in no time and nothing was less appealing than cracked lips with peeling paint on them.

Chastity decided she was as good as she was going to get on such short notice and abandoned the mirror. They were only going for a walk, after all. She shrugged into her thick woolen overcoat, gathered up her fur muff and gloves, and headed downstairs again.

"I'm ready." She stood in the drawing room doorway.

Douglas put down the copy of *The Mayfair Lady* he'd been reading and stood up. "You read this, then?"

"Doesn't everyone?" Chastity responded. "It has a special relevance for us, as you might imagine. After the libel case."

"Ah, yes." He nodded. "That must have been hard for your father."

"It wasn't easy. But it's water under the bridge now." She walked back to the hall.

"I can't remember the details," he said, following her to the front door. "Wasn't he the victim of some fraudulent scheme?"

"Yes," Chastity said, her tone flat enough to discourage any further questions. "Jenkins, we're going for a walk. I'll be back in half an hour. I'll have my bread and cheese then."

"Very well, Miss Chas." Jenkins opened the door for them. "Enjoy your walk. Good day, Dr. Farrell."

Douglas returned the farewell and the door shut behind them. They stood on the top step, bracing themselves against the cold. "It's going to snow," Douglas stated, tucking Chastity's hand into his arm and guiding her down to the pavement.

"How can you be so sure?"

He laughed. "I'm a Scot, remember. From the frozen north. We know such things."

"Ah, and I'm a delicately nurtured southern flower," Chastity returned. "We Hampshire-bred lasses know little of such extremes."

"I'm looking forward to spending Christmas in the country," Douglas said, glancing at her. "That is, if the invitation still stands."

"Of course it does. Where do you want to walk?"

"Is it too far for you to walk to Hyde Park?" he asked, looking down questioningly at her booted feet. "Or we could take a hackney there if your shoes aren't comfortable."

She was not about to encourage that extravagance, Chastity decided. "We'll walk," she stated, thrusting her hands into her muff. "My boots are perfectly comfortable."

He nodded, tucked a hand into the crook

of her elbow, and set off towards Oxford Street.

"So, are you going to explain your mysteries, Dr. Farrell?" she asked after they'd been walking in silence for ten minutes and were now threading their way through the crowded pavements towards Marble Arch.

"I don't have mysteries," he denied.

She laughed. "Oh, you're the most mysterious person I've ever met, Dr. Jekyll."

"Dr. Jekyll?" he exclaimed in mingled astonishment and dismay. "What the devil do you mean?"

"Oh, I was just being fanciful," Chastity said, realizing belatedly that it was hardly a complimentary comparison.

"I would hardly call it fanciful," he said. "More like downright critical."

Chastity sucked on her lower lip. "Perhaps," she conceded. "But you must admit I have some cause."

"Ah." He nodded. "You haven't quite forgiven me, then. I thought it was perhaps a little too good to be true. Or, perhaps, that *you* were a little too good to be true. You'd have to be a candidate for sainthood to forgive and forget quite so readily."

"That I'm not," Chastity stated. "Absolutely no possibility of beatification whatsoever."

Douglas laughed. "That's something of a relief. I'm so far on the wrong side of St.

Peter myself, I might find it uncomfortable in the company of the truly good."

"You need have no fears on that score," she said, looking up at him, liking the way the skin around his eyes crinkled when he smiled. Sensing her gaze he looked down at her and she felt her cheeks warm a little as if she were embarrassed by her thought.

"Why did you become a physician?" she asked abruptly. It was one way to get to the purpose of this walk.

"It runs in the family," he said casually, tightening his grip on her elbow as they dodged the traffic at Marble Arch. He said nothing more until they had entered the park through Cumberland Gate and the clatter of iron wheels and horseshoes and the roar of omnibus engines were behind them.

"Oh, yes," Chastity said, remembering. "Your father, of course."

"And my grandfather. He started off as a young lieutenant in the Indian army. He was about eighteen at the time of the mutiny, and that hideous experience put him off war altogether. He came to Edinburgh and studied medicine, then opened the family practice."

They were walking along the narrow path beside the tan where horses and riders were trotting in relatively sedate fashion beneath the winter-bare trees. Chastity found herself intrigued by this little insight into Douglas's family history. "So, you're the third generation of physicians."

"Fourth or fifth at least. I rather suspect that somewhere down the line of Farrells there was a barber's pole and a knife-wielding barber who called himself a surgeon." He laughed lightly and bent to pick up a shiny horse chestnut. He polished it on his sleeve and held it up for inspection. It was a perfect round, glowing richly burnished in the gray light. He presented it to Chastity with a half bow and all the gravity of a man bestowing a precious jewel and Chastity received it in the same manner, offering a half curtsy in acknowledgment. "It's too pretty to play conkers with," she said, tucking it into her muff. "Did you ever play as a child?"

"Of course," he said. "I had one that was unbeatable one year. We soaked them in vinegar to make them hard. And mine was definitely the champion." His smile at the reminiscence was rather endearingly smug, as if that childhood triumph still gave him pleasure. Chastity smiled with him.

"Tell me about your family," she said.

Douglas glanced up at the overcast sky, pursing his lips. "Do you want the long history or the potted?"

"The long, of course."

He inclined his head. "You may well regret it. It's hard to know where to begin, but I'll try."

Chapter 10

"Six sisters," Chastity said, some while later, sounding awed. "I always thought two were plenty."

"I'd have settled for two myself," Douglas said, stopping at a wrought-iron bench over-looking the Serpentine. "Shall we sit for a little?"

Chastity sat down with some relief. They had walked a long way during Douglas's re-cital. She was thinking that his family story put paid to any idea that he had been dis-owned. Quite the opposite. He seemed to have been swaddled in love and attention from the moment of his birth. And there was no other explanation either for why he ap-peared strapped for cash. His background was both wealthy and titled. It seemed she was no closer to the mystery of what really lay behind this sudden removal to the London slums. Not to mention the need for a rich wife.

"Something on your mind?" he inquired.

“I want to ask you a very personal question and I’m trying to come up with the right words,” she said frankly.

“Ah.” He regarded her with a smile in his charcoal eyes. The cold air had reddened the tip of her nose and he had the absurd urge to kiss it. Ridiculous, of course. “Well, why don’t you just come out with it? I usually find that’s the least complicated way of getting personal. It avoids misunderstandings, at least.”

Chastity smoothed her skirt over her knees and approached the issue from a rather oblique angle, but one that was somehow uppermost in her mind. “I was wondering why you didn’t mention a wife, or a fiancée. Surely there must be or have been some woman in your life.” She watched his expression, afraid that if she’d trodden too close to an invisible line, Mr. Hyde would reappear.

Douglas realized he should have expected the question. It was a perfectly natural one in a truth-telling session. He tried a sidestep, saying with a slightly exasperated laugh, “My dear girl, I am surrounded by women. I have more women in my life than any one man should be expected to handle.”

“You know what I mean. I wasn’t talking about sisters or mothers. Have you ever been married, or thought of being married?” She sat back with a decisive air. “I can’t be more straightforward than that.” *And now let’s see how you answer that, Dr. On the Hunt for a Rich Wife.*

Well, the sidestep hadn't worked, but he hadn't expected it to. "No, true enough," he agreed rather briskly. "To tell you the truth, I haven't given the matter much thought. I've been far too busy." Before she could pursue the subject, he said quickly, "Tit for tat, Miss Duncan. What about you? I see no evidence of a husband, but is there a fiancé? A particularly close friend . . . Viscount Brigham for instance?"

Chastity shook her head and accepted defeat. He wasn't going to reveal to a mere social acquaintance an ambition confided to a professional matchmaking agency. "No, no one special. I have plenty of close friends of both sexes, but . . ." She shrugged. "Marriage doesn't loom anywhere on my horizons." Her stomach suddenly growled too loudly and insistently to be ignored. They'd been out a lot longer than half an hour. "I'm ravenous," she confessed unnecessarily, sniffing the air.

There was a most succulent smell wafting towards them, and then she heard the bell and the loud cry of the barrow boy announcing his wares. " 'Ot pies . . . 'ot pies . . . come an' get 'em. Steak-an'-kidney pies . . ."

"It's a pie man," Chastity said, jumping to her feet. "Where is he?"

"Coming along the path," Douglas said, standing with her. "Let's see what he's got." He waved at the pie man, who carried a laden tray balanced on a thick round pillow on his head.

"Whatcha like, guv, pretty lady?" the man said cheerfully, swinging the tray down and setting it on the bench. His wares rested on a rack above a bed of hot charcoal. "A nice muffin 'ere, or a nice bit o' steak an' kidney . . . just right fer a cold day."

Douglas glanced at Chastity, who, mouth watering, pointed at a golden-crusted pie. "That one," she said.

The man wrapped it in a sheet of newspaper and handed it to her. "I'll have the same," Douglas said, reaching into his pocket for coins. He gave the man a shilling and took his pie. Chastity had already retreated to the bench and was biting deeply into the hot, gravy-filled pastry crust, trying not to dribble juice down her chin.

Douglas laughed and reached into his pocket for a large, crisp handkerchief. "Napkin, madam?" He presented it to her with a flourish.

"Thank you," she mumbled through a mouthful, taking the offering and wiping her chin. "This is so good, even though it's messy."

They ate swiftly and in silence. It wasn't the kind of meal to encourage conversation, but finally Chastity scrunched up the newspaper and gave a little sigh of satisfaction. "That was wonderful."

"It was," he agreed, taking the newspaper from her and going to throw it in a litter bin with his own. "Can I borrow the handkerchief back? Thanks." He took it back and wiped his hands and mouth, then thrust it into his pocket. A flake of snow drifted to the grass at his feet, and then another.

"Alfresco dining in December is somewhat eccentric," he observed. "Let's start walking back. I don't want you to freeze to the bench."

"I'm warmer now I've eaten," Chastity said, but she got to her feet, tucking her hands into her muff. She'd learned a lot about his family but she still didn't know the answer to the most important question and she wondered if perhaps he was now regretting the decision to confide in her and hoping she had forgotten the reason for this little outing.

They started to walk towards Cumberland Gate and after a few steps she said directly, "You were going to enlighten me about yesterday afternoon."

Douglas had been hoping the recitation of his family history had put the other issue out of her mind. He was enjoying her company, as he had done the other evening, and he wanted to keep this light and friendly ease between them. He realized with surprise and dismay that now if she responded in the wrong way to what he had agreed to tell her, it would indeed matter to him, and their present burgeoning friendship would be destroyed. It didn't seem possible any longer to dismiss her as just another spoiled, privileged, Society lady. Something had changed his view of her and he had no idea what. But it was suddenly very important to him that he had mistaken her reaction to his clinic and his patients, that she hadn't been showing the instinctive and immediate revulsion he had automatically expected and therefore assumed.

It would be so much easier not to tell her and therefore not risk the wrong reaction, but as he looked down at her determined expression, the firm set of her full mouth, the glinting lights in the depths of her hazel eyes, he knew she was going to hold him to his agreement. So be it. "Did it strike you as unusual that I would have a medical practice in the city slums?" he asked.

"Well, yes, of course it did. You told me you had an office on Harley Street." She had stopped walking and was gazing up at him, her eyes fixed upon him with a mixture of curiosity and wariness. Snow dusted her hat and the ostrich plume was beginning to look a little bedraggled.

"Keep walking," he said, taking her arm

and urging her forward. "Answer me this, Chastity. Can you imagine why a doctor would choose to serve those people?"

Chastity frowned. This was clearly some kind of test and she had the sense that rather a lot depended upon her passing it. "Someone has to," she said. "Just because they're poor doesn't mean they don't get sick — quite the opposite, from what I saw."

"What kind of doctor should they have, do you think?"

Chastity's frown deepened. She felt as if she were on trial here. She gazed down, watching her feet stepping through the light coating of snow on the grass. "A regular one, I suppose," she said. "Are there other kinds?"

"Unqualified ones."

"Ah." She thought she was beginning to get the point. "I don't imagine it's a particularly well-paying branch of the medical profession."

He smiled but it was bitter rather than humorous. "Not only that, medicines don't come cheap."

"Ah," she said again, remembering how she'd noticed almost all the patients had emerged from his office with medicines of some kind. Now she knew she had complete grasp of the point. "So, in order to provide them you have to supply them."

"And in order to do that I have to have an alternative source of income," he said.

Chastity pursed her lips in a silent whistle of utter comprehension. "Hence Harley Street."

"Hence Harley Street," he agreed.

Chastity's frown deepened, drawing her arched eyebrows together as she considered the implications. She said finally, "Are you saying that those poor souls in Earl's Court are your primary concern, Douglas? That you take care of the rich only in order to take care of the poor?"

"In a nutshell." He couldn't tell yet how she was really reacting to this revelation, but he liked the way she seemed to be looking at it from every angle, reflecting before she spoke.

Now she looked up at him and her eyes were filled with a warm light and her lovely full mouth formed a smile of such genuine pleasure and sympathy that it made his heart sing.

She took her hand from her muff and slipped it into his. "I think that's wonderful, Douglas, really splendid." She was aware of a distinct prickle of discomfort when she thought how she'd disliked him, how she'd talked so contemptuously about him to her sisters. This was a *good* man. A truly good man. Oh, he was awkward and arrogant and confrontational, but that did nothing to blunt the knowledge that she had been wrong, so wrong. Of course he would be a little skeptical of rich hypochondriacs when he worked with such passionate commitment among the truly needy, and of course he had to have a rich wife in order to complete his mission.

And she was going to get him one.

Douglas smiled and tightened his clasp of her hand. "You understand now why I asked you to keep my confidence."

"I always understood that," Chastity said. "What I didn't understand was what you were doing there in the first place. You hadn't exactly given the impression of an altruistic mission-bound man."

"I don't think I would lay claim to such a grandiose description," he said. He glanced at his watch. "We need to take a hackney back. I have a rich patient coming at three and it doesn't do to keep paying customers waiting."

"No, I suppose not." Chastity took back her hand. She shivered suddenly despite her wool coat and reached behind her to turn up the collar.

Douglas unwound the thick muffler he wore and stopped, turning her to face him. He wrapped the scarf around her neck, tucking the ends into the neck of her coat, his movements deft and swift, a little frown of concentration on his brow. He settled the material of her coat over her shoulders, smoothing it out with what seemed a rather lingering gesture. And then he bent his head and very lightly kissed the tip of her nose. Chastity realized she was holding her breath as she tried to pretend it wasn't happening. He raised his head and laughed down at her.

"Your poor little nose is red with cold. I've been wanting to warm it up for a long time," he said.

"Well, that's no way to go about it," she retorted, moving away from him even as she inadvertently rubbed the tip of her nose with her gloved palm. A warm tingle ran down her back, his scent and the warmth of his skin was on the scarf around her neck, and her cheeks were suddenly flushed with more than the cold.

"I thought it might help," he said with a grin that had no remorse in it at all. He turned his head and gave a two-fingered whistle in the direction of a hackney. He opened the door for Chastity, who climbed in before he had a chance to put his hands to her waist. He sat on the seat opposite her.

"I was forgetting you don't like helping hands," he said.

"I don't like overly familiar helping hands," she corrected with an attempt at hauteur that didn't quite come off. Douglas merely smiled and Chastity felt a stirring of annoyance that rather dissipated their earlier harmony.

"One question you haven't answered," she said, her eyes narrowing a little. "Just *why* were you so rude to me? It was more than simply because I stumbled upon your secret, wasn't it?"

He looked across at her. Her mouth was set and he would swear there were little sparks of fire amid the golden flecks in her hazel eyes. She wanted an answer. And in fact he had one. But it was one he was fairly positive Miss Duncan would not appreciate.

"It's a habit," he said.

She stared at him. "A habit? Being rude like that. A habit? That's it? That's the only explanation you have?" Her tone was incredulous and needled him sufficiently to provoke the truth.

"Very well," he said crisply. "If you must know, I made an assumption about your reactions, and because that assumption angered me, I'm afraid I took it out on you."

"What kind of assumption?" She leaned forward to watch his expression more closely.

He sighed. "I am just so accustomed to challenging the preconceptions of the women in my family — in fact, to a certain extent those of almost everyone in the social circles I move in — that I assume most people in general, but women in particular, are complacent, prejudiced, and utterly lazy in their thought processes."

"*What?*" Chastity's jaw dropped. She continued to stare at him until she realized her mouth was hanging open as if she'd lost her jaw muscles. She hastily snapped it closed.

"*Women in particular,*" she said. "Of all the arrogant, prejudiced, unthinking comments. You talk of complacency and lazy thinking . . . ye gods." She blew breath through her lips in vigorous and noisy disgust. "Physician, heal thyself."

A tiny smile touched Douglas's mouth, tugged at the corners. Laughter danced in the charcoal eyes. "Mea culpa," he said, throwing up his hands in a gesture of defeat. "If I'd known I'd be provoking a veritable Boadicea, I would have watched my words."

"Watched them but not revised them," she fired.

"I accept that there are exceptions to every rule," he said solemnly, the gravity unfortunately belied by the continuing smile in both eyes and mouth. "How could I not when I find myself in the presence of one?"

Chastity tried to maintain her own position of dignified indignation but there was something about that smile that made it all but impossible. It was a very appreciative smile with just the hint of rueful acceptance in its depths. Willy-nilly, her own lips curved. "There is more than one exception to this particular rule," she said. "You have, I believe, met my sisters."

"Oh, yes." He nodded. "Not that I had much in the way of conversation with either of them, but I'm sure they're very intelligent, analytical, deep-thinking women."

Chastity folded her arms. "You've read *The Mayfair Lady*. What about the women who write that? Are they lazy-minded, complacent, prejudiced?"

"Probably not," he conceded. "But some of the articles in there are designed to appeal to such women. You have to admit that."

Chastity let that one pass. It was easier than reminding herself that she and her sisters had often expressed very similar sentiments to the doctor's about the Society ladies who formed the lion's share of their readership. "What about suffragists?" she challenged. "There's nothing complacent about them or their cause."

"No," he agreed.

"What do you think of the issue? Should women have the vote?" She was aware that there was an edge to her voice now, as if she was giving him her own test.

Douglas heard it and guessed that this was an issue very close to Miss Duncan's heart. It was also clear on which side of the fence she stood. "I'm not against it in principle," he said carefully.

"But in practice you are." She sat back with a little sigh that seemed to say, *I knew it all along*.

"No, no, wait a minute." He held up an imperative finger. "It's a very complicated question. Most of the women I know wouldn't want the vote and wouldn't know what to do with it. My mother and sisters consider themselves powerful enough in their own sphere, and indeed they are."

"Their *own* sphere," Chastity said. "That's precisely the usual argument. Women have their world and men have theirs and never the twain shall meet . . . and everyone is very clear which of the two is the more powerful and important," she added, thinking she was beginning to sound as didactic as Constance. Ordinarily, she could see both sides of any issue, but for some reason Douglas Farrell caused her to suffer one-sided blindness.

"I think perhaps we should agree to disagree on this," Douglas said. "I'm not against the idea itself, I would merely hesitate to put it into practice until the majority of women have acquired the education and the ability to think outside the domestic sphere to the larger issues that at the moment are men's province." He had thought that was rather a diplomatic way of putting it — his companion, however, didn't think so.

"It's no wonder you don't find the idea of marriage appealing," Chastity observed with disconcerting sweetness. "With such an outmoded and prejudiced view of women, how could you? And I venture to suggest that any woman who might come up to your exacting standards would probably find something unappealing in a man who holds such a generally low opinion of her sex." She folded her arms again, as if punctuating the end of the conversation.

Douglas scratched the side of his nose. "I had hoped we were beginning a rather promising friendship," he observed. "Am I too unregenerate and dislikable to qualify as a friend, Miss Duncan?"

"I don't dislike you," Chastity protested. "It's just your opinions I dislike."

"Oh, is that all," he said, sounding relieved. "I'm sure I can change those."

"If you changed them you wouldn't be the same person," she pointed out unarguably as the carriage drew to a halt outside her house.

Douglas jumped down and punctiliously gave her his hand to alight. He paid the driver and then walked with her up the steps to her door.

"Let me give you back your scarf," Chastity said, pulling the long muffler out of her coat.

"Allow me." He took it from her and unwound it from around her neck. They were standing necessarily very close together on the top step and she could feel the warmth of his breath on her cheek. "So," he said, holding both ends while it still lay around her neck. "Friends, Miss Duncan?"

"Yes, of course," she said.

He leaned into her and touched the corner of her mouth with his. It was the kiss of a friend, of the kind she had exchanged with many men, but then something happened. He pulled on the ends of the scarf, drawing her closer to him, and his mouth was fully on hers. Her eyes had closed and against all reason and logic she returned the pressure of his lips, lifting her hands to his shoulders, holding him. They drew apart together, almost jumped apart in the same instant, and stood looking at each other in stunned silence.

Chastity put her gloved hand to her mouth as she stared at him. He gave her a rather rueful smile. "A seal of friendship," he said, but without much conviction.

Chastity took the way out offered. "Yes," she said. "Friendship. Of course." She lifted the scarf over her head and held it out to him. "Christmas," she said. "We didn't talk about Christmas."

"No," he agreed.

Chastity spoke rapidly and with as little expression as possible. "We're all, at least my sisters and I, taking the four o'clock train from Waterloo on Christmas Eve. If that's convenient, you could travel with us. Unless you prefer to come down on Christmas Day, but I doubt you'll find any trains running."

"I should be delighted to accompany you and your sisters on Christmas Eve," he said with a bow of his head.

"And what about a valet?"

That made him laugh, breaking the awkward tension. "Chastity, my dear girl, after what we've been discussing, how could you possibly imagine I'd have a valet?"

"I have learned, Douglas, that you are not always what you seem," she said with a lofty air that she couldn't possibly maintain. She shook her head with a slight laugh, feeling for her key in her pocket. "No, of course I didn't expect you to be bringing a servant, but I had to ask."

"I can't imagine why," he said, taking the door key from her and inserting it in the lock. The door swung open.

"Thank you," she said. The air crackled between them and she slid past him in the doorway. He reached out and lightly stroked the curve of her cheek with the back of his hand, a fleeting touch that was nevertheless deeply intimate.

"Until later, Chastity," he said, handing her the door key as Jenkins materialized from the shadows of the hall.

"Thank you for the pie," Chastity said, thinking how silly that sounded. She stepped farther into the hall and closed the door firmly behind her.

Douglas walked to Harley Street in something of a daze. He couldn't decide what had just happened. Since Marianne he had avoided any kind of attraction to a woman of his own social circle, and he hadn't found it much of a deprivation. Once bitten, twice shy was a good motto, he reflected as he walked up the staircase to his suite on the second floor. Once he'd started his forays into the miserable slums of Edinburgh, all his emotional and physical energies had been devoted to the desperate souls in need of everything he had to give. He had kept a mistress, a pleasant undemanding courtesan who was happy to have her rent paid and a reasonable stipend in exchange for satisfying his sexual needs, but she was no more interested in emotional entanglements than he, and had moved without complaint to a substitute protector when Douglas left Edinburgh.

He had left that city only when he'd established a thriving clinic staffed by men and women he'd trained himself and funded to a large extent with his own personal trust. Then, in search of fresh fields to conquer, he'd come to London. But the trust fund could only support one clinic, so Harley Street and a rich wife it had to be. There was no room in his life for anything other than a straightforward marriage of convenience, an arrangement where courtesy and consideration prevailed, but where romantic love and all its snares and pitfalls had no place. Dalliance with the Honorable Chastity Duncan was most definitely not in the cards. It would interfere with the primary goal.

The door to his office suite stood open and

he frowned in surprise. He hadn't yet acquired a receptionist and he was a half hour early for his appointment. He stepped inside, called, "Hello?"

"Oh, *Dottore, Dottore.*" Laura Della Luca emerged from the inner office into the waiting room, her arms filled with swaths of material. "I was just trying out a few ideas. The caretaker let me in when I told him I was working with you on refurbishment."

"Oh." The caretaker would have to whistle for his Christmas bonus, Douglas thought with justifiable irritation. He didn't want this woman, or indeed anyone, wandering in and out of his private apartments as if she had every right to do so. But in all fairness he could well imagine how she'd swept over any possible objections of the caretaker like a Covent Garden street sweeper dealing with the market detritus.

"I thought this would be particularly suitable for the waiting room, *Dottore,*" Laura burbled on, quite oblivious of his silence and the lack of greeting. She held up a swatch of flowered chintz. "Just imagine it on the chairs. I have been looking at chairs and I found at a lovely little shop in Kensington some wonderful deep armchairs that would work very well with this material. We would have it made up with skirts to hide the legs . . . legs are so vulgar on chairs, don't you think?"

"Rather necessary, I would have thought," Douglas said aridly.

"Oh, yes, necessary, of course." She waved this little objection aside. "But we don't have to sully our eyes with necessities, do we, *Dottore?*" She shook her finger at him. "Now, I thought this would be really pretty on the windows, looped back, of course, with matching ties and a frilled pelmet." She produced another swatch of chintz that looked identical to the previous one.

Douglas peered at it. "Isn't it the same?"

"No, no . . . men have not the eye," she said. "See, the pattern is different and the colors are different. This has a gold background, this a blue one."

"Ah." Douglas nodded, thinking of the Park Lane mansion. Gold and blue were the predominant themes there too, but at least there they didn't make the place seem like a country tearoom.

"And over the windows beneath we shall have this lovely filmy lace curtain." Laura triumphantly held up a piece of white lace. "Just picture it, *Dottore*. Just picture it." She hurried to one of the long stately windows and held the lace with one hand and the chintz with the other. "So sweetly pretty."

"Yes," Douglas said faintly. *Sweetly pretty.* Dear God, sweetly pretty in the waiting room of a serious practitioner. He'd be the laughingstock of the medical profession.

"And little gilt tables," she rushed on. "I found just the ones. At each chair, I thought. For convenience, you understand." She flung her arms wide. "With flower paintings adorning the walls we shall have an atmosphere of soft prettiness that will welcome the weary and the sick."

More like some old lady's boudoir, Douglas thought. But he didn't wish to be rude . . . it wouldn't do much to advance his suit. If he smiled, nodded, and procrastinated, the whole business would eventually die a natural death.

"And just wait until you see what I have planned for your office," Laura said, gesturing as she went before him into the office. "Here we will have the same lace at the windows to keep out the sun, but gold tapestry curtains with red tassels and a crimson leather top to your desk. Chairs in the same crimson leather, I believe. And a carpet, oh, most definitely. A carpet of multihues, reds and blues and golds. Yes, yes, it will be perfect." She nodded firmly. "Just picture it, *Dottore*."

Douglas did, and shuddered. He would be conducting physical examinations in a room resembling a bordello. He cleared his throat, preparing to find a delicate way to steer her clear of this vision, but she swept on regardless.

"I think Italian paintings on the walls . . .

they are always the best. Italian art, there is nothing like it. No reproductions, of course, so I will have to look carefully for you. It will be expensive but you won't mind that."

Douglas cleared his throat again. "My funds are not unlimited, signorina."

Laura waved a hand in dismissal. "Oh, I will bargain for you. We Italians are so good at negotiating prices. Don't you worry about a thing, *Dottore*. I will arrange everything just so."

"It's most kind of you, Miss Della Luca . . . Laura . . . to go to all this trouble, but I'm afraid . . ." He glanced at his watch. "I am expecting a patient in ten minutes and I must make some preparations."

"Oh, yes, of course. The busy doctor. I wouldn't intrude for the world." She walked back to the waiting room, gathering up her swatches that littered surfaces everywhere. "But you can't expect to build up a practice properly without the right accoutrements, *Dottore*. Can you imagine the King's physician in such shabby surroundings? Oh, dear me, no." She gave another of her little trilling laughs.

"The King's physician?" he queried blankly, wondering where this could possibly have come from.

She laughed and tapped him on the shoulder. "Ambition, *Dottore*. We all must have ambition and I can read yours in your eyes."

A somewhat illiterate reader of character, Douglas reflected, even as he kept his fixed smile on his face. It was beginning to feel as if it was cemented in place. Perhaps he'd never lose it.

"You must leave these things to me," she said with a significant nod. "You have your own concerns, *Dottore* . . . but I must practice calling you Douglas, mustn't I? Yes, Douglas, you have the man's work to do, you must let me take care of the woman's. Indeed you must."

"You are too kind," he murmured. "Let me show you to the street." He escorted her downstairs and out into the street, then he closed the door firmly and resisted the urge to lock it only by reminding himself that a prospective patient faced with a locked door was unlikely to become anything other than prospective.

He returned upstairs wondering how five square miles of one city could contain such vastly different women as Chastity Duncan and Laura Della Luca. And for the first time he felt a niggle of doubt. Was Laura's money and the obvious willingness and ability with which she would throw herself into promoting her husband's career worth a marriage?

He dismissed the cavil with a sweeping gesture of his hand. People made such compromises all the time, and had done so since the dawn of civilization. She was exactly what he needed. And they'd spend little enough private time together. He was sure he could give her what she wanted in a marriage, and she'd give him what he needed.

But the King's physician? Dear God. That he would have to nip in the bud. She could have her chintz if necessary, but not that.

Chapter 11

"Well, that was very satisfying," Constance observed as the sisters walked out of St. George's, Hanover Square, on Christmas Eve, having witnessed Hester Winthrop and David Lucan tying the knot.

"Yes, our first real matchmaking job," said Prudence.

"Not counting Amelia and Henry," Chastity reminded them.

"We can't really count them, Chas, because we didn't charge them anything," Prudence pointed out.

"But then, neither Hester nor David knew they'd been matchmade . . . if that's a word," Chastity said.

"It's not," Constance said. "But it's descriptive enough. Anyway, they paid for the service, or at least their mothers did, although they didn't know it."

Prudence chuckled. "A generous donation to a charity for indigent spinsters. I still think that was one of your best, most devious ideas, Con."

Her elder sister laughed. "It worked, as we saw this morning."

"They were both radiant," Chastity said as they stepped into the barouche where Cobham was holding the horses' heads. "We're going to the Winthrop residence, Cobham, but of course you know that."

"Of course, Miss Chas," he said. "Nice wedding, was it?"

"Lovely," Prudence said. "Everyone was crying."

"Except us," Constance said.

"I was, just a little," Chastity confessed. "Happiness always makes me weep."

"Oh, darling, you're so softhearted." Constance put her arms around her and hugged her. "You make Prue and me feel like a couple of dragon ladies with iron hearts."

"You wouldn't say that if you saw me around Douglas Farrell," Chastity declared. Her reputation as the softhearted sister sometimes irked her, particularly if, as she suspected, it was a euphemism for sentimental. And she really didn't think she was sentimental. "He thinks I'm the most sarcastic, provoking, inquisitive woman." Even as she said this, she knew it wasn't the strict truth. She had said nothing to her sisters about the confusing nature of his so-called kiss of friendship, although she had confided to them the truth about his real mission. Even so, it was simpler somehow to keep up the pretence that she still disliked him as much as ever.

"Well, you do have that side to you," Prudence conceded. "Every one of mother's daughters has it. Yours just surfaces a little less frequently."

"We shall be watching with great interest at Christmas," Constance said as Cobham drew up at the curb, expertly inching the carriage into a space among the throng of vehicles disgorging wedding guests. "If you need help besting him, you know where to come."

"I just might manage without assistance," Chastity said with a toss of her head that made them all laugh. "The only assistance I really need is to keep him interested in Laura. We'll have to find all sorts of ways to throw them together." *And all sorts of ways to keep him at arm's length from herself. Any more of those "friendly" kisses would really jam up the works.* But this too she kept to herself. The awful thought had occurred to her that Douglas, who presumably assumed that she was rich as well as single and available, might switch his attentions from Laura to her.

"You're still prepared to condemn him to the Della Luca even though you've revised your opinion of his gold-digging motives?" Prudence asked as she stepped to the pavement.

Chastity shrugged. "He still wants and needs a rich wife. And he still doesn't care about what kind he gets. His view of women is so Neanderthal, I think all her nonsense will just flow over him. He'll treat her with the same somewhat amused indifference that he treats his mother and sisters. *This is the way women are.*"

"And this is the way to treat them," Constance said, inclining her head in scornful agreement. "You're right, a lost cause."

"What time should I come back for you, Miss Con?" Cobham inquired from the box.

"Oh, around three o'clock, please. We're catching the four o'clock from Waterloo, so we'll go straight there from here."

"Right y'are, Miss Con. I'll bring Miss Chas's bags with me then."

"Yes, they're ready and waiting in the hall," Chastity said, adding to her sisters, "I suppose Max and Gideon have yours?"

"Yes, they'll be leaving at about the same time," Prudence said. "Only in separate motorcars, of course. But they should get to Romsey by seven, in time for dinner anyway."

"I'll be back at three, then," Cobham said.

"Your last official driving job," Chastity said with a smile.

"Aye, Miss Chas." He shook his head. "Not sure what I'll be doing with myself all day."

"You'll be in your garden," Chastity said. "You'll love it."

He chuckled. "Getting under the wife's

feet, that's for sure."

"She'll love it too," Constance declared. Cobham laughed and clicked his teeth at the horses, who set off again at a brisk pace.

"Right, let's go in and greet the newlyweds," Prudence said, joining the steady stream of guests entering the Winthrop mansion.

Douglas surveyed the small pile of prettily wrapped parcels on his dining room table and wondered if he'd done the right thing. He was unsure about the etiquette for Christmas-present giving at a house party but had decided that it was better to go prepared. If it seemed that exchanging presents was not a Duncan tradition then he could leave them in his valise. He had bought gifts for his hosts, deciding to assume that all three Duncan sisters as well as their father would consider themselves hosts. Lord Duncan had been easy to buy for, a particularly fine box of cigars was always acceptable, and since he didn't really know the two elder sisters at all, Douglas had settled for perfume. But Chastity had been a different case. He wanted something more personal for her. Something more suited to a friend and confidante.

It had surprised him how much it seemed to matter that he find just the right present. Something that would suit her personality.

He'd spent a long time trying to capture the essence of her character in his mind, the two extremes, from the sharp, provocative wit to the sympathetic warmth that set her eyes aglow and brought the lovely curve to her mouth.

He finally found what he'd been looking for in a small milliner's shop in a side street off Bond Street. A silk scarf, generous enough to do service as an evening shawl, in a wonderful mélange of colors — greens and honey golds, amber and russet. A perfect match for her eyes and hair. And then his eye had been caught by a strand of amber beads and he knew that they were perfect too. So he bought them as well and only now as he wrapped the beads in the scarf did it occur to him that such personal gifts would stand out among the other more prosaic and impersonal offerings for her sisters.

But he owed her an apology and gratitude too for her empathetic reception of his confidences. They had agreed to be friends and he thought it likely that Viscount Brigham, a close friend, would go to similar trouble to pick out a Christmas present for her. Douglas felt that his relationship with Chastity had moved on to a similar footing. And just to redress the balance he had also gone to some care to find a suitable gift for Laura. He had found an illuminated copy of Dante's *Divina Commedia*, bound in ivory calfskin, so perhaps the present for Chastity wouldn't stand out too dramatically.

He tied silk ribbon around the soft parcel and laid it with the others in his valise. Whistling softly to himself he finished packing. Evening dress . . . riding dress . . . morning dress . . . That seemed to cover all eventualities. He locked up his flat and hailed a hackney to Waterloo.

The station was thronged with harried Christmas travelers, children were underfoot everywhere, porters racing with baggage carts towards the platforms where trains steamed noisily. Douglas made his way to Platform 2, wondering if he was ahead of the Duncan party. Chastity hadn't specifically suggested that they share a compartment but he assumed that was the intention. He had just reached the platform when a familiar voice trilled, "*Dottore . . . Dottore.*" He turned, his face automatically assuming the fixed smile that that trill always produced.

"Good afternoon, Dr. Farrell." The contessa greeted him with extended hand. "How nice that we can share a compartment."

He shook hands, murmuring his agreement, and bowed over Laura's hand. "Let me help you with your luggage." He looked around and saw neither porter nor bags.

"Oh, our maids and the porter have taken our bags to the luggage compartment," Laura said.

"Yes, I'm afraid one could never say we travel light, Doctor," the contessa said with a slight laugh. "We have far too much to stow away in the traveling carriage."

"Then let me find us a compartment. I haven't seen our hosts as yet." He turned to the first-class section of the train. He was about to walk along the platform in search of an empty carriage when a piercing whistle arrested him. He looked up and saw Chastity leaning out of a carriage window a little farther along. She stuck two fingers in her mouth and produced that startling whistle again, all the while waving frantically at him as if he possibly could have missed her.

He strode over to the carriage, laughing. "Where did you learn to do that?"

"From you," she said. "I've watched you do it to call cabs so I've been practicing myself." She waved past him to the contessa and Laura. "We have seats here, Contessa, for you and Laura."

"Can you squeeze me in too?" Douglas inquired.

"Yes, of course. We'll take up the whole compartment and then no one will be able to intrude upon our private party," Chastity said, stepping away from the window so that Douglas could open the door.

The contessa stepped up into the train, Laura on her heels. Douglas tossed his valise up and then climbed in himself, slamming the door shut behind him. "Good afternoon, ladies." He greeted the sisters with a smile and a half bow. "How was the wedding?"

"Delicious," Chastity said. "I wept all the way through the service."

She was looking particularly radiant, Douglas thought, not in the least tearful. Her heart-shaped face was framed in the wide brim of a wonderful turquoise hat with a rather impudent wisp of a veil and a huge lavender bow. "I like the hat," he said.

"Why, thank you, sir." She gave him a nodding bow from her seat in the corner of the carriage. "It's a wedding hat."

"So I see." He put his valise up on the rack, intending to take the seat beside her but when he turned again he saw that Constance had squeezed up beside Chastity and the only available place was next to Laura. Resigned, he took the seat just as the train blew a shrill whistle of steam and began to pull out of the station.

"We've reserved a table for tea in the dining car," Chastity informed the new arrivals. "Apart from the fact that it's always sumptuous it helps to pass the time."

"*Dottore,* I wanted to discuss with you the fabric for the curtains in your office," Laura said, ignoring Chastity's remark. She had dropped her voice as if she were discussing secrets. "I had mentioned a heavy tapestry if you recall."

"Are you helping Douglas redecorate his surgery, Laura?" Prudence asked, exchanging a quick glance with her sisters, sitting opposite.

"Yes, that is so," Laura declared. "Decoration is a special talent . . . not one men have in general. Isn't that so, *Dottore?*"

"Possibly," Douglas said, trying to sound repressive. Somehow he had to nip the signorina's wilder ideas in the bud. "I haven't made up my mind as yet how I wish to redecorate."

"Oh, you mustn't worry about a thing, *Dottore.*" She patted his knee. "Just leave it to me. I guarantee you will love — absolutely adore — the results."

"I'm sure you have impeccable taste, Laura," Chastity said. "Judging by your house on Park Lane." She couldn't help catching Douglas's eye and bit hard on her lip to keep from laughing aloud, he was looking so utterly at a loss. "How fortunate that you and Laura should have met at this juncture, Douglas. Her very special talents will be so helpful for you."

Douglas knew that she was teasing him and quietly contemplated exacting revenge at a more private moment. The prospect gave him some satisfaction. He folded his arms and gave her a sardonic smile that she returned with a distinctly impish grin.

Oh, Lord, Chastity thought. *What was she*

doing? Flirting came so naturally to her, she just caught herself doing it without even thinking. And she certainly couldn't flirt with Douglas Farrell. Not after that "friendly" kiss. She opened her handbag and took out a book, opening it decisively.

"Anyway, *Dottore,* to continue," Laura said. "I found a particular tapestry design that I am determined you shall have. And I think some oriental objets d'art. Urns and such-like."

"Oh, dragons, how about dragons?" Prudence asked. "Two dragons to guard the door."

A muffled sound came from behind Chastity's book and she rummaged in her handbag for her handkerchief, making an elaborate play of catching a sneeze. Douglas regarded the sisters in fulminating silence. All three returned his look with utterly innocent expressions.

"I don't think dragons would be at all suitable," Laura declared earnestly. "I don't think they would give quite the right impression. But perhaps a Buddha," she mused.

"A . . . a reclining one," Chastity suggested from behind her book, a suspicious tremor in her voice. "Or do you think a sitting one would be best, Laura?"

"What are you reading, Chastity?" Douglas demanded severely.

"*Pride and Prejudice,*" she said. "It's so wickedly funny."

"But it doesn't seem to hold your attention," he observed aridly. "Not very flattering for Miss Austen."

"Oh, I've read it so many times, I almost know it by heart," Chastity said, closing the book over her finger. She began, " 'It is a truth universally acknowledged, that a single man —' "

" 'In possession of a good fortune must be in want of a wife,' " her sisters chimed in unison. They all three laughed as if at an old and familiar joke and Douglas was not to know the relevance of the quote to their lives. But he found their amusement infectious despite his exasperation at Chastity's teasing.

"Do you agree, Douglas?" Chastity asked, seeing his reluctant smile.

He shook his head. "I have no opinion on the subject."

"Oh," Chastity said, disappointed. "What about you, Laura? Do you agree with the universally acknowledged truth?"

Laura frowned. The sisters' amusement had completely escaped her and she considered the question with all due gravity. "I believe," she pronounced finally, "that wealthy men *and* women have an obligation to marry. It is a social duty."

"And what about poor men and women?" Prudence asked. "Do they have the same social duty?"

"Indeed not." Laura shook her head vigorously. "Poverty breeds poverty. The social duty of the poor is to avoid propagating their species."

"Species?" Chastity queried, unable to conceal her shock. "They're the same *species* as we are."

"No, there you are quite mistaken, Chastity," Laura said firmly. "They lack something essential in their makeup. It's not their fault, poor souls, but it is unfortunately true."

Chastity looked at Douglas and saw the curled lip, the contemptuous flicker in the charcoal eyes. But his lips were set in a thin line and he looked totally disinclined to enter the conversation. Which didn't surprise her, knowing what she did about his prejudice concerning women's preconceptions. It was dismaying, though, if Laura, by justifying his prejudice, had put him off.

"Ah, you must have read 'A Modest Proposal,' " Chastity said swiftly, hoping to make light of Laura's opinion. "How does it go?" She frowned. "Something about a child well nursed is a most delicious and wholesome food." She turned to her sisters, clicking her fingers. "Help me out here."

"A Modest Proposal for Preventing the Children of Ireland from Being a Burden to Their Parents or Country," Constance supplied. "It was one of mother's favorite Swift essays."

"I don't know it," Laura said with a slight sniff of her long nose.

" 'Stewed, roasted, baked, or boiled,' " Prudence said. "I think that's how it goes."

"Something about serving equally well in a fricassee, or a ragout," Chastity said. The three of them laughed, but they were the only ones who seemed to find Jonathan Swift amusing.

"Tea," Chastity announced into the suddenly awkward silence. She set her book aside. "Let us go for tea. I'm ravenous." She jumped up, shaking out the full skirts of her lavender gown.

"I don't take tea, my dear," the contessa said.

"No, it's a strange habit, this English afternoon tea," Laura announced. "Such an uncivilized time of day to eat, don't you agree, *Dottore* . . . Douglas?" She smiled.

Douglas decided he'd had enough conversation with Laura for the moment. The carriage was beginning to feel somewhat stifling. "On the contrary," he said. "I am an avid eater and drinker of tea. May I join you ladies?"

"Yes, please do," Constance said. She and Prudence had stood up with Chastity. "We should warn you, though, that Chastity will eat all the cakes if you give her half a chance."

"That is such a calumny," Chastity complained, pulling back the sliding door that opened onto the corridor. "Take no notice of them, Douglas."

"I'll try not to." He followed her out. The train took a corner and the corridor swayed violently. Chastity grabbed at the wall as she nearly lost her footing, but she had no need to do so. Douglas had anticipated the movement and had an arm around her almost before the train took the bend. He held her against him until the track straightened, and she could feel the rigid strength, like an iron bar, of the arm supporting her weight, holding her against the broad expanse of his chest. A little jolt of pure and unmistakable physical desire shot through her lower belly.

She pushed herself away from him, her hands on his chest. "Thank you," she said hastily, stepping back from him. "You're very gallant."

"Not gallant enough to catch all three of you, I fear," he said. "Let me lead the way and then I can open the door for you." He moved ahead of them down the corridor, opening the door between their carriage and the dining car. They walked through in single file and were shown to a table by a frock-coated waiter.

Chastity sat by the window and Douglas took the seat beside her, leaving the other two to sit side by side opposite them. The space was small and Chastity's skirt brushed against his leg. Their proximity was such that he could smell the light fragrance of her hair and a lingering scent of some flowery perfume on her skin. His reactions to that moment when he'd held her against him in the corridor shocked and surprised him. He had an almost insurmountable urge to hold that small rounded body against him again, to feel the press of her breasts that swelled so charmingly against the bodice of her dress, to span the neat indentation of her waist between his hands. Her presence filled his senses like a luscious sun-drenched fruit, all tactile warmth and sweet perfume.

The waiter took their order for tea, providing him with a welcome distraction from a sensual reverie that was beginning to have some embarrassing side effects. Constance poured tea for them all and the waiter set a toast rack and a plate of cucumber sandwiches on the table.

Douglas took a piece of hot buttered toast and spread Gentlemen's Relish lavishly. Determined to inject a slightly contentious note that would give him some much-needed distance from the natural intimacy of this tea party, he said conversationally, "So, the Duncan sisters find Miss Della Luca amusing?"

"*Signorina* Della Luca," Constance corrected with a sly smile.

"That's rather what I mean," Douglas said

with a raised eyebrow.

"No, of course we don't find her amusing," Chastity jumped in quickly. "She's so very knowledgeable about art — Italian art in particular — and Italy, and she's so well traveled. She's very interesting. And I think it's wonderful that she's going to redecorate your office with Buddhas and Chinese urns and . . ." Her voice trailed off as she struggled to keep a straight face. "And things," she finished lamely.

"Yes, indeed, Douglas, you must find her very interesting company," Prudence said. "And she's obviously so talented at interior decorating. Of course, Con and I haven't seen the Park Lane house, but Chastity has described it to us in great detail."

"I'm sure she has," he said. He looked at the sisters, at their innocently smiling faces. "You are very wicked women," he declared.

"Oh, no, of course we're not," Chastity protested, spreading clotted cream on a scone. "We're very good-hearted, all three of us."

"I don't believe a word of it." He bit into his toast, chewed reflectively, then said, "Where is Lord Duncan?"

"Oh, he traveled down yesterday with Jenkins and Mrs. Hudson," Chastity said, glad that the conversation had moved from dangerous turf. They wanted to encourage his pursuit of Laura Della Luca, not discourage it. "He wanted to supervise the arrangements."

"Those pertaining to the cellar, at least," Prudence added.

"And your husbands?" he inquired.

"Motoring down with bags and baggage and Gideon's daughter and governess and a positive treasure trove of presents," Constance informed him. "There was no room for wives."

"Anyway, we like to travel together," Chastity said. "How's your toast?"

"It's toast." He was relieved to discover that the effects of his sensual reverie were now completely dissipated.

"But there's good toast and bad toast," Chastity insisted. "Soggy toast and crisp toast, or even burnt toast."

He turned his head towards her with a look of mild incredulity.

"I was only making conversation," she said.

"Is that so? Well, permit me to tell you that I have had more stimulating conversations."

Chastity sucked in her cheeks. "Small talk tends to be a little banal."

"Then perhaps we could avoid it."

"Laura has no time for small talk," Prudence said. "I'm sure you'll find her discourse very stimulating."

"So long as it has nothing to do with toast, I'm sure I shall." They were playing some game but he didn't know the rules — in fact, he didn't even know its object. Whether it was pure slightly malicious mischief or purposeful mischief. He guessed the latter from what he'd seen of the sisters. They seemed to play off one another, relishing the steps in a familiar private dance, but he doubted that they ever did anything just for the sake of it.

"Tell us about Edinburgh, Douglas," Constance invited. "We've never been but it's supposed to be a beautiful city."

It was a safe enough topic and Douglas obliged, describing the city of his birth. To his relief the sisters produced only sensible responses and questions and the conversation carried them through tea and back to their compartment.

It was dark by the time they reached the small station at Romsey. Douglas jumped down to assist the ladies as an elderly porter pushed a trolley towards the baggage compartment, where a pair of rather voluble and excited women awaited him, gesticulating at the baggage conductor on the train as they identified the various pieces of luggage that belonged to their Della Luca mistresses.

"You got any bags, Miss Chas?" a voice rumbled from the shadows of the small station building.

"Just the one, Edward, thank you," Chastity called back as an elderly man in a heavy coat came towards them. "And Dr. Farrell has one too." She indicated the two valises that Douglas had handed down from the compartment.

"We'll need at least two carriages for everyone, Edward," Constance said. "And a separate one for Contessa Della Luca's luggage," she added, looking with some awe at the mountain of bags and trunks piled on the porter's trolley. "Perhaps you should come back for that."

"Oh, no, Mr. Jenkins said to bring the farm cart," he said cheerfully. "Joe's driving that and our Fred's driving the gig, so there's plenty of room for all. Bring it along here, Sam," he said to the heavily breathing porter, and led the way off the platform towards the front of the station where a farm cart, a capacious barouche, and a smaller gig stood waiting.

"Douglas, why don't you go with Laura and the contessa in the barouche?" Chastity suggested quickly. "We three will squeeze together in the gig."

For a man intending to court Laura Della Luca it was certainly the most appropriate and useful disposition, but Douglas heard himself say, "There's really only room for two and a half in the gig, and I take up enough room for one and half, so if I sit in the barouche, there'll only be room for three. Why don't your sisters accompany Laura and her mother and you and I can travel in the gig. Much more comfortable all around, I would think, wouldn't you?" And before anyone could protest he had deftly handed the Della Lucas into the barouche and was politely extending his hand to Constance.

She glanced over her shoulder at Chastity, then with an imperceptible shrug allowed herself to be handed up. Prudence could see no way to alter the arrangement without sounding as if she had no desire to travel with their guests, so she acceded without comment either.

"There are lap rugs, I see," Douglas observed. "I should use them, it's a cold night."

"We have every intention of doing so," Constance said, frowning slightly. This was a gentleman too ready to take charge, but why would he rearrange matters so carefully decided by his hosts for his own benefit?

"Good," he said cheerfully, as if quite unaware of her tart tone. "You don't want to ruin Christmas by catching cold."

He turned away from the barouche and back to the gig where Chastity was already installed, wondering just how Douglas had managed to take the initiative so swiftly. And not just how, but *why*. He had been given the perfect opportunity to pursue his courtship of Laura. Unless it was as she had feared and he was beginning to turn his attention elsewhere.

Dear God, it was getting so complicated. There

was nothing she wanted more than to share this close space with him on a frosty night. And nothing that was less conducive to a successful outcome to the Go-Between's strategy. With an almost defensive movement she took the lap rug off the seat and wrapped it tightly around her legs as if it might insulate her from his physical presence.

Douglas sat beside her. "Could I share the rug?"

It was big enough to be shared, indeed designed to be shared. Chastity released the inside edge and he took it with a murmur of thanks, tucking it over his own lap. Now their knees touched, and at the slight brush of his leg against hers, Chastity again felt that jolt of desire. She sat rigidly upright on the narrow bench.

"How far is it to the house?" Douglas asked, seeming not to notice her stiffness. Except that he had, and he knew its cause. The current between them was almost palpable, a riptide that couldn't be fought. One could only swim with it. What it would do to his plans he didn't know, and for the moment he didn't seem to care.

"About a mile," she replied distantly.

"A beautiful night," he said, tipping his head to look up at the clear, star-filled sky. The air was needle-sharp and so dry, it almost crackled. "See Orion over there, and Cassiopeia."

It seemed a safe-enough topic. Chastity followed his gaze. "Where's his belt? I can never find it."

"Let me show you." He put an arm around her shoulders in a gesture so natural that it took her a couple of seconds to realize she should have resisted it, but it was too late. He pointed with his free hand. "Look towards the east. See the Milky Way? There's Cassiopeia just to the left; it's inverted into an *M* not a *W* at this time of year. Now look farther up and over towards one o'clock. See two bright stars almost in a straight line, and halfway between them a cluster of three bright stars? Those three are Orion's belt."

Chastity tried to forget the arm encircling her as she tipped her head as far back as she could, gazing upwards as she tried to follow his finger. She tried to forget that her head was actually resting on her companion's shoulder. She tried to tell herself that she could be sitting here with Roddie in exactly the same position and it would signal nothing more than the ease of warm friendship. "Oh, yes, I see it now," she said. "I've always found the stars fascinating but I know so little about them."

"If the nights stay as clear as this, I'll teach you," he offered. "Astronomy has been one of my passions since I was a small boy." His fingers played a little tune on her upper arm as he drew her closer against him.

Chastity raised her head abruptly. She could no longer pretend this was perfectly natural and merely friendly. She moved sideways on the bench in a definite gesture of withdrawal and his arm dropped. She felt his gaze on her averted face and resolutely kept her eyes on a point somewhere over the horse's head, and it was with relief that she saw the lights of the house piercing the darkness.

"Good, we're here," she declared, throwing off the lap rug. "I hope Mrs. Hudson has some of her mulled wine waiting for us." She jumped down from the gig almost before Fred had reined in the horse, leaving Douglas to climb down after her.

Lord Duncan stood in the open front door, light streaming forth from behind him. "Welcome, welcome," he said as the contessa alighted from the barouche. "Welcome, dear lady." He took her hands in both of his, beaming as he drew her into the hall. "Come, Miss Della Luca, come in all of you, out of the cold," he said, but it was clear to his daughters that he had eyes only for the contessa.

"Looks like at least one prong of our plan is on the way to fruition," Prudence murmured to Constance as they followed them into the house.

"Mmm," Constance agreed. "Not sure about the other prong, though."

"No. What was all that rearranging about?"

"We'll have to ask Chas." And then the subject had to be dropped as Douglas and Chastity entered the hall behind them. A massive Scotch pine, tiny candles illuminating its branches, dominated the huge raftered chamber. Jenkins came forward with a tray of steaming mugs.

"Oh, mulled wine, Jenkins, wonderful," Chastity said. "It's a Christmas tradition," she explained to their guests as the butler passed around the fragrant mugs.

"Indeed it is," Lord Duncan agreed heartily. "Now come to the fire . . . come, dear lady, you must be chilled to the bone after the drive." He ushered the contessa close to the great fire blazing in the inglenook at the end of the hall and beamed around at the assembled company, his rubicund countenance redolent of good cheer and anticipation.

"Have the aunts arrived yet?" Chastity inquired, burying her nose in the clove-and-cinnamon-scented steam of her mulled wine.

"Yes, Lady Bagshot and Lady Aston are resting after their journey, Miss Chas," Jenkins informed her.

"Did you put them in the usual rooms?"

"Of course, Miss Chas." Jenkins looked slightly offended at the question. Lord Duncan's two sisters, Edith and Agatha, always had the same bedrooms on their frequent visits to Romsey Manor.

Chastity smiled. "I know, of course you did. It's only that my head's been full of arrangements for days."

"Mrs. Hudson and I have everything well in hand, Miss Chas," the butler said, but he was mollified. "I've given Miss Sarah and Miss Winston the old nursery quarters, Miss Prue. I thought Miss Winston would appreciate having her own sitting room."

"Yes, I'm sure she would," Prudence said warmly. "They'll be half-frozen when they get here."

"All the fires have been lit," Jenkins said.

"My dear girl, you might give me some credit for arranging matters satisfactorily," Lord Duncan said in mild protest. "I know how to make our guests comfortable."

"Yes, Father, of course you do," Constance said with a teasing smile. "But you know how managing and bossy Chas is."

Chastity, overwhelmingly relieved to be once more in the safety of numbers, laughingly protested. Of the three of them she was the least bossy and managing. Douglas was standing just a little outside the half circle around the fire and a covert glance gave her the impression that he was observing and assessing them all in a manner that was almost professional. She wondered if, as a member of a big family himself, he was comparing the Duncans *en famille* with the Farrells.

"What a delightful hall, Lord Duncan," Laura said, moving closer to her host. "So charmingly quaint with all those stuffed heads." She gave a little shudder. "The glass eyes are most unnerving." She gave another of her annoying little trills of laughter that always accompanied one of her obliquely critical remarks. "Ancestors must have been so uncivilized, don't you think?"

"Can't think what's wrong with hunting," Lord Duncan said. "Perfectly fine sport. And the stag's a noble animal. Graces any hall, in my opinion."

"Ah." Again the little laugh. "Of course, the English are such fervent aficionados of blood sports." She gave another little shudder.

"So, you won't be joining the Boxing Day hunt, Laura?" Prudence inquired, taking off her spectacles for a moment and fixing her myopic gaze on the other woman.

Laura shook her head with obvious horror. "Oh, goodness me, no. I couldn't possibly participate in anything so uncivilized."

"I always thought the Italians and the French were as passionate about hunting as the English," Chastity said, reflecting that the woman seemed to have only one word in her critical vocabulary. Constant repetition of *uncivilized* wore a little thin. "Look at all those medieval and eighteenth-century tapestries. Someone's always chasing something in them.

And one would hardly call those civilizations uncivilized."

Laura for once looked a little put out. "The French," she said with a vaguely dismissive wave of her hand. "And *La Chasse*, of course." She managed to give the impression that by conceding Chastity's point she had disproved it.

"Of course," Chastity murmured. *"La Chasse."* She turned to Douglas. "I'm sure you hunt, Douglas."

He shook his head. "No, I'm afraid not. I've never seen the point."

"Oh," Chastity said with a bright smile. "In that case, on Boxing Day you and Laura will be able to ride together through the countryside. We have some lovely rides through the New Forest and across the heath. I'm sure you'll both enjoy it."

Before either Douglas or Laura could respond, Lord Duncan rumbled, "Good God, man, never seen the point of hunting. And you a Scot. Some of the best grouse moors in the world in Scotland. Not to mention salmon rivers and trout streams."

"I wouldn't argue with you, sir. And I don't count fishing as hunting," Douglas said with a smile. "Fly-fishing is a true sport. Shooting birds out of the sky . . ." He shook his head. "I don't think so."

"Well, I suppose if you're a fisherman, that's better than nothing," his lordship said, but he regarded his guest with a degree of doubt, as if wondering if he should be housing such a heretic under his roof.

Chastity set down her mug and said diplomatically, “Let me show you all to your rooms. Contessa, Laura, Douglas. I’m sure you’ll be glad to get settled in.” She swept a hospitable smile around the assembly and walked to the stairs, her guests trooping behind her.

Chapter 12

"Contessa, this is the room my father wanted you to have," Chastity said with a warm smile. "I expect your maid will be waiting for you." She opened the door onto a large well-appointed guest room, predominantly decorated in green, where indeed the contessa's maid was busy unpacking her mistress's bags. "I hope you'll be comfortable."

"It's delightful, my dear Chastity," the contessa responded, beginning to unbutton her coat. "A lovely room. Thank you."

Chastity smiled again and backed out. "Laura, let me show you to your room. And Douglas, yours is right next door." She led the way back down the corridor. The rooms she had allocated Douglas and Laura were as far from the contessa's as was possible on the same floor. The contessa would be in blissful ignorance in the event of any sleepwalking between the doctor's room and Laura's. However, such an event seemed increasingly unlikely to Chastity. Laura might be happily assuming the role of interior decorator on Harley Street, but for her to indulge in a clandestine liaison was impossible to picture even with the most willing imagination. Chastity firmly put aside the reflection that the doctor himself was beginning to show less enthusiasm for his pursuit of the signorina. Just as she resolutely ignored the little twinge of satisfaction that this reflection brought her.

Fortunately, Laura pronounced herself contented with the pretty pink and pastel bedroom where her maid was also already busy and Chastity left her giving a series of orders to the maid, who was rushing around like a headless chicken.

"You're in here, Douglas," she said, opening the door to the next-door bedchamber. "It has a view over the churchyard, I hope you're not superstitious."

"Not in the least," he said, closing the door behind him. "I see you're not wholly against dragons." He gestured to the oriental wallpaper.

"It depends where they are," she said. She heard the click of the latch and it sounded rather definite in the sudden hush. She began to talk rapidly. "The bathroom is just down the corridor, the second door on the right. I'm afraid there are very few rooms with their own bathrooms."

"I wouldn't expect otherwise," he said,

leaning against the door, watching her with some amusement and something else that made her skin prickle. She wandered around the room, pointing out its amenities, for all the world like an anxious hotelkeeper, she thought crossly.

"There's usually plenty of hot water," she said. "But it takes awhile to run. Would you like me to send someone up to help you unpack?"

He laughed. "Chastity, my dear girl, you know better than that. Of course I wouldn't. I am perfectly capable of unpacking what I packed myself this morning."

"Yes, I'm sure you are," she said, looking warily at the door. She would have to go through him to get to it and she didn't think she possessed the spirit qualities of walking through solid matter. "I'll see you downstairs, then, when you've unpacked and freshened up. It's traditional to invite the village carolers in on Christmas Eve for mince pies and mulled wine. They usually come at around seven-thirty, before dinner."

"I'll be sure not to miss it," he said. The something else in his eye was suddenly more pronounced.

"Then I'll leave you to it," she said, making for the door.

He moved slightly aside for her and then with a movement that Chastity somehow knew was inevitable he laid a restraining hand on her arm. Prickles rose suddenly on her skin, making her cold, as if the temperature in the room had dropped for some reason.

"Chastity," he said softly. That was all. His eyes said the rest as he took her face between both his hands. He kissed her mouth, very gently, almost experimentally, moving his lips to each corner, and then kissed her eyelids. His lips were warm on her lids and then trailed in little bird kisses over her cheeks, touched the tip of her nose, brushed across her chin, his tongue for a second darting into the deep dimple there, and then coming to rest again on her mouth.

Chastity didn't breathe. She wanted to tell him that this was wrong. He had the wrong end of the stick. Laura Della Luca was his quarry, not Chastity Duncan, who had not a sou of capital to her name, and only the most modest income. Not to mention the monstrous deception she had practiced upon him, the secret identity that had made her privy to a mercenary ambition that, however justified it might be in terms of the greater good, would still be immensely embarrassing for him to have known to a social acquaintance. But the words wouldn't form themselves.

With a sudden sigh she drew breath, inhaling the scent of his skin, a rugged, slightly earthy scent. Her tongue touched his mouth, tasting the spicy sweetness of the mulled wine, feeling the warm pliancy of his lips. She had noticed before that he had a strong mouth and it *felt* strong, muscular as well as pliable, to her exploring tongue.

Then his own tongue joined the little play and her mouth opened to the nudging pressure. She tasted the mulled wine and a lingering flavor of peppermint and his hands on her face tightened their clasp so that she could feel the roughness of his afternoon skin against her own.

Chastity was no naive ingenue, and neither was she a fool. Maybe, at a huge stretch, their earlier kiss could be called a seal of friendship, but by no stretch of the imagination could this one be anything but a passionate promise of future lovemaking.

She drew her head back and stepped away. She touched her mouth where she could still feel the imprint of his lips. "That was not friendship," she said.

He shook his head. "No . . . no, it wasn't." He gave a little rueful shrug. "I've kissed many friends, but never like that." He put his hands lightly on her shoulders. "What shall we do about it, Chastity?"

"Nothing at all," she said with a sharpness that sprang from her own dismay. "There's nothing *to* be done. It was just an aberration. I've disliked you from the first moment I met you." Which was only partially true but she wasn't going to let that stand in her way. She forged on in the tone of one delivering the coup de grâce, "And we've been quarreling since you came to that At Home."

He looked a little taken aback at this vehemence, then shook his head again and laughed. "Oh, I wouldn't call it quarreling," he said pensively. "You *have* had a rather confrontational attitude towards me, I admit, and I don't really know why. I think it's just your nature. You're quite a bantam, really."

"A bantam?" Chastity glared at him, thunderstruck by such a patronizing comparison.

"Yes," he said, stroking his angular jaw. "Small, well feathered, very assertive, and more than a little combative."

"Oh, let me pass," she said in disgust, pushing him aside with a flat hand to his chest as she marched to the door.

Chastity went straight to her own room, too shaken to face anyone until she had decided for herself what had just happened. He was insufferable, worse even than Max and Gideon had been on first impression. She paced her bedroom, following a circular path since the room was too small to give a satisfactory length for one march, and she only stopped when it occurred to her that she must look like a fuming caged tiger. She thumped down on a small armless chair beside the fire and reflectively chewed a fingernail. What an absurd mess to find herself in.

Her personal inclinations were so far at odds with her professional obligations.

A knock at the door brought her to her feet with a startled jump. It was followed by her sisters' entrance and she wondered rather aridly as her heart rate slowed somewhat exactly whom she had been expecting.

"Is everything all right, Chas?" Prudence asked.

"You look as if you've seen a ghost," Constance said.

Chastity shook her head. "No, I was just contemplating how the best-laid plans oft gang awry."

"Douglas," Constance hazarded.

"Tell all," Prudence demanded.

Chastity sighed, took a deep breath, and explained what had just happened. "And the worst of it is," she concluded, "I didn't even try to stop him." She tucked a red curl behind one ear with an air of distraction. "Actually, that isn't the worst of it. The worst of it is that I enjoyed it and I want to do it again."

"Oh, Chas," Constance said, sitting on the bed. "I thought you didn't like him."

"I don't," Chastity said helplessly. "Well, that's not strictly true. Sometimes I like him, until he says or does something to put my back up — like calling me a bantam, for God's sake," she added with remembered annoyance. "But . . ." She bit her bottom lip.

"I desire him. It's as simple — and as complicated — as that."

"What a pickle," Prudence observed, taking off her spectacles.

"Yes, it is," Chastity said almost in despair. "It's all so dishonest. If he knew about the Go-Between . . . that I was the one he met in the National Gallery. Can you imagine how he'd feel? And apart from that, we can't have him distracted from his courtship of Laura."

"But maybe he's not really interested in Laura," Prudence said thoughtfully, polishing her glasses on her skirt. "If he's decided he's not, and there've been no promises or even vague murmurings on either side as yet, then he probably thinks it's perfectly reasonable to turn his attention elsewhere. And here you are." She gestured towards her little sister with an open palm.

"Yes, but he can't," Chastity said. "Apart from the whole deception business with the Go-Between, he has to marry for money, otherwise he won't be able to afford his mission. I couldn't possibly ruin his chances to do that just because I fancy a little dalliance."

Prudence put her spectacles back on. She wondered if her baby sister really meant dalliance, or something more serious. But it was not a question she thought she could ask, since it was possible Chastity herself didn't know. "Well, we can put him right on the money score," she said. "I'll let him know casually that you're as poor as a church mouse, and if that doesn't work, then Con and I will just have to protect you from him."

"From temptation more like," Constance said. "Sorry, Chas, I don't mean to make light of this but it does have its ironical side."

"I know," Chastity said with a heavy sigh. "Here am I trying to set him up with a suitable bride, one who fits his very precise specifications, and he's going off on frolics of his own. It would be fine if he found another bride other than Laura who would fit the bill, but he can't be distracted by *me*."

"Well, Prue and I will hammer home the poverty nail and at the same time try to keep ourselves between him and you," Constance declared. "We'll stick to him like glue and never give him a chance to be alone with you. How's that?"

Chastity shook her head. "He's going to think it very strange."

"It doesn't matter what he thinks," Prudence stated. "For the rest of the holiday one of us will be at his side at every waking moment." She stood up from the deep window seat. "We'd better hurry and change for the evening. The carolers will be here soon. What's everyone wearing?"

"Chas needs to find something utterly frumpy and unappealing," Constance said with a chuckle.

"I don't have anything," Chastity said. "Unless Prue has that dreadful dress she wore when she first confronted Gideon. You know, that dun-colored one that made her look like some dreadfully prim and dour spinster schoolteacher."

"It smelled of mothballs," Prudence said reminiscently. "Poor Gideon, he didn't know what to make of it."

"Well, do you have it down here?"

Prudence shook her head. "Even if I did, Chas couldn't wear it. Gideon would know immediately that we were playing some game and he'd be bound to say something that would ruin the effect."

"I suppose you're right," Chastity agreed with a reluctant nod. "I'll have to make do with what I've got."

"We'll see you downstairs, then." Constance went to the door. "Coming, Prue?"

The two sisters left the room and Chastity opened her wardrobe to survey the contents. She didn't actually possess a single garment that wasn't attractive. There wasn't really any incentive to spend money on clothes that didn't suit one. She didn't want to outshine Laura but that would be difficult to avoid since Laura seemed to favor only the most modest cuts and dull colors for her wardrobe. Whereas Chastity's clothes were almost universally as bright and vibrant as her hair.

With a shrug, she selected an evening dress

of a rich chocolate-brown velvet. No one could call brown a vibrant color, she thought, but without much conviction. This gown had a wonderful luster to it and deeper shades rippling in its generous folds. When she surveyed herself in the mirror before going downstairs she saw an elegant woman in a glowing gown that fitted her body in all the right places. The richness of the color and the material imparted a bloom to her complexion and a luminous light to her hazel eyes that even the most critical self-examination couldn't deny.

She tried to pull her hair back in a severe bun at the nape of her neck, hoping that would counteract some of the effects of the gown, but as usual the bright curls were uncooperative and escaped the pins in an unruly and quite charming cloud around her face. Even the scattering of freckles on the bridge of her nose seemed to have disappeared completely. On the one hand it was infuriating to know that despite all her efforts she looked at her very best, but on the other, shamefully pleasing to her vanity.

Oh, well, she thought, vanity's only human. She would have to rely on the protective wall of her sisters.

The party was already assembled in the great hall when she came down the stairs, and her gaze was immediately and unwittingly drawn to Douglas, who stood talking to Max and Gideon, who must have just arrived. As if Douglas sensed her look, he turned towards the stairs and a slow, appreciative smile curved his mouth. He made as if to move towards the stairs and Constance stepped quickly in front of him.

"You and Laura will enjoy a Boxing Day ride through our Hampshire countryside, Douglas." She smiled at him over her sherry glass.

"Yes," he agreed vaguely, watching over her shoulder as his quarry was lost in the embraces of a pair of elderly ladies at the bottom of the stairs. She seemed to shimmer in that lustrous velvet dress, he thought. "Uh, yes," he said. "I'm sure."

"I believe Laura is a most accomplished horsewoman," Constance persevered. "I only hope we can find a horse in our stables that will suit her exacting standards." She turned to include Laura Della Luca in the conversation. "Laura, I seem to remember your saying you had an Arabian mare, I believe."

"Yes, indeed. I am very fond of riding. Of course, the Italian countryside, particularly in Tuscany, is wonderful. Such delightful hill towns to explore and of course the vineyards of Chianti. Utterly unparalleled."

"Of course," Constance said. "But I like to think that the New Forest has its own delights." She turned to give Douglas an assessing glance. "I think one of my father's hunters will be up to your weight, Douglas."

"Oh, it will be lovely to ride out together," Laura said, with a gracious smile at Douglas. "A delightful excursion, *Dottore*. And we can discuss decorating. I am determined to look at your apartments on Wimpole Street as well. I'm certain they would benefit from a woman's touch."

Douglas's eyes snapped back into focus. He blinked at Laura. This was assuming a little too much. "I find them quite satisfactory as they are," he stated.

"Oh, that's because you don't see them with a woman's eye, *Dottore*," Laura trilled, patting his arm, fixing him with her pale gaze. "When you see what I've done with your offices, you will know exactly what I mean."

Douglas gazed rather wildly about him, looking for salvation. Chastity could not provide it. She had now inserted herself between her brothers-in-law and was talking animatedly to a child, who seemed to have a great deal to say for herself.

But it came in the form of her other sister. "Douglas, let me introduce you to Miss Winston, Sarah's governess," Prudence said, coming up to them with a woman whose plain but pleasant countenance radiated intelligence and humor. "And this is Signorina Della Luca, Mary." She gestured to Laura. "Miss Winston is a mine of information on

Italian culture, Laura, I'm sure you'll enjoy talking with her. You speak Italian fluently, I believe, Mary?"

"I would hesitate to make such a claim, Lady Malvern," Mary said quietly with a modest smile. "I speak it adequately."

"Oh, well, one could only lay claim to fluency if one has lived there," Laura said, regarding the governess with some disdain. "I don't imagine you've done that, Miss . . . uh . . . Winston, is it? Unless you were in service with an Italian family, perhaps?"

It was a very deliberate attempt to put the governess in her place and while Mary showed no obvious discomfort Douglas felt a flash of anger on her behalf. Disdain crossed his eyes as he looked at Laura, her rather small pinched mouth and colorless complexion not helped by a white taffeta evening dress that made nothing of her sticklike figure. Once again he caught himself wondering if the obvious advantages she would bring to a marriage of convenience were worth the irritations of her company. And once again he told himself that they need spend very little time in each other's company. Laura would not want a uxorious husband, just a useful one.

He was a shrewd judge of character and had met Laura's type many times before. She would be quite happy going about her own social business, arranging practical matters for him to suit her own purposes while leaving him to the total absorption of his work. A woman like Chastity Duncan, on the other hand, would demand much more of a husband. She would want an engaged partner, a sympathetic and stimulating companion . . . a passionate lover. His blood stirred at the reflection and he thrust it from his mind. He had had time enough in the last couple of hours to acknowledge that that impulsive kiss had indeed been an aberration. It merely muddled the clear-sighted vision he had constructed of his needs and his future. Chastity would be a good friend, and if there was a frisson of sexual attraction beneath the friendship, that would merely be a bonus. There was no room in his life for emotional entanglements — he'd learned that lesson long since.

But these reflections didn't dull his anger at Laura's discourtesy. He turned his shoulder to her and said warmly to Mary, "Would you say that there were any real similarities between Latin and Italian, Miss Winston? I'm an indifferent classicist, at least outside medical terminology, but I've always wondered if there's any connection. In the way that modern Greek is easily traced to ancient Greek."

"An interesting question, Doctor," Mary said.

"Oh, I don't believe there's any similarity

at all," Laura stated.

Douglas pretended he hadn't heard. He took Miss Winston's arm and drew away from Laura, engaging her in conversation. Laura looked a little surprised, as if wondering what had happened. Constance and Prudence exchanged a speaking glance and with a word of excuse abandoned their guest to her own opinions.

The sound of singing from the driveway beyond the front door provided welcome distraction. Jenkins crossed the hall with stately step and flung open the door, letting in a blast of freezing air. Caroling voices rose in the joyful verses of "Good King Wenceslas" and the house party trooped to the door to listen.

"Merry Christmas," Lord Duncan said, flinging open his arms. "Come in, come in." He was in his element, greeting the adult carolers by name, shaking hands, chucking children's chins. His daughters watched with pleasure. It seemed their father had at last returned to himself, embracing the ancient traditions of the lord of the manor with his old fervor.

Douglas stood with Mary Winston as they listened to the carols. The fine single malt in his glass was frequently replenished by Jenkins or one of his several assistants and the warmth of the occasion seeped into him. His suspicion bordering on contempt for these privileged English aristocratic traditions was blunted by the obvious good humor and general pleasure taken by both lord and tenants. He couldn't discern the slightest hint of social condescension on the part of the Duncan family. The daughters were helping to serve the carolers with mulled wine and mince pies, chatting cheerfully to everyone. It seemed as if they knew something personal about each one of their singing visitors.

Chastity, he noticed, was particularly concerned with the children, often kneeling down to talk to them so that she was at their level. She was smiling her lovely glowing smile, her large green-gold eyes filled with warmth. And try as he might, he couldn't take his eyes off her. Once she looked up and caught him watching her. A slight flush tinged her cheeks, then she gave an almost imperceptible shake of her head and turned away, reaching a hand to another child.

It would be quite natural for him to go over and join her — she was his hostess, after all — but he couldn't leave Mary Winston without someone to talk to. It would be insensitive, particularly after Laura's discourtesy. The child he had seen earlier bounced across to them. "Hello," she said. "I'm Sarah Malvern. I think you're Dr. Farrell."

"You think right," he said with a smile.

"Is this your first Christmas here? It's mine

too. I think it's going to be wonderful. We have the carols this evening and then dinner, only I'm not to stay up for dinner, but Mary and I will have dinner upstairs, roast chicken like everyone else. And I'm not to go to midnight mass, but I don't mind that, I don't really like going to church anyway, but we'll have to go tomorrow after breakfast. And then we have presents before Christmas lunch and then everyone will play games all afternoon and there'll be a cold supper because the servants will have their Christmas dinner in the servants' hall, so we have to serve ourselves. I can be downstairs for supper because we'll play more games afterwards, Aunt Chas says. Sardines and murder in the dark." The child gave a delicious shudder.

"And then the next day, Boxing Day, we're to have the hunt and I'm going to hunt with Daddy and Prue. And then all the neighbors will come in for the hunt breakfast, except that it's not at breakfast time but in the afternoon when everyone gets back, and then Lord Duncan will give the servants their Christmas boxes." She paused and drew what Douglas thought was probably her first breath since the recital had begun. "That's why it's called Boxing Day," she said.

"Sarah's excited," Mary said unnecessarily. "This is her first real Christmas."

"Well, we've had Christmases before,"

Sarah said seriously now and suddenly rather less childishly exuberant. "But it's always been just Daddy and Mary and me." She smiled up at Mary. "Not that it wasn't lovely to be with you and Daddy, Mary, but a big party is different, isn't it? It's a real family affair. All these aunts and guests." She waved an expansive hand at the assembled company.

"A real family affair," Douglas agreed with solemnity, hiding a smile as he noticed Mary Winston was also doing.

"Have you had family Christmases before, Dr. Farrell?" Sarah now asked.

"Many of them," he said. "I have six sisters, you see."

"Six!" Sarah's eyes widened. "Are they older or younger?"

"All older."

"Tell me about them," Sarah demanded.

Mary Winston said gently, "You can't monopolize Dr. Farrell, Sarah. I'm sure other people would like to talk to him."

"Oh." Sarah glanced around. "I don't see anyone."

And neither did Douglas. He still wanted to talk to Chastity; the longer he waited to restore their usual easy manner with each other, the more the awkward memory of that kiss would stand between them, but she was deeply involved with a circle of children and showed no inclination even to glance his way.

"Well, perhaps you should come and meet

Daddy and Uncle Max," Sarah said, taking his hand. "I'll introduce you."

"I have already met them," Douglas said.

"Then come and talk to them some more," Sarah declared. "Mary will come too, won't you?"

"I hardly think that's necessary, Sarah," Mary said. "You and Dr. Farrell go and talk to your father and Mr. Ensor. I shall go and talk to Lady Malvern's aunts." She nodded at Douglas, a friendly nod that somehow acknowledged an understanding, and made her way over to the aunts.

"Come along, then, Dr. Farrell," Sarah said, giving his hand the slightest tug. "Do you know Latin? I'm learning it and I find the grammar really complicated. The order of the subjects and verbs seems so illogical, it drives me mad sometimes."

Douglas almost laughed aloud. The exuberant, excited child had given way to a remarkable Lilliputian grown-up. He knew the process well enough, having watched his myriad nieces go through the various stages of growing up.

"Daddy, I've brought Dr. Farrell over to talk to you some more," Sarah announced.

Gideon playfully tugged her pigtail. "You have to be careful around Sarah, Farrell. She's liable to manage you into whatever situation she considers best for you."

"In that she's not unlike her stepmother

and her aunts," Max observed, taking a sip of whisky. "The Duncans are the most managing family, in case you haven't discovered that for yourself, Farrell."

Douglas laughed. "I haven't had much opportunity to see them in concert. I really only know Chastity."

"How did you meet her?"

"At an At Home in Manchester Square," he said, seeing no reason to conceal the information. "I was looking for someone who I was told would be there."

"Ah," Max said. He and Gideon nodded and both became suddenly absorbed in the contents of their glasses.

Douglas frowned slightly, wondering what it was about what he'd said that caused them both to react so strangely. "I happened to meet the contessa and her daughter there too," he went on, watching them closely. They both merely nodded again and continued to study the amber whisky at the bottom of the cut-glass tumblers.

"And then while I was visiting the Della Lucas on Park Lane, Chastity and her father arrived," he continued into the studied silence. "Lord Duncan invited the contessa and her daughter to join the party for Christmas and Chastity invited me." He laughed a little. "Probably because she thought courtesy gave her no other choice since I was standing right there."

"Oh, none of them do anything they don't choose to do," Max said.

"Yes, there's always a reason," Gideon said. "Sometimes it takes awhile to find it, though." His brother-in-law laughed at this and the two of them grinned.

Douglas felt as if they were sharing a joke to which he was not party. "I can't imagine what reason Chastity would have had for inviting me except simple courtesy and kindness," he said.

"As we said, dear fellow, it sometimes takes awhile to discover the method behind their madness," Gideon said, clapping him on the shoulder in a gesture of fellowship. "Ensor and I know of what we speak, I do assure you."

"I'll bear that in mind," Douglas said, glancing over his shoulder to see what Chastity was doing. She still seemed absorbed with the child carolers, and her sisters and their father were equally occupied with the adults. With a word of excuse he left the two men and made his way through the crowd to Chastity.

"Poor fellow," Max murmured. "He doesn't know what's hit him."

"No," Gideon agreed with a soft laugh. "I wonder if they've decided to turn his life upside down for his own good or whether he's a Go-Between client and actually asked for it."

"Let's hope for his sake it's the latter." They touched glasses in a silent toast and drank.

Prudence waylaid Douglas on his determined path to Chastity. "So what do you think of Romsey Manor, Douglas?"

"A most delightful house, Lady Malvern," he said. "These old English country manors are quite charming."

Prudence nodded but gave a sigh. "And so expensive to keep up. You wouldn't believe the shifts we have to make to keep everything in something resembling good order. Ever since Father's debacle on the Exchange . . ." She smiled as easily as if she had said nothing of any significance, stepped aside, and moved away towards a knot of women gossiping busily with their heads together.

Douglas frowned, wondering what had prompted that particular confidence. He resumed his path to Chastity. "I haven't said good evening," he said as he reached her. He hitched up his trousers at the knees before squatting on his heels beside her. "Hello," he said to the child she was talking to. The small boy regarded him solemnly, his mouth full of mince pie.

"I'm rather busy," Chastity said vaguely. "This evening is for the carolers. We have social obligations to the locals at different times of the year, but Christmas is the busiest. I like to give the children all my attention."

There was no mistaking this dismissal. But Douglas refused to take it. He said quietly, "I just wanted to apologize for indulging an impulse earlier. I don't know what came over me. Can we put it behind us?"

Chastity looked at him, wondering if one of her sisters had already managed to convey the true state of the family finances to him. If so, it had certainly worked, and she could only be grateful. Matters between them would now return to their former friendly footing and she could easily overcome her own inconvenient desires if they were given no encouragement and no outlet. She said with a quick smile, "Yes, of course. That would be best. We won't think of it again."

He nodded, straightened, and walked away in the direction of the aunts. Chastity wiped the child's sticky fingers and stood up herself. The carolers were gathering their belongings, putting on coats and gloves, and making their way to the front door in a chorus of "Merry Christmas." A tiny sigh escaped Chastity, but she didn't know why. Everything was now going smoothly and according to plan.

Chapter 13

In addition to her other charms, Chastity had a remarkably pretty voice, Douglas thought. In fact, all three Duncan sisters had fine voices. He was well placed to judge since he was sitting just behind them in the Duncan family's box pew in the little village church as their voices swelled with the choir into an energetic rendition of "O, Come All Ye Faithful" at the end of midnight mass. The entire party with the exception of Sarah and her governess were in attendance, and Lord Duncan's powerful baritone rose to the Norman rafters of the ancient church, all but drowning the contessa's lighter alto as she stood beside him.

"I always think that sacred music should not be sung with such exuberance, just as if it were a popular song, don't you, *Dottore?*"

At Laura's whispered comment he glanced sideways. She was looking as if she thoroughly disapproved of the present proceedings. "Just a little vulgar, I think," she said with a conspiratorial nod. "The Italians know so much better how to revere the sacred."

Douglas, who was enjoying lending his own tenor voice to the vigorous choir, said in an expressionless whisper, "I hardly think Christmas carols come into the category of sacred music. They're the expressions of popular joy and as such should be sung by the congregation with as much pleasure as they feel."

Laura frowned as if he'd disappointed her. She muttered something about "lack of sensibility," and returned her eyes to her hymnal but maintained a steadfast silence amid the joyful outpouring around her.

Douglas wondered how anyone could go through life criticizing everything and everyone in her path. It must be very wearing. He repressed the reflection that it was also very wearing for her companions. The congregation knelt for the blessing and he dutifully bowed his head while he plotted an escape route from the box that would separate him from Laura and put him naturally at Chastity's side for the walk home.

They'd had no further conversation and he was anxious to underscore the return of friendly relations. At dinner he'd been seated beside Laura at Lord Duncan's end of the table. Chastity had been in the middle but on the same side, so he couldn't even try to catch her eye during the meal. After dinner she'd been inseparable from her sisters or had been too busy pouring and offering coffee for any kind of sustained conversation.

He rose to his feet as the organ struck its first chord for the recital accompanying the congregation's departure. Laura was between him and the door to the box and she took her time about gathering up her belongings, looking all around her on the pew as if she might have dropped some precious object. He ground his teeth in impatience as he waited, politely smiling, for her to precede him into the aisle. Chastity and her sisters with their husbands were already at the church door with Lord Duncan and the contessa when he could at last join the slowly moving throng in the narrow aisle.

The family had stopped at the church door to greet the vicar and were still gathered in a knot in the vestibule, the crowd milling about them, when Douglas and Laura finally made it to freedom.

"An excellent sermon, Vicar," he said, offering the ritual compliment for these occasions.

The vicar beamed. "Christmas services are always the easy ones," he said. "Same thing every year, just what everyone expects."

"I would have thought you might welcome the opportunity to shake up complacency in that case, Vicar," Laura said with a humorless smile. "Isn't it the role of a pastoral shepherd to challenge his congregations' assumptions?"

"I . . . well . . . perhaps so, at other times of the year," the vicar responded, clearly dismayed by this false note in the general bonhomie of Christmas morning.

"I believe we all have enough challenges in our lives the rest of the year, Vicar," Chastity said swiftly. "One day out of 365 can surely be devoted guiltlessly to simple pleasure."

"Yes . . . yes . . . quite so, Chastity, quite so," he said, once more beaming.

"We'll leave you to the rest of your congregation, Dennis," Lord Duncan declared, shaking his hand. "Expect to see you at the meet on Boxing Day."

"Oh, yes, indeed, Lord Duncan," the vicar said. "Wouldn't miss the hunt for the world. And the breakfast," he added. "Nothing like tradition, is there?"

"Nothing like it, m'dear chap," his lordship agreed. "Come along now, people, come along. Let's leave the good man to his flock." He shepherded his own party down the path and through the lych-gate.

"A hunting vicar," observed Douglas, doing a neat sidestep and a little quickstep in order to bring himself up on Chastity's right side. "Positively Trollopian."

"Yes," Chastity agreed, opening the little gate that led directly into the grounds of Romsey Manor. "He likes his claret too. But

Dennis is no Archdeacon Grantly." She turned to Constance. "Did Grantly hunt, Con? Can you remember?"

"I don't recall," her sister said. "Prue, can you remember?"

A lively discussion among the three of them ensued on which of Trollope's many characters had emulated their creator's passion for hunting and Douglas listened with interest on the short and frosty walk home. The sisters' knowledge of the author's oeuvre was considerable, and to Douglas's mingled amusement and relief, rather too erudite to encourage interjections from Signorina Della Luca, who kept opening her mouth to interrupt and then — wisely, he assumed — closing it again.

Hot brandy punch and mince pies awaited them in the great hall. "Are you happy with punch, Douglas, or would you prefer whisky?"

"Punch, thank you, Constance." He took the mug she offered him and inhaled the rich fragrant steam. He observed with a smile, "I find myself enjoying these English Christmas traditions."

"Yes, we love them too," she said, adding with a tiny sigh, "Poor Father, since he lost all his fortune, is always fretting that we can't afford them anymore. But the estate is self-sufficient and generates enough income to cover most of the London expenses, although we do have to economize." She gave a little shrug. "It's hard for him to accept reduced circumstances."

"I'm sure it must be," Douglas said neutrally, wondering why on earth the two sisters had chosen to confide this surely private piece of family business to a man who was to all intents and purposes a near-stranger.

"Well, if you'll excuse me, I must see to my other guests." Constance, message delivered, smiled at him and glided away.

"There is a rather pleasant chintz material in my bedroom, *Dottore* . . . oh, I must get used to calling you Douglas." Laura's irritating little trill broke into his puzzled thoughts. "I think it would be delightful for your waiting room. Perhaps you would like to come and look at it."

"Good God, no, I couldn't do that," he said before he could stop himself, appalled at the prospect of entering this woman's bedroom. It wasn't that he was afraid of her suggesting anything untoward. Laura Della Luca was not in the habit of the untoward, but the intimacy of a tête-à-tête in her bedroom was somehow unthinkable.

"Oh, you English," she said with another little laugh, lightly patting his arm. "So worried about appearances. But I assure you my maid will be there as chaperone."

"Actually, I'm Scottish," he said. "And we Scots do worry about appearances." He tried a smile. "The dour and puritanical Scots . . . the land of John Knox." He waited in vain for the swift witty comeback that he knew the remark would have elicited from Chastity but Laura merely blinked her pale eyes in something bordering on incomprehension.

"Oh, I'm sure you exaggerate, *Dottore*," she said with an attempt at sympathy. "Not all Scots can be puritans, surely?"

"No," he agreed flatly. "Of course not. Can I get you another glass of punch?"

"No, thank you." She offered a thin smile. "It's late. I believe I shall retire." She let him take her empty beaker. "I must take my mother to bed."

The contessa didn't look in the least ready for bed, Douglas reflected as he put the empty beaker on a long refectory table that stood against one wall of the hall and went to refill his own from the steaming punch bowl.

Contessa Della Luca was sitting on a deep and shabbily comfortable sofa before the fire, laughing and talking with Lord Duncan, a beaker of punch between her hands. At her daughter's approach she looked up, listened for a minute, then with a smile that looked resigned to Douglas, set down her beaker and rose to her feet. She was a remarkably handsome woman, he thought. Stately in a bustled gown that would have been fashionable some twenty years earlier. But it suited her and clearly Lord Duncan thought so too. He had risen with her and was now bowing over her hand, then, not satisfied with that courtesy, he escorted her to the bottom of the stairs, raised her hand to his lips, kissed it, and stood looking up until she and her daughter had disappeared into the shadows of the upstairs landing.

It seemed to be the signal for the party to break up. The aunts wafted upstairs in a cloud of feather boas and cashmere shawls and Douglas offered his good nights to his hosts. He took Chastity's hand in his and bent to kiss her cheek in a perfectly proper friendly salute that could draw no untoward attention. "Good night, Chastity. Sleep well."

"You too," she said, making no attempt to return the kiss, although her smile was friendly. "I hope the church bells don't wake you too early."

"I always wake early anyway," he said, dropping her hand. He turned to shake hands with Lord Duncan and then ascended the stairs. Chastity watched him go and took a breath of relief. Christmas Eve was over and there would be so much to fill the next couple of days that she wouldn't have time to dwell on lustful urges.

He was *so incredibly attractive, unutterably desirable, though. Oh, she wanted to kick herself.*

"Gentlemen, will you join me for a nightcap in the library?" Lord Duncan inquired of his sons-in-law. "Never could be doing with this punch . . . too sweet on the tongue."

Prudence and Constance made little shooing gestures with their fingertips at their husbands, who recognized that sitting over a cognac with their father-in-law was a family obligation.

"Of course, Lord Duncan," Max said. "Punch is a trifle cloying, I agree."

"But the ladies like it," his lordship said with a genial smile.

"Father, not all women have a sweet tooth," Constance protested.

Her father regarded her. "You are an exception to the rule, Constance."

"I, on the other hand, am not," Chastity said cheerfully. "I'm off to bed. Good night all."

Max held up an arresting hand. "Before you go, Chastity, Gideon and I would like to talk to the three of you in the morning . . . before breakfast, if possible."

"Oh, surprises," crowed Prudence. "Is this to do with what you've been whispering about for weeks?"

"It might be," her husband said mysteriously. The effect was somewhat lost when he winked at his brother-in-law. "Would eight o'clock be a good time?"

Prudence wrinkled her nose. "I wish you didn't have this predilection for early rising,

Gideon. It's gone one in the morning now."

"Sarah will be up," he reminded her.

"Yes, I know," she said. "Tomorrow's different. We were always up at crack of dawn on Christmas morning when we were children. I was talking more generally. We have a stocking for Sarah that has to go on the end of her bed so that she has something to open as soon as she wakes. Shall I take it in, or will you?"

"That's a Duncan tradition, not a Malvern one," Gideon said, reaching out a hand to draw her against him for a moment. "It's for you to do."

She turned her face up and smiled at him. "I didn't think you'd mind, but some people are funny about family traditions."

"Not when it comes to Duncan family traditions," Max said. "What goes into these stockings?"

"Wait and see," Constance said. "You don't know what you'll find at the end of *your* bed."

Chastity felt suddenly bereft. This light loving banter, the sharing of her family traditions . . . she wanted to be part of it too. "Good night," she said brightly. "I'll see you all in the morning, then."

"Wait, Chas." Prudence moved away from Gideon's arm and came quickly towards her sister. "We'll go up together. The men are going to drink cognac but I'm not sleepy — are you, Con?"

"Not in the least," Constance said. "And there are a few things we need to talk about . . . arrangements for tomorrow and suchlike," she added vaguely, linking arms with her baby sister.

Chastity made no objection. She knew they knew how she was feeling. "If we're going to play silly games tomorrow, we should organize them a little," she said. "Otherwise there'll be chaos."

"There'll be chaos anyway," Prudence said blithely as they climbed the stairs. "No one will be clearheaded enough after lunch to read a playing card straight."

"Just as long as we steer Father clear of the bridge table," Constance said as they went into Chastity's room. "I'm not playing cutthroat bridge with Max if I don't have all my wits about me."

"What do you think this surprise is?" Chastity asked, falling onto the bed.

"No idea," Prudence said with an expressive shrug. "They've been whispering for weeks, but it's something for all three of us, that much we do know."

"Intriguing." Constance yawned, dropping into the chair by the dying fire.

"I thought you weren't sleepy," Chastity said.

"I wasn't downstairs, but now I am. By the way, I managed to drop the subject of straitened circumstances into the doctor's shell-like ear."

"So did I," Prudence said with a chuckle. "He looked totally dumbfounded."

"Well, it is a bit of a strange confidence, coming out of the blue like that," Chastity pointed out. "But I think it probably worked." She told them of her exchange with Douglas. "So, we're back to being just friends again," she finished. "Which is something of a relief."

Her sisters made no comment. Then Constance said, "This isn't supposed to be a sequitur, but I'm getting the feeling we might be running into difficulties with our plan to unite the doctor with the Della Luca. Sorry to bring this up now." She yawned again. "But have you seen the way he looks at her sometimes?"

"She is a pill," Prudence said from the dresser stool, where she'd alighted. "And I don't think her pillness is washing over him. Sorry, Chas. I know you thought it would, but I honestly think, whatever his needs, he's not going to sell his soul to that particular devil."

"Devil's a little strong," Chastity protested.

"No," Prudence said. "They come in all varieties. You didn't hear what she said to Mary."

They talked a little more and then her sisters left Chastity to get to bed. She had a feeling they were right about matchmaking Laura and Douglas. Laura showed every sign of embracing the prospect eagerly, but Douglas was a different matter. As she knew full well now, he *did* have finer feelings, and a boring pedant with hostile opinions about the underprivileged was going to offend them at every turn. It was only a matter of time, she thought, before he realized that.

It was such a nuisance. Now she would need to find someone else for him. Oh, and they would have to find someone else for Laura since none of them could be condemned to too many close encounters with such a step-relation.

Chastity yawned deeply as she pulled her nightgown over her head and reached for her dressing gown. For some reason she felt as if this entire burden rested on her shoulders. It didn't, of course, but her sisters had other concerns, personal concerns that had to take priority on a family occasion. They were not supposed to be working over Christmas, even if Chastity felt that she was. And now she was just feeling sorry for herself. She shook her head in self-reproach and went off to the bathroom that she had always shared with her sisters . . . and now, of course, also with their husbands.

She locked the door behind her, something she would never have done in the past, because no one, apart from the upstairs maid in the morning, came in there except her sisters. Shaving soap and razors on the washstand made it very clear that things had changed.

Her body felt taut as a bowstring, as if she had been holding herself rigid for hours . . . or holding something at bay for hours. And, of course, all evening she had been doing just that — holding emotion and impulse at bay as if they were a pack of ravening wolves. She contemplated running a bath to relax herself and then decided it would take too long and she was too bone-tired. Hester and David's wedding seemed to have happened a week ago rather than that morning. Or rather yesterday morning, she thought through a mighty yawn. She washed her face and cleaned her teeth then unlocked the door and went out into the now-darkened corridor.

The house was quiet, the gas lamps extinguished, the only light coming from the star-filled window at the end of the corridor. She trod softly past her sisters' bedroom doors and had just lifted the latch of her own when she felt someone behind her.

She turned with a gasp and a bitten-off cry. "What the devil are you doing?" she demanded fiercely, as her fast-beating heart slowed.

"I was looking for another bathroom," Douglas said. "Someone was in the one close to my room." He was still dressed, although he'd discarded his coat, waistcoat, and white tie and wore only shirt and trousers. Chastity noticed that his feet were bare, which was probably why she hadn't heard his approach.

"Oh," Chastity said. "There's one just down there." She pointed towards the door from which she'd just emerged.

"Ah . . . right," he said, but he didn't move. They both seemed rooted to the spot. Chastity's hand was still on the lifted latch of her door and as she held it the door swung slowly open. *An escape route, or an invitation?* She had no idea.

A glow of firelight and the soft flicker of a candle illuminated her as she stood in the doorway. Douglas looked down at her and heard himself swallow in the taut silence. Her dressing gown hung open, revealing the thin folds of her white nightgown, her unbound, well-brushed hair framed her face in a dark red cloud. Her hazel eyes glowed huge in the ivory complexion, little flickers of golden fire in their depths. Her lips were slightly parted as if she would say something but didn't know what.

He reached out and touched the curve of her cheek with the back of his hand as he had done once before. And once again the intimacy of the gesture sent shock waves to the soles of her bare feet. "Oh, dear Chastity," he said softly. "This isn't going to work, is it?"

She moistened her lips with the tip of her tongue, overwhelmingly conscious of his physical presence, of the touch on her cheek, of the dark eyes filled with passion resting upon her upturned face. "No," she said, taking a step back through the open door. "It isn't."

He followed her, closing the door gently behind him. Without looking, he turned the key in the lock. Then he came towards her.

Chastity stood transfixed. She couldn't possibly withstand this juggernaut — not the juggernaut of Douglas Farrell but the whole massive and magnificent avalanche of her own desire. And she didn't want to. She thought fleetingly of her sisters, of how they had succumbed to this same overwhelming passion against all reason and logic. Why shouldn't she? Just this once experience what they had?

Douglas reached her. He towered above her, and the intensity of his physical presence turned her knees to butter and sent a jolt through her loins. "Sweetheart, I want you so much," he said, the soft lilting burr in his voice suddenly more pronounced.

"I want you too," she whispered. "So very much."

He slipped his hands beneath the open dressing gown and cupped her shoulders as he drew her towards him. The instant before she closed her eyes she watched his mouth coming closer, the deep fire in his eyes now filling his intent gaze. He smelled of soap and his cheeks were smooth without the rough stubble of earlier. But his mouth was the same, strong yet pliant. She kept very still, concentrating on the sensation. Now that the decision had been made — had made itself — there was no longer any hurry, any need to do anything but enjoy the inexorable building of desire.

Without taking his lips from hers, he changed his grip on her shoulders and the dressing gown slipped to the floor. He ran his hands down her arms to her wrists. He put his hands over the backs of hers, enclosing her hands and holding them at her sides. He took a half step closer so that her body was brought against his.

She could feel his heart beat against her breast and her nipples peaked beneath the thin cotton of her gown. She used her tongue, pushing at his closed lips, and for a second he playfully resisted, then his lips parted and she pushed within his mouth, curling her tongue over his. He still held her hands at her sides and without them Chastity was yet more powerfully aware of the rest of her body as it pressed against his, of the pulsing in her belly, the growing moistness of her loins, the quiver in her thighs. Her feet were bare and her toes curled into the rug, then she rose on tiptoe, reaching to deepen the kiss, to explore his mouth, his cheeks, his teeth, the soft palate.

At last she drew back, letting her heels drop to the floor, tilting her head backwards so that she could look up at him. He smiled at her, a warm, slow smile that seemed to drink her in. "Who were we trying to fool?" he asked, tracing her lips with his fingertip.

"Ourselves," she said, her tongue darting to moisten the fingertip.

"Never a good idea," he said. He ran his hands up her arms to her shoulders again and then lightly clasped her throat, pushing up her chin with his thumbs. "You do the strangest things to me, Chastity Duncan." Then he kissed her again, his mouth hard on hers, his tongue insistent and muscular as he explored her mouth as she had explored his. His hands moved from her neck and slid down her back, pulling her hard against him so that she could feel the powerful jut of his arousal against her belly. He gripped her backside, kneading the firm roundness, finding the little indentations at the base of her spine.

Chastity ran her own hands down his back, grasped his buttocks with a soft exhalation that could almost have been a moan. His backside was as hard and muscular as the rest of him. She moved one hand between their bodies and rubbed the bulge of his penis, hearing and delighting in his own swiftly indrawn breath. She fumbled for the buttons at his waist and he drew back a little to give her more room, although his mouth never left hers. The buttons flew apart as her fingers moved deftly and then she slid her hand into the opening and felt his warmth, the pulse of his penis beneath the thin wool of his drawers.

Douglas began to pull up her nightgown, hand over hand until it was bunched at her waist. He clasped her bottom, ran his hands down the backs of her thighs, and she rose up on tiptoe again in involuntary reaction to the intimate touch.

His mouth left hers. "Lift up your arms," he said softly, and she obeyed, raising her arms as he pulled the nightgown over her head, tossing it hastily to the floor. He stood back, taking her hands, holding her arms away from her body, gazing at her hungrily. "Lovely," he murmured. "Quite lovely."

Chastity shivered with pleasure at the compliment, but also with a surge of sensual delight as the air touched her skin, bringing her to full and vibrant consciousness of her nakedness. She felt his gaze touch every inch of her, lingering on the swell of her breasts, the dark peaking tips, sweeping over the slight roundness of her belly, pausing long on the tangle of red curls at the apex of her thighs, then moving down the length of her thighs, holding for a second on her knees, as if there was something special about them, before continuing to her feet. She felt as if she'd been painted with his eyes.

"Turn around," he said softly, releasing her hands as she did so. She couldn't see his gaze now, but she could still feel it, almost palpably hot on her back, her bottom, the backs of her thighs, the hollows behind her knees.

"You are magnificent, Chastity," he said, stepping up behind her, placing his hands on her hips. She could feel the softness of his shirt against her back, the silkiness of his opened trousers, the hot throb of his penis against her backside. He moved his hands around her body, stroked her belly, dipped a finger into her naval, slid down to cup the mound at the base of her belly, his fingers working through the fine silky bush to the warm damp flesh beneath.

She leaned back against him, parting her legs for his further exploration, her breath coming swiftly now, a light dew misting her skin. And when she had scaled the glorious heights of sensation her knees buckled and she fell forward onto the bed, breathless.

He leaned over her, kissing the nape of her neck, tracing the line of her spine with his tongue, until she groaned in soft protest and rolled over, reaching up a hand to caress his face. "That's enough selflessness," she said with a weak smile. "Take your clothes off, Dr. Farrell."

He laughed softly and threw off his clothes

with rough haste, heedless of where they landed, then he came down to the bed with her, kneeling above her so that her hands could have free rein to make their own exploration. She stroked and kissed and nuzzled, reveling in his soft moans of delight, and when finally he leaned over, grasping her hands palm against palm, holding them above her head on the bed, she raised her hips, her legs clasping tightly around his waist, her heels pressing into his buttocks, and took him inside her.

Chastity had made love once before in her life and it had been nothing like this. This delicious sensation of flesh on flesh, of the swelling, throbbing presence within her, each rhythmic thrust driving him against her womb. Pleasure grew in an ever-tightening spiral. Her nails raked his back, his buttocks, twisted in the dusting of curling hair on the backs of his thighs as she matched his rhythm. His eyes never left her face, watching every fleeting expression, and she kept her own gaze locked with his until the world burst apart and she didn't know whether she was drowning or flying.

When she finally came to herself, Douglas was lying beside her, one hand on her damp belly, his chest heaving, his eyes closed. "Sweet Jesus," he murmured. "We are a fit made in heaven."

Chastity tried to laugh but she couldn't summon the strength. She turned on her side, burying her head in the hollow of his shoulder, and fell instantly asleep.

Douglas reached down to pull the disarranged covers over them both, tried to turn down the gas lamp, couldn't quite reach it without disturbing her, and with a mental shrug closed his own eyes.

A wintry light was falling across the bed when Chastity awoke, groggy and disoriented. She lay still, for a moment wondering what strange pillow her head had found. Her thoughts cleared slowly and she raised her head to look down at Douglas, who still slept. He had enviably long eyelashes, she thought, studying the rich black half-moons on his cheekbones. His eyebrows almost met across the bridge of his Roman nose. She resisted the urge to trace the calm relaxed line of his well-sculpted mouth with a fingertip. She didn't want to wake him, there was something wonderfully peaceful about his quiet rhythmic breathing, the warm sense and scent of him in the tumbled bedclothes.

She lay down again, gazing upwards at the beamed ceiling. Last night she and her sisters had decided, however reluctantly, that Douglas Farrell and Laura Della Luca were never going to make a match, so, without another prospect in mind, she hadn't really thrown a spanner in the Go-Between's works by last night's little episode. *Not so little,* she reflected with a rather smug grin. There had been nothing little about her own orgasmic experience. Losing her virginity had been an unremarkable experience — gentle enough, not traumatic, but unspectacular, no earthquakes to speak of. Last night, however . . .

Chastity hugged herself and stifled a chuckle. Beside her, Douglas slept on. At least she thought he did, but his hands were moving. She lay very still, holding her breath, as his fingers tiptoed across her belly. She felt something hard and growing nudge her thigh and her smile deepened. Slowly she turned on her side to face him, throwing one leg across his hip.

His eyes were still closed on the pillow beside her, but everything else about him was wide-awake. He slid inside her, a hand on her hip pulling her against his body. They moved gently in harmony, none of the explosive fireworks of the night, but a simpler and infinitely sweet melody. She felt a deep sense of loss when he pulled out of her the instant before they both reached their peak, but her orgasm was already rolling over her and the loss was quickly a mere shadow.

"Good morning," Douglas said, curling her into his embrace, his lips brushing through her hair while his hand cupped her breast.

"Good morning," Chastity said, then froze as the door latch rattled. Douglas lay stone-still beside her.

"Chas?" It was Constance. "We promised to meet with Gideon and Max at eight. It's five to."

"Oh," Chastity called, her voice rather muffled. "Yes, sorry. I forgot. I'll be there in ten minutes."

"Why's the door locked, Chas?" Prudence asked. The latch rattled again.

"Is it?" Chastity asked, at a loss.

There was a short silence, a soft murmur beyond the door, then Constance said, "Good morning, Dr. Farrell."

"Merry Christmas, Dr. Farrell," said Prudence sweetly.

Douglas lay on his back with his arm across his eyes and made no reply. Chastity said, "I'll be down in ten minutes."

"Oh, take your time . . . take your time," Constance advised, a laugh now clear in her voice. "I'm sure there's nothing that can't wait on . . . on . . . Well, take your time."

"Yes," Prudence assured. "Take your time." The sound of their receding footsteps came through the door.

Chastity went into a peal of laughter, falling back against the pillow. Douglas kept his arm over his eyes for a minute. Then he sat up and looked down at her. "God help me," he declared. "God help *any* man with more than a nodding acquaintance with the Duncan sisters."

"Oh, that's so harsh," Chastity protested.

He shook his head vigorously. "Oh, no, it's not. I just wonder where this instability — this outrageous unconformity — came from. Your father seems perfectly sane, perfectly normal." He shook his head again. "It must have been your mother's responsibility."

Chastity grabbed a pillow and hit him with it.

"Oh, you want to play, do you?" he said, laughing. "I should warn you, Miss Duncan, that engaging in physical combat with me is a grave error. I've bested men three times your size."

"Oh, have you?" She wriggled off the bed, still clutching the pillow. "And I should warn you, Dr. Farrell, that I have never lost a pillow fight."

She stood there, naked, feet braced, the pillow grasped between both hands, her red curls flying around her face, her hazel eyes shooting golden flames.

"I venture to guess you never went to boarding school," Douglas said, grabbing up a pillow of his own. "If your only combatants have been your sisters, dear girl, you are about to find yourself hopelessly outclassed." He jumped off the bed, pillow flying.

Chastity did her best, but it was a completely unequal battle, and finally she fell back on the bed, gasping for breath, as he reared above her, holding her hands captive high above her head. "You're so big," she complained. "I should have been given a handicap."

"I would never have expected a Duncan sister to demand a handicap," Douglas said, kissing the tip of her nose.

"It depends on the arena," Chastity said with a failed attempt at dignity. "Oh, dear, Douglas, I have to go downstairs, and look what you've started." Her voice was almost a wail.

"Me?" he protested. "*I* didn't start anything. You threw down the glove."

She smiled and pulled at her captive hands. "I suppose I did. But truly, I have to go downstairs, and I can't go down looking like this."

He released her with a resigned sigh. "Entrancing spectacle though it is." His hand stroked over her belly. "This I love," he said thoughtfully. "This little roundness is so utterly delightful."

"I eat too many cakes," Chastity said, pushing his hand away and sitting up. "Go away now and let me get dressed."

He dipped his head and kissed her, then scrambled into his clothes, unlocked the door, and slid out.

Chapter 14

Chastity searched for her dressing gown amid the general tumble of bedclothes. Somehow it had found its way under the bed, together with her nightgown. She shook out the garments and put them on, reflecting that since it was already twenty past eight she didn't have time to dress, and since it was Christmas morning, a little dishabille was perfectly acceptable.

She took up her hairbrush and tugged it through the impossible red tangle. Her complexion had a pinkish glow as if she'd been exercising vigorously in the fresh air and her eyes were very bright. Sex, she decided, was obviously very good for one's looks. The observation made her chuckle with a certain degree of smugness and the mischievous reflection that if her sisters had enjoyed themselves similarly last night, for once she wouldn't feel the odd one out. She searched for slippers in the wardrobe and hurried from the room.

"Merry Christmas, Aunt Chas." Sarah, still in her nightgown, breathless, wreathed in smiles, tousled from sleep and excitement, bounded down the stairs from the top floor that housed the nursery and schoolroom as Chastity reached the landing.

"I had a stocking on my bed!" The girl flourished the woolen stocking. "It had an orange in it, and a rubber ball, and a pencil case, and a complete set of colored pencils, and a hair ribbon, and a set of hair clips shaped like butterflies and dragonflies in all sorts of pretty colors. See, aren't they lovely?"

She rummaged in the stocking for these treasures and Chastity patiently admired them as they were produced, managing to give the impression that she'd never seen them before and the idea of a stuffed stocking at the foot of the bed on Christmas morning was as magnificent a surprise as Sarah had found it.

"Have you been downstairs yet?" she asked Sarah, taking a step towards the stairs.

"No, I'm not dressed," the girl said.

Chastity laughed. "Neither am I, but some rules don't apply on Christmas morning. Go down and see the tree."

Sarah bounced ahead of her down the sweep of staircase and then stopped on the bottom. "My goodness, I've never seen so many presents." The base of the Christmas tree was obscured by piles of wrapped parcels.

"They're for the servants too," Chastity said, watching Sarah's wide-eyed delight with pleasure. It was almost as good as experiencing the wonder for the first time herself.

"Can I go closer?"

"Yes, but no peeking."

Sarah looked shocked. "I wouldn't do that, Aunt Chas. I wouldn't spoil a surprise."

"No, of course you wouldn't," Chastity agreed, and left the girl on her knees gazing awestruck at the treasure while she went in search of her sisters and their husbands.

She ran them to ground in a small family parlor at the rear of the house. A fire burned in the grate and the gas lamps were lit. The clear night had given way to a cold gray overcast that promised snow.

"Merry Christmas," she greeted them, doing the rounds for hugs and kisses. "You all look remarkably tidy — you'll have to forgive my disarray."

"I expect you didn't get much sleep," Constance murmured with a wicked tilt to her mouth and Chastity, to her annoyance, felt herself blush.

She chose not to respond but noticed how Max and Gideon were studiously avoiding catching each other's eye. Obviously Constance and Prudence had shared their explanation for their sister's locked door. Of course, she should have expected them to, and she didn't see much point in denying anything anyway.

"Sarah seems over the moon," she observed casually, going to the table to pour herself a cup of tea.

"Yes, she's never had a Christmas like it," Gideon said with a fond and yet slightly rueful smile. "It seems a shame that an eleven-year-old should never have experienced it before."

"Not if you think that if she had, by now she would be jaded by it all," Prudence pointed out.

"Yes, it would be one big yawn," Chastity said. "She'd consider herself far too old to be entranced by the magic."

"Perhaps you're right." But Gideon didn't sound totally convinced.

"Anyway," Constance said, steering the conversation into happier paths, "what are we all doing in here at this early hour?"

"Not so early," her husband corrected mildly.

"No, that's my fault," Chastity said, sipping her tea. "But what is all the mystery?"

"Ah," Max said. "Ah, that."

"Yes, that," his wife said with amused exasperation. "Come on, spit it out."

"What an inelegant expression," Max murmured, pained.

The three Duncan sisters as one folded

their arms and surveyed the two men, three pairs of variegated green eyes fixed upon them with unwavering concentration, until Max threw up his hands. "I yield. Gideon, the floor is yours."

Gideon turned to the desk that stood in the corner and took up a thick envelope. He lifted the flap and drew out a sheaf of papers. "One for you, Prudence; one for Constance; one for Chastity." He handed them each a document, then went to stand beside his brother-in-law. Both men watched the women.

The sisters read the documents they held, then all three looked up in frowning puzzlement. "What is it?" Constance asked.

"Shoe Lane?" Prudence said, obviously bewildered. "What is it, Gideon?"

Chastity said slowly, "It looks like a lease."

"Precisely," Gideon said, winking at Max. "That's exactly what it is."

"But a lease for what?" Prudence demanded.

"A property in Shoe Lane just off Fleet Street."

"But why?" asked Chastity. "What's it for?"

"You're being a remarkably obtuse trio this morning," Gideon said. "Isn't it obvious?"

"No, it's not," Prudence declared.

Max laughed. "Never did I think to see the day when the Duncan sisters were rendered speechless with bewilderment."

"No, wait a minute," Prudence said, holding up a hand. "Fleet Street . . . newspapers . . ."

"You're getting there," her husband said. "Follow that train of thought."

"Newspaper offices," Constance said.

"*The Mayfair Lady*," Chastity said. She tapped the lease with a finger. "This is the lease on an office space, isn't it?"

"Indeed it is," Gideon said, both he and Max now smiling broadly. "We decided it was time the broadsheet had official business premises, particularly since you're not all living under the same roof anymore."

The sisters exhaled in unison as they absorbed this. "Our own office," Chastity murmured.

"We wouldn't want the name on the door," Prudence said thoughtfully. "We've still got to be anonymous. We wouldn't want people just turning up there with advertisements they wanted to place, or anything for the Go-Between."

"No, I imagine you'll keep the poste restante," Gideon said. "But there is a telephone in the office. There's nothing to stop you putting the number into the broadsheet. It'll speed up business."

"Yes, it will," Constance said. "And of course no one we know would ever be seen dead in that part of London, so we can come and go quite safely."

"Exactly," Max said. "You'll find three desks, three chairs, three typewriters, two filing cabinets, and a telephone there."

"Typewriters?" his wife queried. "But we don't know how to type, none of us does."

"Then I imagine you'll learn," her husband said.

"Yes, of course we will," Chastity agreed, her eyes shining. "Think how much quicker it will be, and so much easier for the printer to read."

"So, you're pleased?" Gideon said, somewhat unsure as to their true reaction.

"Oh, yes, absolutely thrilled," Prudence said, flinging her arms around his neck. "Just dumbfounded for a moment."

"Yes, it's so much to take in," Constance said. "But it's wonderful. Thank you both."

The two men somewhat complacently accepted the triple dose of hugs and kisses that enveloped them but within a few minutes the sisters were huddled in front of the fire in deep discussion about the ramifications of this Christmas present and Max and Gideon left them to it and went in search of breakfast.

It was half an hour later when the door opened and Lord Duncan came into the parlor. "I was wondering where you'd all disappeared to," he said. "We do have a house full of guests, in case you've forgotten."

"No, we haven't forgotten, Father, it's just that Gideon and Max have given us this amazing Christmas present and we're trying to decide what it's going to mean," Chastity said, setting down her teacup.

"Oh? What is it?"

"I'm not sure you'll approve," Constance said with a smile. "Maybe you'd rather not know."

"Nonsense," he declared, clasping his hands at his back. "Out with it."

Prudence explained, and Lord Duncan shook his head and harrumphed a little at the end, then said, "Well, what's done is done, I suppose. They're grown men, and if they want to support their wives in their madness then that's their business." He turned back to the door. "Perhaps you could come out now and start organizing this shambles of a morning."

"It's not a shambles, Father," Chastity protested, standing up, stretching, and yawning. "It's only just breakfast time."

"And you're still in your nightclothes," her father pointed out somewhat tartly. "And your stepdaughter, Prudence, is looking extremely anxious to begin the festivities."

"We're coming right now," Prudence said soothingly. "And Chas is going to get dressed, aren't you, Chas?"

"At once," her younger sister agreed. "I'll be down in half an hour."

Lord Duncan gave another harrumph and marched out, leaving his daughters laughing ruefully. "He certainly seems to be taking his hostly duties very seriously," Chastity observed.

"Oh, that's the contessa's doing," Constance said. "He never worried before about house parties, he was always quite happy to leave the details up to us and the social duties to the aunts."

"Well, I'd better dress before he gets any more agitated," Chastity said, going to the door.

"We haven't talked about what happened last night," Prudence said. "Should we, Chas?"

Chastity sat down abruptly on the arm of a sofa, swinging one slippered foot. "He knows I don't have any money," she said, speaking the thoughts that had somehow populated her sleep even though she hadn't been aware of them. "So he's not going to be looking for anything more than a short, passionate dalliance. I can surely allow myself that Christmas present, don't you think?"

"Are you sure it won't get more complicated?" Constance asked directly.

Chastity sucked on her bottom lip, reflecting with as much clear sight as she could muster. "It can't," she said after a minute. "I couldn't possibly let him know I was the pseudo French woman in the National Gallery . . . he can't possibly know that we three are the Go-Between. He'd be so humiliated, he'd never forgive me. So, I'll just take this Christmas passion as a present from the gods and when we get back to London we'll find him another bride. Last night wouldn't have happened if he was considering Laura as a prospective bride — he's not the type to engage in any out-of-court dalliance if he's seriously courting."

"Are you certain?" It was Prudence who asked, watching her sister with narrowed eyes.

"Yes," Chastity said, and her sisters could almost detect a sigh in her voice. "He's a straight arrow. He knows what he wants and he goes out and gets it. He's not ashamed of what he does or what he needs to achieve in order to go on doing it. But I saw him at work."

She looked up at her sisters, both sadness and conviction in her eyes. "A man with that kind of selfless devotion wouldn't cheat." She dropped her gaze to her swinging foot again, catching the sliding slipper on her toes. "And I'm certain he would consider that I had cheated him with this deception. So, he must never know. And so, it can never become complicated. We'll have a short and sweet liaison." She slid off the sofa arm and gave them a cheery wave as she went out.

Constance raised an eyebrow as the door closed behind her youngest sister. "The lady doth protest too much . . ."

"Methinks," Prudence agreed. "If Chas has fallen hard for Douglas, she's going to be hurt, however much she pretends that it's just another one of her light flirtations."

"Chas doesn't sleep with her light flirtations," Constance observed. "We can't do anything at the moment, but maybe when we're back in London . . ."

"We'll see," Prudence said. "I'd better go and find Gideon and Sarah. We're going to church with Sarah and Mary this morning, although a double dose of Dennis's Christmas sermon seems a bit excessive. Are you and Max coming?"

"I don't think Max will be particularly enthusiastic. He's not what he calls a God-botherer," Constance said with a laugh. "One Christmas service is probably enough."

Chastity opened her bedroom door and stopped in surprise. Douglas was sitting in the armchair by the window reading a copy of *The Mayfair Lady*. He stood up, smiling as she came in.

"I was waiting for you," he said. "I thought you'd have to come in here sooner or later." He set down the broadsheet and crossed the small room, his hands extended. He took hers in both of his, his clasp warm and tight. He bent and lightly kissed her mouth. "Am I intruding?"

She shook her head. "No, but I wasn't expecting to find anyone in here."

"You've been closeted with your sisters for a very long time," he said as if in explanation for his presence, releasing his hold on her hands.

"Yes, I know." Chastity indicated her night attire with a sweeping downward gesture. "I'm still not dressed. Gideon and Max had a Christmas present for us all and it took us a long time to absorb it." Her eyes darted involuntarily to the copy of *The Mayfair Lady* that Douglas had discarded.

He followed her eyes and said, "You seem to be a devoted reader of this paper. I'm always finding it lying around your rooms."

"Oh, well, as I told you, it has a special relevance for us," she said, seizing the opportunity to fertilize the seed her sisters had sown. "My father lost most of his fortune to the man who sued *The Mayfair Lady* for libel. He didn't get his fortune back, of course, but there was some satisfaction in seeing the earl proved a fraud." She opened the door of her armoire. "There's no family money any longer, but we muddle through."

"I'm not sure Lord Duncan's financial situation is any concern of mine," Douglas said.

"Oh, it's public knowledge," Chastity said carelessly, her voice muffled as she riffled through the garments in the armoire. "We have no secrets." She closed her eyes on the lie and burrowed deeper into the wardrobe.

"Well, that's as it may be," he said. "Could you come out of there, because I did have a reason for lying in wait."

Chastity backed out of the armoire, aware that her cheeks were rather flushed. Douglas turned aside to the chair and picked up a prettily wrapped package. "I wanted to give you my Christmas present privately." He held it out to her, a slightly anxious smile on his face and in his dark eyes.

"Oh," she said, taking the parcel, turning it over in her hands. "But I don't have anything special for you. We just bought little things to put under the tree for everyone."

"It doesn't require reciprocation," he said gently. "Open it."

Chastity fumbled with the ribbons and then unwrapped the paper. "Oh," she said again. "Oh, Douglas, it's beautiful." She shook out the folds of the scarf. The amber beads fell to the floor as she did so. Douglas bent to pick them up.

"They're lovely, perfect," she said in delight as he held them up. "And they match the scarf. How clever of you." She reached up her arms to circle his neck and kissed him. "I feel so bad that I don't have anything for you."

"You're not to feel bad," he said with a frown. "It's enough for me to know that they please you. You'll spoil my pleasure in the giving if you start fretting about exact exchanges."

She nodded, accepting that he was right, and kissed him again. "I'll wear them today. I have just the right dress for them."

"Show me." He went to the wardrobe that still stood open.

"What do you know about women's clothes?" she said, teasing.

"With six sisters, a great deal," he assured, flicking through the garments hanging from the clothes rail. "Now, let me see . . ."

"I tell you what," she said, laughing, "I shall go and have my bath and you can choose my clothes."

"All right," he said from the depths of the wardrobe. "Go and do that. If you leave the door unlocked, I'll come in in a minute and wash your back."

"I don't think that would be a good idea," Chastity said, heading for the door. "We'll never get downstairs, and I have guests awaiting."

"Oh, very well." Douglas gave an exaggerated sigh. "I'll just have to contain myself, I suppose."

"Continence," Chastity said. "That's what it's called."

"Continence and chastity," he said, glancing at her over his shoulder, holding a handful of corn-colored silk up to the light.

She laughed, and left him before temptation got the better of her.

She took her bath quickly and when she returned to her bedroom she found it empty. She had to quash a flash of disappointment. The corn-colored silk dress lay on the bed, the scarf draped artfully across it, the amber beads lying on top. She had to admit that it was a perfect combination. Dr. Farrell did indeed have an eye.

Dressed finally, Chastity hurried downstairs. The church party had already left and the breakfast table had been cleared, so she made her way to the kitchen, where Mrs. Hudson presided over bubbling pots, roasting geese, and steaming Christmas puddings.

"Merry Christmas, Mrs. Hudson. Anything I can do?" Chastity asked as she cut herself a piece of bread and fetched butter and marmalade from the pantry.

"No, nothing, Miss Chas," the housekeeper said placidly. "Everything's well in hand. Luncheon will be on the table at one o'clock."

"Wonderful. I haven't seen Jenkins this morning." Chastity spread butter and marmalade lavishly. "I wanted to ask him what time he wanted to do the present-giving tomorrow."

"He's in his pantry with the silver," Mrs. Hudson informed her, her hands plunged deep into a bowl of sage-and-onion stuffing.

Chastity nodded, her mouth full of bread

and marmalade, and made her way to the butler's pantry, where Jenkins sat in a baize apron, polishing the silver cutlery. "Shouldn't someone else be doing that, Jenkins?" Chastity asked.

"Indeed not, Miss Chas. The silver is my duty," Jenkins said, sounding quite horrified. "I wouldn't trust anyone else near it."

Chastity smiled and made no further demur. She asked her question, received her answer, and returned to the main part of the house. She wandered through the various public rooms, looking for people. There was an air of suspended animation, as if the very house walls were taking a breath, waiting for something to start. The candles on the tree were all lit, fires blazed in the inglenook in the hall, in the drawing room and the library, but she couldn't find anyone. She knew Prudence and her family were gone to church and probably the aunts had accompanied them, but there was no sign of her father, Max, Constance, either of the Della Lucas, and most particularly she noticed the conspicuous absence of Douglas Farrell.

"It's startin' to snow, Miss Chas," Madge said, emerging from the kitchen regions with a scuttle of coal. "A white Christmas good an' proper."

Chastity hurried to the front door and opened it, letting in a blast of icy air. She pulled the door closed behind her and stood on the top step, arms folded tightly across her chest, looking up at the leaden sky, where thick white flakes were falling silently. There was no birdsong, no sound of anything as the ground slowly disappeared under a virgin layer of white.

Then she heard voices, her father's deep baritone, the contessa's light, pleasant tones interspersed with Laura's thin trill. The group came around the corner of the house, hurrying through the snow, and Douglas walked a few paces behind them. He looked somewhat disgruntled, Chastity thought, until he looked up from his studious observation of his feet and saw her standing there.

He quickened his step, passing the others as he strode to the front door. "My dear girl, you'll catch your death," he said. "You don't even have a coat on. Get inside." He took her elbow, propelling her back into the warmth of the hall.

"I have my scarf," she said, fingering the delicate material. "It's big enough to be a shawl."

"It's not intended as an outdoor garment," he chided, then smiled. "But it really does suit you."

"Yes," she said, bathed in the warmth of that smile, the knowledge of a shared passion. "I know."

"Come in, dear lady, come in," Lord Duncan was saying as he stamped snow off his feet in the doorway. "We should never have gone out. I knew it was going to snow. Let me take your coat. Miss Della Luca, go to the fire, you look chilled to the bone."

Laura did look chilled, her countenance was white and more pinched than usual, and her lips had a bluish tinge to them. "I'm not used to the cold, Lord Duncan," she declared with an exaggerated shiver. "Such a brutal climate this is."

"Positively uncivilized," Chastity agreed. "Come to the fire and I'll fetch you some coffee, or anything else that might warm you."

"Whisky," declared Lord Duncan. "Only thing . . . nothing like it."

Laura's mouth formed a moue of distaste. "Thank you, Lord Duncan, but I don't touch hard spirits."

His lordship looked a little nonplussed at this, and then, dismissing such an oddity, turned to the contessa. "You, dear lady, will take a glass of single malt. I shall fetch it directly. You too, Farrell. I'm sure you could do with one." Without waiting for a response, he hurried off towards the decanters in the library.

"Would you like coffee, Laura?" Chastity asked, feeling sorry for the woman, who really did look chilled and miserable. "Or perhaps some warm milk, or hot cocoa."

"Coffee, thank you," Laura said. She

sighed. "Of course, no one can make coffee like the Italians."

Chastity raised her eyes heavenward and caught the glimmer of a distinctly sardonic smile from Douglas. The rot was clearly setting in. "We do our best, Laura," she said. "I'll ask them to make it extra-strong for you. Why don't you go into the drawing room, it's less draughty than the hall. Douglas, will you escort Laura and the contessa to the drawing room fire? Or do you perhaps have some medicine to keep away a cold?"

"There's nothing that can protect against a cold," Douglas said somewhat brusquely. "But I have medicines in my bag that can ameliorate symptoms. However, I don't believe you've caught cold, Laura. A warm fire and a cup of coffee will do the trick." Douglas, who was suffering from half an hour of Laura's nonstop complaints about the barbarity of the English countryside and English hospitality in general, offered her one arm, gave his other to her mother, and accompanied them to the drawing room.

Constance came down the stairs as Chastity emerged from the kitchen with a tray of coffee. "I went to fetch it myself," Chastity explained. "Everyone's so busy. The kitchen's like something out of Dante. All those steaming pots and spitting fat."

Constance nodded with a comprehending

smile. “That scarf is stunning, Chas. And the beads. I haven’t seen them before.”

“No,” Chastity said, moving towards the drawing room with her tray. “They were a Christmas present.”

“Oh,” Constance said with another comprehending smile. “I wonder who from?”

“Don’t rack your brains too much,” her sister said, and went into the drawing room. “Coffee, Laura. I made it myself, so I hope it’s to your liking.” She set the tray on a low table. “Do you like sugar? I’m sure it helps to keep the cold out.”

“Just one lump,” the lady said from an armchair drawn so close to the fire, she was almost sitting on the fender. “And the barest tinge of cream.”

Chastity poured the coffee and handed it to her. “Douglas, would you prefer coffee?”

“No, I’ll wait for the single malt, thank you.”

“Ah, good man, good man,” Lord Duncan declared from the door. He carried a whisky decanter in one hand and held three cut-glass tumblers in the fingers of his other. “Constance, my dear, do you care for whisky?”

His eldest daughter shook her head. “No, thank you, Father. It’s a little early for me and I don’t have the excuse of a walk in the cold. I’ll have coffee.”

The slam of the front door and a rising

crescendo of voices heralded the return of the church party. Sarah bounded into the drawing room ahead of her parents, her cheeks rosy with cold, snowflakes clinging to her hat and scarf. "A white Christmas," she declared, flinging her arms wide to the windows. "Isn't it just perfect? It couldn't possibly be more perfect."

"No, it couldn't," Chastity agreed. "And you know what happens now."

"Presents," Sarah said, unraveling her long scarf from around her neck. "I'm so excited. I don't remember ever being this excited. Have I ever been, Daddy?"

Gideon shook his head gravely. "I don't believe so," he said.

"If luncheon is to be at one o'clock, we should not delay the present-giving," Aunt Agatha said. "Don't you agree, Edith? The servants will want to be getting on to their own festivities."

"Yes, of course, Aunt Agatha, you're quite right," Chastity said, exchanging a meaningful glance with her sisters. The aunts liked to maintain the appearance of being in charge of their widowed brother's household, a fiction the sisters made no attempt to correct.

"Give us five minutes to take off our coats," Prudence said. "We're all snowy."

"It'll take me less than three," Sarah declared, running to the door. "Are you coming, Mary?"

Mary Winston smiled. "I'm on your heels, Sarah."

Prudence followed them, pausing to say to Chastity, "Pretty beads, Chas. And I love the scarf. I haven't seen either of them before."

"No," Chastity said. "I didn't have them before this morning."

Her sister's eyes flicked to Douglas Farrell, standing with his whisky beside the hearth. Her eyebrows lifted a fraction, she inclined her head in the doctor's direction, as if giving him a compliment, and followed her step-daughter and husband from the room.

Chapter 15

"A song title?" Chastity guessed as Sarah produced a creditable imitation of an opera singer. The girl beamed, pointing and nodding vigorously. It was after luncheon and only Sarah seemed to have the energy for this game of charades but most of the adults were doing their best for the girl's sake.

The snow was falling even more thickly than before, adding to the feeling of post-prandial lethargy. The aunts had retired for their afternoon naps. Lord Duncan was snoring gently beside the fire and the contessa herself was nodding off in a discreet fashion in a deep wing chair. Laura sat conspicuously engrossed in her Christmas present from Douglas. Now and again, when the game of charades became noisy, she would look up with a pained expression, give a heavy sigh, and then return to her volume. Everyone else stifled yawns and regrets over the second helping of Christmas pudding and struggled to give an impression of lively interest in charades.

Sarah, wrapped in a white bedsheet and flourishing a toasting fork, was doing her best to convey something, tossing her head in a haughty fashion and pointing a finger commandingly. Her audience leaned forward attentively but blankly and the child's mime became increasingly frantic.

Douglas rose to his feet and went to the sideboard to pour himself a glass of port. He stood against the wall, sipping his port and watching Sarah with a frown. Then he snapped his fingers. " 'Rule Britannia,' " he said to her, and her face split in a wide smile.

"You guessed . . . How did you guess?"

"You're a very good actress," he said with a smile.

"Bravo, Douglas," Chastity said, applauding. "And well done, Sarah." The rest of the assembled company with the exception of the sleepers and Laura joined in the applause, and Sarah beamed and took an exaggerated bow.

"Whose turn is it now?" she asked eagerly.

"I think we need to try something else," her father said through a deep yawn. "I have to do something fairly energetic if I'm not to fall asleep in my chair." He got to his feet and stretched. "I wouldn't mind a walk."

"Not in that," Max said, gesturing to the snow-blanketed window.

"We could play another kind of game," Sarah suggested hopefully.

"I know," Prudence said. "Sardines. That'll wake us up." She ignored her husband's groan of protest.

"How do you play sardines?" Sarah asked.

"Well, we each draw lots and the person who gets the short straw has to go and hide. After ten minutes everyone else looks for him or her. When someone finds the person, they have to hide in the same space with them until finally there's only one person left looking."

"Prudence," Gideon said. "I'm too old for this."

"No, you're not," she denied. "We'll exempt Father and the aunts, and of course the contessa and Laura, but everyone else has to play." She picked up a sheet of paper and tore it into strips. "I'm going to put a cross on one of the pieces, and whoever picks it is *It*. Sarah, pass me that crystal bowl on the sideboard."

Sarah pranced across the room to fetch it and brought it over to her stepmother. Prudence tossed the folded pieces of paper into the bowl and stirred them up with her fingers. "All right, Sarah, you take the bowl around."

"We should establish the ground rules," Constance said. "What parts of the house are off-limits?"

"The servants' quarters, obviously, and the bedrooms of those who aren't playing," Chastity suggested. "And the cellars and the attics."

"That still leaves a pretty wide playing field," Max observed, taking a piece of paper from the bowl that Sarah was presenting.

"That's the point," his wife told him. "We all need exercise, we'll get it by running all over the house."

Douglas took a piece of paper, watching as Chastity took hers. The quick glance she gave it told him that she didn't have the marked piece. He unfolded his own then scrunched it tightly in his palm. "Looks like me," he said, setting down his port glass. "How long do I have?"

"Ten minutes," Chastity said. "And don't hide anywhere too small, there's a lot of us to cram in."

"I'll hide where I please, Miss Duncan," he said. He leaned over her, ostensibly to throw the paper in the wastebasket beside her chair, but managing to murmur into her ear, "In your bathroom linen cupboard if I choose." He straightened, ignoring her sharp inhalation, waved a hand at the assembled company, and hurried away.

In the cavernous hall, he paused, listening to the sounds of music, singing, and unbridled laughter coming from the servants' quarters through the green baize door at the rear of the hall. He strode up the stairs, two at a time, and made straight for the bathroom Chastity had indicated the previous evening.

There was indeed a linen closet, a large one with wide shelves piled high with sheets and towels and enough space for a man, even one as big as he was, to sit on the floor and stretch out his legs. He pulled the door to but not closed, leaned his head against the wall, and waited.

It wasn't long before he heard the hue and cry, voices calling, running feet. And then finally the door to the bathroom eased open with a slight creak. He pushed the closet door a fraction so that he could see through the crack. He smiled a rather wicked smile, reached through the crack, and grabbed Chastity's hand.

"Oh," she gasped as he pulled her into the closet. "I can't believe you would tell me where you were going to hide. You of all people. It's so unsporting." She sat down abruptly as he pulled her on top of his legs.

"Nonsense," he said, running his hands up her back. "If we've got to play this ridiculous game, it seems only reasonable we should amuse ourselves in the process." He kissed the nape of her neck, sending a delicious shiver over her skin. He slid his hands around to cup her breasts, rubbing the nipples until they rose hard beneath the silk of her dress.

He nuzzled her neck, inhaling the fragrance of her warmed skin, then slowly began to inch her dress and petticoat up over her stockinged legs. Chastity held herself very still. She couldn't turn around in the confined space and neither could she use her own hands to return the caresses that slithered up over her thighs, slipped between them, pressing the fine cotton of her drawers into the now-damp hot cleft of her sex.

"Lift up a little," he murmured, taking his hand from her for the moment it took to unbutton the waist of her undergarment. She complied, helping him to push down her knickers so that now she could feel the rough tweed of his trousers against her thighs and backside. He worked his hand beneath her bottom and she bit her lip, trying not to make a sound, barely daring to breathe. If anyone should come into the bathroom, think to look in the closet . . .

She felt the hard thrust of his penis as he released it from his trousers, and raised herself just enough for him to slide deep within her while his fingers continued to play with her. She moved slowly, lifting and lowering herself onto him, hearing his breathing quicken in the dark closet, feeling his breath hot and damp on her neck. Perspiration misted her brow with the effort to keep silent even as the pressure built until it could be contained no longer. He put a hand over her mouth, stifling her cries, and she could taste herself on his fingers. And then it was over and she found that she was laughing silently as the glory of release receded.

She fell back against his chest, too weak for the moment to do anything about her disordered dress or even to worry about discovery. Until the bathroom door opened. She froze and felt Douglas go still as stone beneath her for a second before his hands swiftly rearranged her skirt so that it covered both their legs. Everything would appear perfectly normal to a quick and incurious glance.

The closet door opened.

"You found us, Con," Chastity said obviously. "There's not much room in here."

"No," her eldest sister agreed. "I'll hop up on the shelf above you. It's deep enough and there's just enough headroom if I lie flat." She suited action to words, commenting as she arranged herself, "This is a very inconsiderate hiding place, Douglas."

"Yes, forgive me," he agreed, feeling Chastity's helpless laughter shaking her body. He tapped her hip, trying to get her to raise herself enough so that he could at least pull up her undergarment and fasten his own trousers. She complied, still shaking with silent laughter.

"What are you two doing?" Constance demanded.

"Nothing, it's just rather cramped and I'm stiff," Chastity mumbled as somehow Douglas managed to fasten the waistband of her knickers.

"If you don't want to be found, you shouldn't talk," came Max's voice from the bathroom. He opened the closet and looked in. "Oh, Lord, Farrell, couldn't you have done better than this?"

"Oh, no," Douglas said. "Absolutely not."

Chastity gave up and yielded to a peal of laughter. Max looked down at her, then up at his wife. "Am I missing something here?"

"If you come up and share my shelf, we might find out," Constance said.

"I'll have you know that I'm a Cabinet Minister," Max declared, clambering with great difficulty onto the shelf. "And this is most undignified for a man in my position." His voice was muffled, because his head was almost on his chest as he tried to avoid bumping into the shelf above. His legs dangled down into Chastity's lap.

"Who's left?" Chastity wondered. "Prue and Gideon, of course. And Sarah. Mary's not playing, is she?"

"I hope for her sake she's not," Max grumbled. "And the very next person who comes in here is going to have to hide in the bath."

The bathroom door opened again and Sarah said, "I found you. You left the closet door open."

"That's because there's not enough room in here for all us if we shut it," Chastity explained. "But you're small enough to climb onto the top shelf. Can you do it?"

"Easily," Sarah said confidently. She scrambled over Max and Constance and curled up on the top shelf. "This is fun."

"That rather depends on the length of your legs," Max muttered.

Prudence's arrival a few minutes later was too much for him. "That's it," he declared. "I'm not waiting for Gideon."

"You don't have to, he's here," said Gideon from the doorway. He laughed at the sight of them. "How very inconsiderate of you, Farrell."

"It is called sardines," Chastity protested in Douglas's defense. "The whole point is to be crammed in."

Max jumped down from his shelf, pressing his hands into the small of his back. "Do you have anything for backache in your medical bag of tricks, Farrell?"

"I'd be inclined to prescribe a large whisky," Douglas advised. He was reluctant to move Chastity off him with everyone around since he had only a hazy idea of how well buttoned they both were.

"Help me down, Max." Constance reached out her hands to her husband, who half lifted her off the shelf. He reached up to Sarah, giving her his hands to help her jump down.

"Are you two getting out of there?" Prudence inquired of Chastity and Douglas from the edge of the bath, where she was sitting.

"I'm actually quite comfortable," Chastity said. "Aren't you, Douglas?"

"Oh, yes," he agreed, lying through his teeth. "Perfectly comfortable."

Max peered in at them, then cleared his throat. "Well, we'll leave you in peace, then." He straightened, and made a sweeping gesture towards the door. "Come along, people. Let's go and devise some other devilish game to play."

"Do you think they guessed?" Chastity asked, as the door closed behind the group.

"I'm assuming that's a rhetorical question," Douglas replied, easing her off him. "Let me up, for God's sake, before I lose all feeling in my legs."

"I didn't think it was your legs you were worried about," Chastity said, crawling out of the cupboard. She stood up, hiking her skirt and petticoat up to her waist so that she could refasten her knickers and check her suspenders.

Douglas groaned and turned his back on the entrancing sight while he adjusted his own clothes. "Ready?"

"Ready." Chastity checked her appearance in the mirror, licking a fingertip and smoothing her eyebrows. "I'll bet there are going to be winks and smart remarks when we appear."

"Well, we only have ourselves to blame," he said cheerfully.

"I beg your pardon, Dr. Farrell, we only have *you* to blame," she corrected. "You started it all."

"Oh, yes, so I did," he agreed with an amiable smile. "But don't tell me you didn't enjoy it."

"I wasn't going to," she said, heading for the door.

Douglas didn't immediately follow her. Thoughtfully, he turned towards the mirror above the washbasin and examined his reflection. He looked the same as always, but he *wasn't* the same. In fact, if he thought of how he'd been behaving in the last twenty-four hours, he hardly recognized himself. He wasn't a man who would engage in sex play in a linen cupboard, for God's sake. He was far too serious to indulge in play of any kind . . . far too devoted to his work. His life was well regulated, ran on the tracks he'd carved out for himself many years ago. He didn't give in to passionate impulses, and his instincts for self-preservation were usually sufficiently honed to ensure that he didn't become entangled with utterly unsuitable women. And Chastity Duncan — irreverent, combative, playful, and too clever by half — was about as unsuitable a woman for a man with his needs as any could be. He couldn't afford to be distracted by passion, not in the real world of single-minded devotion to his work, and he knew without a shadow of a doubt that Chastity, once admitted, would be impossible to forget for a minute. She would be as vital and distracting a presence in his mind and imagination as in reality.

He told himself all this but it didn't seem to have any impact or to hold any real meaning for him and after a puzzled moment or two he decided that for now they were inhabiting some alternative universe where the usual rules didn't apply. Just the thought of her brought a smile to his lips, filled him with a deep and satisfying pleasure. Whereas the thought of Laura Della Luca brought merely irritation and an amorphous dislike. Not that he was considering the signorina as a prospective bride any longer. He would not have tumbled into bed with Chastity if that were the case. He hadn't articulated it to himself, but it was true.

So, now what? He shook his head. He didn't know the answer and he seized on the comforting reflection that it wasn't necessary to find one now anyway. He wasn't going anywhere for the next few days, so he might as well explore this new and surprising side to his character that had been so suddenly revealed. He realized that he was smiling at himself in the mirror. A fatuous, utterly self-satisfied smile. God in heaven, he really didn't recognize himself.

* * *

"We won't get the hunt out in this," Lord Duncan declared later that evening. He stood looking out of the drawing room window into the swirling darkness, his hands clasped at his back. "Bloody weather. I beg your pardon, Contessa," he said with an apologetic bow to the lady.

"Don't mention it, Lord Duncan," the contessa said with a wave from the bridge table. "I've heard a lot worse."

"Damnable business, though," his lordship said, turning back to the window. "Boxing Day meet, hunt breakfast, canceling the whole thing . . . damnable."

"Has the Master sent a message to cancel it?" asked Constance, selecting a card from the hand she held.

"Not yet, but he's bound to. Couldn't run the hounds in this, let alone the horses." He returned to the bridge table and took up his cards again. "What's that you put down?"

"The ten of diamonds," his eldest daughter said.

"Oh, you're drawing trumps, are you?" He hemmed and hawed, then with a disgusted sigh threw down the jack of diamonds and watched as his son-in-law laid the queen on top. The contessa discarded a heart.

Constance laughed and gathered up the trick. "Our rubber, I believe, Max."

The front doorbell chimed at the same

time as the great knocker was plied with considerable vigor. "I'll get it," Chastity said. "It'll probably be a message from Lord Berenger."

She got to the front door just as Jenkins, looking rather flushed, his customary dapper appearance a little disordered, emerged from the kitchen regions. "It's all right, Jenkins," she said over her shoulder. "I can manage. Go back to your party."

It was a measure of the butler's generous consumption of Christmas good cheer that he merely bowed a little unsteadily and retreated.

Chastity struggled with the lock and pulled open the door, letting in a blast of wind and a flurry of snow. She greeted the visitor with some surprise. "Merry Christmas, Lord Berenger, we were expecting a message from you, but didn't think you'd brave the storm yourself."

"Oh, just thought I'd pop over with the bad news myself, Chastity. Your father's bound to be disappointed." His lordship, Master of the Hounds, stepped into the hall, stamping his feet vigorously, his normally rosy cheeks reddened by the cold.

"Well, come into the warm," Chastity said, reflecting that George Berenger, a middle-aged widower with no children, had probably had a lonely Christmas.

"Ah, George, come in, come in," Lord

Duncan greeted his neighbor with an expansive gesture. "Whisky, cognac . . . name your poison."

"Whisky, Arthur, thank you." He allowed Chastity to take his coat and scarf and came to the fire, rubbing his cold hands. He took the whisky his host proffered and bowed as introductions were made to the strangers in the company. "Don't let me interrupt your bridge." He gestured to the card table.

"Oh, Max and I have just won the rubber, Lord Berenger," Constance said with ill-disguised complacency. "I doubt Father and the contessa will be eager for another defeat this evening."

"You'll overreach yourself one of these days, mark my words," Lord Duncan declared, shaking a finger at his daughter. He turned back to the visitor. "So, the meet's canceled, eh?"

"Afraid so," Berenger agreed with a sigh.

"Well, never mind." Lord Duncan sounded surprisingly sanguine. "Sit down, dear fellow." He gestured to the sofa where Laura sat, still occupied with her book. Lord Duncan himself sat opposite, next to the contessa, to whom he said, "You weren't going to hunt tomorrow anyway, were you, my dear?"

"No, it's not a sport I particularly enjoy," the contessa said with a smile.

The Duncan sisters exchanged a significant look. It seemed that the contessa's lack of participation in the hunt explained their father's swift recovery from his disappointment.

"Ah, I see you're reading Dante, Miss Della Luca," Lord Berenger said, leaning over to look at the book Laura held. "And in the Italian. I've always considered works lose much of their essential meaning in translation."

"Indeed." Laura looked at him with a somewhat startled interest. "Are you a lover of Italy, my lord?"

"I lived there for three years," he said. "In Florence. I studied at the university there."

Laura's eyes widened. *"Firenze,"* she said. "My home." She laid a hand on her meager breast. "It is a city that lives in the heart once one knows it, don't you agree? You speak Italian, of course."

He responded with a fluent stream of Italian that had Laura nodding and smiling with clear gratification. She interrupted him in the same language, waving her hands about as if she was conducting a full orchestra. Who would have thought George Berenger, a bluff and seemingly unsophisticated country squire, could have such hidden depths, Chastity reflected. Was this a situation that could be turned to the Go-Between's advantage? She glanced at Prudence, wondering if the same thought had occurred to her. Prudence raised her eyebrows and rose from the backgammon board where she'd been playing with Sarah and wandered casually over to the pianoforte.

"Are you going to play, Prue?" Constance asked, following her. "Shall we try a duet?"

"I'll turn the music for you," Chastity said, going to join her sisters. "What do you think?" she whispered, rustling sheets of music as if she was selecting a particular piece.

"How do we get him to London?" Constance murmured, as she too examined the pile of music.

"If we can throw them together over the next couple of days, he might take care of that himself," Prudence whispered.

"We could invite him to spend tomorrow with us, now that the hunt's canceled," Chastity said. "He must be so lonely, snowbound with no friends or family. We can sit them together at luncheon."

"What are you three whispering about?"

They jumped guiltily as Douglas suddenly came up behind them. "Music," said Chastity. "Just trying to find a particular piece of music. We seem to have mislaid it." She turned back to the room, asking hastily, "Laura, do you sing at all . . . in Italian, perhaps?"

"But of course," Laura said. "All the great music is Italian. Think of the opera . . . only the Italians can write opera. Do you not agree, Lord Berenger?" She turned her intense pale gaze upon him.

"It is the language of the opera," he agreed, and to the immense astonishment of the company, rose to his feet and launched into an aria from *Don Giovanni*.

Laura gazed at him with rapt attention, her hands clasped to her breast, and when he ceased, looking somewhat astonished himself at his impulsive performance, she applauded with a cry of "Bravo! Bravo, signore."

"Good God, man," Lord Duncan said faintly. "Didn't know you had it in you."

"Oh, I studied the opera — took singing lessons — in Florence," George Berenger confessed with clear embarrassment. "Of course, never touched it after m'father died, you understand. Had to return to England, take up the reins of the estate. No time for such indulgence." He sat down again and wiped his brow with a large checkered handkerchief.

"Hardly indulgence, my lord," Laura said. "The finest music in the world. And you have such a wonderful voice. How sad that with such delicate sensibilities you were obliged to return to such a mundane existence." She waved an all-encompassing hand at the unpoetic evidence of their bucolic surroundings. "To stifle such a talent . . ." She gave a heavily dramatic sigh. "Tragic."

"Well, I would hardly call it tragic, Miss Della Luca," he demurred.

"Oh, don't deny yourself — and, please, I would be honored if you would call me Laura." She took his hand between both of hers.

"Looks like *Il Dottore* has lost the ascendancy," murmured Chastity, forgetting that Douglas was still standing beside the piano.

"What was that?" he demanded.

"Oh, nothing," Chastity said, trying to stifle a laugh. "Nothing at all."

Douglas continued to look at her suspiciously. Prudence sat down at the piano and struck a chord. "Any requests?" she announced.

Chapter 16

"Just what *was* that smart remark about *Il Dottore?*" Douglas asked later that night. He was lying on Chastity's bed, clad in a dressing gown, arms linked behind his head, lazily watching her undress. "And don't say 'Nothing' again in that airy fashion either."

Chastity glanced at him over her shoulder as she unbuttoned her petticoat. "It wasn't anything important," she said. "Just a private joke."

"Well, if it concerned me, I don't consider it to be private," he said.

"Now, what makes you think it concerned you?" She pushed the opened petticoat off her shoulders.

"As far as I know I'm the only *Dottore* around here at present." His eyes roamed the smooth line of her back, eagerly anticipating the moment when she'd take off her knickers. She was unfastening her suspenders, peeling off her stockings, and his breathing had quickened.

Chastity turned slowly towards him, the nipples peaking on her bare breasts. Her eyes narrowed as she slowly unbuttoned the waistband of her knickers, then slipped them off her hips and kicked them free of her ankles. She smiled, placing her hands on her hips, offering herself to his now hungry gaze.

"Closer," he said, crooking a beckoning finger. She stepped to the edge of the bed. He put a hand on her hip.

And that, Chastity thought with satisfaction, was the end of that dangerously awkward conversation. But she was wrong. He pulled her down to the bed, his hands moving over her with wicked precision. "Tell me what you and your sisters are up to, Miss Duncan."

Chastity groaned. "Not now," she said, her thighs parting under the insistent pressure of his hands.

"Yes, now. Your brothers-in-law told me that you and your sisters never do or say anything without purpose. So, just what are you up to?" His hand cupped the moistening mound of her sex, his busy fingers bringing her ever closer to the edge.

"We're not up to anything," she denied. "Max and Gideon must have been teasing you."

"I don't think so," he said, lifting his hand from her.

"Douglas, don't stop," she begged. "Not now."

"Then answer my question."

"You are so cruel."

"No, but I *will* have an answer." He stroked her belly, then moved his hand down, his fingers playing a tantalizing little tune.

Chastity groaned again. "We're trying to marry off our father," she said, and was rewarded with a more purposeful caress.

"To the contessa?"

"Mmm." She closed her eyes, losing herself in sensation.

"So, where does *Il Dottore* come into this little scheme?" He lifted his hand again.

"He doesn't . . . you don't," she said desperately. Her heart was beating fast. *How in the devil's name was she to get out of this? He mustn't suspect that the Duncan sisters had ever intended to match him up with Laura. He'd put two and two together in no time.*

"It was just a little joke," she said again. "Because she seemed to like you, and was paying so much attention to you . . . what with all that decorating business. And then she seemed to have switched her attentions to George Berenger. We were just laughing about it. That was all."

"Was it indeed," he murmured. Everything she said was perfectly plausible, but something didn't ring quite true.

"Please go back to what you were doing," Chastity pleaded.

He didn't immediately comply. "Why do I

think there's something you're not telling me?"

"I've told you everything," she stressed. "We're just trying to make our father happier. He's been so lonely and depressed in the last few months. We wanted to take him out of himself."

He shook his head, gazing down at her. How could he possibly quibble with a motive as pure as filial affection?

"Come on, Douglas, play fair," Chastity said. "I answered your question."

He shook his head again. "I wish I could believe that you did." Then he laughed. "But I'm not enjoying this deprivation either — so, where was I?"

"Here," she said, putting his hand in the right spot. "Just here."

That had been a very close call, Chastity thought, when she could think again, but he didn't seem to have made any connection with his introduction to Laura through the medium of the Go-Between and his invitation to Christmas at Romsey Manor. At least, he hadn't yet.

She stifled a sigh, turning her head into the pillow. Everything was getting out of hand. She had thought she could indulge herself with impunity in a passionate fling and then just pick up the strands of her life once this interlude was over. But now she wasn't so sure. The deception she was practicing on Douglas stuck in her craw, and she could no longer ignore it. Her fear when she had thought he might discover the truth had been all too real. She could only imagine how he would react if he knew the truth, and her skin crawled at the prospect. It all seemed so grubby, no longer a light and harmless subterfuge, and she felt dishonorable, besmirched somehow. And she knew in her heart of hearts that the interlude had to come to an end. She couldn't go on deceiving him, and she couldn't bear to tell him the truth.

She burrowed deeper into the pillow, aware that she was instinctively trying to bury her thoughts as if the man breathing rhythmically beside her would be able to read them. It would be all right if she didn't care for him, but she did. There was no point continuing to fool herself into thinking that this was just a passionate romp, a whirlwind affair with no strings. She hadn't fallen into bed with Douglas on a whim. She loved him. She loved *him,* not just his body. And *that* she loved to distraction. She inched backwards, fitting herself against his side; at least her body didn't lie to him.

Douglas left her bed just as the first faint pink of dawn showed low on the horizon. Chastity murmured a faint protest in her sleep as his skin left hers, then she rolled into the warm indentation left by his body and slept on. Douglas slipped into his dressing gown and crept out to the corridor. He felt uneasy, unsettled in some way, and he didn't know why. Their lovemaking had been as glorious as ever, but he'd sensed a slight discordance, and he couldn't lose the feeling that Chastity had not been completely open with him about the sisters' plans for their father. Not that it was really any business of his, he told himself, but without conviction.

He took a leisurely bath, dressed, and went outside. The snow had stopped overnight and the air was crisp and cold, the sky a clear, sunny blue. He tramped through the snow for an hour, trying to clear his mind. He felt as if he had arrived at some kind of watershed where his carefully drawn plans no longer seemed to have any relevance. He thought of the plan to acquire a rich wife and found it an absurd idea. Soulless and mercenary. He now couldn't imagine how he had ever believed that a marriage of mutual respect and convenience would satisfy him. But that said, money *was* essential for his plans, and emotional entanglements *did* get in the way of single-minded commitment. Chastity, it appeared, had no money, and no one could call the feeling he had for her anything but an emotional entanglement.

He stopped in front of a frozen ornamental

lake and stared frowning fiercely across to the far side, his hands resting unconsciously on his hips. Why not put a name to the feeling? Not to put too fine a point upon it, he was in love. And it was a vastly different emotion to what he had felt for Marianne. He had adored Marianne with a thoughtless, almost doglike devotion. Utterly superficial when compared to this deep-rooted sense of belonging he felt when he was with Chastity. She had somehow crept up on him, ambushed him, and he was caught, hopelessly ensnared. He saw her faults as clearly as he believed she saw his. He had seen no flaws in Marianne until she had shown him her feet of clay. The shock and disillusion had been all the greater for his blindness. He didn't see how Chastity could spring any unpleasant surprises on him.

He turned back to the house, aware that he was hungry. The household would be up and about by now and so too would Chastity. The memory of her warm body against his stirred him anew and his step quickened, crunching through snowdrifts along the driveway towards the front door. It was a good feeling, this longing to see someone, this need to be with them. For the moment he was content to savor the feeling, to live in the moment. He would have to make some decisions soon, but not immediately.

Chastity was coming down the stairs as he

entered the deserted hall, stamping the snow off his boots. "Good morning," he said, his eyes crinkling in a smile. "Did you sleep well?"

"As if you didn't know," she said, trying to sound lighthearted as she reached the bottom of the stairs. "Have you had breakfast?"

He shook his head. "Not yet. I went for a walk, but I'm hungry as a hunter now."

"Don't bring up hunting this morning," she said, turning towards the breakfast room door. "It'll set Father off on one of his lamenting tirades. He seemed resigned last night, but the sunshine this morning is bound to produce regrets."

"Well, at least you can do a little more matchmaking," Douglas said, looking at her closely. "Encourage him to spend the morning with the contessa."

Chastity felt her cheeks warm but she attempted to laugh off the remark, saying, "Oh, I don't think he needs too much encouragement. Let's go in to breakfast."

Douglas had seen the quick flush and he sensed a tension in her that he hadn't been aware of before. Her laugh was a little too brittle and her cheerful greeting to the assembled company around the breakfast table seemed almost false. He helped himself liberally to kidneys, bacon, and mushrooms and sat at the table.

As the day progressed he realized with

mingled fascination and somewhat shocked amusement that whatever plans the Duncan sisters had for their father and the contessa, they had others for Laura Della Luca. With varying degrees of subtlety they managed to engineer the continued presence of George Berenger throughout the day, ensuring that he and Laura were neighbors at the table, partners at cards, and singers of Italian duets. Lord Duncan, he noticed, seemed able to take care of himself when it came to the contessa, requiring no encouragement to be her escort or companion at the fireside, and the lady herself appeared more than content with the arrangements.

Douglas had to admit that he wouldn't have been aware of any of this clandestine activity if he hadn't been alerted to it. It was an unsettling recognition. He could well understand why they would promote Laura's burgeoning romance with George Berenger. If their father did indeed marry the contessa, they would be gaining more than a stepmother if they couldn't get Laura established under some other roof. And they had all made little attempt to hide their opinion of the signorina. Perhaps, he thought, it was only that aspect of their plans that Chastity had been keeping to herself last night, nothing more than that. But he still had the sense that something was not quite right. She seemed distracted and once or twice he caught her looking at him covertly but when he tried to acknowledge her gaze she looked away or became absorbed in something else.

He strolled into the library after luncheon to find Gideon and Max ensconced before the fire in a haze of cigar smoke, brandy snifters at their elbows. "Come and join us, Farrell," Max invited, gesturing to the decanters. "We're trying to escape being co-opted for something called murder in the dark."

"Cigar?" Gideon proffered the humidor.

Douglas shook his head, "Thank you, but no. Never took to it myself. I'll join you in a glass, though." He helped himself and sank into a deep leather armchair. "What happens with this murder game?"

"We are not entirely sure," Gideon said. "But knowing our wives, something totally unsuited to men of substance. They are no respecter of persons in certain situations."

Douglas drew in a deep breath, inhaling the cognac in his glass. He sipped, then asked curiously, "Do you know what else they're up to, those three?"

"That rather depends, my dear chap, on what exact aspect of their various nefarious activities you're referring to," Max said lazily.

"I rather got the impression they were trying to throw Laura into Berenger's arms."

"Ah." Gideon took his feet off the fender and reached for his glass. "Yes, that seems highly likely."

"I daresay Chastity doesn't fancy sharing a roof with her if the contessa marries Lord Duncan," Douglas observed, swirling the brandy in his goblet.

"That would be our guess," Max agreed.

"Do they do much of this matchmaking?" Douglas inquired.

His two companions drank deeply and didn't immediately answer him. Then Max said carefully, "They will assure you that they only turn people's lives upside down in the interests of the greater good."

"And you believe that?"

Both men shrugged. "They managed us," Max said.

"Yes," agreed Gideon with a chuckle. "And on the whole we're agreed that the greater good is served." He reached for the brandy decanter. "Relax into it, dear fellow. It doesn't hurt too much."

Douglas smiled a little ruefully. "You mean Chastity, of course."

"Of course," Max said. "They're quite unstoppable, the Honorable Duncan sisters, once they decide upon something."

"Mmm," Douglas murmured thoughtfully. "I'm beginning to think it's time I took the initiative."

"I rather thought you already had," Gideon said, blowing a perfect smoke ring. "Or was that Chastity's initiative?"

"Don't be embarrassed if it was," Max

said. "Constance shamelessly seduced me in this same house."

Douglas considered this question, then shook his head. "No," he said definitely. The passionate impulse that had felled them both simultaneously had come out of the blue. "As far as I can remember, there was no initiative."

His companions nodded as if they understood this perfectly well. "Something in the nature of Zeus's thunderbolt, I daresay," Gideon observed. "Well, as long as you have no aspirations towards a quiet life . . . ?"

"I can't remember now," Max said consideringly, "but I may have had such aspirations once."

The library door opened and the three men turned warily towards it. Sarah stood there holding a handful of playing cards. "We're going to play murder in the dark," she said. "Prue says you have to come, Daddy, and you, Uncle Max, and Dr. Farrell."

"But it's not dark," her father protested, trying to buy time.

"It is in the attics, and that's where we're going to play." Sarah came over to her father and seized his hand, tugging on it. "Come on, Daddy. It'll be such fun. Even Miss Della Luca and Lord Berenger are going to play."

Gideon groaned and got to his feet. "All right, I'm coming. And I'm not going alone," he declared to his companions, who rose with as much reluctance and followed them to the drawing room.

"It's all very simple," Prudence said. "Whoever picks the ace of spades is the murderer." She tapped the rules off against her palm. "The king of hearts is the detective. Everyone else is a potential victim. The first person to feel a hand on his neck screams as loudly as possible and the lights go on. Then the detective has to try to find the murderer. Hand out the cards, Sarah."

"How the hell did you get the *signorina* to agree to this farce?" Douglas demanded of Chastity in an undertone as he took his card.

"I didn't," she said. "George Berenger did. He said he'd played as a child every Christmas, and would love to play again. He's so lonely, poor man."

"So, you're going to match him up with Laura?" He sounded a little caustic.

Chastity shrugged, said carelessly, "No one can match someone up with someone else. They have to decide that for themselves. We're just putting opportunities in their way."

"Yes, so I'd noticed," he said dryly. "For their own good, of course."

"It doesn't do any harm," Chastity said, hearing how defensive she sounded. The whole topic touched her on the raw and it was not a conversation she wanted to have. Deliberately, she turned her attention to her playing card, examining it behind her hand.

"Everyone ready?" Prudence, who seemed to be mistress of ceremonies, called. "We're going up to the attics." She led the way, the rest of the party trooping behind her.

In the dark attics there was much scuffling and giggling, as shadowy figures moved around, trying to avoid each other. Douglas, who, since he hadn't drawn a significant card, decided he could opt out without spoiling anyone's fun, found himself an ancient armchair smelling of dog's hair in a dark and deserted corner where he was sure he wouldn't be discovered and settled down to wait it out. The postprandial brandy had made him sleepy and he allowed his eyes to close.

A squeal very close to him shattered his doze. A light and laughing voice declared in the most ridiculous accent, "Oo-la-la, take ze 'ands off me, m'sieur. You take ze liberties."

Douglas squinted into the darkness. He had heard that fake accent before. His blood pounded in his ears.

"I'm not taking liberties, madam wife," Gideon said indignantly. "I am merely trying to strangle you."

"Oh, murder . . . murder most foul!" Prudence shrieked, abandoning the French maid persona and collapsing backwards into her husband's arms. After a few minutes of shuffling, shifting chaos, oil lamps were lit and the participants looked expectantly around at each other. Prudence lay on the floor. Gideon, looking both guilty and bewildered, stood over her, holding the ace of spades.

"Well, that wasn't very good, Daddy," Sarah declared. "Now we all know it was you who murdered Prue, because you said so."

"I'm sorry," Gideon said, bending down to give his wife a hand to pull her to her feet. "I don't think I've fully grasped the concept of this game."

"Well, we'll try again," Prudence said, seeing how disappointed Sarah looked. "One more round. Everyone give me your cards."

Chastity handed in her card and wondered what could have happened to Douglas. She was sure he had come up with them, but he certainly wasn't there now. Maybe he'd gone to take a nap. It wasn't as if there was an obligation to join in these parlor games.

She found him in the drawing room when the party finally went down for tea. He was ensconced in a deep armchair, reading an old copy of the *Times*. Chastity brought a cup of tea to him, together with a thick slab of Christmas cake. "You didn't care for the game," she said, smiling as she set down cup and plate on a little side table. "I don't really blame you. But Sarah enjoyed it."

"I found myself falling asleep," he said. She thought he seemed rather grave, his eyes so dark as to be almost black, and curiously expressionless. He broke off a piece of icing from the cake. "I've just had a telephone call from a patient. I'm afraid I must go back to London on the first train tomorrow."

"Oh," she said. "So soon."

"Yes, I'm sorry. An emergency." He crumbled marzipan between his fingers.

She forced a smile, said quietly, "We have tonight, though. One last night."

He looked up at her, his expression unreadable. "Yes, one last night," he agreed.

Chastity nodded and moved back to the tea table. She had known it had to happen. There was always going to be one last night. When they were once more in London, this interlude would be over. But she had hoped . . . No, she hadn't hoped, but she wasn't ready for it. She hadn't had time to prepare herself.

And there was something desperate about their passion that night. A hunger that somehow could not be sated. It was like some kind of drug, Chastity thought as she moved over Douglas's body, licking every available inch of him, nuzzling him like a puppy at its mother's teat. She was drugged with lovemaking, and she wouldn't allow herself even to think that after tonight she wouldn't have this anymore.

She straddled him, running her hands over his torso, playing on his ribs with her fingertips. She lowered her mouth to his, driving her tongue deep between his lips. He slid his hands beneath her belly and lifted her hips so that he could move upwards and within.

Chastity held her breath as she felt him inside her, for the moment quite still, just an inhabiting presence that slowly filled her. She let out her breath in slow measure and leaned back, resting her hands on his thighs, using only her body to keep them both hovering on the edge. He held her hips lightly, allowing his own body to follow her initiative. She smiled down at him, her hands now at her waist as she sat upright, driving herself down upon him. Sensation grew, spread from her loins to her belly. She tightened her thighs. His fingers dug into her hips, his eyes closing as he drove upwards, lost in her body, and she held him tight inside her and gloried in the possession.

And when it was over, she fell forward, her mouth pressed into the hollow of his shoulder, her hair spread in a red cloud across his chest, her sweat-slick skin glued to his. "How could that be possible?" she murmured weakly.

He didn't answer immediately, then he said, "I don't know," and there was a strange resonance to the simple statement, a mingled anger and sorrow and confusion. Chastity heard it, and heard it as an echo of her own feelings of loss and frustration that something this good had to be given up. Holding her waist, he rolled sideways with her in a slow disengagement that even so left her feeling bereft. She curled tightly against him, fitting her curves to his hollows.

They lay in silence. Douglas listened to her breathing, hearing it deepen. Once it had settled into the rhythms of sleep, he slid out of bed and pulled the thick quilted coverlet over her. He stood looking down at her in the dim glow of the fire. He had intended to say nothing. This lovemaking would be their last, a bittersweet farewell, and then he would leave, and say nothing. But now he realized he couldn't. He needed her to feel the sharp sting of his hurt and his anger and his disappointment. He had suffered Marianne's rejection in silence, as if he had somehow deserved it, but now it felt as if he had to exorcise that hurt too with this other woman who had so deceived him.

Chastity awoke about half an hour later. The room was quiet, except for the slight crackle of the fire. The space in the bed beside her was empty. She struggled onto an elbow. Douglas, in his dressing gown, was sitting in an armchair by the fire, watching her, and she felt a stab of fear as those charcoal eyes rested impassively on her countenance.

"It was you," he said. "The Go-Between . . . in the National Gallery. It was you."

"Yes," she said dully, resignation sweeping

through her. There was nothing to be done now, and nothing to be salvaged. "It was me."

He said nothing, merely looked at her. His anger was an almost palpable force and she wondered if perhaps that was what had awakened her. But there was more than anger in his eyes. There was sorrow and, even worse, disappointment. It made her feel crumpled and dried out like a shriveled leaf.

"How did you know?" she asked, not that it mattered.

He gave a short laugh. "That absurd accent. Your sister used it . . . as a joke, I assume."

"I didn't notice," Chastity said in the same dull tone. "It's just a useful way of disguising our voices. It's not meant to sound authentic."

"I imagine in your business one needs a bag of such deceitful tricks," he said, getting to his feet. "How else would you get your clients, if that's what you call them, to reveal themselves so completely? People you rub shoulders with on a daily basis . . . social acquaintances . . . people who assume you're something you're not. People who trust you." He walked to the door as he spoke. He set his hand on the latch and looked across at her. "Good-bye, Chastity."

The door closed quietly as he left her, the slight breeze sending a sharp spurt of flame rising from the dying fire.

Oh, God. Chastity lay on her back, her arm covering her eyes, where tears stung behind her closed lids. She understood now that he had loved her. The bitterness of his hurt told her that. This had not been a light fling, a casual loving interlude for Douglas any more than it had been for her. And she could not for the life of her think how she could have changed anything.

She lay wakeful throughout the rest of a night that seemed eternal, and fell into an uneasy sleep just before dawn. She awoke to a brilliant day of clear blue skies, cold sunlight sparking off the snow, and dragged herself out of bed. Douglas had said he would be taking the first train back to London, so he would be long gone by now.

Chastity dressed and went downstairs. Jenkins was crossing the hall from the breakfast room, an empty coffeepot in his hand. "Morning, Miss Chas."

"Good morning, Jenkins. Did Dr. Farrell get off all right?" She tried to ask the question lightly, as if it was the mere casual inquiry of a thoughtful hostess.

"Fred took him to the station in the gig about an hour ago," Jenkins said. He regarded her closely. "Everything all right, Miss Chas?"

"Yes, of course," she said airily. "I daresay we'll see him when we return to London."

She smiled and made her way to the breakfast room, where everyone was gathered but the contessa, who always took breakfast in bed, and Sarah and Mary Winston, who had already breakfasted and were out exploring the winter wonderland.

Lord Duncan looked up from his plate of kidneys and bacon. "Morning, my dear. Beautiful, isn't it. Perfect hunting day." He sighed.

Chastity nodded absently and sat down between her sisters.

"Pity we had to lose that Dr. Farrell. A decent chap."

"What kind of medical emergency was it, Chas?" Constance asked. "Did he say?"

Chastity shook her head, tried a laugh. "Patient confidentiality," she said, taking a piece of toast from the rack. She saw that her fingers were quivering and put it down quickly, contemplated picking up the coffeepot to fill her cup and decided against it.

Constance took up the coffeepot and filled her youngest sister's cup for her. "Drink it," she said softly. "You look as if you need it, love."

Chastity's smile was wan, but she picked up the cup and managed to drink from it without spilling, conscious of her sisters' anxious and rather puzzled looks. They had known last evening that Douglas would be leaving this morning, he had made his farewells before bedtime, so there was no explanation for Chastity's clear and present distress.

"What plans do we have for today?" Constance asked brightly, reaching for the butter.

"Fresh air," Max said. "And plenty of it."

"I told Jenkins we'll take the guns out," Lord Duncan said eagerly. "Try for a few ducks on the lake . . . a goose or two. What d'you say?"

"Well, you men can do that," Prudence said. "The women are going ice-skating. I promised Sarah."

Gideon looked alarmed. "How do you know the ice is safe?"

"Gideon, my love, the water in the horse pond is only a foot deep," Prudence said with a smile that managed to be both patronizing and affectionate. "You didn't think I'd let Sarah on the lake, surely?"

"How was I to know there was a horse pond?" he asked. "I don't know anything about country life. I've only ever seen the lake."

Chastity nibbled her toast, thankful that for the moment no one was paying her any attention.

"Will you come skating, Laura? Or do you have other plans?" Constance asked.

Laura bridled, then blushed a little. "I believe Lord Berenger suggested that if the weather was clement we might walk over to his house. He has some splendid Italian artifacts from his stay in *Firenze*. I am most interested in seeing them."

"That's splendid," Constance said. "And your mother?"

"Oh, the dear lady is going to come in the gig and watch the shooting," Lord Duncan said. "I suggested it to her last night, if the weather made it possible, and she seemed most anxious to have a taste of fresh air. Jenkins will bring a luncheon to the pavilion on the lake."

"Well, that all seems highly satisfactory," Max said, getting to his feet. He touched his wife's hair fleetingly. "We'll see you three later this afternoon, then."

Constance reached up and stroked his wrist. "Yes. Teatime probably."

Chastity stood. "I'm not really properly dressed yet. I'll see you all shortly." She made for the door and her sisters let her go, knowing that she would be waiting for them upstairs.

In her bedroom, Chastity sat at the dresser, her steepled hands to her mouth as she tried to absorb what had happened. It had been so fast, as if a freak whirlwind had entered her life, turned it upside down, and then swept out again, leaving chaos in its wake. Her eyes looked curiously hollow in the mirror, blank, as if they were no longer reflecting thought or light. She didn't move even when the tap at the door she had been expecting brought her sisters into the room.

Prudence closed the door behind her. Constance came over to the dresser and put her hands on her baby sister's shoulders. "What happened, Chas?"

Chastity took a deep, shuddering breath and told them.

"Oh, God," Prudence said. "I never thought for one minute, up in the attic, when I used that stupid accent . . . Gideon and I often play around like that . . . since the trial, when I first used it. I'm so sorry, Chas." She looked worriedly at her sister's reflection in the mirror. "I'm so sorry," she repeated helplessly.

"It wasn't your fault, Prue," Chastity said. "I thought it was over anyway, only . . ."

"But you love him," Constance said, with barely a question mark.

"Yes," Chastity said flatly. "And now I know that he loves — loved — me. He wouldn't have reacted with such hurt, such pain and disappointment, if it had been only a fling. He would have been angry at the manipulation, yes. And embarrassed at what he'd revealed. But it was much more than that . . . much more." She propped her elbows on the dresser and buried her face in her palms. "How could I have made such a mess of things?"

"You didn't make a mess of anything,"

Constance declared. "Circumstances got everything muddled."

"Quite," Prue agreed. "And what we have to decide now is, what we do to untangle this mess."

"Nothing," Chastity said. "Nothing at all."

Chapter 17

Douglas shoveled more coal onto the miserable fire in the grate at St. Mary Abbot's. It did little to warm the waiting room, with the wind howling outside. He'd seen at least three cases of frostbite that morning, many of his patients coming in with old newspaper and rags wrapped around their bare feet. It was too cold in his office to examine a patient properly. He really needed better premises, but better premises, even if he could find something in this area, drew higher rents.

He was back to square one, he thought dourly. Actually, it was worse than that. He had come to London with a clear plan of action. A rich wife, a substantial establishment practice, and a thriving clinic in the slums. And now the first two aspects of that plan filled him with acute distaste. He still wanted the last, wanted it with the same passionate fervor and commitment as ever, but he no longer knew how to go about getting it. He had thought he could have a pragmatic marriage, a civilized union that suited the needs of both partners. He had thought he would be happy with that.

And now he knew that he couldn't possibly settle for anything less than he had glimpsed with Chastity Duncan.

He realized he was still squatting on his ankles in front of the fire, still holding the empty coal scuttle. He set it down and stood up stiffly. The cold dampness of the room seemed to have seeped into his bones, certainly into his spirit. Perhaps it was time to abandon this plan, leave this city and go home. There at least he could plunge himself into the work of his slum clinic. It was already thriving but there was always more work to be done. It could be expanded into other parts of the city. He could establish other branches.

But that would be running from failure. And he knew he could not do that. It was not in his nature and never had been. And he wouldn't just be running from failure. He'd be running from Chastity. From the deeply personal failure she represented. He loved her. Still loved her. He was angry with her, but he was angry with himself too. Whenever he thought of that meeting in the Rubens gallery he went cold with embarrassment and self-contempt. He heard his words, so callous and mercenary. *The only essential quality in a wife was that she should be rich.*

He had been so annoyed that the supercilious, veiled Go-Between had made no attempt to hide her contempt. He had thought then only that she had no right to pass judgment on a situation of which she knew nothing at all. But it was pure arrogance on his part. He couldn't be bothered to explain himself to someone whose services he required and was prepared to pay for. If he *had* explained himself, then perhaps she would have explained *herself.* He thought of the sisters' apparently gratuitous efforts to inform him that there was no family money, and mortification swamped him anew. Could they possibly have thought he was pursuing Chastity for her money? Thought that he had decided she answered his needs for social position and wealth? It didn't bear thinking of.

He took his greatcoat from a peg by the door, looked back at the fire, hoping it would stay lit for a good few hours in case any poor soul needed a little shelter, however inadequate, on a bitter January day. He blew out the oil lamps, and went out to the freezing street. It was time to assume his other persona. He was expecting a certain Lady Sydney, an obstetric patient who said she had been referred to him by Lord Brigham's sister.

He had not been to his Harley Street offices for several days. The city was still largely deserted and his patients were thin on the ground, although he expected that to change when the London Season was in full swing. As he turned onto Harley Street, he saw a large, covered dray drawn up outside his building, two massive cart horses tossing their heads, breath steaming in the icy air. Two men appeared from the house, burly men in baize aprons, wrestling with a massive oak desk. *His* oak desk, Douglas realized in a sort of horrified trance. He watched as they hefted the desk into the back of the dray and then turned to go back inside. Other men appeared, this time carrying leather armchairs, the old cracked leather armchairs from his waiting room. They too went into the back of the dray and the men returned inside.

Was he being evicted? Of course not, he'd taken a year's lease on the suite. Signed and paid for. He broke into a run. When he reached the dray he stared inside at the contents of his suite piled any which way in the dusty interior. His downstairs neighbor emerged from the door as he turned in bemusement towards it.

"Afternoon, Farrell." Dr. Talgarth lifted his pince-nez on the gold chain and peered amiably at Douglas. "Doing a bit of refurbishment? Always good to see the tenants doing improvements. Raises the tone of the building." He waved a hand in farewell and marched off down the street, his belly leading the way.

Douglas raced into the hall, dodging a man carrying a large oil painting. A particularly gloomy hunting scene that had hung between the windows in the waiting room. He took the stairs two at a time and burst through the open door to his waiting room. It was warm, a good fire in the grate, the gas lamps lit. And it bore absolutely no relation to the room he had been in two days earlier.

"*Dottore, Dottore,* I had hoped to be finished before you arrived." Laura emerged from his office holding up an ornate gilded lamp with a crimson tasseled shade. "I will just put this here . . ." She set the lamp on a gilded table beside a chintz sofa and turned to him with a triumphant smile. "Is it not beautiful . . . is it not perfection, *Dottore?*" She gestured expansively at the country tearoom that had once been a doctor's waiting room. "So welcoming . . . so comforting for the sick."

Douglas looked around. She had done exactly what she had threatened. The walls were eggshell blue with pale pink moldings. Flower paintings caught the eye at every turn. Chintz and lace at the windows, chintz on chairs and sofas. The carpet beneath his feet was a field of cabbage roses. He blinked, feeling dizzy at the riot of color. In a daze he walked into his office. Brocade, tapestry, more cabbage roses, more lace. An ornate screen concealed the examining table in the corner.

Laura was behind him. "The screen," she said. "Such a perfect touch. So charmingly reassuring."

Douglas peered at the screen's three gilded panels. They seemed to represent some kind of Roman orgy, or was it the sacrifice of a vestal virgin? He thought of Lady Sydney's imminent arrival and shuddered. He was at a loss, he had no idea what to say. He turned slowly to Laura, his mouth half open as he tried to find words.

She seized his hands, pumping them vigorously. "I know, *Dottore,* I know. You don't know what to say . . . but there is no need to say anything. I promised I would do this for you and I always keep my promises. It has been a pleasure, a true pleasure to put my talents to such good use." She gave him a bridling smile. "You know, perhaps, that Lord Berenger and I are affianced."

"Congratulations," Douglas managed to say. "Um . . ." He looked helplessly around, his hands waving in the air as if they had nothing to do with him. "All this . . ."

"Not a word, *Dottore,*" Laura said, seizing his hands again. "Not a word of thanks. It has been my pleasure." Her smile grew more coy. "And it gave me a little practice . . . a little preparation . . . for refurbishing dear Lord Berenger's house. My next project, of course."

"Of course," Douglas said.

"Well, I must be on my way." Laura gathered up a fur stole with a glassy-eyed fox's head that dangled over her shoulder, a handbag, and gloves from one of the chintz sofas. "You'll find the bills on the little table over there, *Dottore*." She waved airily in their direction. "You will see how well I negotiated on your behalf." She moved to the door, pausing for a moment to indicate a gilded palm tree beside the door. "Isn't that the most perfect hat stand? I was delighted when I found it. I knew it would be exactly right." And she was gone.

Douglas felt as if he'd been run over by a steam train. He didn't dare look at the bills. Dazed, he took off his overcoat and reached automatically to hang it up on the hat stand, then he stopped, his eyes glazing as he stared at the palm tree, the coat hanging from his hand. He turned his back on the abomination and went into his office, throwing his overcoat over a chair and slinging his bowler hat onto the windowsill. Desperately, he realized he had a patient coming at any moment. He couldn't think about any of this. He had to exude confidence and control. He *was* in control. He smoothed down his black suit coat and gray waistcoat and walked back into the waiting room.

"Dr. Farrell, is there anything — oh, my!" The woman who managed Dr. Talgarth's office downstairs appeared in the open doorway of his office. She stared around. "Oh, my," she said again, rather faintly.

"It's only temporary, Miss Gray," Douglas said, trying to sound confident and in control. He *was* in control, he told himself again.

"Yes . . . yes, of course," she said, her eyes still wide as platters. She cleared her throat. "Is there anything I can get you before your patient arrives?"

"No, nothing, thank you, Miss Gray. It's good of you to work through your lunch hour." He offered what he hoped was his usual suave, employer's smile.

"My neighbor makes Mother a sandwich on a Friday," the woman said somewhat distractedly, her head still swiveling from side to side like a fascinated marionette. "I always pick up some fish and chips for supper on the way home as a special treat to make up for it."

Douglas forced himself to concentrate on the matter at hand. He could hardly redecorate his suite before the arrival of his patient. "I'm very grateful for your help," he said truthfully. Miss Gray was a real stroke of luck. The practice couldn't support a full-time receptionist, and when Miss Gray had offered to fill in when she wasn't working for Dr. Talgarth he had jumped at the prospect. He guessed she needed the extra money and was probably not that keen to spend the free time afforded by Dr. Talgarth's less than arduous office hours alone with her mother in the small flat they shared on the Bayswater Road. And she was very good at her job.

"If you could show Lady Sydney into the office when she arrives," he said, and went back to his office. He stood looking at the screen, then bent to examine the tapestry panels more closely. On close scrutiny it appeared they did not represent an orgy or a virgin sacrifice. It was some pastoral scene in a Roman temple. Or at least he decided to believe it was.

Lady Sydney, by some miracle, was on time. Douglas was learning to accept that his time was not considered nearly as valuable as his patients', and for the time being he held his tongue. Once he was established, he would probably unleash it. Against all expectation he found he liked Lady Sydney — but then, he had liked Chastity's group of friends that night at Covent Garden, which seemed an eon ago. He would probably like the Duncan sisters' friends as a matter of course. It was not a helpful reflection. He tapped his pen on the desk blotter, noticing for the first time that the leather edging had some kind of runic engraving. Laura had probably thought the hieroglyphics depicted ancient remedies or apothecaries' recipes.

"Dr. Farrell . . . Dr. Farrell?"

He became aware that his patient was staring at him in puzzlement. "You were saying something about iron."

"Yes, of course." He resumed briskly. "Liver, and cod liver oil. You should include those in your diet at least three or four times a week. Pregnant women become anemic very easily."

"I loathe liver," the young woman said, wrinkling her nose.

"You want a healthy baby," he said with something approaching a snap, thinking of all those women who couldn't afford the foods that would ensure that outcome.

She looked disconcerted. "Yes, of course. I'll do everything necessary, Dr. Farrell."

He smiled, hoping to dissipate the effect of his snap. "I'm sure you will, Lady Sydney. I'll see you in a month. If you'd like to make an appointment with Miss Gray on the way out . . . ?"

She rose to her feet, gathering handbag and gloves. She held out her hand to him. "Your office . . . such unusual furnishings," she said. "For a physician, I mean. Not that they aren't charming, perfectly charming," she added rather hastily.

"My predecessor's choice," he said smoothly, shaking her hand.

"I expect his wife had some influence," Lady Sydney said.

"Yes, I expect so," Douglas agreed. His visitor took her leave and he sat staring at the screen and the crimson tasseled shades on the lamps and exhaled slowly. Miss Gray came in with an armful of files. She looked around in clear puzzlement.

"The filing cabinet, Doctor," she said. "It appears to have disappeared."

"It's probably disguised," he said. "Like the hat stand."

"I wonder what as," the woman said, a little laugh shivering in the back of her throat. "It's quite intriguing, really. I'm sorry, Doctor, but —" The laughter got the better of her and she dropped the files onto the desk and laughed as if she couldn't stop. After a minute, Douglas yielded to the absurdity himself and joined her. The room rocked with the sounds of their hilarity.

"Oh, dear," Miss Gray said eventually, wiping her eyes with her handkerchief. "I don't know what came over me, Doctor. I can't remember when I've laughed like that."

"It did me good too," Douglas said. And it *had* done him good, in more ways than one. He felt purged. No bitterness, no desire for vengeance, not even a shred of mortification remained. He now knew exactly what he wanted — well, he'd always known that, but he now knew exactly what he had to do to get it.

He waited until Miss Gray had left, still wiping a tear of laughter from her cheek with her gloved finger, then opened a drawer and took out a plain sheet of paper, dipped his pen in the inkwell, and very carefully printed his missive, signing it with a completely indecipherable scrawl. He blotted the sheet, folded it, inserted it into an envelope, and with the same care printed the address of Mrs. Beedle's corner shop.

"I don't seem to be able to get the hang of this," Prudence complained as she tapped with two fingers on the typewriter's keyboard. "My *B*'s keep becoming *N*'s."

"I'm not sure my thoughts flow as quickly as they do with a pen," Constance said, leaning back in her chair at the desk in *The Mayfair Lady*'s new premises on Shoe Lane.

"It's just adapting to a different technique." Chastity slapped the carriage backwards with a merry ring. "I think I have it down pat. It's so much quicker to answer these agony aunt letters. Maybe I'm not as cerebral as you two."

"And that, you know, is nonsense," Prudence said. "You're just more adaptable."

"I doubt that," Chastity said with a tiny shrug, and continued with her tap-tapping.

Constance stretched and flexed her hands and wrists. "I think it's time for luncheon," she said. "Three working women are entitled to a luncheon break."

"Agreed," Prudence said, jumping to her feet. "Let's try that little café on Fleet Street where all the newspapermen go. I'd love to see how they react when we walk in."

"Prue, we can't," Constance demurred. "We'll draw far too much attention. Let's go to Swan and Edgar's."

"You two go," Chastity said, still tapping away. "I'm not very hungry. I'll finish this and then take the omnibus to Mrs. Beedle's. We haven't picked up the post in a week."

She didn't turn around as she spoke, leaving her sisters to look at the back of her head. "You must need luncheon, Chas," Constance said.

"Oddly enough, I don't," her youngest sister responded. "You two go."

Prudence sucked on her lower lip, wondering whether they should force their way through this thicket that Chastity had thrown up around herself, and then decided that they couldn't. She glanced at Constance, who simply nodded and took her coat off the rack.

"Can we bring something back for you, Chas?" she asked. "We could bring you some soup."

"No, I'll go and eat lardy cake at Mrs. Beedle's," Chastity said, still without turning around. "I haven't had a good chat with her for ages."

"All right. See you later." Prudence and Constance left the office. They didn't say anything until they'd gained the pavement.

"I'm worried about her, Prue," Constance said.

"I know. So am I. But I don't know what to do."

"No," Constance agreed. "Neither do I."

Chastity finished typing her letter and then leaned back in her hard office chair, aware of a crick in her neck. Typing was certainly quicker than penmanship but it was physically harder work. Maybe once she became proficient it wouldn't be such a strain.

She needed a break, though, and a walk to the omnibus would be welcome exercise. She walked briskly, muffled in a scarf, her felt hat pulled low over her ears, her gloved hands thrust deep into her pockets. She wasn't allowing herself to think these days, or at least not about anything that didn't concern *The Mayfair Lady* or her father's developing relationship with the contessa. Only at night did the longings plague her, the regrets that she didn't know what she could do to assuage.

She got off the omnibus at Kensington High Street and walked quickly to Mrs. Beedle's. Involuntarily she found herself glancing at the passersby, wondering if she would see Douglas. But of course he would have no reason to be around here now. His slum surgery was some walk away and he now lived in the upper reaches of Wimpole Street. He would have no need to visit Mrs. Beedle.

"Why, long time no see, Miss Chas," Mrs. Beedle greeted her with wreathing smiles. "It's a Happy New Year to you too. How was Christmas?"

"Nice, thank you, Mrs. Beedle. Very nice," Chastity said, hearing how lukewarm she sounded. "Cold and snowy," she added, trying to infuse some enthusiasm into her voice. "Sarah had a wonderful time."

"Oh, well, that's good," the shopkeeper said comfortably. "Nice for the little lass to have a real Christmas. Got some post for you." She lifted the hatch in the counter, inviting Chastity through.

The kitchen was warm and inviting as always, and the smell of baking filled the air. "Jam roly-poly," Mrs. Beedle said. "You'd like a piece with custard, Miss Chas. Straight out of the oven, and the custard's just made."

Pudding for lunch, Chastity reflected, suited her mood. There was no one to tell her she had to eat her meat and vegetables first. "Yes, please, Mrs. Beedle," she said, unwinding her scarf as she sat at the table.

"And here's your post." Mrs. Beedle reached up to the shelf and took down a batch of envelopes, setting them beside Chastity before she went to dish up an enormous portion of jam roly-poly liberally smothered in thick yellow custard.

Chastity glanced at the envelopes, then put them in her handbag and turned her attention to her pudding. Mrs. Beedle was chatting cheerfully about her children and grandchildren and seemed to require little or no response. Once or twice the shop bell rang and she went out to deal with a customer. In her absence Chastity scraped her plate clean. That was going to put back a few of the curves she'd lost in the last couple of months, she thought.

"And how's his lordship doing?" Mrs. Beedle asked as she bustled back into the kitchen.

"Oh, rather well," Chastity said with a tiny wink. "He has a lady friend."

"Oh, my goodness me," the shopkeeper exclaimed. "Well, now, isn't that wonderful. I always say, however good the marriage, the one left behind should be open to fate."

"A good maxim, Mrs. Beedle," Chastity said. "Mother would have agreed with you."

"A wonderful woman," Mrs. Beedle said. "Such a great heart."

"Yes," Chastity agreed with a smile that was just a little sad. "She was and she did have." She reached for her hat and coat. "That was wonderful, Mrs. Beedle. I could stay all afternoon, but I have to go."

"Well, don't be a stranger," the woman

said. "And give my best to Miss Con and Miss Prue."

"Of course. And they send theirs." Chastity kissed the woman's round cheek in farewell and braced herself for the cold outdoors. Roly-poly pudding and custard had their uses when it came to padding against the wind, she thought.

She went back to the office and found her sisters already returned, Prudence balancing the books, Constance writing a rather wicked account of the New Year's Eve party at Elizabeth Armitage's.

"How was Mrs. Beedle?" Constance inquired, glancing up from her two-fingered pecking.

"Well. She sent her best." Chastity hung up her coat, then reached into the pockets for the post. "There are a few letters."

"Did you eat anything?" Prudence asked, trying not to sound anxious. "We brought you back a sandwich just in case."

"I had the most enormous helping of jam roly-poly and custard," Chastity said with a laugh. "Not at all good for me, but good for the soul."

"Then good for you," Constance said. "Let's have a look at the post."

Chastity laid the letters on the central table and they scooted their wheeled chairs over to look at them. Prudence, by custom, wielded the paper knife. "Two agony aunts for you,

Chas," she said, passing them across. "And this one's some kind of tirade against that article you wrote about Freud's book, Con."

"*Three Contributions to the Theory of Sex,*" Constance said, reaching for the letter. She glanced at it, pronounced disgustedly, "What a bigot. Some ignorant country vicar who thinks publications of our kind should cater to the delicate sensibilities of ladies, not go out of their way to offend them."

"Shall you answer it?" Chastity asked somewhat absently as she perused another of the letters Prudence had handed her.

"What do you think?" Constance said.

Chastity smiled reflexively. "This is another Go-Between. Odd writing, though. It's all printed."

"Perhaps he — or is it she — can't manage cursive," Prudence suggested.

"I think it's a he." Chastity passed the letter over. "But the gender is definitely a little obscure."

Her sisters read the letter. "No one who reads *The Mayfair Lady* is unable to write cursive," Constance said. "Perhaps he has a reason for not wanting people to know he's sent the letter."

" 'Curiouser and curiouser, said Alice,' " Prudence quoted. "Who's going to meet the mystery?"

"I will," Chastity said without too much enthusiasm. "The Rubens room at the National Gallery works well. I'll tell him to carry a copy of the broadsheet, as usual."

"Are you sure you don't mind doing this?" Constance asked. The Rubens gallery was where Chastity had first met Douglas and it might rub salt into old wounds.

"No," Chastity said with an unwavering smile. "Interviewing Go-Between applicants is my job. Of course I'm happy to do it." She took the letter and scooted her chair back to her typewriter. "It's Friday today, so I'll suggest next Thursday. That should give him plenty of time to make whatever arrangements he has to, to make the rendezvous."

Chapter 18

The following Thursday was crisp and clear as Chastity strolled across Trafalgar Square, tossing corn to the pigeons as she went. The brightness of the day had lifted her spirits a little but she knew from experience that it wouldn't last. Once the evening drew in and the prospect of the long night lay ahead, the now familiar depression would swamp her anew.

She was swathed once more in her loose alpaca dust coat, her face obscured by the opaque chiffon veil, her Feydeau accent well prepared, although just the thought of it filled her with distaste. She hurried up the steps and entered the ground-floor hall, then climbed the stairs towards the atrium, turning to the left at the half landing, a copy of *The Mayfair Lady* prominently displayed in her hand.

She made her way through to the Rubens gallery and sat down on the circular bench in the middle of the room, as she'd specified in her letter, and opened up the broadsheet, its title page facing outwards. The Go-Between's client couldn't fail to identify her.

He didn't. Douglas entered the gallery and spotted the veiled, swathed figure immediately. A smile touched his mouth as he approached. "Madam Mayfair Lady, we meet again," he said.

Chastity looked up. She stared at him in bewildered incredulity. "Douglas?"

"The very same. May I sit down?" He didn't wait for an answer, merely sat next to her on the bench. He reached out and lifted her chiffon veil, folding it carefully over the brim of her hat. "Surplus to requirements on this occasion, wouldn't you say?" He raised an eyebrow even as the smile in his eyes deepened. "Since we have no secrets from each other."

Chastity was unable to respond for a minute. Her first thought was that this meeting was accidental; her second, that of course it wasn't. She was overwhelmed by his presence, by his scent and his smile, by the crinkles at the corners of his eyes, the large hands that were now stripping off his gloves. His deep-set eyes were darkest charcoal, and his long angular jaw had a disconcerting jut to it, as if he had determined on some course of action.

"You wrote to the Go-Between?" she asked, feeling stupid.

"I took a gamble that it would be you who answered, not one of your sisters," Douglas said. "I need you to come with me." He took her hand, standing up as he did so, drawing her inexorably to her feet.

"Come with you where?" Chastity thought she should be making some protest but for some reason couldn't summon the will to do so.

"You'll see," he said. "I want you to see the consequences of your actions." Still holding her hand he drew her firmly beside him and began to walk out of the gallery.

Chastity made no protest as they walked across the upper hallway, down the great flight of stairs, and out into the bright afternoon. In truth, just the feel of his fingers on her wrist set her senses awhirl. If she'd wanted to, she could have pulled away, but the idea never crossed her mind. She had no idea what was happening, or what he intended, but he was here beside her and she could sense none of the cold hurt and anger that had marked their parting.

Douglas hailed a hackney and when the cab drew up he lifted Chastity into the interior and climbed in behind her. She contemplated a form protest and then with an unconscious shake of her head dismissed the idea. She hadn't minded, why pretend she had? He was sitting beside her and now took her hand again, enclosing it in his own but saying nothing, seemingly content to sit quietly side by side in the swaying carriage.

"Where are we going?" she asked finally.

"Harley Street."

"Why?"

"You'll see." He smiled again, a very private smile, and said nothing further until they were inside the ground-floor hallway of his office building. "The second floor," he said, gesturing to the stairs.

Chastity, with one questioning glance, went up the stairs ahead of him. She couldn't help drawing a shocking comparison between this opulent building and the tumbledown hovel of St. Mary Abbot's. It must be so difficult for Douglas to move between the two, she thought, stopping outside the single door on the second floor.

He leaned across her shoulder with a key in his hand and unlocked the door, pushing it open. Chastity stepped inside. She stopped dead. "Dear God," she whispered, a tremor in her voice. He moved to stand beside her and she turned her head towards him. "Laura," she said in the same awed whisper. "She did this?"

"To the letter," he agreed impassively. He gestured. "Go in. There's more."

Chastity took another step, and then another. She looked all around, her hazel eyes stunned. "Is there a Buddha?" she asked.

He shook his head. "No, she spared me

that. But there's a palm tree." He pointed.

Chastity gazed at it, her hands now covering her mouth. "Sweet Jesus," she murmured.

"You realize that you are entirely responsible for this," he said, leaning against the door, arms folded, little flickers of laughter in his eyes.

"Me?" she said. "No . . . how . . . how could I be?"

"Well, I was under the impression that you, in the guise of the Go-Between, had attempted to make a match between me and the Signorina Della Luca," he observed.

"Well, yes . . . but . . . but I didn't suggest you make her your interior decorator," Chastity protested.

"Neither did I," he said aridly.

Chastity looked around again, then almost tentatively went towards the door that led to his office. She stood there in silence, then turned slowly back to him. "I am so sorry."

He came over to her, took her face between his hands, looked down at her with a smile in his eyes that was half rueful, half amused. "So am I, sweetheart," he said. "So very sorry."

She reached up to grasp his wrists. "I didn't know what to do," she said. "I didn't know how to stop it. Everything seemed to spin out of control."

"I know." He kissed her gently, and then

more urgently. "I hurt you. Forgive me." The words rustled over her lips, his thumbs pressed into the soft skin beneath her chin.

"I deceived you. It must have been so wretched for you." She raised a hand to caress his cheek.

"It was, but I brought it upon myself." He kissed the corner of her mouth. "Such crass stupidity to imagine that I could . . ." He raised his head and stared almost angrily at the wall behind her.

"I love you," she said, touching his mouth with a fingertip. "Douglas, I love you."

The anger faded from his eyes. He held her tightly against him, his mouth finding hers again, his lips firm and possessive, his tongue demanding entrance. She felt his body harden against her, felt the liquid jolt in her loins, and laughed with the sheer joy of desire. "Where?" she asked, laughing and yet urgent, sucking on his bottom lip as if it were a ripe plum, pressing herself against him, suddenly devoured by need.

He bore her backwards to the large desk adorned with an elaborately decorated blotter. Her legs curled around his hips as she fell back onto the smooth surface. She twisted her fingers in his thick hair, pulling his mouth down on hers as he pushed up her skirt and petticoat. She lifted her hips as he pulled down her knickers, tightened her thighs around him, barely aware of the hard wood beneath her, and then with a little gasp of delight felt him inside her. He slipped his hands beneath her hips, holding her on the shelf of his palms as he moved within her, his mouth pressed to hers.

He raised his head, looked down at her transported countenance, said softly, "Chastity, I love you," and drove to her core as she rose to meet him, her heels pressing into his backside. They were laughing as the world reasserted itself, laughing at the absurdity of their position, laughing with heady relief, laughing with sheer unadulterated pleasure.

"I hope you weren't expecting any patients," Chastity said, taking the hands he held out to pull her into a sitting position.

"No, I usually schedule appointments with some care," he said, releasing her hands to tuck his shirt into his trousers before buttoning them. "Today was no exception."

Chastity slid off the desk. "Oh, so you planned that."

"Not exactly," he said with a rather wicked smile. "But I had my hopes."

Chastity was busy buttoning and tucking herself. She glanced over her shoulder. "I think you're going to have to keep the desk," she said. "I've grown rather fond of it."

"And the blotter," he agreed. He reached for her, taking her shoulders, kissing her brow. "But what in the devil's name am I to do with the rest of this . . . this . . ." He ran his hands through his hair.

"Send it back," Chastity said. "You have the receipts?"

"I have the bills," he said. "Five thousand pounds' worth." He reached into the desk drawer.

Chastity grimaced. "It's astonishing what people will pay for bad taste." She glanced through the sheaf of papers he handed her. "We'll let Prue handle these. She's an expert at sending back merchandise. She was always having to do it when Father ordered things we couldn't afford."

"I don't want to involve your family," Douglas said, reaching to take them back from her.

Chastity put them on the desk. "You're not," she stated. "You're part of the family, therefore you're not involving them, they are involved." She regarded him through suddenly narrowed eyes. "Unless, of course, Dr. Farrell, you are merely trifling with me, and have no intention of making an honest woman of me."

He was pleased to note that he was taken aback for no more than an instant. "Are you asking me to marry you, Miss Duncan?"

"Why certainly I am, sir." She swept him a curtsy. "Dr. Farrell, would you do me the honor of becoming my husband?"

"The honor would be all mine," he said with a formal bow.

"Good, so that's over with," Chastity said cheerfully. "So, we're agreed we'll let Prue deal with returning this stuff. I promise you, Douglas, she will have the shopkeepers begging to take it back before she's finished with them. There'll be no problem there."

"Maybe not, but there *will* be a problem," he said. "I shall be left with an unfurnished suite."

"Oh, that's easy," Chastity said. "As long as you don't want new stuff." Her tone suggested that anyone desiring such furniture would be showing a serious lack of good judgment.

Douglas shook his head in hasty disclaimer. "No," he said. "Not at all."

"Then it's simple. We have so much in the attics, both in Manchester Square and at Romsey Manor . . ." She paused, seeing his expression.

"I sat in an armchair in the attic at Romsey Manor that reeked of dog," he said neutrally.

"They don't all," she said, coming across to him. She put her arms around him. "We are at peace now, aren't we?"

"Oh, yes," he said into her hair. "Utterly at peace, my love."

Much later, in the full dark of late evening, in Douglas's flat on Wimpole Street, Chastity stirred against him and murmured, "At the risk of opening old wounds, we ought to discuss what we're going to do about money for your clinic, since I don't have any."

"Well, you're not going to be an expensive wife, are you?" he asked, his voice teasing in the dark.

"No, of course not. We're all three of us financially independent," she said with a touch of indignation.

"That's all right, then. As long as I don't have to support you." He moved over her, tracing the contours of her face with a fingertip. "And you do have the right social contacts to scare up some rich patients for me, don't you?"

"I could do that," she murmured. "And maybe we could find some philanthropic backer for the clinic. That would help."

"It certainly would," he agreed solemnly. "But what would help most at the moment is if you would just lift your hips a fraction . . . that's it, perfect." He slid his length deep within her. "I can do anything, Chastity, my love, if I have you."

She smiled up at him in the darkness. "Together," she said softly, "we shall move mountains."

Epilogue

"Do you realize," Chastity observed, "that this time last year we didn't know that Max, Gideon, or Douglas even existed, and now look at us all." She drew a silk stocking up to her thigh.

"Don't forget Father and the contessa," Constance said, passing her sister a ruffled garter.

"I suppose garters are more romantic for a wedding night than suspenders," Chastity said, tying it high up on her thigh.

"Most definitely," Prudence said, handing her the second one. "For the Flying Scotsman, only garters will do."

Chastity laughed. "You are referring to the train, I trust, Prue."

"It was intended as a double entendre," her sister said.

"Well, the train doesn't leave until ten tomorrow morning, so I'm spending my wedding night in the honeymoon suite at Claridge's." Chastity slid her feet into a pair of ivory kid slippers. "And I don't know how Douglas is paying for it."

"I don't think it would be politic to ask," Constance said, shaking out the folds of an apple-green chiffon evening gown before dropping it over Chastity's head.

"I'm not a complete idiot," Chastity protested, her voice muffled in the yards of material. She held out her arms for her sisters to button the tight sleeves of the gown. "This is so pretty, isn't it?"

"It's lovely," Prudence agreed. "Unlike her daughter, the contessa has superb taste. It was a lovely stepmotherly gift."

"Does Laura know what happened to her decorating attempts?" Constance asked, fastening the last tiny button.

"No, she hasn't been near Harley Street since," Chastity said. "She's been far too busy remaking poor George."

"He doesn't seem to mind the process," Prudence said with a chuckle. "He adores her."

"Each to his own," Constance said.

There was a brisk knock at the door and Max called, "Mrs. Farrell, your husband grows impatient."

"Tell him some things take time, Max," Constance instructed. "Chas isn't going away in her petticoat."

"I doubt he'd object," her husband said, "but I'll pass it on."

"We had better hurry," Chastity said, clasping the amber beads around her throat. A ray of the setting sun caught the fire opals on her finger. "Wasn't it clever of Douglas to know that only people born in October can wear opals?" She held her hand out to the sun. "Look how they change color . . . so iridescent."

"They are gorgeous. As are the earrings. Put them on, Chas." Prudence handed her a pair of opal drops.

"Here's your evening bag, gloves, cloak," Constance said, passing each garment to her baby sister. "You look utterly beautiful, love, just as you have all day."

Chastity took a deep, shuddering breath, and tears glistened for a moment in her hazel eyes. "I know it's not the end of anything, but it feels as if it is."

"No, it's not, love. It's the beginning," Prudence said firmly. "For all of us. Now go to your Flying Scotsman." She gave Chastity a little push towards the door, then pulled her close again and kissed her, her own eyes suspiciously shiny. Constance encircled them both in a tight hug and for a moment they clung together, then Chastity stepped back.

"All right," she said. "I'm ready."

Her sisters preceded her down the stairs to where the wedding guests were gathered to see off the newlyweds. Douglas stepped to the bottom of the stairs, his eyes on his wife.

Constance whispered as she passed him, "Take care of her, Flying Scotsman."

He looked at her, startled, then Chastity was beside him and he could only drink her in, take her hand, and kiss her on the mouth to the general applause.

"The carriage awaits, sir," Jenkins announced. "Mrs. Farrell, please accept the congratulations of all the staff."

"That's the one and only time you may call me that, Jenkins," she said with a misty smile as she kissed him.

"Certainly, Miss Chas," he said, bowing.

Douglas tucked her hand into his arm and they walked between the two columns of guests. Laura, with Lord Berenger at her side, tossed a handful of white rose petals. "An Italian custom," she trilled. "So civilized." Chastity smiled at her, happy to have civilized rose petals adorning her hair.

Lord Duncan and his wife stood beside the front door that Jenkins held open. Lord Duncan took his daughter's hands in both of his in a fierce clasp. "The last one," he said. "Your mother would have been so proud."

Chastity leaned close and whispered in his ear, "Less than a year ago, Father, you had despaired of ever walking any of us to the altar." She kissed him as he laughed and hugged her.

"I was never any good at predictions," he said, reaching a hand to his newest son-in-law. "Farrell, take good care of my youngest."

"I will, sir," Douglas said. "But Wimpole Street is no more than a five-minute walk."

"We shall be delighted to see all and any of you whenever you have the time to visit," the contessa said with an understanding smile. "Will we not, Arthur?"

"Oh, yes, m'dear. Yes, certainly. Whenever convenient." He put an arm around his wife's waist. "But young people have their own lives to lead."

Douglas gently urged Chastity through the door and down the steps. She turned to smile and wave at the guests gathered now at the top, then obeyed the hand that turned her to the carriage, a very splendid open carriage drawn by two magnificent Shire horses.

"You're going to pick me up, aren't you," she said with a tiny sigh of resignation.

"It's customary," he returned, his eyes sparkling.

"It's a pagan custom, and it's only over the threshold," she protested.

"I have more than a little of the Scots pagan in me," he said, and scooped her into his arms. Before he put her in the carriage, he said, "What was that your sister said . . . something about a Flying Scotsman?"

"Oh, that . . . probably a reference to the pagan Scot," she said airily as he deposited her on the wide leather bench amid a round of cheering applause from the top step of 10 Manchester Square.

About the Author

Jane Feather is the *New York Times* bestselling, award-winning author of *The Bride Hunt*, *The Bachelor List*, *Kissed by Shadows*, *To Kiss a Spy*, *The Widow's Kiss*, *The Least Likely Bride*, *The Accidental Bride*, *The Hostage Bride*, *A Valentine Wedding*, *The Emerald Swan*, and many other historical romances. She was born in Cairo, Egypt, and grew up in the New Forest, in the south of England. She began her writing career after she and her family moved to Washington, D.C., in 1981. She now has more than ten million copies of her books in print.